CH

BY KAREN MARIE MONING

THE FEVER SERIES
Darkfever
Bloodfever
Faefever
Dreamfever
Shadowfever
Iced
Burned
Feverborn
Feversong

GRAPHIC NOVEL
Fever Moon

NOVELLA
Into the Dreaming

THE HIGHLANDER SERIES
Beyond the Highland Mist
To Tame a Highland Warrior
The Highlander's Touch
Kiss of the Highlander
The Dark Highlander
The Immortal Highlander
Spell of the Highlander

HIGH VOLTAGE

KAREN MARIE MONING

HIGH VOLTAGE

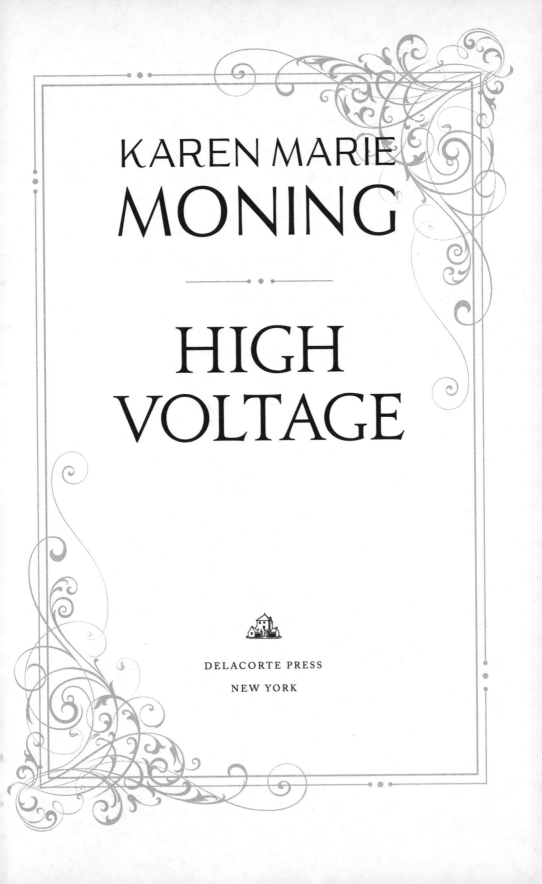

DELACORTE PRESS

NEW YORK

Copyright © 2018 by Karen Marie Moning, LLC

Published in the United States by Delacorte Press, an imprint of Random House, a division of Penguin Random House LLC, New York.

DELACORTE PRESS and the HOUSE colophon are registered trademarks of Penguin Random House LLC.

Hardback ISBN 978-0-399-59366-6
Ebook ISBN 978-0-399-59367-3

Printed in the United States of America on acid-free paper

randomhousebooks.com

2 4 6 8 9 7 5 3 1

First Edition

Book design by Caroline Cunningham
Title-page and part-opener frame by iStock.com/ANGELGILD

For all you "Dani's" out there.

Ad astra per aspera.

Move the stars.

Rise.

In loving memory of Sam Rae Moning

1994–2017

We deny, at our own peril,

the cry of the soul to stand in our truth.

You stood strong.

GLOSSARY ALERT

---•◦•---

I F THIS IS THE first book you've picked up in the Fever series, I've included a guide of people, places, and things to il-
luminate the backstory at the end of this novel.

If you're a seasoned reader of the series, the guide will reac-
quaint you with notable events and characters: what they did, if
they survived, and, if not, how they died.

If you're reading an ebook, factor this into your expectation
of when the story ends, which is a bit before the final page count.

You can either read the guide first, getting acquainted with
the world, or reference it as you go along to refresh your memory.
The guide features characters by type, followed by places, then
things.

THEN

Men rarely (if ever) manage to dream up a god
superior to themselves. Most gods have the
manners and the morals of a spoiled child.

—ROBERT HEINLEIN

Everything you think you know is wrong.
Mortals possess short lives, shorter memories.
You can't even spin the same story twice without
bastardizing the facts. When politics come into
play, human canon becomes convenient at best,
dispensed with entirely at worst. You have no
bloody idea who your gods are.

—CONVERSATIONS WITH DAIRE

I have no gods. My demons ate them.

—DANI O'MALLEY

STARDUST

· ● ·

He WOULDN'T HAVE SEEN the shooting star if the woman in his bed hadn't fallen asleep, overstaying her welcome, filling him with the restless desire for a solitary walk on the beach.

The ocean at night always made him glad to be alive, which was why he'd chosen to live so near it.

Alive was the one thing he'd always be.

Tonight, the sea was a shiver of dark glass, harboring secrets untold in her depths while on her tranquil surface stars glittered like diamonds. Life-giving, life-stealing, beautiful, a challenge to handle, worth learning to ride, full of fresh wonders every day—if he'd had a woman like the ocean in his bed, he'd still be there.

He wasn't a man that believed in signs from the heavens. He'd lived too long for that and knew if he were to receive a sign of any kind, it would explode from below in a shower of sparks and brimstone, not descend from above, a wonder to behold.

For a few moments he watched the star scorch a path across a black velvet sky, leaving a streak of shimmering stardust in its wake.

Then he turned away and stripped off his clothes to go for a swim. He was nearly to the water when he realized the star appeared to be headed his way and was much closer than it initially appeared. In fact, it seemed—if it continued on its current path—it might land on his beach. What were the odds of that?

He arched a brow, considering its trajectory. Although he couldn't gauge its velocity, the star certainly seemed to be on a direct collision course.

With him.

His laughter was deep, mocking; how rich that would be. After so many eons, was he to be felled by a shooting star? Had he finally managed to offend both those who resided in the heavens and those that dwelled beneath? Was his sentence finite after all?

He watched its approach, amused, daring it to find its mark. End his life. Obliterate him.

He growled, "Do your best," and closed his eyes, waiting for the impact. He'd seen the end come too many times to care in what guise it appeared. He didn't need to watch. He knew what death was.

Never final. Not for him.

He waited.

And waited.

Finally, he opened his eyes. The star had slowed to a crawl and was no longer speeding across the sky but tumbling slowly, lazily, directly overhead, perhaps a mile above him.

He didn't move a muscle. *Come on, you bitch. Do it.*

The star plummeted abruptly, acquiring velocity as it fell.

When it crashed to the beach a dozen paces away, impact buried it in a soft explosion of sand.

One brow arched, he contemplated the indentation. The only other time the universe had singled him out for attention, it hadn't gone well. He was intrigued in spite of himself; this was an unusual turn of events for a man to whom nothing was unusual anymore, and hadn't been for a very long time.

Approaching the depression, he knelt and began to dig. When at last his fingers closed on the thing that had fallen from the sky, he muttered an oath and yanked his hands from the sand.

It was blisteringly hot. And now it was covered again.

He sat back, stretched his legs around the hollow, and excavated it more carefully, until a black chunk the size of his hand was revealed, with jagged, broken edges that glowed red as burning embers.

So much for signs.

So much for death.

It was only a flat chunk of molten rock that had coincidentally plummeted to his beach while he'd happened to be out walking.

He pushed up and began to lope toward the sea, but as he moved away from the fallen star a sudden breeze gusted a fragrance after him that stopped him in his tracks. The monster within growled and inhaled greedily.

Ah, the smell! What *was* that smell?

He glanced back, nostrils flaring. Returning to the object, he stood above it, eyes closed, breathing hungrily, tasting the aroma with his mind. His monster was pacing now, restless and alert.

Woman.

The rock smelled of a woman: dark and vast, complex as the

sea. She was life and death, mercy and ruthlessness, joy and grief. Complicated. Hard to handle. Worth learning to ride.

Where had it come from?

Consumed by the mystery, he opened his eyes. Although he healed with remarkable speed, he was in no mood to burn his hands again so he stalked to a nearby tumble of rock and selected a long narrow wedge.

Returning to the far-flung star, he nudged it with the stone, working it up the side of the sandy indentation so he could flip it over and examine it. Even with his hands a fair distance from the object, it cast enough heat to blister his skin.

He, who believed in neither signs nor death, who, truth be told, believed in nothing at all, stared down for a long time, no bloody idea what to make of it.

On the opposite side of the fallen star, etched by a quill of stardust, three words gleamed:

I'M OKAY I'M

EARTHDUST

THE SOULSTEALER HAD NO idea how long it slumbered.
It didn't know it *was* slumbering.

It thought it had died.

Strains of music shivered into the earth, burrowed deep into fertile soil, through rock, clay, and rock again, sinking deeper into iron, lead, copper, silver and gold, then an alien, immutable alloy until, at last, the ancient melody penetrated the tomb and nudged the deadly leviathan awake.

Awareness dawned in slow stages.

It remembered then.

The arrival of the Faerie, the endless, unwinnable war, the lies and deception, the loss of power. The torture. The conquest. The brutalized face, the mask. The incarceration, the disease that claimed it, until finally it was a shade among shadows. Mask clattering to age-old stone, it had become as insubstantial as air.

At the end, with the last vestige of its awareness, it managed no more than a feeble protest.

It had once believed itself obdurate, eternal, unstoppable.

It would make certain of that this time.

ONE

———•———

The pupil in denial; I can't take my eyes off of you

"I SMELL BONES!" SHAZAM EXPLODED, whiskers bristling with excitement. "Bones *everywhere*. Thousands and thousands of them! You take me to *all* the best places, Yi-yi!" He slanted me an adoring look before launching himself at the earth and digging, sending tufts of grass and dirt flying.

"Stop digging," I exclaimed. "You can't eat those bones."

"Can, too. Watch," came the muffled voice.

"No, I mean, you're not *allowed* to eat them," I clarified.

He ignored me. Dirt continued to fly, mounding rapidly behind him.

"Shazam, I mean it. You promised to obey my rules. My expects," I reminded, using his often-stilted manner of speaking, "bars on your cage."

Head buried in the dirt, he said in a muffled voice, "That was then. This is now. Then, I didn't have a home."

"Sha*zam*," I said in the warning tone I knew he hated. But heeded.

Pudgy body wedged halfway into his hole, my Hel-Cat stiffened and inched out—exceedingly slowly and begrudgingly—and glared at me. Dirt dusted his broad nose, his silver whiskers, and clung to his long, silver-smoke ruff. He sneezed violently, licked his nose then scrubbed it with a furious paw. "But they're *bones,* tiny red. They're already dead. I'm not killing them. You said I couldn't *kill* anything. You didn't say I couldn't eat things that were dead." His eyes narrowed to violet slits. "You bofflescate your expects. You bofflescate my head. Who even *does* that?"

Bofflescate wasn't a word I knew—he had many of those—but I intuited the meaning. "These bones are different. They matter to humans. We bury them in certain places for a reason."

He spoke slowly and carefully, as if addressing a complete idiot. "Me, too. So they're easy to find when I'm hungry."

I shook my head, a smile tugging at my lips. "No. These are the bones of people we care about." I gestured at the dark silhouettes of gravestones that stretched for acres around us. "We don't eat them, we bury them so—"

"But nobody's doing things with them and they're rotting!" he wailed. Slumping on his haunches, he splayed his front paws around his pudgy white belly. "You give bones. I find bones. Same thing. One good reason why I can't eat them," he demanded.

I debated trying to explain human burial rituals to him, but many of our traditions defied his comprehension. A bone was a bone was a bone. Convincing him that graveyard bones carried an emotional and spiritual attachment to humans, unlike the cow or pig bones I sometimes brought him, could take all night, and leave him just as bewildered as he'd begun. And me exhausted.

I gave him the only answer that worked at a time like this. The answer I'd hated as a kid. "Because I said so."

He rose to his full height, arched his back and hissed at me, baring sharp fangs and a long black-tipped tongue.

I returned his snarl. With Shazam, I didn't dare yield or say "just one bone, just this time" because in his mind if a rule could be violated once, it was no longer a rule and never would be again. Unless, of course, it worked in his favor.

His eyes turned flinty.

Mine cooled to emerald ice.

He cut me a look of scathing rebuke.

I switched tactics and flayed him with an expression of reproach and disappointment.

His violet eyes widened as if I'd struck him. He shuddered dramatically, toppled over, collapsed on his back, and began to weep with great, hiccupping sobs, clutching his paws to his eyes.

I sighed. This was my best friend—the last remaining Hel-Cat in existence. Powerful, often brilliant beyond comprehension, most of the time he was a wildly emotional hot mess. I adored him. Sometimes, when he flashed like wildfire between feral and neurotic, feeling every facet of his life so intensely, I saw myself as a kid—too much to handle.

I'd been kept in a cage for most of my childhood.

I didn't own a cage and never would.

I moved across the damp grass, sank down beside the sobbing, shaggy-pelted chimera with traits of an Iberian lynx and the supple lazy posture of a koala bear, and tugged the fifty-pound beast toward me. The moment I touched him, he howled bloody murder and began to growl, then made himself stiff, un-wieldy, and mysteriously heavier. With all four legs sticking straight up in the air, sharp black claws extended, spine rigid, hoisting a hostile hyena onto my lap might have been easier.

He stopped growling long enough to snap, "Don't touch me. Find your own dimension. You're cramping my space." Then he collapsed across my legs and his head lolled back. "Comb my neck, it's tangled again," he wailed.

I bit my lip to keep from laughing; Shazam got his feelings hurt easily in this state. Using my nails, I groomed the thick pelt of his chin, his shaggy neck, and around behind his ears until I heard a deep, contented rumble in his chest.

We sprawled in the grass in the graveyard behind Arlington Abbey, beneath a cobalt sky glittering with rose-gold stars and a full amber moon, enjoying the moment. It was the middle of March but fat-blossomed velvety poppies bobbed in nearby urns, and exotic, trellised roses adorned graves, scenting the night air with indefinable Fae fragrances. A night symphony of crickets and frogs filled the air.

Dublin's climate had been uncharacteristically mild since the queen of the Fae used the Song of Making to heal our world last November. We'd had no winter; a long, fertile spring had morphed seamlessly into an extraordinary summer, splashed with brilliant Fae colors and new species of plants.

There'd been little peace in my life. I tended to find myself embroiled in one melodrama after the next but, aside from a broken heart that wasn't healing on the timetable I would have preferred, life was good. I had Shazam, I had friends, I would heal and there was endless potential for new adventures once I did.

Eventually the Hel-Cat squinted a lavender eye open and

peered up at me. I caught my breath. There was nothing feral or neurotic in his gaze now, only an ancient wisdom wed to remote, timeless-as-the-stars patience. I'd learned to listen carefully when he looked at me like this.

"Remains of the one who danced you into love are in the ground, Yi-yi. That's why you don't want me to eat the bones. Do what you came for. I will hunt only the tasty night moths." Smirking, he added, "And I will kill as you do—with love." He surged from my lap in a suspiciously graceful leap, given the heft of his body, and bounded into the darkness beyond the graves.

I rolled my eyes as he vanished. I'd been trained to kill at the age of nine. Before then I'd killed without training. Shortly after I rescued Shazam from Planet X, he asked how my killing was different from the killing I'd forbidden him to do, aside from me wasting food by not eating my prey. I told him that when I killed, it wasn't with the hatred that once blazed in my heart, but with love for the world I was trying to protect. I did it only when necessary, as quickly and mercifully as possible. Killing with violence in your heart, or worse, a complete dearth of emotion, made you a killer, plain and simple. Killing because it had to be done, because there was no other way and it was the right thing to do, made you a necessary weapon.

Do what you came here for. I wasn't sure what that was. Nothing of Dancer remained in this macabre memorial to the dead behind Arlington Abbey. I found that a terrible thought—that his essence might be trapped in a box buried beneath the dirt. *When I die, cremate me and cast me to the stars.*

Still, I pushed to my feet, skirted a bank of low hedges and wide planters, and moved to stand at the foot of his grave.

Time slid away; it was four months ago and I was kissing Dancer's cold lips and closing the lid of his casket.

God, I missed him.

We'd played with the innocence and impunity of kids who believed themselves immortal (at least I had), conquering video games, watching movies, dreaming together about what our futures might hold, gorging on ice cream and candy and sodas, racing out into the night in search of adventure.

I smiled faintly. We'd found plenty. We'd plunged into life with similar enthusiasm and devil-may-care bravado. Caring, thoughtful, and brilliant, he'd been one of only two people I've ever met that I thought was as smart, possibly smarter, than me.

We'd grown up, become lovers.

Dancer Elias Garrick, never the sidekick, always the hero.

I shoved my hands into my pockets and stared down. I'm not a woman who often looks back. I measure actions by results, and peering into the past rarely yields any. Reflecting on something that hurts you only prolongs your pain, and when death is involved, the pain is often compounded by a relentless sense of guilt that attacks the moment you start to heal, as if duration of grief somehow proves the depth of your love for the person you lost.

If that were true, I'd have to grieve Dancer forever.

Born with a flawed heart, he'd lived fearlessly. The unfairly penalized muscle in his chest had given out on him before he'd turned eighteen, while I was sleeping next to him in bed. I'd woken after a night of lovemaking to find him forever gone.

I'd melted down. It got ugly. My friends got me through it.

Guilt had definitely led me here, but not spawned by lack of grief. A sheer abundance of it made me do something stupid last night.

I tried to erase my pain in another man's bed. It had seemed like a good idea at the time.

It hadn't worked. The first man I'd had sex with taught me how beautiful it was.

The second man had shown me how ugly it could be.

"I miss you," I whispered to his grave, and waited.

Shortly after he died, he spoke to me twice. I'd felt his presence, as if he was standing right there behind me, sunshine on my shoulders, reaching through the slipstream to comfort and counsel me.

A few weeks ago, however, I'd become aware that intangible warmth was gone—vanished while I slept—and I knew in my gut he'd moved on. Somehow he'd managed to linger in the ether to make sure I was all right and when he was satisfied, he'd raced off for the next grand adventure.

As he should have.

As we all should when it's our time.

That thought didn't make me feel any better. Thoughts rarely do. The heart has its own mind, measures its own time, and if it consults with the brain, doesn't always heed the advice. My brain was screaming—*stop hurting already*. To a deaf audience.

I'd never fully grasped the meaning of the word "forever" before. I'd lost my mom long before she died. It wasn't the same. I'd grieved her while she'd still been living.

But the idea that I would never see Dancer again was more than I could stand. All I had left of him were memories and we'd not had time to make nearly enough.

My gaze drifted to the headstone east of his marker. JO BRENNAN. We'd laid another of my friends to rest beside him. I smiled faintly, remembering her breaking into my dungeon cell to save me. We hadn't always gotten along but she'd been a genuine, good constant in my life and didn't deserve to die the way she did.

ALINA MCKENNA LANE. Mac's sister was buried beside her. There'd been so much death in my life.

"All the more reason to live," came the deep, exotically accented growl from behind me. I could hear traces of many languages in it, a consensus of none.

I bristled. Not many people can sneak up on me without my preternatural senses kicking into high alert. Ryodan defies the odds in countless, irritating ways. "Stay out of my head."

"I wasn't in it. Didn't need to be. When humans stand at graves, they brood." He was beside me then, in that sudden, silent, eerie way of his.

Humans, he'd said. Whatever Ryodan was, he wasn't one of those and he'd stopped making any effort to conceal it from me. Whether urbane, sophisticated man or black-skinned, fanged beast, he was all the supers I was, plus an awe-inspiring, aggravating assortment of others. When I was young, I'd felt like Sarah from the movie *Labyrinth*, dashing around Dublin having grand adventures. Ryodan was Jareth, my Goblin King. I'd defied him at every turn, defining myself in opposition to him. I'd studied him, incorporating his ideologies and tactics into my own. Silverside I'd functioned by the code: WWRD? I'd never tell him that.

I turned and scowled up at him. Beautiful, cool, aloof man. Two things always happen to me whenever he shows up. I get an instant jolt of happiness, as if every cell in my body wakes up and is glad to see him. It pisses me off because my brain rarely agrees. Ryodan and I are enthusiastic foes, wary friends. I tell him things I don't tell anyone else, and that offends me, too.

The second thing baffles me. I often feel like crying. I've wept on his flawless, crisp shirts more times than I care to remember.

"Because I understand," he murmured, staring down at me with those glittering silver eyes. "And I can take it. I wasn't sure about the happiness, though. Nice of you to clear that up."

"What part of 'stay out of my head' didn't you understand?"

"Your face, Dani. Everything you feel is on it. I rarely need to delve deeper."

He'd glimpsed such raw emotion in me recently that I'd been avoiding him. As Jada, I was respected, feared. As Dani, I sometimes felt like I vied with Shazam for Hot Mess Poster Child of the Month.

I could only hope what happened last night was nowhere to be seen on my face. I'd never before experienced what an average woman with average strength contended with on a daily basis: physical vulnerability to the opposite sex. It had been humbling and horrifying and awakened a fierce compassion in me, making me even more protective of my city, especially women and children.

In bed with a stranger, my heart felt like it was going to explode. I'd tried to leave the man and that empty thing I was doing but the intensity of my emotions shorted out my *sidhe-seer* strength, leaving me a frighteningly normal five-foot-ten woman who weighed in at 142, in a locked room with a six-foot-four, 240-pound man.

Who'd called me a cock tease and turned violent.

I hadn't killed him. I'd wanted to. If he'd succeeded in raping me, I'm not sure what I would have done. "No" is "no," no matter when it's said. As it was, I'd be watching him from a distance to make sure he never crossed that line again. And if he did, well: violate other's liberties, lose your own.

"Ah, Dani." Ryodan touched my cheek, brushing a stray curl

back and tucking it behind my ear. "Men can be bloody bastards. But not all of them. Don't let it shut you down. Be fearless. Don't be afraid to fall. Taste it all."

My eyes flashed mutinously. Not because of what he'd said but rather what he hadn't said. It was there in his voice. Mac and Barrons left two weeks ago to deal with the revolt happening in Faery. She'd reminded me time moved differently there; a week for her might be as much as a year for me. He was leaving, too. "That sounds suspiciously like goodbye."

He smiled but it didn't reach his eyes. There's a palpable coolness, a distance in Ryodan's gaze most of the time, a thousand-yard stare that's seen and done things that change you forever; a big picture view. I understand it. I see the same look in my own eyes sometimes.

"There's something I have to do."

I knew it. I said coolly, "Great. Me and Shazam will come with you."

"You can't."

"Sure, we can. They've elected a council for the abbey, gone back to popular vote like old times. I'm merely a consultant." I wanted it that way. Freedom to come and go as I pleased.

"Not this time."

"You just told me to taste it all. I'm merely taking your—"

"Nothing. You're taking nothing," he cut me off harshly. "I can't take you with me now. You don't belong with me now."

Gone was the polished, sophisticated man. The black-skinned beast he sometimes became stared out at me through cold, incalculably ancient eyes, flecks of crimson glittering in their depths. The beast's atavistic presence reshaped the planes and angles of his face, changing and elongating his jaws to accommodate the sudden appearance of fangs.

Once, I'd kissed him, felt those fangs graze my teeth as pure high voltage had arced between us. Once, I'd offered him my virginity. He'd rejected me and I'd vowed he'd never get another chance.

His gaze shuttered and he was Ryodan again, a man with even white teeth and the clearest gaze I'd ever seen. A man who played the long game and suffered no conflicts being what he was. Ruthless. A prick. My friend.

"Remember the cellphone and the tattoo," he said. "It doesn't matter if the cell towers are up or not. IISS will always work. Use it only if you must."

IISS, code for I'm in Serious Shit, was a number programmed into my phone that would activate the spelled tattoo Ryodan had inked at the base of my spine at my request. According to him, he could find me anywhere, virtually instantly. "I know the rules. Only if I'm dying."

He was leaving. This was really goodbye. My hodgepodge family pieced together of extraordinary friends was falling apart. I took comfort in knowing he was near, in my city, and I could see him anytime I chose. Not that I had lately but I liked knowing the imperious king was holding court eternal in his glass kingdom high above the rest of us, that Chester's nightclub was open and it was business as usual. I may not have gone inside over the past few months but I'd certainly made a point of passing it frequently. I keep an eye on the things that matter to me.

My heart chilled and I let it. Dancer, Jo, Mac, Barrons. Now Ryodan.

"Don't do that," he growled.

"Don't tell me what to do," I growled back. "You're leaving. You don't have a say anymore."

"I always have a say. I don't need your permission."

I clipped, "Clearly." He was leaving Dublin without it. Did he think I would beg him to stay? Never. People had to *want* to stay, choose to be with you, or it meant nothing. There were physical cages and there were emotional ones. Holding onto someone too tightly made it hard for them to breathe, and eventually, inevitably, they'd do one of two things: suffocate or run, leaving you feeling like hell either way. I waved a dismissive hand. "What are you waiting for then? Go."

His nostrils flared and a muscle twitched in his cheek. Moonlight silvered a face I'd once thought uncaring and remote. I'd traced the sharpness of those cheekbones with my fingers, the shadow beard of his jaw, the scar that bisected the thick column of his neck. I'd experienced the rare emotional ferocity of the man. He made me uneasy in ways I didn't understand. I sighed and said, in spite of myself, "When are you coming back?"

"It'll be a while."

"Be precise. Weeks? A month or two?" When he didn't answer me, I gaped, incredulous. "*Years? Are you kidding me?*"

His eyes narrowed and he spat in a savage rush, "Listen to me and carve everything I'm about to say into that giant complicated brain of yours. You're right about killing with love. Keep the light shining in your heart; death is a hungry darkness. It *wants* to swallow us. You're different and will always be misunderstood—never let that touch you. You're a terribly real thing in a terribly false world. The world is fucked up, not you. Stay close to Shazam; you need each other. Don't return to Dancer's grave again; he's not here and you know it. If he could see you now, standing at his grave, he'd kick your ass right out of this cemetery and ask if you'd lost your bloody mind. You don't grieve love; you celebrate that you had it. Choose the men you take to your bed by these criteria: they see the finest in you, en-

hance and defend it. When you fuck a man you are giving him
A. Motherfucking. Gift. Be certain he deserves it. And bloody
hell, don't have one-night stands. Commit to the action. Make it
matter. Feel it and ride it all the way through."

I fixated on his final words with aggrieved incredulity. "Says
the king of the infamous nod and one-night stands?" I'd had no
intention of having sex last night. I hadn't even vaguely entertained the notion. But my heart hurt so damned much, and the
man standing next to me in the pub was good-looking and flir-
tatious, and I'd needed desperately to dump some of my emotion. I thought it might make me feel better, perhaps even
refueled, like hugging. I thought I might pour out some of my
pain through my hands, dump it on another man's body, get up,
walk away clearer, more grounded.

"Never dump emotion, Dani. Channel it. Find an equal that
can handle it. But don't waste that precious commodity."

"Is Lor going, too?" I demanded. "What about the others?"

He made no reply but I didn't need one. I could see it in his
eyes. They were all leaving—or had already gone. I had no idea
where or why. But one thing was clear: I wasn't invited. "Who's
going to run Chester's?" I said, as if that alone might make him
stay. Constructed of chrome and glass and a mysterious alloy
Dancer and I had never been able to identify, Chester's-above
was the hottest nightclub in Dublin, offering dozens of subclubs
that catered to all types of clientele, while below was the Nine's
kingdom, containing their private residences and clubs. Level
after level stretched for miles beneath the ground, powered by a
vast geothermal array that, knowing Ryodan, probably tapped
the magma itself. Suspended above the club was Ryodan's see-
through glass office, equipped with the latest electronic surveil-
lance devices, serving as the lofty throne from which he surveyed

his world. I had no idea how long they'd lived there but I suspected it was a very, very long time.

"It's been closed. Stay out of it."

Chester's was dark? I'd only ever seen it that way a few times, and I'd hated it, like a carnival packed up to quit town, leaving behind only a muddy field of tattered flyers and tarnished dreams. "I'll bloody well go wherever I want. Once you're gone, it's not yours anymore. Maybe I'll take it over, re-create it as my own club." But I wouldn't. I'd have to kill half his patrons; Ryodan was an equal opportunity host, catering to the best and worst of men and monsters. However, I certainly wasn't averse to poking around after he'd gone to see if he'd left anything interesting lying around.

"I said 'stay out.' And don't worry, you'll be protected. I've taken precautions."

Protected my ass. I didn't need protecting. Nor did I want it. I *wanted* my family. I wanted him to stay in Chester's where he belonged so he'd be there in case I decided I wanted to see him. I resisted the urge to fist my hands. He'd notice. He'd draw conclusions. The man didn't miss a thing. "When have I ever needed protecting?"

He snorted. "As if keeping you alive hasn't been a bloody full-time job."

Once Ryodan made up his mind, nothing changed it. There was only one thing to do: tell him goodbye and wish him well while making it clear I didn't need him and wouldn't miss him. I opened my mouth and said, "I hate you."

He threw his head back and laughed, stymying me. Who laughs when you tell them you hate them?

Then his hands were in my hair and his lips were against mine. Soft, easy, neither provocation nor invitation but instant, electrifying current arced between us, the same as it had the last time we'd kissed, as well as the first time, when I'd meant it mostly to mess with him. It had messed with us both. I leaned into him. It would have been wiser to go to him to dump emotion last night. Safer. At least in body.

His hands tightened on my scalp and he said with sudden fury, "I wouldn't have let you. Don't come to me like that, Dani. Never fucking come to me like that."

That was the last straw, the final blade-sharp words I would let him cut me with. Our kisses had taken on a grim pattern: we shared one, we insulted each other, we stalked away. "Fuck you, too, Ryodan."

But he was gone, already halfway across the cemetery, slipping between gravestones and trees.

He was leaving.

For years. And I didn't even know how many.

It hurt me in places I didn't know I could hurt. If he'd been trying to get my mind off Dancer, he'd succeeded. There was nothing like a fresh, unexpected wound to make the pain of the older one feel slightly less crippling.

I narrowed my eyes, trying to separate him from the night, determined to watch him until the very last second, until he was finally, fully beyond my vision, beyond my reach. It wasn't easy. Ryodan in his natural state is a shadow among shadows, a subtlety of darkness, a whisper of power, a ripple of grace. Immortal. So damned strong.

Unbreakable.

I wanted to be him. I wanted to run with him. I wanted to run away from him and never look back.

Just before I lost sight of him, I thought I heard him murmur, "Until the day you're willing to stay."

TWO

My blood type's Krylon, technicolor type A

I WANDERED THE CEMETERY, KEEPING an eye out for Shazam, without calling for him in case he was hunting dinner. We'd agreed that he could eat like any wild creature, taking a single kill a night, as long as it was something he could catch and devour in his current form. No turning into the genocidal version of himself, capable of devouring civilizations. Despite his sentience and ability to talk, he was still a hot-blooded beast that relished the hunt. I understood that.

Besides, I'd reasoned, it was possible the exercise might slim him down. Although I loved every inch of his cuddly girth, being awakened in the morning by a fifty-pound pounce on a full bladder was brutal.

Not, however, as brutal as Ryodan and the rest of the Nine packing up and leaving Dublin. My city was starting to feel like a ghost town despite the hordes of people immigrating from all over the world. There weren't many cities as fully functional as ours. People came drawn by our technology, supplies, and the relative safety and order we'd managed to achieve.

Years ago, before I got lost Silverside and ended up with no idea how old I am—which is somewhere between nineteen and twenty-one—my world was pretty much perfect for a short spell. Well . . . before Mac found out I was the assassin who'd killed her sister. Then things got a bit dicey.

Point is, I'd had a small group of people I thought of as mine. Some of them I'd liked better than others, depending on the day of the week, but after our last adventure together saving the world, my group of sharp-edged, brilliant, deeply committed friends had become my family.

Now, most of them were gone, I still had Kat, Enyo, and the *sidhe*-seers, and I thought I still had Christian MacKeltar, although I hadn't seen him in a while. But Mac, Barrons, Ryodan, and Lor, they were like me: powerful, strong, invested in doing their best to understand their ever-changing place in an ever-changing world. Though I was reluctant to admit it, each of them was, in their own way, a role model of sorts, a challenge I'd relished to get stronger, smarter, faster, better.

"I can't believe they even trust me by myself," I muttered. There was a time they wouldn't have. "I shouldn't be left alone and unsupervised. They know that." But trying to make light of things to conceal my true feelings no longer worked as well as it once had, so I did what I always do if I can't change anything about what's bothering me—partition off a quiet place in my mind and tuck it away. Don't pick at it. Go on with life. Time had a funny way of teasing out the most complicated knots.

While part of me wanted to mull over the things Ryodan

had said, particularly what I'd thought I heard him say at the last, I refused to indulge myself. Assuming I drew any conclusions, what good would it do?

He was gone. For years. I refused to allow the bastard to consume my brain in his absence. He'd like that.

Ergo, open box. Shove in. Close box.

When he returned, I'd open the box again.

Dancer, however, I left rattling around in my head. He hadn't left by choice. I would work through the grief. It would change me, but I knew I'd like the woman I'd be by the time I was through, and Dancer would, too.

Meanwhile, I needed a mystery to take my mind off things. Finding one in Dublin, AWC—after the wall crash—and ATS—after the Song—should be as simple as heading back to the city.

Shazam would catch up with me as soon as he'd eaten—he can find me anywhere—so I glanced up to set my bearings by the stars. After wasting so many years staring at a TV from behind bars, I spent a lot of time looking up now. I'm obsessed with the sky, especially at night. It has a way of making me feel utterly irrelevant while part of a vast, timeless whole. I'll never forget my first week free of the cage. At night I slept on the ground in the middle of wide-open fields, drifting off with my arms behind my head, marveling at the immensity of it all; a child whose entire universe had, until then, been forty-two square feet.

Position noted, I hurried to the drive to circumvent gravestones before kicking up into the slipstream. During that perilous first instant or two before I enter the higher dimension in which I've learned to move, I can still crash into things. Once I'm up, I'm flawless. Coming down is even trickier than going up, and how I get most of my bruises.

I paused on the pavement, glanced around to lock down the many variables on my mental grid—and froze, a chill of horror licking up my spine. Not many things do that to me.

"What the—" I bit off the hushed curse and went as still as one of the corpses in the ground, adjusting my breath to minute, shallow inhales. *I'm not here, I'm not here,* I willed.

What I was seeing was impossible.

The Song of Making had been sung. The Unseelie had been destroyed by it. All of them. I no longer carried flashlights or a MacHalo.

The life-sucking Shades were gone.

Nonetheless, I was surrounded by them, hemmed in by countless inky shadows rising from the earth, bursting from graves, exploding from headstones, ghosting out windows of crumbling mausoleums, even clawing their ghastly passage through pavement.

Dozens—no, a hundred or more!—filled the cemetery.

One fought its way free of the blacktop five feet from my left; another hovered a few feet in front of me; there were three of the lethal things to my right.

I didn't dare glance behind me because they hadn't seemed to notice me yet. Perhaps they'd gorge on grass, flowers, and trees and move on, sated, if I held very, very still.

I locked down my limbs but my mind raced: it had been nearly four months since the new queen of the Fae sang the exquisite, dangerous melody that repaired the rifts in the fabric of our world. It was common knowledge that nothing Unseelie could survive that Song, and nothing Unseelie had been seen since.

I've always been massively suspicious of common knowledge, clearly with good reason. The cemetery was packed with Shades, nearly as many as had broken free of the poisoned D'Jai Orb on Halloween when the wall between the worlds of Fae and Man had been destroyed.

How did they survive the Song? What else had survived it?

Amorphous vampires, Shades live in the darkness and suck the life from anything or anyone foolish enough to stumble across their path. Not that I'd been doing any stumbling, nor had I been foolish in thinking I no longer needed a bloody MacHalo. I had every reason to toss my bike helmet adorned with dozens of LED lights onto a shelf. The Unseelie were dead.

Not.

When Shades dine on humans, they leave behind small sundaes of papery husks, garnished with shiny fillings, watches, implants, and other oddities. They suck even the sap and insects from trees, strip the soil so clean not a speck of bacteria remains. My sword is useless against them. All weapons are. Shades can't be killed and the only thing that can save you from a gruesome death is light. If you have enough, you can hold them at bay.

My cellphone wouldn't cast enough light to protect even *one* of my hands.

Take that, Ryodan. You leave, I die. May you be crushed by a mountain of guilt.

I slammed the lid of that box back down.

The Shades were moving, swarming, drifting near, slithering away. The cloud of darkness directly in front of me listed nearer, and hovered ten inches from my left boot. No way I could try to kick up into the slipstream. It was too close; I'd collide with it before escaping to the higher dimension. If I'd been High Fae, I could have sifted. But freeze-framing—what I do—is clumsier, slower, and not nearly as elegant. Fae can blink out and reappear half a world away. I'm far more limited.

There was no way I was calling for Shazam. I wouldn't put him in danger. I wasn't sure how powerful he was against something like this, and losing him would positively gut me.

My cellphone was in my back pocket. I calculated the odds of getting it out, pressing it on and managing to thumb up IISS before the nearest Shade devoured my foot.

Not good.

I went for it anyway. Some folks suffer a delusion that life is about making the right choices, implying there is a right choice in every situation. I don't know what kind of life they live but in mine the only course of action is often a bad one. I die doing something or I die doing nothing. Although I loathed calling Ryodan for help, I loathed the idea of dying more and I deeply despised that I hadn't been able to manage life on my own for an entire ten minutes after he'd gone.

My hand cleared my side, slid beneath my sword and plunged into my back pocket.

The Shade swallowed my left boot.

I gaped down in horror as I fumbled my phone from my pocket and thumbed up the contacts, furious at the epic waste the tattoo Ryodan inked on my skin had already proved to be. Who had time to search through their phone contacts when they were being attacked by Shades?

The Shade swallowed my left knee.

There went my right knee.

I'd vanished from mid-thigh down.

Even if I were able to dial IISS now—and I couldn't because I had a lot of numbers in my cellphone and couldn't find the bloody thing—even if he arrived instantly and somehow managed to do the unthinkable and kill it, my legs were already gone.

I wasted a fraction of a second wondering whether I wanted to live without legs.

There it was—IISS!

My thumb paused slightly above it, refused to move.

I could feel my legs. They were icy but there.

I peered down. The Shade was motionless, an inky, oily sleeve around my lower body.

I frowned. This wasn't how Shades behaved. When Sorcha, a fellow *sidhe*-seer died, Clare had seen it happen, and said Sorcha vanished into her own boot as she pulled it on, thanks to a Shade tucked in the darkness within. This particular caste of Unseelie devoured their prey instantly and with one swift inhalation, then belched a small pile of crumbs. Or in her case, left them in her shoe.

Was it possible it wasn't a Shade? If so, what was it? I realized with a distant part of my brain that my legs weren't the only part of me that was cold. My left hand was freezing. And itching. I glanced at it. It was completely black, with dark veins crisscrossing my pale wrist. It was the hand I'd used to stab the Hunter with years ago when something of the ancient beast seemed to slither up my sword, infecting me.

The Shade was on the move again, inching upward.

I had no idea what might happen—if anything at all—but I sliced my cold black hand down into the inky cloud as if it were a blade.

The Shade recoiled violently and reared away. It stopped a dozen or so feet from me and hung suspended in the air. I was struck by the sudden certainty that it was assessing me. I could feel a sentient mind taking my measure, evaluating me, determining what to do next.

I glanced around. All the Shadelike things in the cemetery

had gone still, and I deduced, from the slight lean of their amorphous forms, that they were peering at my attacker, as if listening. What the bloody hell was this? A collective swarm of evolved Shades? The thought was terrifying.

The cellphone was still in my hand, the screen lit, waiting for me to press IISS.

I thumbed it off. I was not calling for help. He'd left me on my own? I'd handle it myself.

"Get out of here!" I roared, lunging for whatever-it-was.

The shadowy shape recoiled again, vanishing on a sudden gust of wind then resolidifying in the same spot. More breezed over to join it, settling on either side, until I stood glaring at a nearly solid wall of blackness fifty feet wide.

I gestured threateningly with my left hand. "I'll destroy you. You picked the wrong woman to mess with on the wrong bloody night. I was already in a bad enough mood!" I snarled. I paused and did that thing I used to do when I was young, when I was still killing with hate in my heart, enough to Kevlar all the Garda in Dublin. I embraced my rage at the injustice and hypocrisy of the world, welcomed it, let it fill my body, shape my limbs, backlight my eyes. I knew what I looked like when I let it happen— Ryodan on his worst day.

There was steel in my spine and death in my eyes when I swaggered toward the menacing wall. "You have two choices," I said in a terrible voice, my left hand raised high. "Leave. Or die."

The wall vanished.

I blinked, murmuring, "Well," mildly surprised and majorly skeptical. I knew I could be intimidating, but I was a single person and there were hundreds of them.

I stood for several long moments, scanning the cemetery, unwilling to act rashly, from a misguided belief they were gone. The monsters that stalk our world are devious, patient, and sly. So are a lot of the humans.

While I waited I evened out my breath. It was a constant reminder of how I lived: Bold, Ruthless, Energy, Action, Tenacity, Hunger; B-R-E-A-T-H. I wanted to kick up into the slipstream and rush to the nearest pool of light but I don't run from the things I fear anymore. They chase you, gaining substance and power the longer you run.

When several minutes passed without any of the shadows reappearing, I shoved the cellphone back in my pocket and turned to walk through the cemetery, eyes peeled for clues. I stumbled smack into a gravestone, tripped over it, rolled, sprang up and stood motionless, running a rapid internal assessment. I felt oddly shaky, weak as if my legs might go out from under me if I moved suddenly. Brushes with death usually invigorate me but this one had rattled me more than I'd realized. On the off chance I was simply hungry—a far more palatable conclusion to both tongue and ego—I crammed a protein bar in my mouth and resumed walking, taking careful mental notes about the locations from which the unknown entities had come, their shapes and sizes, their actions, and filed it all neatly away in my mental vaults.

I'd wanted a distraction.

I'd certainly gotten one. A mystery wrapped in an enigma, topped with a bow of suspense and danger.

I was whistling a cheery tune by the time Shazam bounded out of the night to join me, blood on his furry muzzle, delight in his violet eyes. We moved together and I rested my hand on his shaggy head as we padded into the night.

Still, I made a mental note to be a bit more careful about the things I asked the universe for in the future.

NOW

All men have limits.
They learn what they are and learn not to exceed
    them.
I ignore mine.

—BATMAN

Great spirits have long suffered violent
opposition from mediocre minds.

—EINSTEIN

What they said.

—DANI O'MALLEY, STILL AS MEGA AS EVER

THREE

The roads are fragile food for city crooks

on a starry night

"ANOTHER THREE OF THEM, Dani?" Rainey Lane exclaimed as she threw open the door of the townhouse.

The light from the cozily furnished home spilled into the night, glistening on cobblestones damp from a recent rain. Backlit, the fifty-four-year-old woman looked like the radiant, matronly angel of mercy she'd proven to be since I'd brought the first of the orphans to her.

"Four," I corrected, motioning to the eldest of the children huddled behind me. Her name was Sara Brady, she'd told me grudgingly, and she was eleven years old. Her brother, Thomas, was seven, the girl holding his hand was five, and the baby a mere ten months.

As I reached behind Sara to unfasten the satchel that held her sleeping sister, she tensed, rising to the balls of her feet, and knocked my arm away, thin shoulders trembling. Poised to run, her eyes darted nervously as she considered her odds: the chilly, dangerous night or the warm, inviting light.

"You agreed to come here with me," I reminded. "You'll be safe and well cared for."

"How long have they been on their own?" Rainey asked quietly.

"Nearly two months. Like most, they've no idea what happened to their parents."

"*I* do. The Faerie took them," the boy blurted. "I saw it, I did, with my own—"

Sara's mouth thinned to a line as she kicked him sharply in the shins. "Hush Thomas, you're not to be speaking of that!"

The boy began to cry, tears trickling down grimy cheeks. He rubbed his eyes with his fists then shook one at her. "But it's true! I saw it! It was one of the Faerie! You know it's true, Sara! You—"

When she kicked him again, harder, I moved between them and drew one to each side, resting my hands on their thin, knobby shoulders. "You'll be safe here. This is Rainey Lane. She helps run the foster center."

"Where they'll split us up!" Sara hissed, pulling away from me.

Rainey spoke swiftly. "We never separate siblings. If we're unable to find a good home for the four of you, you may stay in the center as long as you like."

That was one of the things I'd been counting on when I'd brought Rainey the first of the abandoned children I'd discovered, half dead in the streets. Her adopted daughters were biological sisters: Alina and MacKayla Lane. Family was everything to her. Still, it wouldn't be long before the recently formed center became too full to continue offering such an alternative.

Sara Brady squinted up at Rainey through damp, tangled hair, hostility blazing in her eyes. Silently, I applauded her bravado. The terrified eleven-year-old had managed to take care of her infant sister and her young siblings for nearly two months, without the many *sidhe*-seer gifts I'd had at her age. She was a fighter. But she was an eighty-pound-dripping-wet fighter, and Dublin, AWC, was no city for lightweights.

"You know who I am and what I do," I said to Sara softly. "Have you heard such terrible things about me, then? Or the foster center?"

"I've not heard of your 'foster center' at all," she said stiffly. "But kids on the telly *always* get split up." *And dreadful things happen to them*, the shadows in her eyes said.

"What about me?" I said.

"What about you?" Sara said, with a dismissive sniff.

I smiled faintly. She knew who I was. I was a legend. My talents coupled with the infrequent appearance of Shazam had seen to that.

"You're some kind of superhero!" the boy exclaimed. "And your sword," he gestured to it where it was sheathed across my back, "crashes like lightning when you fight. And you have a great, fat cat with superpowers!"

I winked at Thomas. "Never call him fat. It makes him grumpy. Nor is he . . . quite a cat." Well, he was a *Hel*-Cat, but that was an entirely different thing.

"There's no such thing as superheroes," Sara scoffed. "And if you *are* one, why didn't you stop the Faerie—" She clamped her mouth shut.

These weren't the first children I'd found who believed the Fae had stolen their parents. It made no sense. Fae didn't abduct adults, they lured them off with glamour, illusion, and lies. "Where else will you sleep tonight? They firebombed your squat and burned you out," I reminded.

For no reason. In a moment of boredom, a diversion for the three bullies who'd done it. They'd laughed as the children fled the blazing shell, screaming. Sent three half-starved kids and a helpless baby out into the deadly night. I'd been torn between going after the kids or the bastards who'd tossed the bombs. I'd gone for the kids.

First.

Sara fisted her hands at her sides. "It wasn't fair! I found that house. No one else was living there. I watched it for five days before we took it! And they *burned* it. A perfectly good place to live. They didn't even *want* it! Why would anyone do that?"

A house with running water and electricity; a thing she'd needed desperately to keep her family alive. But possession was nine-tenths of the law only if one was strong enough to enforce that law, and her ragged troop wasn't.

During the day, Dublin, AWC, was a normal, bustling, safe city, if there was such a thing with the walls down between Fae and Mortals, two-thirds of the world population gone, fragments of Faery drifting free, Light Court Fae living openly in town, establishing cultlike settlements around the country, and gangs warring to control supply and demand.

At night all bets were off. The predators came out to play, and if you weren't one of them, you were meat. There were only three types of beings that dared trespass beyond the protected Temple Bar District after dark: the very powerful; the very foolish; or the helpless, driven there by one threat or another.

"Just stay here with me for the night," Rainey said gently. "See how you feel in the morning. No one will force you to remain with us. May I see the baby, Sara?" She extended her arms. "I believe we've a diaper that needs changing."

Sara shot a quick glance over her shoulder and sniffed. Then glared up at Rainey.

"I suppose you've no diapers," Rainey went on in a low, soothing tone. "No food, or change of clothing. We've plenty of that here."

Of course, Sara had nothing, I thought with a rush of bitterness and relief. She hadn't been in the streets long enough to realize a child on her own needed many, many places to hide. All that she'd managed to beg, borrow, or steal was stashed in the house that was taken from her.

It was time for tough love. I said, "Do you want your baby sister to get diaper rash? Or catch cold from the weather? How will you get medicine if one of you gets sick? *You* might be able to survive out there, Sara, but the others won't. What if something happens to you? What will your sisters and brother do then? You're responsible for them. You have to be strong enough for four. Now isn't the time to be shortsighted and selfish."

Sara flinched and cried, "I'm not selfish!" Fear, isolation, crushing responsibility, she woke up to it, lived it all day, and fell asleep with it—a too-heavy stone in her too-empty stomach. I wanted to hug her. Take her in my arms and promise her life would be good again. Not selfish at all. Selflessly doing everything she could. But I needed to get her inside the door of the townhouse. There were three bastards skulking around out there, preying on the innocent, with my sights on their backs.

I knew what she was thinking, freedom conferred a certain solace: When it's only you taking care of your world, you feel as if you have some control over the many things that might go wrong. When you widen your circle to trust others, the risks increase exponentially.

As if she'd just ended an inner debate on the same thought, Sara Brady tensed, rising onto the balls of her feet again, trembling but determined.

I shot Rainey a look that said, *She's going to bolt.*

On cue, Rainey pushed the door to the townhome open all the way, allowing the scent of baking bread and a slowly simmering stew to waft out.

I watched Sara carefully. I'd had to drag a few kids inside, kicking and screaming, and had no problem doing so now. But more often than not, what words failed to accomplish, the promise of a hot meal did. It was easier for them in the long run if they took that first step willingly.

"Sara, I'm *hungry*," the younger girl cried plaintively. "And *thirsty* and I need to *pee*! Just tonight, okay?"

"Can we, huh, Sara, *please*?" Thomas chimed in. "I'm cold!"

Sara looked from my eyes to Rainey's and back again. Few adults probed gazes with such intensity. But the fate of her entire family was in her eleven-year-old hands. I wanted to tell her how proud I was of her. That she impressed me with all she'd done to keep them alive and together. But Rainey would say all that and more.

"Okay," Sara Brady said tightly. "But just for tonight. One night," she repeated, glaring at her siblings.

Once my charges were tucked safely inside and the door was closed, I smiled as I melted into the night.

That was what they all said, at first. Then found their fears were no match for the breadth and scope of Rainey Lane's heart.

Seeing Mac's mom was always uncomfortable for me. Given the unspoken that lay between us.

She'd never been anything but welcoming and kind. It was why I'd chosen to bring the first of the children to her and her husband, Jack, that bloody night, months ago. And why I would continue bringing them, assured she would always grant them safe haven.

Anyone who would welcome someone like me could never turn away a child.

π

I tracked my prey into Temple Bar and out, across the River Liffey and back again, debating whether the trio was so powerful, so drunk or drugged, or just so bloody stupid that they brazenly walked the killing fields of our city.

Their deaths would save countless lives.

Still, my sword hand itched so much from not being allowed to use it to kill the Fae now that Mac was queen, I'd begun to question my sentencing methods. I'd been taught a taste for the kill at a young age. Patterns like that are hard to break. I was good at it and someone had to do it. Then Dancer died and the finality of death took on new meaning for me. I still haven't found mercy—with the exception of kids and animals—but I've discovered creative sentencing. I had a few choice fragments of Faery—IFPs, Mac used to call them—I'd begun using for prisons.

Speaking of my sword hand, it really *was* itching, and scratching it through my fingerless glove wasn't working so I peeled it off.

My palm was black and cold as ice. The last time I'd seen it this bad was years ago, standing in a cemetery, watching shadows explode from the graves. Shadows I'd been hunting for the past two years, with no success. No one else had seen them that night, and no one had seen them since.

I watched as the darkness spread, creeping around to the

back of my hand then shooting up into my fingers. A sudden, sharp pain stabbed beneath all my nails. Black veins exploded up my wrist, vanishing into the sleeve of my jacket.

I stripped off my coat. Inky veins and black streaks marbled my left arm, nearly to the shoulder.

I was fourteen when I stabbed a Hunter through the heart with the Fae Hallow, the Sword of Light. The giant winged beast gushed black blood and shot me an incomprehensible look before closing fiery eyes. I thought I killed it but when I returned to snap photos for my newspaper, the enormous dragonlike creature was gone. My hand turned to dark ice within the hour, making me worry something of the creature had seeped up my sword and infected me. I was enormously relieved when my hand regained its normal color and temperature a few days later. I'd since discovered spells work better when etched with that hand and if, occasionally, I woke in the middle of the night to find it dark and freezing, I considered it a static oddity.

It was no longer static. Something had changed.

I waited to see if the darkness under my skin would continue to spread. When it didn't, I put my glove on and shrugged back into my jacket.

There was nothing I could do about it. I couldn't unstab the Hunter. I'd think about it later.

My hunt took me in the direction of Barrons Books & Baubles. I liked seeing the lovely, spatially challenged bookstore that was sometimes four floors, sometimes six, slicing the night, bastion eternal, spotlights blazing on the rooftop. It was a promise, made of timeless stone, polished wood, wrought iron, and stained glass: One day, Mac and Barrons would come back. One day, I'd bang in that door again. One day, the people who mattered to me would return.

Through the many disasters and riots that had befallen our city, even the ice age of the Hoar Frost King, Barrons Books & Baubles had remained untouched. I wouldn't be surprised to learn it had stood there since the dawn of time. There's a special feeling about the spot, as if once, a very long time ago, something terrible nearly happened at this precise longitude and latitude, and someone or -thing dropped the bookstore on the gash to keep the possibility from ever occurring again. As long as the walls stand and the place is intact, we'll be okay. Some people have churches. I have BB&B.

I turned a corner, anticipating the familiar sight, the rush of warm memories.

The bookstore wasn't there.

I narrowed my eyes, blinked and looked again.

Still not there.

I scowled down damp, fog-wisped blocks at an empty concrete lot. Then I kicked up into the slipstream and devoured the distance, stopping shy of where the front wall of the bookstore should be. If the building was concealed with glamour, I had no intention of crashing into it. I sported fewer bruises these days and liked it that way.

Beyond the empty lot, Jericho Barrons's epic garage was gone, too. In its place was another empty, concrete-surfaced lot.

My stomach clenched.

I reached out and felt around. No wall. I took a few steps and groped blindly about again. I strode forward until I was standing dead center in the rear seating area of the bookstore. Mac's fireplace should have been to my right, the Chesterfield behind me.

There was nothing.

I got a sudden chill. "Nothing" wasn't quite the right word. The bookstore was gone. But a thick, gluey residue lingered, as if something cataclysmic had transpired here, leaving a miasma of emotional, temporal, or spatial distortion in its place. Perhaps all three.

"This is bullshit," I growled. I'd had it. Enough was enough. Chester's nightclub at 939 Rêvemal Street had gone dark two years, one month, four days, and seventeen hours ago, not that I was keeping track or anything; the Fae-run club Elyreum on Rinot Avenue had taken its place, the Nine were gone, and the last I'd heard Christian was somewhere in Scotland, holed up in an ancient crumbling castle (shades of Unseelie King anyone?) with powerful wards placed at a seventy-five-mile perimeter around him to keep everyone out. Or him in. No one seemed sure.

Now someone or something had taken my bookstore. The universe continued erasing the best parts of my life.

Squaring my shoulders, I stalked to the empty lot where the garage should have been and studied the concrete, looking for wards, spells, any hint of illusion or glamour.

Nothing. Both buildings were simply gone.

As was my promise.

I knew nothing about what was going on with Mac, and had no way of contacting her. Had she established control over the Fae court? Taken them away and tidied up after herself? The bookstore was a site of immense power that she and Barrons would never leave lying around for someone else to exploit or claim.

Feeling oddly lost without my Mecca—Dublin just wasn't Dublin without BB&B—I spun away and was nearly back to the street when I felt a rumble beneath my feet, paused and cocked my head, listening intently. There it was again faintly, so faintly I'd almost missed it, even with my superb hearing. The baying of an animal. A wounded animal from the sound of it. Badly wounded. Not a wolf. Something . . . Fae? Terrible sound. Pain, so much pain.

I'll never let you be lost again.

Out of the blue, Ryodan's voice exploded in my head, deep and faintly mocking. I had no idea how that memory escaped incarceration from the high security ward of my disciplined brain. All my "that man" memories were under strict house arrest, locked down tight. I didn't think about Ryodan anymore.

There'd been a time the sheer number of superheroes in Dublin had annoyed me. Now I was a wolf without a pack. There'd been a time everyone had wanted me to open up, let them in. I'd complied; a word I can barely think inside my head even when it's the right thing to do, without hackles sprouting like poison ivy all over my body. And what did they do?

Left.

I was feeling as volatile as my Hel-Cat but the bookstore's disappearance was the last straw.

It began to rain, further dampening my mood. Rain is just what Ireland does. You'd think I'd be used to it. I hold a deep, personal grudge against rain: it makes my hair go curly and wild, completely undermining the cool, composed look I like to project to the world.

Breathing deep, I kicked up into the slipstream where I could avoid the raindrops. Unless animals began attacking Dublin, whatever was baying wasn't my problem. It sounded like it was dying anyway. And if such an attack did come, I knew one very hungry Hel-Cat that would relish the job.

I turned my focus back to what I excelled at: the hunt.

Dublin, or *dubh-linn*, "the black pool," with its many colorful inhabitants, was my city now, more so than it had ever been, given every bloody damned one of my fellow warriors had bloody well decamped.

I would protect it.

π

I lost my prey at the mirror.

Or rather, I let them go, unwilling to leap blindly into a Silver with an unknown destination.

I'd been closing in fast when the three men ducked into the entrance of an abandoned, crumbling brewery on the north bank of the River Liffey. I'd shadowed them through the gloomy industrial interior and was about to ease up into the slipstream to nab them when they abruptly vanished into a wall.

I approached with caution. When the Song of Making was sung, repairing the fabric of our world, I'd thought reality would return to a semblance of normal; the Fae-induced changes to our planet would reverse; the Light Court would retreat to their own realm despite the lack of a wall between our worlds, and society would resume its usual bleating, morally ambiguous course.

In retrospect, I don't know why I thought any of those things. Perhaps I'd just wanted a happy ending.

None of it happened. Post-Song reality was one in which the rules only became clear by interacting with them, often with unpleasant consequences. Children were being born with unusual gifts—although I'd call some of them curses; objects didn't always function quite like one had every rational reason to expect; doors didn't consistently go where you thought they would; and mirrors were the most unreliable of all—even human ones.

Magic burned in the planet, more potent than ever, as if the ancient melody had penetrated deep into the Earth, crooning in dangerously random fashion *"Awaken."* Everything had gotten more juice, even us *sidhe*-seers.

The many new elements of unpredictability had changed my behavior. I traveled in the slipstream only for short distances now, under calculated circumstances. There was too much I needed to see, less I could take for granted, and I absorbed few details moving in a higher dimension.

I skirted a large vat to get a closer look at the Silver. Embedded in stained and crumbling brick, a narrow black opening rippled in the wall, three inches from the floor, stretching all the way up to decaying rafters. Something about the slender, dark aperture made my blood run a little colder.

A gust of stifling air belched from the shivering surface, reeking of wood smoke and—I cocked my head, sniffing—old copper, perhaps blood. Distantly, I heard a rhythmic chant, thousands of voices—perhaps tens of thousands—repeating something over and over in a nearly hypnotic cadence.

It wasn't English. I didn't recognize the language.

I eased warily closer, kicking through several inches of litter and broken bottles, sending a small horde of roaches skittering into shadowy corners of the room. All mirrors debut on my dangerous list; few of them work their way off it. I wasn't even willing to put one in my bathroom until it underwent rigorous testing.

A person with normal hearing would have heard nothing coming from the dark glass, but I'm not normal. I catch the gentle whoosh of air displacement as people move; if I lay my ear to the earth, I hear countless insects wriggling and tunneling in the top layer of soil. I still couldn't decipher the words but the indistinct chant was now threaded by thin, distant, bloodcurdling screams.

I narrowed my eyes, focusing my *sidhe*-seer gifts on the inky darkness as if I might penetrate the veil. Still, I saw nothing but a narrow stream of roaches, climbing the few inches of wall and vanishing into the glass. Too bad I didn't have one of Dancer's handy little wireless cameras to attach to one, see if I could get a glimpse at the other side. I wondered if they were normal Earth roaches, or part of the disgusting Papa Roach that used to hang at Chester's. Unfortunately, they're indistinguishable to me.

I backpedaled from the wall and squirted up into the slip-stream a half a second before the mirror exploded, spraying razor-sharp splinters of dark glass across the floor.

I'd felt it coming. A vibration on the other side, as if the blow of whatever implement or spell had struck it required a second or more to reach my side of the portal.

By the time I dropped down again and crunched across broken glass and still more roaches, the wall was just a wall, access to my prey gone.

It changed nothing. Four children had been driven into the streets to their certain death. For amusement. There aren't many things I hold sacred. Kids are one of them.

I never forget. Never stop until I finish my job. The men's faces were etched into my memory. Their time would come.

I stalked through the brewery, restless, unsatisfied. It was nearly dawn, that liminal time when night became day, villains vanished, and vengeance got shelved. I spend my day doing normal things like laundry, cleaning, checking in at the orphanage, modifying and monitoring my many obligations, dropping by the abbey to train Initiates and catch some time to read the latest translations. I derive a great deal of satisfaction from doing my part to make our world safer. Tonight I'd failed and it would be twelve long hours before I got to try again. As dangerous as night in Dublin was, day ran fairly smoothly, as if darkness and light had struck a compact of their own, apportioning order to the day and chaos to the night.

I like the nights better. *Carpe noctem* not *diem*. My days drag. Night's when I feel most alive.

I banged out the door and exploded into the wet, foggy morning, tucking my head against a hard drizzle.

As I was about to kick up into the slipstream, a sudden movement from above caught my attention. I paused and glanced up to watch something roughly the size of a playing card falling from the sky, end over end.

I have a theory about people. Actually, I have a lot of theories about people but this particular one goes: if someone throws something at you, you're either a catcher or a ducker. I've never been a ducker. I've learned the hard way that it's sometimes wiser to be.

Still, instincts being instinctual and all, I jumped and caught the object while it was a few feet above my head.

"Ow!" I exclaimed. The edges were sharp and cut the tips of my fingers as they closed around it. Cursing softly, I wiped the blood on my jeans before turning my attention to the card.

Four inches by three, about a quarter of an inch thick, it was fashioned of alternating strands of green and black metals, woven together in an intricate, repeating Celtic knot pattern. It was beautiful. I'm Irish to the bone and proud of it. I love my country, my heritage, the fierce resilience and pride of the Irish people. This was fine work, done in the old way, lovely but slightly rough, as if smelt and beaten by a blacksmith. I had no idea what it was or why it had fallen from the sky. Shrugging at yet another mystery, I turned the metal piece over.

was chiseled into the metal in light green letters. A dozen instant responses took vague shape in my mind. Seriously? It was a bloody long list. I rolled my eyes and was about to toss it in the gutter when I saw something shimmering at the border and retracted my hand to inspect the card more closely.

I dropped it, as if burned.

A spell was etched into the metal, nearly undetectable, in slightly darker shades of green on green around the perimeter. A person with normal vision would never have seen it. Years ago I'd have instantly blamed Ryodan for any spelled thing I found, but he was gone and, in our new, magic-enhanced world, the possibilities were vast. Another *sidhe*-seer, Enyo, had told me just last week that some of the Fae lording over cultlike encampments in the rural areas were believed by many to not be Fae at all. None of her wary sources had been willing to elaborate on what they really were, but they'd insisted the charismatic, powerful beings hadn't descended from the True Race and that those of us at the abbey should give them a wide berth.

Which, of course, only made me want to go exploring.

I stared down at the metal card on the pavement. What was its purpose? What did the spell do? I shivered, grateful I hadn't muttered a wish aloud. I like wards. They're practical, straightforward, and don't usually bite you in the ass when you use them. Spells, on the other hand, are convoluted, dangerous, and unpredictable things. Especially when blood's involved.

I glanced down at my fingertips. Then back at the card.

My blood was smeared along the top edge.

Bloody hell.

I wasn't picking it up again, on the off chance I hadn't already activated whatever the spell was meant to do. I'd learned more than I ever wanted to know about blood-spells from the monstrous Rowena. There was no way I was giving it a second shot at me. Nor was I willing to leave it lying around for someone else to cut themselves on.

I toed the thing into a nearby gutter, watched until it vanished down the drain, disappearing into the vast, watery tunnels and caverns of Dublin below, then kicked up into the slipstream and headed home.

FOUR

- • -

And Shazzy's got stormy eyes

"SHAZAM, WHAT IS GOING on here?" I wrinkled my nose as I stepped into my bedroom, peering through the gloom.

The dark room smelled funny, like a zoo. Fecund. I've always liked that word. Just not in my room.

The glow of Dancer's stereo cast enough light so I could see Shazam had either doubled in width or there was something next to him on my fluffy, freshly laundered cloud of a white comforter. Coupled with the strong animal odor, it could only mean one thing. "You know the rules, no eating in bed," I rebuked. No blood, no guts, no gristle in my sheets. I didn't think that was too much to ask.

"I'm *not* eating. That's all you think I do. I do *other* things, too," came the derisive sniff from the darkness.

My eyes fully adjusted now, I could clearly see the outline of a carcass lying next to him, furred and lifeless. "Like what, saving leftovers for later?" I slid my sword off over my shoulder, propped it against the wall, and unzipped my jacket.

He said smugly, "I have a mate."

Holy hell. I froze, half out of my jacket. Thoughts collided in my brain too fast to process, leaving a single horrid image: sharing a bed with a mating Hel-Cat.

I'd take blood, guts, and gristle any day.

I flipped on the light and nearly burst out laughing, but I'm not foolish enough to laugh at a Hel-Cat who might be mating.

Shazam was sprawled on the comforter, one massive, tufted paw clamped tightly around the neck of an utterly terrified, exhausted creature, keeping it pinned to the bed.

It was no wonder I'd thought it was dead. Stretched on its side, it was barely breathing, round golden eyes wide and fixed on nothing. There was froth on its muzzle and whiskers.

Good grief, Shazam had brought home a Pallas cat.

"This is Onimae," he informed me proudly.

I shook my head, not certain where to begin with this latest escapade of his. He certainly kept things interesting. "Shazam, you're a sentient, talking, highly evolved being. That," I stabbed my finger at it, "is a cat, and barely a quarter your size. Let the poor baby go." She looked traumatized. Deeply.

"You're not the boss of me."

"Am, too," I reminded. "You agreed to that. Where did you find her? Have you considered that she may already have a mate, a family of her own?"

He smirked. "Brought them, too, tiny red."

I dropped my jacket to the floor, guns and knives forgotten, and glanced hastily around, realizing I should have seen this coming. Shazam had been obsessing over wildlife DVDs for the past few months; looking for new game to spice up his nightly hunt, I'd thought. But he'd been searching for a girlfriend. Solitary creatures that lived in grasslands and steppes, Pallas cats were the size of a domestic cat, with stocky bodies, shaggy, dense fur, stripes and ringed tails. I wrinkled my nose again. They were also known for scent-marking their territory, which explained the foul odor in my bedroom. "How many and where?"

He shrugged nonchalantly. "Don't know, don't care. They aren't Onimae."

I dropped to the floor and peered beneath my bed.

A dozen yellow eyes glared out at me from fluffy faces, regarding me with identical expressions of hostility: low-set ears flattened to their heads, a single side of their mouth drawn up in an Elvis-like sneer.

Sometimes I feel like I live in a cartoon. There were six Pallas cats from the far reaches of Asia sneering at me from beneath my bed. As they began to growl, I bit back another laugh—once I began laughing I would either hurt Shazam's feelings or lose what little respect I managed to command with him at times like these—and said firmly, "Shazam, you will return all of them to wherever you found them."

"Will not."

I poked my head up and glared at him. "Will, too."

"Can't make me," he said airily.

Technically that was true. Handling Shazam took patience and tact. I pushed myself up from the floor. "When did it, er— Onimae eat last?"

"She will eat after we mate," he said grandly.

"Does it really look like she's about to jump up and mate with you anytime soon?"

"She's gathering her strength."

"She's scared out of her wits." My first goal was to get the small, terrified cat away from him. "She needs food and water. Earth animals can't go as long as you without eating. Let her go and I'll get some food for, er—" I glanced under the bed at my sneering, growling companions and sighed. "—our guests."

Shazam had been in Dublin with me for over two years and I knew it had been a big adjustment for him. I'd found him on a planet in the Silvers, living in another dimension, half mad from long solitude. He was the only one of his species left, and I could only imagine how lonely that must be. Perhaps he *should* have a mate. Perhaps the Pallas cat might grow to like him. Who was I to say he shouldn't have a family of his own? Could he have a family of his own with an Earth animal? Did Pallas cats have large litters? What the bloody hell would I do with half a dozen Pallas/Hel-Cats? My brain thinks in Batman quips under pressure, a defense mechanism that keeps my chin up while the world goes to hell around me. This time it married an old Star Trek episode to my favorite comic book hero and pronounced: *Holy tribbles, Batman, we've got trouble!* Swallowing my mirth, I demanded, "Can you have babies?"

He gave me a strange look. "Children? Of course."

"Is that what this is about? Do you want to make them with her?"

Violet eyes gleaming, he chuffed with amusement. "That is not how children are made. One day you will know how children are made."

I raised my brows. I'd figured out how children were made when I was five years old, sitting unsupervised in front of a TV all day with the remote control. I wasn't sure I wanted to hear how he thought children were made. "If she doesn't eat, she may die." Assuming she didn't expire from shock first. "I'll be back with food and water." As I turned toward the door, I shot a withering look over my shoulder. "I mean it. Let her go. She's terrified of you."

He sniffed. "Riveted by my prowess."

"Catatonic with shock."

"Overcome by my magnificence."

This could go on all night. "Pinned by your paw," I said dryly. "If you're so certain of yourself, try removing it and see what happens."

"She will remain in my thrall," he said confidently.

I shut the bedroom door as I left. The last thing I needed was a horde of hostile Pallas cats coming after me, attacking my ankles. I could imagine too many ways things could get even weirder than they already were.

I had seven Pallas cats in my bedroom.

It wasn't the first time Shazam had brought something unusual home with him, but none of those things had ever been alive and required sustenance. Although I stock fresh meat and blood for Shazam, there was no way I was taking bowls of it into my clean, cream-carpeted bedroom, which already sported an odor challenging enough to eradicate. No doubt I'd be tearing the damn carpet out. Or moving again.

My eating habits have changed over the years. Unlike most people, I have little to no emotional attachment to food. I see it as necessary energy and prioritize it in that order: fat first, protein next, carbs last. I need it fast and efficient so I stock my various residences with canned tuna, canned coconut milk, chocolate bars, and high carb snacks.

I glanced at the closed door of my bedroom, down the hallway, and finally let my laughter bubble free as I grabbed bowls and began opening cans of tuna.

π

Twenty-five minutes later the Pallas cats had devoured nineteen cans of tuna and nearly a gallon of water.

They were going to need to pee. And do other bad-smelling things. Not that I believed the odor in my bedroom could get much worse. I spend my nights in the dirtiest parts of the city. I like to spend my days in tidy surroundings.

I was stretched back against the tufted velvet headboard of my bed, legs crossed. Shazam was sitting on the dresser, alternating between peering beneath the bed at his "mate" and her family and giving me the evil eye.

I waited in silence. He tended to come around to my viewpoint more quickly if I gave him time to work things through himself, offering the occasional gentle nudge.

"I did nothing wrong," he said finally, sourly. "I get bored when you're gone."

"So, come with me. You used to all the time."

"I miss something, Yi-yi," he said plaintively.

Oh, my friend, so do I. Many things. I said softly, "What?"

"Something," he said, his eyes filling with tears. "I don't know."

Beneath the bed I heard claws scratching the carpet as it was prepared for use as a litter box.

"If you return them, Shazam, we'll figure this out. I don't want you to be lonely. If it's a mate you want, we'll find one. But you can't abduct a wild animal and her family and decide she's going to be yours. You have to move slowly, give her time to get to know you. And it has to go both ways or it's ownership. Living things aren't property. You can't take them simply because you want them." It was my job to teach my bombastic, powerful friend how to live among us and I took it seriously. I didn't cite the rules and expect him to obey; I tried to help him understand why the rules mattered.

He slumped in a puddle of depression. "She can't talk and she hardly even thinks. She doesn't know the world is bigger than her cage, or this room. She's never seen the stars and hunted on wild planets. *I'm* not what terrifies her. *Everything* terrifies her." His head drooped to the top of the dresser and he put his paws over his eyes.

"She's not your equal and never can be," I said, vocalizing what was bothering him.

He said wearily, "She is not."

I smiled wryly. Over the past few years I'd done what passed as dating for someone like me. Each time I tried, I ended up feeling more alone, not less. Fascination isn't love and pedestals are hard, uncomfortable, and only big enough for one. Some people get a home with family and friends, some people get a pedestal. Perversely, those on the pedestal hunger for the normalcy of a home and family, while those with the home and family hunger for the glamour and excitement of a pedestal. Further compounding things, the magic of the Song enhanced my *sidhe*-seer gifts. I'm physically stronger and have to hold back all the time. Careful, restrained sex is an oxymoron in my book. I get more release from exploding a few of Ryodan's punching bags.

"Will you return her, then? All of them," I added. Precision was a must with my moody beast.

"*Yes,* Yi-yi," he said with a gusty sigh. After a moment, he lifted his head from the dresser. His violet eyes narrowed and shot a meaningful glance at my left hand, which was still cold and black. "It's happening again."

"I know."

"Bigger now. It doesn't hurt?" he fretted.

"No. I'm fine."

He assessed me intently, as if seeking reassurance of that, then his body disappeared and only his head remained, his large, expressive eyes gleaming with love.

I smiled. "I see you, too, Shazam."

His disembodied head nodded regally. "I will return after I've hunted, Yi-yi." Then all of him was gone.

I dropped to the floor, peered beneath my bed, and watched with relief as the Pallas cats popped out of existence, one by one.

π

I stood beneath the spray of a long hot shower while he was gone, washing my hair, shaving my legs, and considering my left hand. The stain had retreated to beneath the crook of my elbow. Although my hand was still black, even the nails, my fingers were no longer quite so cold.

I had no idea why it happened or what caused it, if anything. It was possible it was simply random. Sometimes when my hand turned black, I was in the midst of a dangerous situation. Other times, I could tie it to nothing threatening in my vicinity. Each time it happened, I felt oddly shaky afterward and had found eating helped allay the strange enervation.

I flexed my hand beneath the warm spray. It didn't hurt. Well, aside from the brief stabbing pain I'd felt earlier when it shot up beneath my nails. The wraiths in the cemetery had been repelled by it.

What had the Hunter done to me that night so long ago?

I hadn't seen any of the enormous winged beasts in our skies for years and I'd been watching, waiting. I had questions.

I'd found no reference to the Hunters in the abbey's vast libraries. But then, I still had the lion's share of the collections to wade through. It was slow going, sorting through the bits and pieces of my *sidhe*-seer heritage. I read for hours a day, sitting with those at the abbey who were scanning the ancient fragile scrolls and books to create an electronic library with cross-referencing tags that will never decompose. It should have been done long ago, but the prior headmistress of our order had been more inclined to let our secrets rot than share them.

I turned off the water, wrapped a towel around my body, and used a second one on my hair. As I toweled it dry and sorted through the damp tangle of long red curls, I turned my thoughts back to the problem of Shazam.

He'd been different lately, with fewer moments of lucid brilliance and more of emotional angst. I was worried about him. When he got back, we were going to have a long talk, and I wasn't going anywhere until I figured out what to do to snap him out of his funk. If an emergency came up, he was going with me to take care of it. I should never have let him stay at home while I'd gone out patrolling the past few months. After nearly seven years together I knew being alone and unseen, as he'd been on Olean, was the worst thing for him.

I smoothed a light oil into my hair to keep it from going completely wild, grabbed my clothes off the counter, tugged on a pair of faded, ripped jeans and one of Dancer's old, faded tee-shirts, a white one with HOLY SHIFT, LOOK AT THE ASYMPTOTE ON THAT MOTHERFUNCTION! emblazoned on the front. Wearing his clothes made me feel like a part of him was here with me, although I wasn't sure he'd be particularly impressed with my life. Lately it positively brimmed with . . . routine. Epic adventures were a thing of the past, Fae battles forbidden.

Sighing, I retrieved the sword that I wasn't allowed to use for its universe-given purpose from its perch within reach of the shower.

I love my sword. I pet it; it soothes me. Cold, hard, frequently bloody, we're two of a kind. Made for war, but with a bit of work we shine right back up again. Double-edged, the straight blade swells in thickness and width as it nears the guard. The blade, apart from the hilt, is 34.5 inches long—most of the time. In battle, I've seen that length increase and decrease. Dancer was never able to identify what it's made from but it's oddly light yet weighty at the same time, razor-sharp, and has proved unbreakable.

Although the blade shimmers alabaster, the grip is fashioned from engraved lengths of ebony and ivory metals woven together. The guard is dark as midnight and resembles narrow wings that arc back toward my hand. The heavily engraved pommel is formed from the same obsidian metal as the guard and is always cold. Ornate dark symbols—a cipher that has never ceased to stump me despite the considerable time I've wasted over the years with pen and paper trying to work it out—flow the length of the blade on both sides. The symbols often move, swirling too rapidly for me to transcribe. When I fight, my sword burns incandescent, and I often find those undecipherable symbols seared into the flesh of our victims.

Most of all, it feels good in my hand. As if it was made just for me. And one day, I just know deep in my bones, I'll get to use it again.

I padded out into the bedroom.

My fingers tightened on the hilt.

There was a man sitting on my bed.

Not Fae.

But considering he'd breached my many booby traps to gain entrance, there was no way he was human either.

FIVE

— • • —

I put a spell on you

"B Y LOKI'S BALLS," THE man said, shaking his head, "you're not at all what I expected."

Expectations limit your ability to perceive things. I try to have few. I leaned against the doorjamb, assessing him, sword deceptively at ease at my side.

He scanned me back, absorbing the bare feet, the holes in the knees of my jeans, the face void of makeup, the tumble of wet hair. His gaze hitched briefly on my left hand and his eyes flared infinitesimally then narrowed. "But you're a mere child. How did something like you get your hands on the Faerie sword?"

On February twentieth of this year, my last birthday, I'd decided to commit to an age. As I was somewhere between twenty-one and twenty-three, I split the difference and settled on twenty-two. Casual and without makeup, I knew I looked several years younger. It worked for me; strangers often underestimated me.

I shrugged and said nothing.

"Well, hand it over and let's be done with it," he said, pushing up from the bed, hand outstretched, eyes fixed possessively on the softly glowing blade at my side. "Time is short, I've much to do."

I laughed in spite of myself. He was shorter than me, with a lean build, wearing black jeans, boots, and a green shirt. Wavy raven hair swept back from a high forehead above a narrow face. His eyes were nearly as emerald as mine, with tiny amber flecks, and alight with amusement. I was the one holding the sword. As far as I could tell, he wasn't carrying a single weapon. "I don't think so."

"We made a deal. You will honor it."

"I made no deal with you."

He spanned the distance between us in a sprightly leap, smiling broadly. "Oh, but you did." He caught my hand in his and lifted it to his lips, kissed it then held it between us and glanced meaningfully at the cuts across my fingertips.

Right. He was wearing black and green, like his calling card. His hair was black and his eyes were green. What was with people? Wasn't anyone normal anymore? Was having a color theme the new trend? "That was a cheat," I said irritably. "You made the edges razor sharp and flung it at me."

He cooed brightly, "And you caught it. There will be no welshing. You plucked it from the sky, offered me your blood, and made a wish. I granted it. You owe me."

"I didn't make a wish and you didn't grant anything. And I didn't offer you my blood. You took it. Through deceit."

Green eyes danced with mischief. "I just love that part, don't you? Blood is blood no matter how you obtain it." His gaze shifted, swirling with menace and mockery.

"That's a trap. You can't sucker people into spells."

He clasped his hands together beneath his chin and sneered, "Oh, please, as if your history isn't positively mired in tales of stupid humans lured into unsavory deals and contracts. *And* their repercussions." He snapped his fingers sharply beneath my nose. "Wake up, child. Pay attention. Fools fall. It's what they do."

I growled, "I'm neither a child nor a fool."

"By my standards, you're both. You didn't have to catch it. I presented an opportunity. You took it. Pay up. The sword is mine."

I said coolly, "I didn't make a wish and you didn't grant one. I'm not giving you the sword."

He hopped with delight and did a fast, merry dance in a tight circle, as if pleased with himself beyond enduring. I half expected him to kick his heels together and break into a sprightly jig. Then he spun about to face me, applauding with gusto—clearly himself, not me. "That's the very, very, *very* best part," he gushed, eyes sparkling. "I *did* grant your wish. You just don't know it yet."

Not good. Which of the many half-formed desires that had sprung to my mind when I read his calling card had he chosen, and in just what convoluted manner would it be granted? History was full of genie-gone-wild tales and rabbit-paw stories. You never got what you asked for. You got a version of a wish as razor-edged as his calling card, something that would either harm me or benefit him, or both.

I still wasn't giving him my sword. He was going to have to take it. If he could.

"Oh, I can," he leered, leaning nearer until our faces were inches apart.

I went motionless, searching his eyes. Flinty eyes narrowed with cunning antiquity, something old and deadly lurked beneath his sprightly demeanor. I'd underestimated him. He employed prancing gaiety for the same reason I allowed people to think I was younger than I am. "Who are you?"

"A name for a name," he cooed.

A small price to know my enemy. "Dani O'Malley."

His eyes twinkled with mirth. "You may call me AOZ; that's A-O-Z, and all capitals, by the way."

"Gotcha, the A is silent," I mocked. He'd pronounced it *Ahhhs*. "*What* are you?"

He laid a long finger to the side of his thin nose as if pondering what answer to offer. Finally he said, "Those who belong here." His face shifted and changed, the bones sharpening, skin drawing taut and far too pale, eyes narrowing, all playfulness gone. I caught a sudden reek of soil, blood, and bones on his breath when he hissed, "Unlike the treacherous Faerie who think to take what is ours, not once but twice. Give me the sword, child, and do it now."

The command affected my head, my limbs—similar to something Ryodan had once done, although he'd merely forced me to eat a candy bar when I was hungry, not give away my most prized possession—and I was horrified to feel my hand rising, preparing to hand him the hilt of my sword. Apparently, the spell agreed with him; we'd made a deal and I had to honor it. I was ensnared by his power.

"Stop!" an imperious voice thundered, and my hand froze, fingers locked on the hilt.

AOZ spun to face the intruder, hissing, "Get thee gone, Faerie!"

I blinked, startled. Inspector Jayne had just sifted in, joining us in my bedroom, and stood a dozen paces away, on the opposite side of my bed. He wrinkled his aquiline nose and said, "By the bloody saints, what *is* that smell, Dani?"

I shrugged, taking pains to avoid direct eye contact. Meeting the gaze of a Fae prince is never a wise thing to do. First your eyes bleed. If you hold their terrifying inhuman gaze too long, it's said your mind will hemorrhage as well. I've never tested that theory. My brain is my finest weapon. "Don't ask." I hadn't seen the inspector in years. Not since he'd undergone the transformation from human to Fae. I nearly hadn't recognized him. The head of the old Garda, Dublin's police force, had once been a rugged, barrel-chested Liam Neeson look-alike.

No more. He'd become a towering, otherworldly being with a stupefying gaze of opal-kissed skies threatening thunderstorms, hair the color of sunshine glinting off fast-running streams, and the lithe, beautifully muscled body of the Light Court. He smelled of fresh dew on morning petals, the crush of spring grass beneath my boots, the fertile, earthy promise of forest awakening from a long winter and raw, to-die-for sensual pleasure. All trace of rugged humanity was gone.

Mac hadn't changed that way. Sure, her hair had lightened and lengthened, but she'd remained human, like us. I scanned him intently, found nothing to define him as having been born of our race. Inspector Jayne was Fae with finality.

I eased my sword down a notch, keeping it at the ready. Trusting no one in the room but myself.

As the inspector, Jayne had once taken it, leaving me in a trash-filled street, badly wounded, on the verge of bleeding out. Was I supposed to believe he'd now sifted in to prevent me from losing it? I narrowed my eyes and assessed AOZ. I'd drawn conclusions while we'd talked. Not Fae, not human, but magical, and smelling of earth, blood, and bones.

There was an old Earth god in my bedroom and he'd cast a spell on me.

And now there was a Fae prince in my bedroom, too, carefully muted at the moment, for which I was grateful. But who could say how long that would last?

AOZ despised Jayne and, apparently, the entire Fae race.

I said to AOZ's back, "You want my sword so you can use it to kill Fae."

He whirled on me, eyes narrowing to slits of green fire. "Better us than them. Give it to me now, you fool!"

In spite of myself, my hand arced upward.

"Dani, don't," Jayne murmured.

My hand dropped again.

I'd have nearly liked Jayne at that instant, if he hadn't added in a voice of coercion, "You will give it to me instead."

My hand went back up and my feet began a traitor's walk toward him.

A puppet. I was their bloody puppet. It incensed me. Enough to want to stab them both with the weapon they coveted.

AOZ said coldly, gaze fixed hungrily on my sword, "My spell was first. Hand it to me now, child, or I will raze your motherfucking world."

Torn between commands, my hand went still and I pondered its motionless state. Spell to my left, voice of power to my right. If they kept tugging at me, what might happen, not to me, but them? Especially if I added my left hand into the mix.

I eased black fingers around the hilt of the sword and laced my hands together.

Jayne's gaze fixed on the subtle coupling then shot to my face, searchingly.

Still, he continued to work at my will, as did AOZ. I could feel ancient, inimical power rolling off them and knew, though neither was speaking, both were furtively attempting to bend my hand their way. Excruciating pressure escalated inside my head, so I tucked the bulk of my brain into one of my boxes and braced myself. I'd learned long ago how to distance myself from pain.

Two very different forms of power crept over my flesh, slithering under and around, seeking control: one brilliant and summery, one dark and earthy. Two arcane arts met on my hands, mingling perhaps with something of the Hunter's ancient power, and mixed as badly as oil and water with an undercurrent of dynamite.

There was a swirling tornado of magic-gone-bad building, growing larger and more flawed with each passing moment, then abruptly power exploded from my hands and slammed back into them. Jayne roared and flinched. AOZ shrieked and clawed at his face.

Both turned to snarl at me.

I shrugged, flexing my fingers to make sure they were under my control again. "You shouldn't try to take a woman's sword."

Jayne said sternly, "Dani, that weapon is far more dangerous than you know. Only a Fae can handle its power now."

AOZ snorted. "Don't listen to him. The Faerie seduce and lie."

"But gods don't?" I said derisively.

His eyes narrowed and he gave me an appraising look. "Perhaps not entirely a fool."

"Neither yours nor his," I warned.

Jayne said, "Dani, what happened to your hand?"

"Yes, what?" AOZ asked, eyes narrowing.

"No clue." That was the truth. But I was done answering questions. I'd formed theories and I wanted answers. "Let me guess; the gods are back, awakened by the Song. Long ago you warred with the Fae. You've decided to start that war up again and, to do so, you need my sword."

"Pretty much," Jayne said flatly.

"And how long have you known this without bothering to tell any of us?" I fired at Jayne.

"Not very," he said, bristling at my tone. "They returned weak and hid, biding time until they regained power. Only recently have they begun to show themselves."

"We were weak because of what *you* did to us!" AOZ hissed at him then snarled at me, "We didn't start the war. They did, turning your race against us. Once, your race prayed to us and we listened. We were good to you. Once."

"Try to take my sword again, you'll die."

"I'm not the only one who will come seeking it. Others won't be as generous as I. You don't want *him* to come after it. You never want him to come. It won't be only your sword he takes. Do yourself a favor and hand it over to me. You'll be glad you did. If he comes for you, you'll discover the true meaning of Hell."

I let my eyes go empty and cold. "I'm not afraid of Hell. I lived there once. And if I have to go back again, I'll swagger through those gates with fire in my blood and war in my heart. And I'll. Take. No. Prisoners."

I meant it. I have little fear. I have a great deal of fury. Inequity, injustice, incites a slow burn inside me that consumes me with deference for neither self-injury nor casualties. I sometimes think I'm a hair trigger away from becoming something . . . else. A thing I don't understand.

AOZ said sneeringly, "Good luck with that. His Hell is a place you can't begin to imagine. Eternal. No escape."

"Or," I said with acid sweetness, "I could give my sword to Jayne and you could try to take it from a prince. But, oh, wait, if that were possible you would have taken it the last time your races warred. Seems to me, giving it to Jayne would pretty much shut the old gods down."

"Yes, Dani," Jayne said quietly, "it would."

AOZ hissed, "You're so certain you prefer the human race answer to the Faerie over us? We guided you. We didn't turn our backs on you until you betrayed us."

"I prefer the human race answer to no one but itself. We don't need, or want, either of you. I'm standing here with two alien races, both vying for control over man—"

"We're native to this world, not alien," AOZ growled at the same time Jayne cut me off with, "That's not true, Dani, and you know it. I once was human. I still hold the same hopes and fears for our race as you do, and adhere to the same priorities I once did."

AOZ said derisively, "You're Fae. You don't feel and you don't belong on our world."

"This is *our* world," I said coolly. "And as far as I'm concerned, neither of you belong here. And I don't care if you were human once, Jayne. You're not now."

"Dani, I'll take the sword to the queen," Jayne said.

"For which I have only your word. No thanks. I'll be keeping it. Or," I fished, dying to see Mac again, "you could bring the queen to me and I'd consider handing it over." Jayne was a mostly good man. With a fatal flaw. Well, two. One, he was a Fae prince now. Two, he'd not been able to resist taking my sword once before for the sake of the "common good." Pretty much every phrase that begins with the word "common" instills unease in me. Common knowledge, common good, common welfare. Somehow, "common man" never seems to have much of a say in those "common" definitions. Politicians and kings make those decisions and it's the "common" man who dies when kings go to war.

"It seems we have an impasse," AOZ said with silky menace. "Two of us don't require sleep. You do." He folded his arms over his chest. "It's only a matter of time and we've an infinity of it. Once you've wearied, one of us will take the sword. Or you may choose your successor."

I glanced at Jayne and knew instantly he wasn't willing to wait that long. He was already changing, no longer concealing his power, but allowing the facade he'd adopted in order to shield me drop away infinitesimal bit by bit, permitting me time to cave before he turned the full, mind-numbing beauty and horror of a Prince of the Court of Seasons on me.

I shivered. Fae princes are sexual beyond human tolerance. They can instill desire in us, amplify it, feed off it, and throw it back at us a thousand times more potent than it began. It's too much for us. It chars a woman down to ash inside her own mind, leaving nothing but a willing slave.

I might have run Jayne through with the sword—if he hadn't already begun letting his glamour fall. Now, if I were to lunge for him, he'd simply blast me with the full strength of it, and I'd be on the floor with no thought left of killing him in my smashed mind.

"You wouldn't," I said icily.

"I'm sorry, Dani, but I don't dare let it fall into their hands. This isn't personal."

He'd said the same thing to me years ago when he left me lying in that trash-filled street. "Spell check," I growled, "when you do something to a person, it's *person*al. That's the funny thing about us persons." I laid down my mental grid and kicked up into the slipstream.

Nothing happened.

I sighed. Extreme emotion and extreme arousal can short out

my *sidhe*-seer powers, and it always happens at the worst possible times. I'd been working on the extreme emotion flaw and had made progress with it. It wasn't quite as easy to master the other fault: I had to get aroused to work on it and . . . well, that hadn't happened in a while. I cast rapidly about for another option, finding only one. It was a long shot.

"Give it to me now," AOZ commanded, "and I'll kill him with it. The Faerie permit only slaves to live and demand worship. We aren't and don't."

As Jayne's glamour continued to fall by slow degrees—still allowing me time to hand it over willingly—I glanced down to where both of my hands were wrapped tightly around the hilt of my sword. I shuddered as his inhuman sexuality began nudging the edges of my mind, looking for a sweet spot, an easy way in. He was trying to do as little damage as possible. For the moment.

Shivering violently, teeth chattering, I ground out, "Y-You're w-w-willing to sh-shatter my m-mind for it?" *What do you think your queen will do to you?* my eyes blazed. I felt tears slip from them as I met his gaze, and didn't need a mirror to know I was weeping blood.

He said sadly, "Ah, Dani, she will most certainly kill me. But she will have the sword. I'm willing to die to protect our race and yours from these vermin."

He'd said "our race," and "yours." There it was. I knew it. His allegiance was to the Fae, not us. I closed my eyes, grinding my teeth together against the cruel teeth of power now tearing aggressively into the edges of my mind. When I was younger, I experienced a Fae prince's compulsion twice. And survived. I was older and wiser now.

I took my long shot, focused on the ice in my hand. I welcomed it, beckoned it to spread throughout my body, course through my veins with absolutely no idea what I was embracing. In a battle for your life, your sanity, your race, the weapon you have is the one you use.

I felt a sudden prick of pins and needles through my entire body, a buzzing deep in my flesh as if my limbs were waking up from a long time of being numb. My skin cooled and shivered on my bones, feeling strangely elastic and supple. Blood thunder crashed in my head, slamming against the confines of my skull, as whatever the Hunter had left beneath my skin responded.

And flexed.

And grew.

A wave of dizziness took me and I nearly stumbled as sudden stars exploded behind my eyes and I had a fleeting glimpse of a vast, nebula-drenched nightscape superimposed in the air in front of me. Then it was gone and the inside of my head felt calm and cool and silent as the deepest reaches of space.

I didn't have time to analyze it. Didn't think. Just opened my eyes and flung my left hand at Inspector Jayne.

The prince sifted out a mere fraction of a second before the bolt of pale blue lightning exploded in the precise spot he'd been standing. The crackling energy struck the south wall of the room, blowing it apart from floor to ceiling. Plaster exploded, wood splintered, and bricks tumbled away, leaving a gaping hole where the wall had been.

My dresser listed dangerously on the edge then plunged four floors to the street below.

Snarling, I whipped my gaze to AOZ.

He dematerialized instantly into a cloud of murky green fog that compacted, narrowed down to a tight stream, and shot out through the opening blasted in the room.

I stood there a moment, leveling my breath, waiting, while the energy surging through my arm ebbed, until at last it was gone. My legs felt like noodles and my hands were trembling.

So much for my warding abilities. They'd failed to keep out both old god and Fae. Push come to shove, I might end up having to sleep on the heavily warded private residence levels of Chester's, and I so didn't want to do that. Then again, I had no idea if they were warded against gods.

I pushed the sleeve of my tee up and inspected myself. My arm was black all the way up to my shoulder, with thin tentacles of dark veins spreading across my left collarbone.

I let the sleeve drop and looked out over my bed into the pale morning beyond where a sea of rooftops stretched, and farther out, the whitecaps of a slate gray ocean. A heavy drizzle had begun to fall, and a sudden breeze gusted rain in, soaking my fluffy white comforter.

I rolled my eyes. My bedroom had been through hell in the past few hours.

But every rain cloud really did have a silver lining.

At least it didn't smell so bad anymore.

ASSASSIN

W hen I was nine years old, Rowena told me a dangerous caste of Fae had infiltrated our city. Slender, diaphanous, beauti-ful, with a cloud of gossamer hair and dainty features, they were ca-pable of slipping inside a human, and taking over their limbs and lives completely.

Once they assumed a human "skin," they were no longer detectable to sidhe-seers and, thus camouflaged, vanished forever beyond our reach to prey endlessly upon our race.

This made them a most deadly threat to our order, she told me in a hushed voice, who could possess her charges at the abbey at any time; in fact, she confided, they had.

But—and there was always a but with the old bitch—she had a special charm that she, and she alone as Grand Mistress of sidhe-seers, could employ to see inside a person to the despicable, life-stealing Fae within.

At nine, nothing seemed far-fetched to me. I'd fully expected to *find the world beyond my cage as densely populated by superheroes and villains as my world on the telly.*

For nearly a year Rowena steered me down the corridors of our abbey as she inspected her girls, guided me out into the streets and alleys and businesses, where we hunted the dastardly villains, a secret team of two tasked with a great, secret mission that made me feel important and good.

And when she'd identify a Gripper with the charm that never worked for me, we'd return to her office at the abbey where, with great gravity and ceremony, she'd place the luminous Sword of Light across my upturned palms and command me to save our order, perhaps even our world.

She taught me to be quick and stealthy about it. She told me how and where to stab and slice and kill. No one suspects a child, not even when they carry a sword. Most thought it a toy. I rarely needed to employ extreme velocity to complete my mission. It was easy to get close. Adults fret over lost, crying children.

Do whatever you must to save our world: no deceit or ploy unjust, she'd taught me. The end justifies the means.

I've come to understand the means define you.

Although they are exceedingly rare, Grippers exist.

That wasn't a lie.

There is, however, no charm that allows anyone to see them.

I took twenty-three lives that year and I don't know why. Mothers, fathers, daughters, sons, I carved holes in their families, shattering their hearts and their worlds. Perhaps they crossed her in business dealings. Perhaps they looked at her wrong at the post office. Regardless, none of them had been possessed. In one of her journals that I didn't find until I was older, chronicling her own greatness with chilling narcissism, Rowena had penned: "The child was sent to Me to ad-

dress my grievances and right those wrongs done Me, controlled by a penurious toy I purchased from a street vendor."

I don't know why she stopped either. Perhaps there were only twenty-three names on her most-hated list. Perhaps so many murders by sword garnered too much attention from the Garda and she'd not wanted me caught and placed behind bars. Though she'd instructed me to hide the corpses, many were eventually found. The universe has a way of betraying those secrets we endeavor to hold near.

The day I learned what I'd done, I decided there were only three courses of action open to me.

Kill myself because I was a monster, too.

Live the rest of my life hating myself, unable to ever atone, consumed by a heart of darkness that would cast no light into a world that badly needed some.

Or lock the past up in a box with those other murders and carry a heart—as pure as it had once been—into the present, determined to do better, inscribing the Latin motto on the tatters of my soul: Actus me invito factus non est meus actus. Acts done by my body against my will are not my acts.

I knew each of my victim's names and was able to locate most of their families.

I protect them still.

SIX

— • • —

High voltage, the unforgettable sound

I PARKED MY MOTORCYCLE IN front of the abbey, grabbed the backpack that held a change of clothing for later, and loped into the front entrance of the ancient fortress wearing ripped jeans, boots, and a white tank top that did nothing to conceal what was wrong with my arm. I wasn't going to hide whatever was happening to me; isolated soldiers are a sniper's favorite target. My sword was slung over my back, knives in my boots, but in deference to the children on the estate, I carry no guns inside those walls. I can't bear the thought of an innocent coming to harm as a result of my carelessness.

I love Arlington Abbey.

With accommodations for a thousand *sidhe*-seers, the fortress is riddled with secret passages behind bookcases and fireplaces, has dozens of concealed nooks and cubbies, and has always held an air of irresistible mystery to me.

From the meditation pavilion hemmed by shaped topiary

that legend claims once lived and breathed, protecting the abbey, to the elaborate maze that spans seven acres near the lake, it was once a badly run motherhouse for women trained to be reclusive, cowed, and uncertain.

Things have changed. We train, we fight, we get dirty and bloody and push each other harder all the time. The abbey's filled to capacity, with a waiting list a mile long to get in.

Entry-level *sidhe*-seers, Initiates can spend anywhere from two to ten years in training as they learn to use their gifts. Those gifts we've been seeing, since the Song of Making restored magic to our world, are unlike anything we've encountered before.

Apprentices, who've achieved a level of proficiency sufficient to pass a series of difficult tests, will spend another few years in additional training. Some might never graduate to the final level: the Adepts, those of us who've harnessed our gifts and serve as trainers for the Initiates and Apprentices.

Then there's the Shedon, the council of popularly elected *sidhe*-seers that govern the abbey.

The motherhouse is no longer a tyrannical prison of coercion and tightly controlled, skewed press. In my youth I'd blasted through those corridors at full throttle, feared and distrusted by everyone around me. I used to hate that, seeing the fear. It made me feel alone. But I've galvanized my truths. Life is funny, it makes you choose sides all the time. Fearless people are outsiders. The fearful have many places to belong. They're the fluffy white sheep that stick close to shepherds, let others feed, fatten, and shear them, and spiral in a tight, panicked knot if a wolf draws near.

When I'm surrounded by that herd, I can't understand the conversation that usually goes something like this: *I'm scared, what do you think we should do? I dunno, what do you think we should do? I dunno, let's ask somebody else.*

Panic ensues. *Baaaaa.*

I'm the dingy gray sheep, the one no one wants to shear and everyone forgets to feed, the one that gets pissed off and, with plumes of steam shooting from my ears, rather than lazing in the sun under the care of a master I have no guarantee knows how to survive any better than me, goes trotting off alone to hunt for wolf-slaying weapons.

I'd rather be fearless and criticized than fearful and approved of.

That's the bloody choice sometimes.

Still, I've learned in recent years to bleach my coat, the better to blend. And when they aren't looking, I'm as gray as I need to be. It's easier on all of us that way. I think that's what Ryodan does, too, concealing his inner beast with casual elegance, behind cool gray eyes. I miss him. When I let myself think about him. Which is never.

Today I stalked down vaulted stone corridors to the library, offering greetings and returning smiles. Though many of the women stared at my arm, it was without censure, only a lifting of brows and curious meeting of my eyes.

When Shazam hadn't returned by the time I awakened from a quick nap on the sofa, I'd packed up and headed out to start my day. He has a way of finding me wherever I go and I suspect he's often perched above me in a higher dimension, manifesting when he feels like it. I understand the need for time alone and don't normally pressure him but after last night's escapade, once he appeared again, I planned to do everything in my power to keep him engaged and by my side.

"Hey, Kat," I said as I entered the library.

The tall, athletic brunette glanced up from a computer screen and swept me with a level gray gaze. "Och, and it's grown."

Kat was part of the Shedon, her *sidhe*-seer gift a dangerously sensitive empathy. Possessing the ability to read the emotions of those around her at their truest level, I've found her incapable of lying.

"What do you feel? Read me." I dropped over the back of a chair and sat down across the table from her.

She stared at me a long moment, eyes drifting out of focus, then said lightly, "You feel like you always do."

"And how's that?"

"Like Dani. Light and energy, a bubbling sense of humor, an exacting sense of personal responsibility and justice, and a heart the size of Ireland." She was silent a moment then added, "And many, many private vaults that never open to see the light of day."

My eyes narrowed. "Can you get in them?"

"No."

"That means you've tried."

"I have."

An unwilling smile tugged at my lips as I thought both "How dare you?" and "Good for you!" She'd changed, toughened, moved beyond courtesy to necessity. We live in hard times. You can't keep your blades sharp by polishing them with a chamois, you have to sharpen them on stone.

"The day I get in, I'll tell you. And the moment I do, I'll back out without looking around. I've no desire to know secrets you've no desire to tell me, Dani. But the vaults of your mind are the greatest challenge I've found."

And would forever remain that challenge. She wouldn't get in. I restructure my brain regularly and meticulously, planting decoys everywhere. Not even Ryodan got very far past the surface. I changed the subject. "I had a visitor last night. Actually two." Nine if you counted the Pallas cats, which I didn't and hoped never to smell again. As I filled her in on what happened, she listened intently.

"The old gods," she finally murmured, "at war with the Fae? Bloody hell. Does it never end?"

"Mommy said a bad word," came a breathless, little-girl voice from behind Kat. Her daughter Rae peeked around her shoulder and I crinkled my nose at her and smiled. Usually, when I first see the dazzling-ray-of-sunshine child, I catch her up in my arms, kick us both up into the slipstream, and twirl her around in a dizzying starry explosion of light because I live to hear her unfettered belly laugh, but from the way she was peeping at me, I could tell she was in a hide-and-seek mood today. I'd chase her later, up and down halls, perhaps into the maze behind the abbey.

"Shazzy?" she asked hopefully, luminous dark eyes rounding with excitement.

"On a walkabout," I said, and her face fell. Rae adored Shazam and the feeling was mutual. When, a few years back, Kat suddenly had a baby, seemingly out of nowhere, we'd all been shocked. We had no idea who the father was, although many believed it was her childhood love, Sean O'Bannion, who, like Christian and Inspector Jayne, had begun transforming into a Fae prince when the original princes were killed.

One of the many unpredictable things about the Fae race was, on the rare occasion the princes or princesses were killed, the nearest raw matter, mortal or Fae, that met some mysterious requirement was selected to begin a painful transformation. Mac told me the Unseelie King said the Fae were like starfish and would always regrow essential parts. Lesser Fae weren't considered essential. The High Court was.

Unlike Jayne, Sean O'Bannion had turned Unseelie and hadn't been seen for years. Kat never offered the name of Rae's father and we didn't ask. She made it clear it didn't matter: Rae was her daughter, end of subject. Whatever *sidhe*-seer gifts the girl possessed hadn't yet begun to manifest. Rae certainly looked like she might be Sean's, with raven curls, brown eyes flecked with amber, and the complexion of a Black Irishman's daughter.

I wasn't interesting enough without Shazam to keep the curious, energetic child's attention today, and Rae ambled off to play as Kat opened a word document and made notes about our conversation, nudging me for as much detail as I could recall. "And this AOZ mentioned another who might come for the sword?"

I nodded.

"But no name?"

I shook my head.

She studied me a moment, then, "Do you believe the sword would be safer with a Fae?"

I said irritably, "I'm half tempted to give it to the strongest god I can find and let the races kill each other."

Kat sucked in a breath.

I raised both hands in placation: one pale Irish, the other dark as ebony. "But I won't. Mac's queen." And I'd die before I put a weapon into the hands of someone who might hurt her. She and I had been through so much together; she was the sister I'd never had. "I don't think that's the answer, Kat. I was able to protect it last night. If I hadn't been, I'd be open to the possibility, especially if I could somehow get it to Mac."

I trusted neither gods nor the Fae with one of the only two hallowed weapons capable of ending an immortal life. Any Fae who got their hands on it could amass an army and go to war against their queen, and many of them despised the human who'd been chosen as their ruler's successor. "Perhaps the sword is right where it needs to be and this power is awakening so I can keep it safe."

Kat said dryly, "Or perhaps it's merely coincidental and our world's gone as mad as it seems while we bumble about foolishly trying to ascribe patterns to chaos."

I laughed. There was that.

"The wish, Dani. Have you any idea what AOZ meant?"

I'd tried to figure it out on the ride here, reflecting on the moment I'd picked up the spelled item. I'd responded primarily with raw emotion, secondarily with actual thought. AOZ might have sorted through a dozen half-formed desires and selected whichever one he thought might bite me in the ass the hardest. I shook my head and said grimly, "No clue. Kat, what do you think about this god business? I read the Book of Invasions a long time ago and found it to be . . ." I try not to insult anyone else's beliefs. I dangle first and let them finish, see how they go about it. I've learned diplomacy. It doesn't come easy to me so I like to practice when I can.

"Pure tripe?" she said with a wry smile.

"At the very least heavily redacted, with enormous poetic license taken," I agreed. "Do you think these gods might be the reality of the stories of the ancient Fomorians, awakened by the Song?"

"It's certainly a theory worth exploring. According to the Book of Invasions, the Fomorians battled the Tuatha De Danaan, were widely regarded as monsters, and were driven into the sea, never to be seen again. But the timetable of those events was severely condensed, to reconcile history with Christianity, forcing the entire period from creation of the world to the Middle Ages to fit within the events of the Bible. I've long suspected those events happened far longer ago than we can imagine. History is murky business, rewritten again and again until the original story is lost to us. That's why it's critical we translate our ancient scrolls. They'll be closer to truth than anything scribed in the past few thousand years, influenced by political and religious agendas. We've been hearing stories from all over Ireland. People in rural areas have encountered beings they claim have Faelike powers. Were you able to sense AOZ with your *sidhe*-seer senses?"

I shook my head grimly. "No. My gut got nothing. My brain registered empirical evidence that made me believe he wasn't human."

She nodded again and rose, gathering her notes. "I'll meet with the Shedon, pass on the news, see what they know."

I kicked back in the chair, propped my boots on the table, grabbed the latest stack of translations and began to read.

π

"Nothing," I muttered several hours later. "Bloody nothing."

"We have no way of determining what the books and scrolls are about before we begin to translate them. Most of them have no titles," Bridget said mildly, head bent close to a tiny journal in her hands. In her late forties, streaks of gray feathered her short dark hair. The day shift of translators had settled in at the long, wide table with me shortly after I'd begun reading.

"True," agreed seventeen-year-old Fallon, whose specialty was ancient dialects. She'd come to us five months ago, bearing a sealed letter from a sister-house in Wales beseeching us to train her, as she'd recently developed latent powers they'd no experience with. Chameleonlike, she'd begun melting into her surroundings, the strength of five men infused her petite frame, and I suspected from how quickly and silently she could move that she might one day be able to join me in the slipstream. Glossy chestnut hair swept her shoulders, framing a face wide through the cheekbones that tapered to a broad jaw before narrowing sharply to a pointed chin. Aquamarine eyes narrowed with frustration as she added, "And we suspect Rowena took the most important books. Saints know where she hid them."

Bridget said, "The council delegated a team to begin exploring the Underneath next week. Perhaps we'll find a stash there. Anything discovered underground will get translated first," she assured me.

Two years I'd been waiting to hear those words—we were finally going to turn our attention to the unexplored realm beneath the fortress. Like a Janus head, the abbey was split into halves: The Upstairs, which held fascinating mysteries of the mostly nondeadly kind, and the Underneath, rumored to hold secrets too powerful, too terrible, for anyone to know. The council had long been wary of the Underneath. The *Sinsar Dubh* was once contained in that subterranean maze.

Rowena had forbidden anyone to enter the Underneath but I'd been there, once, years ago, tailing her past her many wards and traps, lingering to kill the Fae she'd been nibbling on for who knew how long, to increase her power and extend her life span. I'd caught glimpses of countless snaking passageways, heavily locked and warded doors, vaulting caverns, and I'd only been on a single level. I'd passed dozens of curved stone stairwells, spiraling down to seemingly bottomless pits.

I'd hungered to explore it further once she was gone, but I'd committed to our order and toed the council's line, which was: *Si vis pacem, para bellum*—if you want peace, prepare for war. We'd focused on locating the most powerful *sidhe*-seers, testing and training them while we monitored Ireland, the world beyond.

We knew it wasn't over and wouldn't be so long as the wall

between our world and Faery was down. Our races coexisted in a powder keg where the slightest spark could make everything blow. If Mac were unable to gain control of the immortal race, we'd be right back where we started, slaughtering each other in our quest for control of the world.

"Who's heading the team?" I asked Bridget.

"Enyo," she said.

I approved the choice. Born in a war zone in Lebanon, Enyo had been a soldier long before she'd found us. Smart, driven, and hungry for challenge, she was the perfect choice. I looked forward to spending time with her while we explored.

I bristled with anticipation. I *would* be on that team.

I glanced at the clock above the fireplace, noted the time, and shoved back in my chair to head back to Dublin for an appointment I'd made that morning, at the same time Bridget—who I'd not realized had gotten up and was now behind me—leaned over my shoulder to add another page to my stack for when I returned.

We collided.

Or rather, her forearm brushed my left shoulder.

Raw, high voltage exploded from my arm with a thunderous BOOM and my skin crackled with energy. There was the sudden stench of burning hair followed by popping sounds, met with a high-pitched scream that terminated as swiftly as it had begun. Then there was the racket of furniture crashing to the floor, and what sounded like one of the old, massive bookcases behind me splintering, and chilling, wet splats.

Then the stillest of silences.

Half out of my chair, I froze, hands splayed on the table.

Fallon was staring past me, mouth gaping on a silent O, eyes wide with shock and horror.

I couldn't make myself move for a long moment, just stood there, muscles flexed to move but not obeying my command. My legs were noodles again, my hands shaking.

I'd felt the enormity of what had flared to instant life inside me. I'd seen what it had done to my bedroom wall this morning.

Perhaps it had simply knocked her out. I hadn't intended any harm, quite the opposite. Nor had I flung my hand as I did with Jayne, or even moved it at all.

She'd merely brushed the bare skin of her forearm against the bare skin of my shoulder.

"Fallon?" I begged with my eyes: *Say it's not true. Say she's okay.*

The Apprentice began to hyperventilate, gulping air, unable to make a sound. Shoulders shaking, tears spilled from her eyes.

I slumped back into my chair, doubled over and puked violently, retching the contents of my stomach on the floor until nothing but a thin stream of bile dribbled from my chin.

I didn't need to look behind me to know Bridget was dead.

SEVEN

Secluded in a marker stone not only deadlier

but much smarter, too

CONFRONTED BY EXTREME EMOTION, I box it and take action; do something, anything, whatever most immediately needs to be done.

My heart was screaming: *You killed Bridget, you're a liability, dangerous to your friends, run away and hide because you're a monster and, as your mom liked to say so often at the end—the world would be better off if you'd never been born.*

My brain said with cool efficiency: *You made this mess, clean it up.*

I stumbled into my chair, knocking it over, yanked it back up and locked my knees and began to collect parts and assemble them in a small, neat arrangement.

Normally, as soon as I see Rae, I catch her up in my arms. My deadly, killing embrace.

I begged every god to forgive me for killing Bridget and thanked every god that it hadn't been Rae. Then I begged every god to forgive me for making such a distinction, as I picked up pieces with only my right hand because I had no idea what would happen if I touched them with my left, and no desire to find out.

Holding what appeared to be a fragment of the soft-spoken, effortlessly kind woman's pale, bloody arm, I muttered, "I did this," unaware I'd spoken aloud until Fallon snapped, "Dani, stop it. It wasn't your fault. It was an accident. And for God's sake, stop trying to put her back together!"

I hadn't realized I was. I carefully placed part of Bridget's hand and three fingers to the right of the macabre puzzle I was working.

The door flew open and I spun toward it, vibrating, shivering, dangerously close to losing control and vanishing in the slipstream. I hungered to disappear, escape gazes certain to condemn. I fisted my hands at my sides, right hand dripping blood, left hand ice-cold, and forced myself to breathe in a rhythm I'd perfected Silverside when sniping hostile targets. Inflate gut, wave the breath up to my chest, breathe out. Stop breathing. Shoot. Repeat. There's a still, silent flawless dimension that exists on the trigger of a gun, and I could live in that place. It feels good there. Unbreathing, remote, I never miss a shot.

Kat stood in the doorway.

Bridget's pain ended as swiftly as it had begun. But mine was a mushroom cloud of toxic emotion she must have felt and come running to discern the cause. She took stock of me, assessed Fallon, squared her shoulders, and glanced left at the demolished bookcase, the bits of bone and flesh, the mangled remains of Bridget.

I gave her enormous kudos that she didn't double over and puke, as I wiped the last bit of bile from my chin.

"What happened?" she said quietly.

"I killed—"

"Shut up, Dani," Fallon said sharply as she moved to join me. But not too close; she stopped a few feet away. "Dani didn't kill Bridget," she told Kat. "Bridget bent over her left shoulder as Dani was standing up. The black part of her is dangerous and she didn't know it."

"How can you exonerate me? She's dead."

"How can you convict yourself?" Fallon retorted, eyes flashing. "It was an accident. I saw the entire thing. You had no idea she was behind you. You had no idea anything about you was dangerous."

"I should have known."

"How *could* you know?"

"It's my arm. That makes it my fault."

"Stop it, Dani," Kat said quietly. "You won't be carrying this one, too."

Yes, I would. But saying so would only make Kat and Fallon work harder to excuse me. "Kat, what if I'd picked up Rae like I usually do?" My voice broke on the words at the same time my knees gave out. I sank to the floor, tucked my head in my arms, half expecting my own head to blow up, fighting tears. I would weep. But in private. Alone. I would dance until I was too exhausted to hold it in any longer then I would cry. And deal. Like I always do.

"Get buckets of hot soapy water and trash bags," Kat instructed Fallon. "Bring mops, Enyo, and a few of the Adepts."

I glanced up and watched Fallon leave with a sharp stab of pride. An Apprentice, she'd not fallen apart. She'd lost it for a moment, then become the warrior that was needed.

Kat closed the door behind her, moved into the room and sank to her knees a few feet from me. "I'd take you in my arms and comfort you but we seem to have a wee bit of a problem."

"A wee bit?" I mocked darkly. "I just killed an innocent woman. A good woman with a good life ahead of her. Done. Gone. End of story. Thanks to me."

"I know some of what Rowena did to you."

I stiffened. I know a truth—most people can't handle the truths of my life. The *sidhe*-seers perform surgery on our world with anesthesia when at all possible, employing a deft technique. I hack out the cancerous spots, in brutal fashion, armed with whatever weapon is handy. The way I was taught. The way I did it the first time. I began lying young. Made compartments to store them all in, to keep track. Lying is a pain in the ass. It complicates the brain, mandates the creation of more files, consuming valuable space.

"She kept a hidden cache in her suite. When I stayed there, I discovered a collection beneath a floorboard. Some were maps of the abbey, which will prove useful as we explore beneath. There were two journals."

I narrowed my eyes, searching her gaze. How much did she know?

"Pawns are not to blame for the actions of kings. Children are not to blame for the atrocities of adults. You know now that your arm has become dangerous. That information was gained at a terrible price. But," she said in a voice that was laced with steel, "do *not* damage yourself further than the world already damaged you. You're becoming something powerful. Don't abort that birth because of an accident. We live in a time fraught with peril, abilities we don't understand, changes occurring so quickly it's impossible to keep up. Put this in one of your vaults. War is coming. We've both been feeling that dark wind blowing down on us for a long time. Soldier up. This new gift of yours may be precisely the thing we need to tip the balance of the future in our favor."

I knew Bridget's death was an accident. I'd never have harmed her, and I didn't know it was dangerous to touch me. But this was different than "the actions done by me against my will." This had happened due to my carelessness. I'd assumed something about my arm with no basis for that assumption. I'd assumed I was safe to be around. I wasn't and let's be brutally honest here, I've never been to one degree or another; that's why my mom locked me in a cage in the first place. That's why I miss my crew so much. They aren't human. They're much less breakable.

Kat whispered, "Och, so much pain." She was silent a moment then said sternly, "And that's the damage that was done to you unfairly. Your mother gave up. Instead of fighting, she panicked. It wasn't you. It was her. Don't let those voices win. You're not the wrong one or the bad one—"

"When did you become a bloody mind reader?"

"I'm not." She paused then said carefully, "Kasteo taught me a few things."

I said incredulously, "Kasteo? The one that speaks to no one?" I knew she'd worked out with him at Chester's, but he'd taught her other things, too? I'd give my right arm for lessons from one of the Nine. Preferably, my left at this point, if someone would take the damned thing.

"Accept what happened. Grieve. But do it gently. You would never have harmed Bridget. You can't undo it. Logic dictates you incorporate the lesson and move on."

Same advice and absolution I'd have given to another. Same grace I never permit myself. A life ended. Because of me. Christ. Her last breath was the one she'd breathed as she'd stood behind me. She had a boyfriend. She had dreams. "The others will blame me." I'd be walking corridors of condemnation again.

"Some will. Especially those who envy your gifts, and there

are many. Living legends have long been targets for small minds. You won't listen to them. You'll let it roll off you and continue doing all you can to help our world and our people. Such is the price of power. Great power comes at great price. And you, Dani, my love, have always been strong enough to pay it."

Fallon bustled into the library then with Enyo and four Adepts, buckets of soapy water, trash bags, and cloths.

We soldiered up and began cleaning the remains from the walls and floor in grim silence.

π

I took the long, circuitous way home, knowing I'd only sit, staring, playing Bridget's death through my mind, seeing images of the bits and pieces of her being reassembled into a bloody whole that could never be made whole again.

There were many things I should do, as dusk took my city.

At the moment I was sitting on my idling bike in the empty lot above Chester's nightclub. The rubble littering the pavement was hauled off years ago by the Dublin Cleanup Crew, leaving only a fractured concrete surface with deep jagged cracks and a heavily warded trapdoor.

Not, however, too heavily warded for me, and besides I'd found the back way in two years ago.

That was the night I'd discovered, locked in a storage room deep beneath the club, a small printing press and reams and reams of paper. I also found the initials RKS at the bottom of a pile of legal documents, granting Ryodan title to properties all over Dublin. I'd entertained myself endlessly trying to guess his last name. Depending on my mood, they'd ranged from exotic and sexy to absurd.

How many dragons had the man launched into my sky for

me, trying to keep me too busy to get myself killed? The *Dublin Daily* was once the bane of my existence, occupying hours of my time, inspiring me to write smarter, try harder, take myself more seriously. It, and WeCare, which I sometimes suspected he'd created as well, had kept me fighting faceless entities rather than racing out into the streets seeking more tangible, deadly foes.

"Come back already," I muttered at the empty lot.

I missed him and the simple way he saw me, without any filters. I missed feeling the way I felt around him. He was gasoline to my fire, matches to my dynamite. He'd enjoyed my fire, my dynamite. And, whether I'd liked it or not—and most of the time I hadn't—he'd kept me from blowing myself or too many others up with it.

Life wasn't the same without him around. Although I love my city, my life, Dublin without the Nine, without Mac and Barrons, is a Big Top Circus without a single lion, tiger, or bear. Not even elephants. Just chimps, clowns, and sheep. Oodles and oodles of sheep. And snakes—those are the Fae. I used to like being the only superhero in town. I'm so over that.

Countless were the times I'd considered calling him on my cellphone.

Countless were the times I'd shoved it back in my pocket, accepting his absence for what it was: a desire to be somewhere else that was not with me. The man who'd launched my dragons didn't care enough to call or text me a single time in over two years to see how I was doing.

Or if I was even still alive. Leaving was one thing. Never checking in was unforgivable.

"Rot in purgatory, Ryodan," I growled as I put my bike in gear.

π

Shaz and I have code names for our many residences. I doubt I need them. I suspect he can find me anywhere, anytime he wants, and thinks it's funny to humor me by pretending to read the notes I scrawl telling him where I am.

Before I'd left this morning, I'd scribbled the word "Sanctuary" across the bedroom wall in Sharpie. An enemy would have no idea what it meant. Shazam would know he'd find me in the penthouse flat that occupied the top floor of a building on the north side of the River Liffey. I prefer to live up high, with a clear view of my city below. On those rare occasions I'm not patrolling at night, I love to sit on the fire escape, beyond the tall arched windows that line the wall floor to ceiling, and watch the river slide by, the lights twinkling like fallen stars in the streets.

Sanctuary is a study in grays and blacks and whites, the most colorless of my abodes. I crave its Spartan elegance when something's bothering me, eschewing the distracting brightness of the world to think surrounded by soothing monotones.

I dislike doing anything uniform or predictable that might allow an enemy to track me, yet a risky number of my residences are penthouses, as they afford tall windows and vaulted ceilings. I accept the liability in exchange for space, room to breathe, and a place to burn off restless energy. In Sanctuary's enormous living room that's void of all furniture, on a polished black floor that I can see my own reflection in, facing a wall of windows, with a line of fire burning behind glass at my back, on hard nights in my chronic town I dance like I once danced on another world, beneath three full moons, abandoned to a song only I can hear. I dance to get it all out, the emotion that builds up inside me. I dance until, exhausted, often weeping, I sleep.

My kitchen is a sleek modern affair of quartz, chrome, and black marble floors. Those floors spill throughout the entire flat, and are easy to mop blood from. Usually when I seek Sanctuary, I'm bleeding.

Tonight there was no blood, just an arm as black as my floors.

Shazam was sprawled fatly across the ivory island, occupying half of it, tearing flesh off the skull of—

"Is that a pig?" I said disbelievingly. "You ate an entire pig?" From the amount of blood staining the counters, dripping down the sides, and the size of the hooves he'd left uneaten, it was a full-grown pig, too.

Shrugging, he said nothing, only studied a distant space in the air and licked innocently at a paw, tail twitching with audible thumps against the quartz.

"Good grief. You might have at least saved me a flank of bacon," I groused as I rummaged in the pantry for a can of coconut milk and a couple of protein shakes. My stomach was queasy but I needed energy. During our time together in the Silvers, Shazam had often hunted for me, and I'd hacked the flanks off more animals than I could count, filleted and roasted them over a fire. I might seem a bit barbaric to the rest of the world. The world seems barbaric to me.

I tossed back the coconut milk, followed by the protein shakes, wiped my mouth with the back of my hand then turned to find Shazam standing, back arched like a horseshoe, porcupine bristles ridging his spine, lips drawn back in a silent snarl as he stared down the long ebony-floored hallway that, after a right turn into a small foyer, led to the front door. Anytime he does that, a chill ices my spine. He's never wrong. My Hel-Cat's hearing and sense of smell is more acute than mine. It's kept us alive on many occasions, both in Dublin and as we wandered hostile planets in the Silvers.

When he freezes, I freeze. And prepare.

Still, anything that might come through a door doesn't worry me overmuch. The truly dangerous things don't need doors.

Shazam tipped his regal shaggy head to look at me. Violet eyes lingered on my left arm, moved up to the shoulder, then to my face. Whiskers trembling, he whispered, "It's changed again."

"Is something at the door?" I whispered back.

"Yes. Are you all right, Yi-yi? Does it hurt?" he fretted.

I shook my head. Only the things I'd done with it hurt. My heart ached. A part of it would ache eternally for Bridget. I'd cut a good person's life short. Some people try to pay for their mistakes by punishing themselves. I don't. Not only doesn't it undo the mistake you made, it turns you into a nonproductive liability, and makes everyone who has to put up with you miserable. The way I see it, if you screw up you have two choices: kill yourself or try harder.

His luminous eyes grew dewy. "Make the black skin go away. Tell it to leave. It's hurting your heart, Yi-yi."

I considered that, eyes darting back to the long hall leading to the door. Faint but there, a wet snuffling, a scraping against the threshold. I considered my arm, the terrible power it held. The sword I needed to protect. The world I'd chosen to guard. Assuming it were possible, would I do it? Turn my back on power I might use for good, if I could learn to control it?

I didn't find what was happening to me a terrible thing. I found my lack of understanding and inability to control it the problem; one I intended to quickly remedy.

Shazam knows me well. I'm unguarded around my quixotic, unconditionally loving friend, my normally shuttered gaze open, expressive.

"Oh, Yi-yi," he whispered, tears filling his eyes. "You wouldn't unchoose it if you could. You *want* it."

I did. I inclined my head and smiled faintly. He smiled back, albeit tearfully. It's strange to see Shazam smile, thin lips peeling back from sharp fangs, curving up into his cheeks. It always reminds me of something but it's proved an elusive memory.

A volley of thuds hit the front door and I heard it splinter with a thunderous crash.

Shazam vanished, leaving me alone to face it.

I rolled my eyes at the half-stripped bloody skull on the island. "Coward," I muttered as I closed my fingers on the hilt of my sword and began to pad stealthily down the long hallway toward the door.

EIGHT

—— • • • ——

Demons dreaming, breathe in, breathe in,

I'm coming back again

I've FACED MANY MONSTERS in my life, in Dublin and on countless worlds in the Silvers. I've battled on planets of endless night, and scorching desert worlds with multiple suns. I survived by detaching from everything I know, think, and feel and engaging fully in the fight. Some say I've done unspeakable things. I disagree. I've simply done things I don't like to speak about and they wouldn't like to hear.

I could hear it, down the hallway, around a corner, in the foyer near the guest bath (as if I ever had guests), but even without the labored panting of its breath that hitched infrequently on a chilling, snakelike rattle, or the ponderous impact against the floor of whatever appendages on which it prowled (from the sound, my intruder weighed a good four to five hundred pounds), I could feel it.

It had presence.

Massive, dark and hungry. Not Fae.

Staggering power. Familiar in some way, yet . . . not. I cocked my head and opened my senses, siphoning energy off that deep inner lake from which *sidhe*-seers draw power—those of us descended from the six ancient Irish Houses mutated eons ago by the addition of the Unseelie King's blood—but the vast, dark expanse had nothing to offer me. No rune, ward, or gift of foresight to help me discern what lay ahead.

My hand itched relentlessly, as if allergic welts were sprouting beneath my skin. Gritting my teeth against the distraction, I began to pad forward again.

A grunt was followed by a long, guttural groan and a wet snuffle. There was a dull thump, as if my enemy had stumbled against the wall.

Good, a weakness: it was clumsy. Some of my most lethal foes had possessed enormous strength but moved with such heaviness of limb, I'd danced around them as they'd died.

I bent and drew a six-inch military knife from my boot with my left hand, releasing the switchblade with a nearly inaudible *snick*. Since I hadn't blown up my bike when I'd grasped the handlebars on the way back to Dublin, I figured I was safe wielding a weapon. Apparently, I only blew up living things. Lovely. Still, I wasn't willing to put my sword in that dangerous hand, so I was going to be fighting handicapped. I eased the long gleaming sword free with my right hand and crept forward again.

There was another softer grunt that ended on a slobbering sigh and sounded . . . pained?

Was my enemy already injured? Perfect. I could end it fast. I had more important things to do tonight. I knew my left arm was deadly—bare flesh to bare flesh—but I needed to know if, wrapped in layers of clothing, that killing touch was neutralized. If so, the solution was simple: sleeve and glove up. I needed to hunt tonight, and not a blasted animal. I required a human to test my theory.

Sounds of a heavy body moving on . . . I listened intently . . . four feet, followed by another thud then the console table in my foyer crashing to the floor, taking vases and a crystal lamp with it.

Followed by a long, shuddering groan of agony. A ragged exhale.

Then silence.

Two possibilities: it was either a trick to lure me near, sucker me into believing my enemy wounded and helpless; or a massively powerful creature had, for reasons unknown, come to my flat to die and was going to wreck my furniture in the process. Sanctuary was the only flat I'd furnished myself, and the truest reflection of my taste. Bloody hell, as if there wasn't already enough blood in my kitchen to clean up!

Often on distant worlds I'd been so exhausted from prior battles, I'd learned not to rush into future ones. Waiting frequently yielded more information, or goaded an increasingly bored enemy into rash action.

I leaned back against the wall and bided my time. Three minutes passed, then five. I could still feel its presence but it hadn't made a single move. I listened to faint, irregular, shallow breaths and counted between them. The thing, whatever it was, breathed once every two minutes or so.

By ten minutes I was bored out of my skull and had decided it was definitely option two. Something was dying or dead in my foyer and I was growing increasingly chafed by the thought of it bleeding out on my floors, staining the grout and probably soaking into my walls. I hate cleaning. It's something I can't do in the slipstream. I have to slow-mo Joe around my flats and dust and mop like everyone else. Blood on grout takes bleach and a scrub brush. Bleach on marble is a bad idea.

Peeling away from the wall, I glided soundlessly forward. When I reached the corner, I inhaled deeply and ducked my head several feet lower in case unfriendly fire was coming, focused hard (isolating a single part of my body is difficult, if I'm not careful I can sprain every tendon and ligament attached to that part), put myself in freeze-frame from the neck up, snatched a hasty look and retreated.

Then, rubbernecking wildly, I did a double take.

"*Oh, shit!*" I exploded.

An enormous black-skinned beast was collapsed on the floor of my foyer and, from the looks of it, was dying!

It was one of the Nine.

I couldn't believe one of the immortals had finally surfaced in Dublin for the first time in years and, holy hell, I'd been crouching around the corner listening to him die!

I scanned the creature for identifying features but found none. As beasts, I can't tell them apart. I'm not sure anyone could. Was this Barrons? Did that mean Mac was injured? Ryodan, Lor, or one of the others? What was wrong with him?

I approached with care. Before I'd met Shazam Silverside, I'd had to trap my own kills. I hate killing animals but I had to eat. One night I'd caught a beautiful llama-like creature in a trap I designed for a small boar. By the time I'd found it, it was mortally injured but still alive, and nearly insane with hunger, pain, and fear. I'd wept while I battled its great, thrashing hooves to get close enough to slit its throat and end its suffering.

The beast on the floor reminded me of that half-mad creature, tormented past endurance. I paused half a dozen paces away. He didn't weigh anywhere near the four to five hundred pounds I'd thought. Perhaps he once had but now his ribs were sharp-edged razors beneath a black hide. Nine feet tall, dangerously thin, sprawled on his side, stomach caved in, barely breathing, he weighed maybe three hundred pounds. I'd thought he was heavier because it sounded like he'd been nearly collapsing with each step.

His face was sharp-planed, primitive with a ridged forehead and a tangle of long dark hair. Three sets of lethal horns flanked his enormous head, with the rear set curving toward his back. Deadly fangs as long as my fingers protruded from a mouth limned with spittle and foam.

As I inched closer he dragged his head from the floor to gaze at me.

I froze.

Burning crimson eyes with vertical pupils locked with mine, and I jerked from the sheer intensity of his gaze. When he unhinged impossibly large jaws and growled, revealing long sharp fangs, I nearly inched backward, despite his weakened condition. Even dying, he saturated the foyer with fury, hunger, madness.

I said, "I know you're one of the Nine. You came to me for a reason. Let me help you." I could see no wounds on this side of his body. Would he roll over for me? Would he let me touch him; was he strong enough to stop me if I tried? Holy composite, rational, perfect square numbers, one of the Nine was finally back! Kaleidoscopic colors gushed back into my world again with the force of an unchecked fire hydrant.

The beast growled again but tapered off to a whimpering moan as he dropped his head to the floor with an audible crack of bone on tile.

My eyes narrowed. Five days in a cage. Five days my mother didn't come home to feed me. I'd collapsed the same way. Although she'd wept as she finally fed me, her tears hadn't moved me like they used to. My hands fisted. I can't stand to see anyone starved, helpless.

"I'll be back with food," I said, although I doubted he understood me. His gaze was dimming, his head lolled to the side, eyes closing, then a single one snapped back open and a flash of crimson fire tracked me as I left.

Thanks to Shazam, my flats are amply stocked with meat. He hunts only once a day but he's incessantly hungry, binge-eating like a bottomless black hole. I get him pig blood from the butcher on Parnell Street; keep some frozen, some thawed. That's another reason I don't have guests. The contents of my fridge are difficult to explain.

I grabbed a container of blood and a package of ground beef, a bowl from one of the shelves, and dumped it together then hurried back to the beast. He didn't move a muscle as I approached this time so I placed the bowl near his head and waited for him to slide one of his massive appendages with long cruel talons around the bowl. Though his nostrils flared slightly and he exhaled with a low, rattling sound, he made no move for the food. He was too weak.

Cursing whoever had done this to him, I scooped up a handful of the bloody meat and leaned in. My hand was inches from his face when I realized I was using my dominant, dangerous left hand and yanked it back in horror. I dropped the food into the bowl, scraped meat off my palm, scrubbed the blood from my hand on my jeans, stuck my killing hand in my back pocket then scooped again with my right.

"Don't bite my hand off," I said sternly as I drizzled more blood on his muzzle. I'd seen what those deadly fangs could do in the heat of battle. I needed at least one good hand.

He still didn't move. I'd just begun to contemplate how I might force apart his mandibles and feed him with only one hand when he twitched weakly and licked the blood with a long black tongue.

I dropped the beef back into the bowl and scooped up only blood. He could barely lick; he certainly couldn't chew. I couldn't imagine the formidable strength of will he possessed to manage to shatter my door in his condition.

I scooped and repeated again and again as he lapped weakly.

By the tenth cupped handful of blood he was licking with a whisper of animation and a murmur of life flickered in his crimson eyes. By the twentieth fistful the bowl was empty, but the beast was deeply exhausted from his meager effort.

Still, when he dropped his head to the floor this time, it met the tile more gently.

"I'll be back with more," I promised as I hurried back to the kitchen.

π

Two hours later I'd rehung my door on its frame, fortifying it with drill, screws, and the addition of two leafs from the dining table that had never been used, and the beast was unconscious in my bed, a limp puddle of black skin and bones against a white fitted sheet.

I'd gotten three bowls of blood into him and was going to have to head out to raid my other flats. The butcher wasn't open on Tuesdays, and breaking in would shatter the fragile trust we'd attained. He makes no effort to hide how disturbing he finds my frequent purchases and I don't explain.

I couldn't bear to leave the beast passed out in the foyer with his ribs jutting into the floor so I'd hefted the unconscious creature onto a comforter and lugged him to my bedroom. Though starved, his hide was glossy black velvet, his body warm, and I felt a solid though infrequent pulse in his leg.

I can lift a staggering amount of weight, but not even I can haul nine feet of limp beast in an upward direction with a single hand (two hands would have been a breeze), so I dragged my mattress down to the floor and rolled the beast onto it. Then I tucked the comforter around his body, burning with questions. What was going on? What villain was powerful enough to capture one of the Nine and contain him, and why starve him to death? How had he escaped?

I stared at him a long moment, releasing a pent breath I felt like I'd been holding for two long years. Then I inhaled a deep, enormous breath that felt like the first to fully expand my lungs for an equal amount of time. Sheep are social by nature. Deprived of sheep companionship they'll flock with dogs, goats, cows, whatever's available.

As will I.

But this was my kind of company. And I was bloody well keeping it.

There was no way he was dying on me. Sure, he'd come back—but where would he go? I highly doubted he'd return to me. The Nine are irritating like that, master of their own sea, they chart their course and don't consult.

I sleeved, gloved, and weaponed up, then glided out into the night, hoping to kill two birds with one stone before returning to Sanctuary.

NINE

— • • • —

Chronic town, posters torn, reaping wheel

Night in Dublin beyond the TBD, or Temple Bar District, is a graveyard: solitary, eerie, and silent.

No people walk these sidewalks, there's no blat of angry horns, no screech of tires in the streets. Few in Dublin have a car. Fewer still live on this side of the river, which lends the empty alleys and lanes the disturbingly surreal ambience of an abandoned movie set. Most of the population clusters on the south side of the river, clinging to the normalcy of rebuilding the city and reporting to various jobs as if they don't live in the midst of invaders with astronomical power that would delight in erasing us from the face of our own planet.

Without Ryodan and the rest of the Nine who are feared even by the Fae, only I stand between the imperious, immortal Court of Seasons and what they want. Their desires are as bottomless as they are ancient, and I've been neutered by Mac.

The Fae are blatantly contemptuous of mankind. They see us

as puny and inconsequential, marching from birth to death in the blink of an eye. They slake their twisted desires in our world, with no one to fear.

Not. Even. Me.

For Mac, I've turned my back on them, forced myself to pretend they don't exist. I've never been inside Elyreum—not once. I watched it being built, hands fisted, jaw clenched, and did nothing. When queues of sheep spool around the blocks waiting to get in, I detour around them, don't spare them a glance.

If I did, I'd be in trouble. I'd see their pending deaths and my wires would get crossed and sparks would fly because that's what happens when my wires get crossed, and I'd end up starting a war all by myself. Knowing my luck, Mac would have just negotiated peace and I'd be the one who blew it all.

So, like a good little soldier (who doesn't have a single ounce of meaningful backup) I fist my hands and Kevlar my heart and give it a wide berth. I focus my efforts on the differences I can make in this world, while staying alive. Dead, I'm no good to anyone.

I figured out a long time ago that if enough sifting Fae came after me, I could lose. If they've figured that out, too, they've accepted my truce. Perhaps they also realize that if they killed me, Mac, and many of the Nine, would rain down hell on their race. We exist in a chilly, volatile détente.

I choke on it some days. It takes me to a dark place. At night I hunt with that darkness. But I know this fact: if Mac fails to gain the Light Court's loyalty, they *will* come for my sword. It's likely only a few weeks have passed in Faery. Likely they're still playing nice with each other, feeling her out, trying to decide how much of the power the ancient queen passed her that she's figured out how to use, and how far she's willing to take it.

I know another fact, and holy hell I'd like to talk to Mac about it.

To govern a cruel race, one must be cruel.

I hope Barrons's Rainbow Girl can be cruel. It comes easier to me, but we weren't raised the same. Mac grew up drenched in love and approval, waltzing through rainbow-colored days.

Objectively, I entertain the possibility that if the Fae killed me, she'd learn to be cruel instantly. You have to consider all the cards you have to play when the fate of your world is at stake.

I spotted two of my three arsonists lurking in an alley on the north bank of the River Liffey as I headed for another of my northside flats to get more blood for the beast.

My body an adrenaline-infused weapon, I glided silently near, a shadow on their heels, swiftly revising my plan into one that would take out three birds, not two, with a single stone tonight: find out what they were up to; test my theory about my arm on one of them and, if it still blew him up through my clothing, take the other as food for the beast. If their deeds were as villainous as I suspected, I'd kill them anyway. No point in wasting blood.

I pegged the men as brothers, one a few inches taller than the other, moving with the same shambling gait, cut from identical genetic cloth with brown hair, the saggy, bloated skin of lifelong drinkers, mirror-image blunt features, and shifty, cunning eyes behind glasses. I know those eyes. They're the eyes of frightened, small men who serve a dark master to stay alive, taking delight in the torment of others because each obscene task they perform is a way of convincing themselves they're exempt: they chose to be predator not prey.

Was their master on the other side of that slim dark mirror? Might he be the "him" AOZ had threatened me with?

I'm not a predator. Nor am I prey. I'm the thing that crouches in the shadowy places between the two, native to no land but my own.

"We can't go back empty-handed." The shorter one sounded worried as he adjusted a slouchy, rolled beanie on his head.

I was an invisible wind on the salt-kissed breeze behind them, half into freeze-frame, but not in the slipstream. I'd spent a lot of time analyzing how Ryodan moved and had achieved a degree of his ability to melt into his surroundings. It took intense mental effort. I had to keep myself partially in an alternate way of moving, and partially not. It was like compressing myself to fit in a doorway, making myself no wider than a few inches, but occasionally part of me popped on one side or the other if I was startled by something or lost focus. I'd been getting better at it, though, working with Fallon, our young chameleon, determined to learn from her.

"Not tonight," the other agreed with a curse. "He wants an even dozen. Told all of us to come back with no less. How the fuck are we supposed to manage that? We're not bloody miracle workers! He's got so many of us in this city, we're stepping all over each other's turf!"

I assessed them but discerned no sign of weapons. Perhaps they had a knife concealed somewhere, but most people didn't walk these streets without a gun. I had a Glock tucked in my waistband, my PPQ in an inside hip holster on my right.

"Yah, it's bullshit. My back still hurts from last night, and I swear I sprained my shoulder," his companion complained. "Fuckin' fat-ass people. Where do they even find enough food to be fat?"

His brother laughed, a thin, cruel sound, as he tipped a flask back and swigged. "No shit, right? Well, they don't stay that way long." He guffawed again but it died swiftly and he shuddered, shoving the flask and his hands deep into the pockets of his coat.

I narrowed my eyes, pondering that comment. They didn't stay fat. Was it possible whoever they worked for had been holding the beast in my flat? But what was the point in starving people and/or animals to death?

"He needs to cut us some slack for it being so hard! They're afraid now and not going out at night. We took too many. He's gotta let us move again," the shorter of the two complained.

"Never gonna happen, Alfie. Some bloody reason, he wants us here."

"Fuckin' bastard! How's a man supposed to do his job with his hands tied?"

"Fuckin' just like the world was before. Average guys like us is the ones doing all the hard work!"

It went on like that for a while, as I tailed them. Bitching about the world as if they were the good guys, badly abused by everyone, and how terrible it was they were being taken for granted and inconvenienced.

I swallowed the bile of irritation so many times I was about to vomit it when suddenly one of them whirled and I felt a tiny piercing pain in my left breast, just above my nipple.

I stiffened.

The poison hit my blood instantly.

TEN

———— • • • ————

Honey, I'll rise up from the dead, I do it all the time

A T LEAST NOW I knew why they weren't carrying.
Expectations. They trip you up every time. I'd scanned them for the usual, human weapons, not some kind of . . . tiny dart? I stared dazedly down at the dark, two-inch quill protruding from my left breast as I kicked up into the slipstream.

I went down instead, crashing to the pavement on my knees, foaming at the mouth.

My body was going numb. I couldn't even persuade my hand to reach for a gun. Bloody hell, they'd complained about weight— was that because they were paralyzing and dragging people off somewhere? Were these men the reason so many adults had gone missing lately, the cause of the orphans in our city? Then they came back and bullied the children for the sheer, nasty fun of it? But why did kids end up thinking Fae took their parents? These were average, human men.

My mouth worked but nothing came out. I couldn't feel my breasts or my stomach. My hips were tingling, fading.

"Stupid cunt didn't think we knew you were back there." The taller of the two tapped his beanie. "Fooled you," he smirked and leered down at me as the drug took effect. "Damn," he raked a gaze over me, "Alfie, get a load of that sword." Thick, grimy fingers clenched in anticipation.

Alfie moved to join him. "What kind of woman carries—aw, shit, Callum, you know who we got ourselves here?" He laughed. "We caught us a bona fide vigilante. Bitch that keeps taking those kids, stealing our fun."

Callum's eyes narrowed, sharpening. "Well, we ain't taking her to *him*."

Lust has many faces. Some of them are ugly. I tried to push up from the pavement but my arms were noodles, my legs beyond central nervous system control.

"Nah, we'll take her to him after," Alfie said. "We can't be wasting bodies like that. We don't want to end up on one of his other crews, like the excavators." He paled.

"If there's enough of the bitch left to take," Callum conceded. "But I get the sword. I hear it's got some kinda special powers." He bent and tugged my sword from the sheath across my back, tucked it beneath his arm then kicked me viciously in the ribs, shoving me from my fetal side-curl onto my back. Then he patted me down and stripped both guns from my body, tucking them in his own waistband. "Goddamn," he breathed, eyes narrowing further. He reached down and plucked the quill from my chest then closed his hand on my breast and squeezed, hard.

I was screaming inside. Frozen, unable to stop him or spew a single of the many threats on my tongue. The toxin they'd used had magical properties—it was taking me way too fast; my insane metabolism burns off normal toxins—and I'd bet it was given to them by whomever they worked for. But how had they seen me following them? He'd touched his beanie when he said he'd fooled me.

Callum relinquished my breast with a sneer. "You want some of this, bitch?" He grabbed his crotch and laughed. "Don't worry, bitch, you're gonna get plenty. More than you know what to do with." He turned and walked away, ordering over his shoulder, "Bring it. But don't damage the goods. Much. Let's get it off the street, enjoy it somewhere nice and private-like."

Alfie whined, "Why do I always have to do all the work?"

Grab my left hand, grab my left hand, I willed silently.

"'Cause you're younger and stupider, that's why."

Grunting, Alfie turned, bent, and grabbed my right hand with his left and began dragging me down the sidewalk on my back. I employed one of Shazam's tricks—made myself heavier. I used to do it when I was a kid. I have no idea how it works, I just know it does. Kat's daughter, Rae, often does it to me, especially if I'm trying to pick her up to put her down for a nap. I needed him to grab my left hand, too, see if my killing touch worked through fabric.

He made it a dozen paces before snapping, "Bugger, the bitch is heavy!" He stopped, reached behind him and grabbed my left hand with his right and resumed trudging.

My theory had been tested: only bare skin to bare skin was deadly. One goal down.

"Hey, Cal," Alfie called excitedly to Callum, "maybe she makes up for not getting more. We could say it took us all night to capture her 'cause she's some kinda superhero. That'd give us plenty of time to have fun with her first."

Callum was silent a moment. "Dunno. Maybe if we add in the sword. But I ain't sure the bitch's worth giving it up."

"The fuck she ain't, look at the tits on her. We don't get many like this. Bet she's red all over, got the fire down below, you know? Jaysus, you can see it in her eyes. Give him the sword and tell 'im it's got some kinda magic, thought he'd want it more. You know he thinks we're stupid and eager to please. C'mon, let's take her back to the arcade."

Another silence, then Callum said, "But we bust ass and bag his dozen tomorrow. I don't want to get on his bad side."

"All he's got is bad sides."

"Hustle it. 'Spect I might take all night with this one."

"I get my turn," Alfie protested. "You ain't the only one got needs."

"Your turn'll last about as long as your dick, while I blink once."

As they devolved into juvenile bickering about the size of their genitalia, and speculative attributes of mine, all I could think was they'd done this before. How many of the people they'd abducted were women? How many paralyzed, helpless women had they raped?

Callum and Alfie were going to die tonight.

π

They dragged me four city blocks before Callum finally came back to help Alfie haul my boneless body up a steep flight of stairs, into an abandoned office building that housed several businesses on the first floor.

The back of my biker jacket was no doubt shredded but I didn't think my back was. Yet. I had enough scars and was proud of each one, but scars from getting stupidly ambushed and being dragged were not something I wanted to sport. I'd been off my game, brooding in a corner of my mind about Bridget, worried about Shazam and the beast in my flat. I'd been as stupid as my prey.

I'd pondered two things while being dragged, staring up at the clear, starlit skies, unable to close my eyes: Where exactly was the paralysis spell inside me, and how would events unfold? Would they undress me, or only the necessary parts? How far down my chest had the blackness beneath my skin spread? Would I blow them up if they touched my bare breast without my consent? I liked that thought. Problem was, it would only take care of one of them. The other might take my sword and vanish, leaving me lying there paralyzed.

As they half walked, half dragged me through a door into a retro-eighties-style arcade, I searched deeper for the magic that had given my central nervous system orders to stop functioning properly. Spells that entered the bloodstream invariably latched onto some part of the brain, pressuring and reshaping it. But where was the bloody thing and how did I neutralize it?

I envisioned my brain, rummaging around in it, seeking an anomaly. I don't know if other people see their brains like I do. Perhaps years of confinement tortured me into forging pathways I'd never have developed otherwise. Perhaps whatever Rowena did to me made me different. Regardless, I have an acute, detailed awareness of what's inside my skull, and the ability to experience it with multiple senses. I have files and vaults and I'm constantly moving things around, optimizing functionality. You have to take care of your brain. It's your greatest weapon.

Aha, there! A shimmer of silver, a bead of possession, nestled close to the pain center in my head. I've spent a lot of time working on that spot. When I used to hurt so bad from hunger, I'd mentally stuff soft cushy pillows in my stomach to absorb the acid, and cocoon the pain center in my brain with cozy, warm comforters. It passed the time more tolerably.

"Not too close to his fucking door," Callum snapped.

"Why? He never comes through. He ain't gonna leave."

"Hang onto her while I set things up. Gonna be at her awhile."

Callum left Alfie supporting me crookedly while he rummaged audibly about in a part of the arcade beyond my ability to see, preparing a place to rape me.

My eyes were unseeing anyway, turned inward as I teased at the small silvery knot spiking tendrils of control into the complex membranes inside my skull, whispering commands to my body.

It was powerful magic. Old magic. Old earth god, I was willing to bet. Perhaps whipped up with a bit of sap from a sacred tree that no longer grew, blended with minerals found deep in the soil, ground with mortar and pestle to a thin, vile poison, enhanced by arcane arts.

I had magic, too. I envisioned a single black vein of the Hunter residue beneath my skin expanding across my collarbone, encouraged it to creep up my neck, where it glided effortlessly, almost eagerly, into my brain, meeting the silvery knot, seeping into it and nullifying—

Holy hell, my head jerked!

"Jaysus, Cal, she bloody jerked!" Alfie exploded, flinching.

"No, she didn't," Callum scoffed. "Nothing moves after a hit from one of those darts. Not until he says so."

"She did, too," Alfie insisted.

I don't know what else was said then because for a time I simply wasn't there.

I was drifting in space, sailing between stars, tumbling head-over-heels through nebula-stained wormholes, gliding along the edges of gaseous rings encircling planets. A deep, hauntingly beautiful gonging resonated in the enormous vacuum of space around me—a technical impossibility—vibrating into my soul, expanding outward to the stars, and the stars answered. Space was a living ocean, lapping gently at the stars, planets, suns, moons, and asteroids. The sound, the vision, was so exquisite a part of me wept. It was . . . heaven. It was . . . peace. Nothing hurt, nothing was wrong, everything fit and made sense and I could stay there forever and nothing could ever touch me again.

But. I thought.

My. What was it that mattered to me?

World.

No peace for me.

I thrust away the lovely vision and returned my attention to the silvery knot, cramming it full of Eau d'Hunter.

The spell holding me motionless shattered.

I blessed the day I'd stabbed the Hunter through the heart. It had somehow gifted me a stunning, gargantuan power that I looked forward to exploring further. And learning to control. No more accidents.

"I'm telling you, she moved," Alfie was still arguing.

I was lying on my back, on a wood pallet that bit into my spine. They'd relocated me while I drifted inside my head. Made us a "bed" of lumber and old magazines; I could smell the musty pages, old ink.

Callum and Alfie towered over me.

I slammed my hands to the floor behind my head, pushed off and vaulted to my feet in a sleek movement, startling them so badly they stumbled backward, gaping at me, slack-jawed.

"Wanna play, boys?" I purred with acid sweetness. "Because you definitely got me in a mood."

ELEVEN

———— • • ————

And you are not me, the lengths that I will go to

"WHAT THE—" CALLUM BEGAN.
He never finished.

Right hand around his throat, I crushed his windpipe and watched him die. Quick, a far more merciful death than he deserved; the kindness that separated me from him.

I whirled and caught Alfie, the shorter of the two, by the back of his shirt, flung him across the room, slamming him into a wall so hard it shuddered. Then I lunged for him as he leapt for the narrow black opening a few feet to his right. This Silver leading to that hot, unknown realm was smaller, wider than the last, but the same acrid breeze gusted from it, smelling of wood smoke and blood. Like the last, this had no ornate frame, or wide black border found on Fae Silvers. The mirrors they used for travel were something different.

I snatched Alfie as he was about to plunge into the dark

abyss and hurled him back into the room. He crashed into a silent, dark Pac Man upright, shattered the frame, went skidding into a pinball machine, bounced off and hit the floor. He pushed up and tried to scramble away but I kicked him in the side and dropped him back to the floor.

"On your knees, hands behind your head," I commanded. "Don't run again or you're dead."

"Y-Y-You're gonna k-kill me anyway!" Alfie cried, clutching his ribs.

"On your knees," I snarled.

"You killed my brother, you cunt!"

"Last chance," I said softly, cramming more menace into a whisper than a shout.

"There's somethin' wrong with you, bitch!"

"You have no idea," I agreed.

"Fuckin' eyes of a psycho!"

"You should talk. Knees. Now."

Trembling, casting furtive, wild-eyed glances at me, he clambered awkwardly, groaning loudly, to his hands and knees then sat back on his heels, gasping as he placed his hands behind his head. I'd kicked him a little harder than I'd realized. His glasses were broken, askew on his nose, beanie drooping. The glasses were thick with heavy black frames. Thin silver wires were exposed by one broken flange.

As he knelt, trembling with rage and fear, I caught a flash of something metallic in the dark folds of his cap and smiled faintly. Dancer might have created a similar gadget for me.

"Camera on your head, your glasses tie into it. Gives you one eighty vision."

"Infrared," he said sullenly.

"You saw my heat behind you."

"He don't send us out without tools."

"Who?"

Alfie's thin lips clamped together, his jaw jutted defiantly.

"Who do you work for and what is he doing? Answer me or die."

Still, he said nothing.

"Answer me or I'll shove your ass through that mirror with a message carved into it that says you spilled everything and I'm coming for him."

"Fuck you will! You got no clue what you're messing with! You can't touch him! Nobody can! And you don't *wanna* touch him! You don't want him to even *look* at you!"

"Who? I won't ask again."

"What'cha gonna do?" he sneered. "You ain't gonna torture me. I know your kind. Stuck up, tight-ass vigilante, saving worthless kids. Think you're above the rest of us. Think you're on the right side, but sweetheart, the right side is the *winning* side—and you ain't on it."

That he was right about part of what he'd said chafed. I needed information. Torture would get it. But I've always avoided crossing that murky line. I needed a sidekick that had no such problem. Still, a little pain wasn't torture.

My switchblade flicked out with a small *snick.* "Carve. Message. Choose."

He glanced at his brother, dead on the floor, then behind me at the dark aperture in the brick wall.

"You won't make it," I said with an icy smile. "You won't get past me."

Brown eyes met mine. Fury burned in them but was diluted

by fear, tainted with a grim resignation. He was more afraid of his master than me.

Alfie smiled coldly back. "Then I'll die trying."

He did.

π

The mirror vanished the moment Alfie's heart stopped, neat trick, that. Whatever master they served, he had formidable power. I felt the temperature in the room drop and spun instantly but I was too late. The wall was brick, the portal closed.

I kicked through faded popcorn sleeves and empty beer cans, scattering roaches, as I retrieved my sword and collected my guns, acknowledging I'd probably not have gone through it anyway.

If their "him" was the same "him" AOZ had referenced, delivering myself straight to his lair, without a plan or backup, without anyone knowing where I was going, bordered on suicidal and that's something I've never been.

Still, I'd have liked time to inspect the glass.

I searched both bodies, patting them down, stripping the cameras from their beanies, hooking the unbroken pair of glasses over the neckline of my shirt for later inspection. I tucked two thin metal cases the size of wallets that contained a few dozen of their lethal quills into my jacket. In an inner pocket of their coats, I found hideous Halloween masks and rubber skeleton gloves. Of course, children thought they were Unseelie. In the dark of night, after the horrors the human race had witnessed, it was a fair assumption.

My search yielded no other particularly useful information but the evening had. I had much to mull over, cull for clues, posit theories. Theories are a fluid road map for solving a mystery and, if broached with an open mind and scrupulous attention to detail, they grant the answers you seek.

At the moment, however, I had a cruelly starved member of the Nine in my bed that might already have some of those answers.

And the blood in the corpses was cooling.

π

Once, a few weeks back, on a warm, starlit evening, I'd walked the Temple Bar District, doing nothing but enjoying myself. I need to do that every now and then. Keeps me connected to my world.

Within the confines of those protected streets, patrolled by the New Guardians and, I suspected, warded by the queen of the Fae herself, affording humans a safe haven where they might do more than merely survive, they could *live*, I forgot about my many responsibilities for a few hours.

I tapped a foot along with street musicians. I stopped in pubs and danced with patrons. I threw darts with a hen party, intentionally missing a lot and gushing over the bride's picture of her dress, acutely aware my future would afford few occasions for beautiful dresses and never a wedding gown. I sipped a Guinness and grabbed a bite to eat at my favorite fish house.

Before leaving the seemingly spelled haven I stared across the street, between passing, boisterous partiers, through the glass pane of a restaurant, watching a family celebrate their daughter's birthday with a chocolate layer cake, my mouth watering. Chocolate is one of very few foods I have an emotional reaction to.

I wondered what it would be like to have that kind of life. I couldn't fathom it. I'm wired differently. I wouldn't be able to enjoy it. I'd be incessantly scanning my environment, knowing someone was out there, in need, and I was eating cake. Situational awareness is instinctive for me. I can't override it.

Back in my apartment I leaned against the wall in the foyer, stretched my legs long and crossed them at the ankles, watching the beast eat the bodies I'd hauled up four flights of stairs because the elevator in my building was on the blink again and, since no one actually lived here, I'd have to figure out how to fix it myself. I'd dragged the deeply exhausted creature out into the foyer on my comforter to feed him there. No blood, no gristle, no guts in my bed is an unbreakable rule.

The beast roused the moment he smelled the bodies, making quick work of one before moving to the next.

I stopped watching and stared out the bank of tall windows, mulling the day's events.

When at last the beast rolled back onto the comforter, which was now bloody and meant I would have to do my version of shopping again, since no amount of bleach ever gets all the bloodstains out, I tugged him back to my bed and cleaned up the mess that remained on the foyer floor, then sanitized the kitchen of the remains of Shazam's feast, thinking about chocolate cake the entire time.

π

Later, I stood in my bedroom with the slumbering beast and stripped, inspecting my clothes. The back of my jacket was destroyed and the butt of my jeans worn so thin I'd split them if I wore them again, so I tossed both in the trash.

I don't shower multiple times a day unless I'm covered with blood that doesn't come off with my clothing, but sometimes I feel the need to rinse a more intangible filth from my body.

After I dried my hair, I inspected myself in the mirror. The blackness of my skin was static with a small exception: a single obsidian vein trellised the left side of my neck and disappeared beneath my curls.

"Well, damn," I muttered as I pulled a long-sleeved, close-fitting black shirt over my head. I tugged on the same nylon glove that had served as protection from my lethal touch earlier while pondering what to do about my neck. I couldn't think of any reason someone might touch that six-inch expanse of my skin and I despise turtlenecks, they make me feel like I'm choking. Still, I had no guarantee that—Bloody hell, Rae always flung her arms around my neck.

I considered the thinness of the fabric of my glove, a silky, nearly transparent nylon, then rummaged in the vanity drawer, retrieved a roll of Duck Tape—don't ask why I have it in my bathroom, my life is strange—and taped the side of my neck, deciding as thick as my hair was, it would protect anyone who touched my head.

I tugged on a pair of faded sweatpants and draped a well-worn quilt over the enormous sleeping beast. After a moment's deliberation, I shrugged and curled up on the small amount of available mattress to catch a few hours of sleep, sword at my side.

π

I dreamed of being helpless, in a cage, and knew, even in the dreaming, the sensation of being paralyzed, about to be raped by those despicable trolls had triggered a difficult memory I keep locked in one of my highest security vaults.

I dreamed I really did pick up Rae at the abbey, and the lovely child exploded in my arms. Little girls are meant to be cherished, protected, and raised into powerful young women.

Something inside me died with her, and my heart turned to a dark, ugly bit of useless stone.

I dreamed I stood at Bridget's grave, weeping blood while black shadows rose from the earth. Then something was behind me and it was going to starve me worse than I'd ever starved in my cage, and whatever the thing was, it wanted me to say its name over and over. But I didn't know its name.

I dreamed of the night, years ago, when Mac came to the abbey, insisting she hadn't meant to stab the *sidhe*-seer who'd attacked her but the spear was in her hand, and the woman lunged and they'd met in lethal fashion. When she moved through the cluster of women and hugged me, I could feel her, smell the scent of shampoo on her hair. *Life is an unavoidable accumulation of transgressions. None of us are exempt. Let them go and work harder to make miracles,* she whispered against my ear, kissed my hair and vanished.

I dreamed my left forearm sprouted darkly beautiful obsidian thorns, so many it became a black-studded opera glove, lethal to the touch. Then it spread, consuming me, and I became lethal to touch. Isolated by my own skin, never again to be held or hugged or permitted any physical contact at all.

I dreamed the beast in my bed licked my shoulder, the nape of my neck. That might have been real. I didn't feel teeth so I didn't worry about it.

I dreamed Ryodan was bending over me, etching symbols on my forehead, my cheeks, my chest, murmuring, *Ground zero, woman. Let it go, let it go. See only beauty. Know only joy.*

Then I dreamed the infinite, dazzling nightscape I'd traveled when I embraced the power inside me.

Nebula-stained, nova-kissed, I drifted, eyes wide with awe and wonder, among the stars.

TWELVE

———— • • • ————

A dark divine intervention, you are a shining light

KAT SIPPED HER TEA as she waited for the others to join her in the parlor.

The Pheasant Room was one of her favorites at the abbey, furnished with lovely century-old black and cream velvet sofas, white ottomans embroidered with black Celtic knot patterns, gleaming black side tables, and curio cabinets of zebra ebony. Faded gray and ivory Persian rugs covered the floors. Burgundy pillows and throws dotted the chairs.

But it was the south wall of floor-to-ceiling windows opening onto the meditation garden that made the expansive room one of her favorites.

The room had drawn its name from the silk wall covering of tan and gray pheasants on an ivory background that stretched from wainscoting to acanthus-embellished crown molding. In Rowena's day the heavy, dark, dusty drapes had been eternally drawn, protecting (or hiding as she'd hidden everything of value) their cherished heritage from the sun and prying eyes.

No more. Both the sun and the lovely, illuminating rays of the moon would, by God, shine in this abbey, if Kat herself had to shred every bloody drape in the place. There would be no darkness, no secrets within these walls.

Well, perhaps a few.

Sean had found a man who could do a paternity test once the child was born. How he'd located him, she had no idea. Those with medical training of any kind were in high demand and short supply.

Kat had been heavy with child at the time. *You think I've been unfaithful,* she'd said. She had. Not willingly, but she had.

Have you? he countered. *We were taking precautions.*

Indeed, they were, unready to bring a child into an uncertain world.

Do you love me? she asked quietly.

Och, and you know I do. Whatever, wherever, I am, it's you, always and only.

Then how could it matter, if I pledge my fidelity to you for the rest of our lives?

Are you willing to, Kat?

Aye.

He'd been an Unseelie prince by then, wings forming on that dark, beautiful back she so adored running her hands down.

He'd been half mad at times, from pain, tortured by fear that the twisted magic of the Unseelie had selected him because he, like all the Black Irish O'Bannions, was deeply, irrevocably flawed.

Still, she'd have chosen him. Her childhood confidant, her lover, her soul mate.

Jealousy, a twisted emotion she'd never felt in her sweet Sean, had thundered so violently in his heart, it terrified her. This wasn't her best friend, the man she knew nearly as well as she knew herself.

He'd said, *I can't accept that. I need to know.*

What difference could it make? she'd said wearily. *Would you be asking me to give up the child if it's not yours? Do you think we can just send it back? Is that what you want of me? It's my child, too.* Either he could love them both or he couldn't. By then a mother's love had awakened, fierce and protective. She could feel the life within her, tiny and lovely. She'd already resolved her struggle. If the child were Cruce's there were two options: kill it—which was no option at all; or give it away—which was no option at all. It was half of *her*, and if the worst were true, the child could have no mother better than Kat. Another woman would have no idea what she was raising. Her only choice was to trust in the power of love.

A love Sean clearly didn't feel. She hadn't seen him for over two years. She ached to see him. She struggled to not think about him, to not think about many things.

"Evening, Kat," Enyo said, dropping down in a tufted chair next to her. Kicking her legs over the side, the tawny-skinned soldier nudged the butt of her gun, tucked in a hip holster, to keep it from digging into her ribs, and slid her automatic, suspended by a band across her chest, over the arm of the chair. Dagger hilts gleamed, tucked into her boots. Enyo was a crack shot, sniper or close-range, responsible for training all the women at the abbey that wanted to learn. None were pressured. Still, all eventually came.

"Good evening, Enyo," Kat replied with a smile that wasn't returned, but Enyo rarely smiled. Energy thrummed beneath her skin, intelligence flashed in her dark eyes. Though Kat would never voice them—it wasn't her place—she knew some of the woman's secrets. They were painful and had made her the hardened warrior she was. Born inside a military tank under heavy fire, war was where Enyo Luna thrived.

As the rest of the Shedon filed in, Kat focused outward, lowering her guards, assessing the room. Her gift gave her many unfair advantages. She used them.

There were eight members of the Shedon: herself; the fierce French-Lebanese Enyo; the ethereal Rhiannon from Wales whose specialty was shattering wards and neutralizing spells; quiet Aurina from Derrynane, County Kerry, who could commune with animals of every kind; sharp-edged Ciara from Ulster-east, with her wild fire-magic; Colleen MacKeltar from Scotland, who over the past two years had become, under one of her uncles' tutelage, an expert in the druid arts; the lovely, aloof, chocolate-skinned Duff from their powerful Boston sisterhouse, who possessed a terrible gift; and the cynical, jaded Decla, who'd traveled the world with a military father and who possessed far darker *sidhe*-seer talents than she owned up to.

These women were the new rule. Duff and Decla took a bit more time to assess than the others but Kat ruthlessly scanned each of them in turn, assessing, seeking rotten spots in the shiniest of their apples.

She found none.

Tonight.

But maintained eternal awareness that one day, her elegant, brutal invasion might fail to yield such happy results.

Perhaps even with her own daughter.

The Song of Making had changed everything. War was coming, there was no doubt of it. Sides would be taken. None of them black and white; there were acres and acres of gray as far as she could see, evidenced by changes even on their estate. Six months ago a caste of tiny Spyrssidhe had taken up residence in the abbey's gardens and labyrinth. They were as simple and kind as could be, lovingly nurturing the foliage, openly seeking the *sidhe*-seers, pledging their loyalty, eschewing their own race, outcast by them. Begging sanctuary to live among humans. Initially Kat had feared they were spies, but she'd turned her gift on the tiny sprites and found them as pure and simple as the dawn. Earth elementals, a type of Fae she'd never imagined existed. *Good* ones.

Though she'd been horrified to discover them capable of reproduction.

There was one Fae name she never permitted herself to think.

A name Rae would never know. He was dead. There was no reason to know. And no need for a paternity test.

Time would tell.

"Any luck?" she asked the room, as the women settled in armchairs and sprawled on divans. A dozen of their *sidhe*-seers, Adepts, had gone missing.

Duff said grimly, "Not yet. We combed Temple Bar from end to end and we plan to fan out into the outskirts tonight. Decla and I went into Elyreum, tried to ask around, but if you're not willing to fuck Fae," she spat with a dark scowl, "you get nothing but suspicion in that club. I don't know how they survived their shifts there."

"They knew it was necessary," Kat said, with no small measure of regret. "We sent only volunteers." The twelve were spies, mature women, Adepts, sent into Elyreum because the Shedon had finally unanimously agreed they could no longer go on without gathering intelligence on the state of the Fae court. For two long years they'd waited and prepared, giving the Fae wide berth. Never going near them, as Mac had demanded.

But rumors had been growing that the Fae had changed, and how could they hope to prepare for a war if they didn't know their enemy? The team had gone in with full awareness of what they were getting into. What was being asked of them. They'd been working the shift for a week. And each morning, when they returned from having sex with the Fae, Kat had used her gift on each in turn, painfully aware of how ruthlessly, overwhelmingly seductive the Fae could be. To a woman, their dozen *sidhe*-seer spies at Elyreum had remained true. Night after night they'd let their bodies be used, while protecting their minds, mining for tidbits of information. Had sunk to the depths necessary to infiltrate the club, while holding onto their essential selves. And for so little gain. All they'd been able to tell the Shedon thus far was that the Fae were definitely more powerful, to degrees unknown, definitely changed by the Song, but there was an inner circle of High Fae cloistered deep within their own private club, to which a highly select few were ever granted access. None of the twelve had yet gained an invitation.

Now they were gone. All of them. Vanished without a trace. They'd left for the club, as usual, Saturday evening and failed to return Sunday at dawn. They'd been missing for two days now, and she feared the worst.

"What did Dani say?" Colleen asked. "Has she had any luck searching for them?"

"I didn't tell her they were missing for the same reason we agreed not to tell her we were sending spies in. Had she known, she'd have insisted on accompanying them. If she knew they were missing, she'd storm into Elyreum, demanding answers at the tip of a sword. We all know what outcome that would have."

Enyo said, "Our oath to the Fae queen would be broken. That sword is part of Dani's soul. She can't not kill Fae. The only way she's managed it this long, and kept her word to Mac, is because she won't allow herself to go anywhere near them."

"Precisely. That's why we can tell her nothing. Continue your search. Continue your silence."

Nodding, the Shedon rose and prepared to head back into the city to find their missing sisters.

π

"Mommy, why are the Fae bad?" Rae said later as Kat tugged off her shoes and began to run her bath.

"Not all of them are," she replied absently, mulling the day's events with half her mind.

She realized what she was doing and forced herself to put away the abbey's business for a time. Her daughter deserved her full attention, a thing she'd never known from her own mother. She'd been deemed a worthless implement by both her parents; handicapped with such extreme empathy, she'd seemed broken, even insane, as a child.

Rae was her world. An unexpected gift. A treasure she would forever cherish, protect, and love, and do all in her power to raise well. The love of a child from her own flesh was the purest an empath could know.

Her daughter had been slow to start talking but, given her own childhood, that hadn't concerned her. Then suddenly, a month ago, Rae had begun blurting words she'd no idea her daughter even understood, stringing them together into impressive sentences.

"The Spur-shee like me," Rae announced happily. "They say I smell good to them."

Kat froze, her hand tightening on the edge of the antique, enameled, claw-foot tub in their suite. "Did they say what you smell like?"

Rae shook her head, black curls bouncing, eyes dancing merrily. "Just that I'm yummy. They smell yummy to me, too."

"Like what?" Kat asked.

Rae nibbled her lower lip and thought. Then scrubbed at her nose and laughed. "It tickles my nose. Just good."

Pollen, Kat thought. Many of the tiny Fae, banished from their own court, lived tucked inside human blossoms, made homes in fragrant, herb-drenched thickets and nests in piney glades. Lately, some of the *sidhe*-seers had taken to building diminutive wooden houses for them, painted bright colors. She'd half expected the earthy Spyrssidhe to protest the humanlike structures, but the other day she'd watched a couple—they mated for life—battle a surprised, hostile sparrow at their door, protecting their new abode.

"Come, love, your bath is ready."

"Bubbles?"

"Not tonight. Only on hair-washing nights." Rae's hair was so thick and curly, it was a chore to wash. They only did it every third night, and then bubbles in her bath were her reward for the time she had to sit while Kat detangled her hair.

"Mommy," Rae said, "my back itches. I can't reach it."

Smiling, Kat held out her arms, and when Rae stepped into them, snuggling to her chest, she tugged her daughter's shirt off over her head.

"It itches bad."

"Turn around and let me see it, pumpkin," Kat said.

"I'm not a pumpkin. Today I'm a dragonfly."

"Well, then, little miss dragonfly, turn—"

But Rae had already turned and bent forward. "Mommy," she huffed, "itch!"

"Did you lay on something today?"

"I always lay on things."

"Like what? Rocks? Something sharp?"

"Just things. Grass and stuff."

"But there might have been rocks in the grass."

"Don't 'member any. Itch."

Kat raised a hand that trembled only slightly and scratched her daughter's beautiful, smooth skin that was so much like Sean's, fair yet with the slightest sun it turned golden.

There were two identically sized, round, pink blemishes.

One on each shoulder.

THIRTEEN

◆ ● ◆

Raise a little hell, raise a little hell, raise a little hell

I WAKE UP GRUMPY AND discombobulated most of the time, unless I'm under attack. Then I wake up sleek, cool, and lethal. Lack of pressure turns me into a high velocity Ping-Pong ball that bounces off anything it encounters. Adversity molds my finest shape.

Today was a disturbing anomaly. I woke feeling bright, focused, alert. More well-rested than I could recall being in years.

Something was definitely wrong.

I snatched my sword, vaulted from bed, and spun in a tight circle, seeking intruders. There were none. I was alone in my bedroom and the beast was gone.

I forfeited a split second of situational awareness to seething about that, then resumed analyzing my inexplicably fine mood. There was no other explanation for it; there had to be a threat somewhere in my flat.

I set to clearing every room, closet, and cubby.

Nothing.

I headed back to my room to search it a second time, and as I crossed the threshold, I felt it. I would have noticed it the first time but high alert focuses me like a laser on potential intruders, not innocuous doorways.

I glanced down, squinting, peering in a sideways I'm-not-really-looking fashion. Wards can be tricky to see. Especially good ones, and this was exquisite: A slate so dark it was nearly indistinguishable from the black marble threshold into which it was carved, the ward had seven distinct layers of design, painstakingly embedded atop each other, plus the softly shimmering hint of two more layers I couldn't make out. The more intently I studied them, the more elusive they became, shifting into indistinct designs.

Oh, yes, damn fine wards. Protected by a spell of obscurity to prevent them from being duplicated; the mark of a true artisan. It took blood, sweat, and time to work such a spell into cold marble, plus skill I don't possess.

I moved to the windows. Located the same wards at each sill.

The beast had draped his version of a well-worn quilt around me before he'd left.

I recognized the elaborate symbols and runes. They're etched at thresholds of Barrons Books & Baubles and there isn't a Faery in all existence that can cross them. Possibly not even Mac, unless he wove it with an exception for her, which would have required her blood as well.

Did that mean my cruelly starved visitor was Jericho Barrons? And, if so, where did he go and why? What did he think, my flat was a convenient Stop N Go where he could pop in unannounced, get fed, then go tearing off without a word, thinking to appease me with the gift of a few wards?

Don't get me wrong, I was grateful for them. I'm incapable of working such formidable magic myself. Their presence made Sanctuary infinitely more valuable to me. I now had a flat with a room that was safe from the sifting Fae who could simply appear smack in the middle of any of my flats, if they felt so inclined.

But I didn't want wards. I'd survived just fine without them for two years. I wanted answers.

I wanted my beast back.

I wanted to no longer be the only supercar revving my engine in Dublin. I wanted the entire primal fleet of growling, high-performance Lambos and Ferraris and big, black, badass military Humvees making thunder in the streets of my city.

Besides, I'd pretty much convinced myself the beast was Ryodan. Not from a wealth of empirical data, but an unshakable gut feeling. I'd thought he'd stay. I'd wake up and find him here. We'd catch up. Get mad at each other. It'd be like old times.

Not.

My bright, alert, true-north-pointing mood took a steep nosedive south. Fuming, I stalked into the bathroom, muttering beneath my breath. I'd lived two long years without a single glimpse of the Nine and when I finally got one of them back, he'd snuck off while I was sleeping. After everything I'd done for him.

I'm rarely—okay, never—a houseguest, but if I was, I'd offer both a hello and a goodbye. Especially if my host had saved my life.

The Nine drive me batshit crazy.

Still, the beast might be floating around Dublin somewhere.

After brushing my teeth and scraping my tangled hair back into a messy ponytail—not about to brush it, time was of the essence—I tugged on black combat pants and stuffed the many zippered pockets and pouches with weapons, then tucked my Glock in my waistband. I fastened a belt around my waist that became three different weapons and hooked a choker at my neck that became a fourth. Slid on a cuff that concealed razors.

I pulled on a long-sleeved shirt and boots, gloved up, Duck-Taped my neck, slid my sword over my back, and headed for the kitchen to gulp down protein and fat while scanning my text messages.

As I hurried for the door I called out to Shazam, telling him to catch up with me ASAP, that I loved and missed him and would enormously appreciate his extraordinarily acute sense of smell that was so vastly superior to mine, and would he please join me on an adventure today? His recent, long absences were really worrying me.

Then, with thunder in my step that held belligerence I didn't bother to conceal, I exploded into the fog-kissed Dublin morning, woman on a mission.

Hunt beast.

I prowled the streets, scanning my surroundings up, down, and sideways, sniffing the air, listening intently, while tallying my priorities for the day.

Rainey had texted while I was sleeping, letting me know she'd found a home, not only for Sara Brady and her siblings but two other orphaned families. No children were placed until I inspected their new homes myself. I won't save innocents only to lose them to another's corruption.

In my teens, I'd have also prepped a *Dani Daily* about recent events, but Dublin had a paper again and, these days, I merely jotted notes, snapped photos, and left the info outside their offices down by the O'Connell Post Office. They'd proven reliable about printing the things I considered important so I stuck to my gracious noncompete. I didn't get a byline but at least the news got out there.

Also on my list was book shopping. Since my bookstore of choice, with its kickass motto—*You want it, we've got it, and if we don't, we'll find it*—was MIA, I was going to have to patronize Bane's Bibliotech & Bagels (seriously—copy much? Get your own original thought) with its concrete floors, stark fluorescent lights, dog-eared, smelly, secondhand, over-priced books, and even more overpriced café.

The euro still ruled, second to brute-force and black-market racketeering. Dublin had quickly relapsed into that elaborate conspiracy of pretending meaningless pieces of paper were worth something, which worked for me. I'd pilfered a pile of currency I found stashed in a storage room deep in Chester's. One of *ten* storage rooms, crammed with currency from too many countries to count, much of it intriguingly ancient.

Though cell towers functioned reliably for the most part, the Internet was in sad shape, vast chunks of it missing. With so much of the human race gone, enormous areas of the planet lacked both the power and manpower to run things. Compounded by magic making things unpredictable, books once again commanded a premium.

I needed information about Ireland's gods and goddesses. I'd never given them much of a thought. I preferred superheroes and had spent far more time poring over comics and graphic novels. Who was AOZ and what was his modus operandi for tripping people up with their own wishes?

While uncovering their legends perhaps I'd stumble across a story about a god that had long ago been wont to abduct adults, leaving their children behind. Discover the why of it, a name. A way to defeat him. Granted, a contemporary book wouldn't yield nearly the detailed information of the abbey's private libraries, but it was as good a place to start as any.

Beast first.

I decided, even though BB&B was gone, to head straight there. Not only was it closer, but the wards were decidedly Barrons-esque. Perhaps both owner and establishment had miraculously reappeared; one could always hope. Besides, when I'd discovered it missing the other day, I'd not scouted the lots with my customary attention to detail, aggravated by its disappearance and on the trail of prey. If BB&B yielded nothing, I'd head straight for Chester's.

As I moved briskly across Ha'Penny Bridge and entered the south side of Dublin, I encountered my second anomaly of the day.

It was Saturday, but this morning at seven-thirty the streets teemed with people in suits and dresses who looked suspiciously as if they were going to work. As a pedestrian plowed down the sidewalk toward me—a woman in her late twenties or early thirties who was peering intently down at her cellphone—I said politely, "Pardon, what day is it?"

She raised her head, absorbed me, noting the hilt of my sword poking over my shoulder, the many bulges in my pockets, perhaps she just didn't like my face. Her eyes narrowed, she clutched her purse more tightly and darted around me, sprinting off in high heels.

I glared at her retreating back, "Right, because monsters *don't* exist and you *don't* need people like me in the world," I muttered as I reached for my phone. When I'd read my text messages earlier, I hadn't paid any attention to the date. There'd been no reason to. I sleep a few hours at most and can go days without it. But yesterday was a bit more eventful and I'd slept closer to four hours.

I gaped down at the screen.

It was Tuesday.

I shook it. Hard. It still said Tuesday.

That was impossible. I narrowed my eyes as the tatters of a dream I'd had last night—or rather *days* ago—surfaced in my mind. Ryodan. Tracing symbols on me. Murmuring.

That prick. I'd awakened feeling so unusually fine because he'd spelled me into sleeping from Friday night until Tuesday morning!

Bristling, I pivoted sharply and stormed in the opposite direction, crossing Barrons off my suspect list. Ryodan had used his powers of "relaxation" on me in the past. This was a Machiavellian move, taking me out of the game so he could leave Dublin on his own timetable.

If Ryodan wasn't at Chester's, I was wrecking the place. Trashing. Maybe torching. No, I wasn't done searching it. But definitely wrecking.

Nobody knocks me out for days. Especially not after being gone for two years. Especially not after I saved his ass.

As I stalked toward 939 Rêvemal Street, my brain processed a third anomaly: an inordinate number of blue-collar workers, laborers from the looks of them, were marching in the same direction, belts swaying, heavy with tools. They were bright-eyed, ruddy-cheeked, talking loudly with excitement.

I moved in behind the fast-moving throng to eavesdrop.

"I heard there's a year's work, maybe more," one of the men exclaimed.

"I heard two. Christ, that'd be something."

"Ballocks, it's good to be working again! The construction business has been deader than a bloody doornail. Too many buildings, not enough people to fill a tenth of 'em."

"Nice to see someone willing to put the money into new construction."

"Right, that. With folks worrying about what tomorrow might bring."

Part of me was pleased by this turn of events. Someone was building. Making jobs for those who had none. Electricians, plumbers, specialty skills were still in demand. But builders, men that cut lumber and hung drywall, metal workers, men who tiled and framed, simply weren't needed anymore. No one was building anything new and probably wouldn't for a long time.

It wasn't as if these men could get additional training to learn a more useful skill. We were back to low- or no-wage apprenticing, a long way from staffing universities again. There was too much unrest, a deep unease about the future. We were a society fractured in countless ways. Those gainfully employed filled essential positions: food production, crucial technology, law enforcement, news. Jobs were hard to find, hence the high rate of crime in our city. And it got a lot worse the farther out you went.

"Who's funding the project?" a newcomer to the conversation said.

"What's-his-name . . . bugger, it's right on the tip of my tongue. Weird name. Riordan? Same guy that turned things around a few years back, when those black holes were everywhere and we were running out of food. Got the papers out. Put the city back on track. He's been gone awhile. Glad to hear he's back. We could use more men like him around this city."

I scowled. A bigger part of me was distinctly not pleased.

I'd been here, humping the grind every day for the past two years, working tirelessly to save my city. And what did I get? Scowled at and run away from, merely for asking a polite question. My hands fisted and my frown deepened.

I was willing to bet half the money I'd stolen from Ryodan that these ebullient, newly employed men were headed for Chester's.

And if my suspicion was correct, that person in the premier spot on my shit-list this morning, that pain in my ass who hadn't been doing a bloody thing to help Dublin for the past two years, was about to get sainted by my city again.

FOURTEEN

———•◦•———

COCKROACHES SLITHERED IN STONE-DUSTED crevices, under and over rocks, reassembling beyond a jagged
outcropping, deep in shadow, into a squat, gelatinous body with
two legs, six arms, and a small head with a beaklike mouth.

His fragile, uncertain form disgusted the roach-god. He
craved a solid existence among men, or at the least, a return to
the lofty position he'd once enjoyed.

When Titans warred, it wasn't the giants that survived. It
was those who made themselves small and inconspicuous that
passed beyond their enemies' regard.

At this the one called "Papa Roach" by mortals excelled. He'd
been the insects beneath humans' feet, reviled, assaulted merely
for poaching small morsels of food for longer than he cared to
recall. Modern man found him grotesque and, with caustic, cor-
rosive chemicals, drove him from their bright world, into the
darkness of foundations, walls, caves, and sewers. Turned him

into a creature of furtive stealth and petty displays of scratching his back on their toothbrushes while they slept, spitting into their glasses, smearing small crusts of feces along the rims, dropping more in their utensil drawers. His beggarly amusements: they shared their world with him whether they wanted to or not, whether they knew it or not. The darkness was his; his exploits began when theirs ended in sleep.

In his venerable prime, his countless bodies, their enviable endurance, agility, and ability to penetrate the most secret places, had been much acclaimed and sought after. He'd been respected, feared, admired, his counsel deemed invaluable. Women had put out food for him at each meal, beseeching his presence beneath their table, preparing tempting dishes to entice him near so they might importune his aid. There'd been a time he'd benevolently assisted them. Enjoyed them. Cared.

No more.

By the blood of the *sidhe*, what did they expect? When you treated things badly, things behaved badly. Who was inclined to seize moments of persecution to demonstrate their finest nature? Idiots. Fools. He'd been there from the first, long before the Faerie, had watched humans make their first slithering passage onto solid ground. Had applauded them as they'd evolved, become more.

Now they were so much less.

Glistening mandibles ground together as he rubbed shiny, black carapace against carapace to grate in a hiss, "My name is Gustaine."

It had been thousands of years since he'd said the words. Since he'd called himself anything but "roach."

The Titans had fallen, most forever slain, the rare few, the impossible to kill, perhaps a hundred of them, imprisoned in the earth. The handful of gods who'd both survived the catastrophic wars and escaped imprisonment had, like him, found a way to hide.

Gustaine enjoyed an intimacy with the planet few gods knew. He, who'd once dined on the finest the world had to offer, now subsisted on its refuse, burrowed deep into its septic waste, had come to relish the diverse flavors of shit, for the knowledge it afforded him. He could taste the sickness in human offal; knew what disease was killing them. In days of yore he might have fetched them the right herb, root, or oil to correct the imbalance. Rot faster, he cursed them now. Blow yourselves up, kill your race off and get out of my way.

He'd even burrowed of late, beneath human skin, dining on the succulent fat of their bodies, nestled within them, privy to many of their thoughts and feelings. He crept anywhere and everywhere, knew all their secrets yet lacked the power to do a damn thing with it. Merely shaping himself into a form that could communicate was taxing. His arms and legs tended to crumble into individual segments if overexerted.

Yet . . . the timeless melody had been sung and it had changed the world, waking some things, killing others, but most dazzling of all, giving rise to the possibility of a new order that might restore the position he'd once enjoyed. Elevate him from the gutters and sewers and endless attacks that were his existence. The Earth felt the same as it once had to him, over a million years ago.

The ancient Song had not, however, improved or altered him in any way. The imperviousness of the cockroach ran deep into his insectile core. Virtually indestructible, he alone remained unchanged by the relentless march of time, by the magic that waxed, waned, and waxed anew. He was, as far as he knew, the sole exception: the obdurate Gustaine.

He'd pledged his allegiance to a few during his darkest times: a half-mad witch from the Caspian mountains, a dead man who'd risen to hunt the night, an ancient, primal beast that was neither god nor Faerie but possessed the *Lanndubh*, the hated black blade that could destroy him; and finally, recently allying himself with a prince of the very race that had corrupted and crushed his. With his brothers and sisters gone, he no longer cared who held power, so long as he had a share.

But now one of his own was back and strong enough to merit attention. Powerful enough to reclaim the *Lanndubh* and free him. And from what he'd witnessed thus far, quite possibly capable of becoming deadly enough to eradicate the Faerie from their world.

Gustaine dispersed his many bodies, reclaiming and molding them into a misshapen head atop one of the many corpses littering the stifling cavern, with its glowing rocks and bonfires, and watched the great god command his legion of worshippers.

The great Soulstealer, Balor, had returned.

The gods had been tricked by their Faerie enemies; deceived, manipulated, and crushed. But they'd lacked advantages they now possessed, assets Balor had already begun to exploit, as evidenced by a recent acquisition: a dozen women, many of them badly beaten, chained to a column near his altar.

Even now a slim dark aperture rippled near the towering dark god who'd once been worshipped more devoutly, and with more terror, than any of the others, as he stripped still more human souls from their bodies, increasing in power with each one he claimed.

Once, the gods had cared about humans. That affection had been destroyed long ago. This time things would be different.

This time the gods would win.

Unlike Gustaine, Balor had changed, as had his method of exploiting his—he chuckled dryly at the pun—God-given gift. And why not? With such enormous power, it was a wonder he'd ever been kind.

He'd watched long enough. This was the master he would serve. A gargantuan, ruthless deity who shared his own grievances, goals, and desires. Who'd already begun drawing other powerful gods near, as even now the devilish, bloodthirsty, wish-granting AOZ danced devious attendance. Balor had a plan, and a fine one. Gustaine was more than ready to see the human race wiped out. And when it was, Balor would be powerful enough to kill even the Faerie.

Gustaine scattered into a sea of insects, scuttling over the grooves and crevices, making his way across the enormous cavern in a dark, glistening wave. He approached the god, where he stood near the black mirror and mound of bodies. Though many were maimed, they were not beyond repair or prolonged use.

He waited respectfully while Balor finished removing the paralysis spell from a tumble of bodies before assembling a precarious form and grinding out a formal troth, "I am at your service, great and powerful Balor."

The immense god whirled from the bodies in a rustle of long black robes, his limp barely noticeable. Ah, yes, he was stronger than before!

Half his magnificent face curved in a blindingly beautiful smile, the other half was completely concealed behind an elaborately embellished glossy raven mask.

As he glanced down at the roach god's squat form, he laughed. "Ah, Gustaine, my dear old friend, I'd hoped you'd survived and would find me here. Your skills have always been invaluable."

"It is a pleasure to see you," Gustaine said. "How may I serve?" One day he would never say those words again.

"AOZ has just apprised me of a human who has something that should belong to me. Scour Dublin and find her."

"I would be honored to aid your cause. Who do I seek?"

"AOZ will give you the description. When you locate her, return to me with her location. Take no action. I will collect this body myself."

"Have you a name?" Gustaine eavesdropped everywhere, on everyone, invisible at their feet, in crevices and refuse. A name would help.

"She calls herself Dani O'Malley."

FIFTEEN

— • • —

I'm awfully underrated but came here to correct it

SURE ENOUGH, THE BASTARD was rebuilding Chester's.
    I stood on the sidewalk, hands fisted, a muscle working in my jaw, assaulted by such acute duality that I'd locked my limbs to keep them from ripping me apart, as they attempted to obey polar opposite desires.

Conflicted is not my natural state.

I'm an arrow to the goal, focused, unwavering. I pick a side and stick with it where every single facet of my life is concerned.

Except for one.

That. Man.

Half of me wanted to punch my fist into the air and shout, "Bloody hell, my sidekick's back and it looks like he plans to stick around for a while this time!" while I dashed below to confirm the auspicious event with my own eyes.

The other half of me wanted to slam my fist into Ryodan's face and break bones.

No, I reevaluated my percentages, half wasn't quite right. Thirty-eight percent of me was in favor of caving to an idiotically happy smile, while sixty-two percent of me was incensed, infuriated, enraged, with thick plumes of steam threatening to erupt from my ears.

I don't get headaches often but I was about to have one. There was too much pressure in my body and no way to vent it.

While he'd kept me out of commission without my consent, he'd made mind-boggling progress. A framed structure now stood on the previously empty lot above Chester's underground nightclub. Several hundred workers were rushing to and fro, prepping for the next phase of the project.

Footers had been poured and were curing, there were steel beams and girders waiting to be placed. Bobcats growled, there was even a small crane maneuvering stuff around. Here, piles of lumber rested on pallets, there, enormous blocks of smoky stone were stacked high.

He had to be running three shifts a day, working through the night. Ryodan was like that. Once he wanted something, he wanted it yesterday. He'd wait if he had to, with the true patience of an immortal, but if he could bypass that waiting he would.

Why now? His bloody club had been wrecked years ago and he'd not once made any effort to rebuild the facade aboveground! What message was I supposed to take away from this—you may have worn yourself out helping Dublin for two long solitary years but I've gained their fealty in a mere matter of days?

Not that I thought he was doing it to mess with me, which—given how much he used to mess with me would have been a fair assumption—but I no longer think everything he does is about me.

Still, my super ears were picking up way too many compliments about him.

"Hey, miss? Miss?" a man said behind me.

I ignored him. I was no doubt in his way and he wanted me to move so I wouldn't delay a single second of the great Ryodan's planned re-creation of the world, which the bible of Dublin would soon be rewritten to immortalize.

"Miss, is that you? I thought it was!" The man circled around, stopping in front of me. Plucking his cap from his head, he stood, clutching it in his hands, a warm smile creasing his ruddy face. "Nobody else with that sword. Top of the morn to you, m'dear! The missus keeps asking if I've seen you again. She'd like you to join us for supper of an evening."

I retrieved his name from my mental files: Connor O'Connor. Some parents should be shot on naming day. After I'd visited them six months back, I'd approved Rainey placing eight-year-old Erin with the middle-aged couple who'd lost their children when the walls fell.

I managed to unclench my jaw but forcing a smile was out of the question. My bones were connected by too-tight rubber bands. Nodding tightly, I said, "That'd be lovely, thank you. I'll drop by when I can. How's Erin?"

"The wee lass is fine as can be. She still has the occasional bad dream, but they're fewer and further between."

"Wonderful. I knew she'd be happy with you." I still couldn't unclench my hand so I jerked a fist at the commotion. "What's the plan here? How many stories?"

"At least half a dozen, I hear, but I've not seen the plans. The boss is below. You might ask him. I hear he's got an eye for the ladies, and a beauty like you could dazzle him into telling you anything." He winked at me.

His opinion and reality were clearly suffering massive disconnect. Answers from Ryodan? As if. Beauty like me? I had Duck Tape on my neck, a scowl embedded in every muscle in my body, and I hadn't even brushed my hair.

"Well then, Miss Dani, I'll be leaving you to your business but I'm hoping you'll find time to drop by. You changed our lives, gave my missus her sparkle back, and when that woman's happy, my world's right as rain. There'll always be a seat for you at our table, and my Maggie's a fine cook." Blushing, he tucked his chin down in a nod of sorts and ambled away.

An eye for the ladies?

That was pretty much all my brain retained.

If Ryodan was nodding from the top of his arrogant, womanizing staircase again, I was going to saw his head off. I had no idea why and didn't care. I just would.

Hands fisted, jaw clenched, I sped across the lot in half-freeze-frame, adroitly navigating machinery and men, to the door in the ground that led to Chester's-below and began my descent into Hell, to raise some of my own.

SIXTEEN

---•◦•---

I feel stormy weather moving in (it's raining men)

A S THE SHINY NEW steel trapdoor closed behind me on
its shiny new hydraulic arm, I descended the (also-new)
stairs that had replaced the clumsy ladder once welded to the
wall.

As a teen I'd watched the See-You-in-Faery girls in their
skintight short skirts paired with insanely high heels navigate
that tricky ladder with a derisive snort, thinking, Please, wear
panties!

The stairs were a definite improvement.

There used to be two sets of trapdoors and two ladders before
you reached the foyer of Chester's-below. That was no longer the
case. The entry must have been the first thing Ryodan set his
crew to modifying. The foyer was now a single mammoth vesti-
bule, with a long, elegantly curved staircase framed in enough to
use, but not yet finished, that ended on a black marble floor so
highly polished it served as an obsidian mirror.

I clenched my hands so tightly I nearly broke my own fingers. He'd clearly admired the floors of my flat. And copied them.

New, colossal double doors soared twenty feet, made of thick matte black steel embellished with fantastical panels of wrought-iron twisted into complex designs, undoubtedly laced with wards ready to be activated at a moment's notice. Ultramodern charcoal consoles inlaid with onyx and a dozen white leather and chrome chairs graced the perimeter of the foyer.

I stalked across the room and shoved the massive doors open with a scowl. I had to put my shoulder into it, which meant the average human would need to be let in from the other side. I stood between the parted doors for a long moment, breathing deep and slow, taking in the view.

Interior lights blazed the entire width and breadth of the many-terraced club and there was that duality again: CHESTER'S WAS LIT! competing with *What else did that bastard copy of mine?* I, too, had white leather and chrome chairs in my foyer, next to my charcoal console. I'd stolen them from some rich guy's penthouse. I enjoyed decorating because I'd never gotten to do it before and I see things in structures and patterns, and decorating is a way of arranging things to achieve maximum visual happiness. If his kitchen had been remodeled with *my* counters and back splash, he was dead. Death might be brief for him, but temporary was enough to make me feel better.

Urban sophistication wed to industrial muscle, Chester's was London haute couture slumming with Irish mob in the best possible way. The club was divided into countless tiered subclubs that would soon be filled to overflowing again. When the world goes to hell, people party. They need to. Who am I kidding? I need to. It spring-cleans my brain, refreshes it like a blast of detritus-removing sanitizer. The days look brighter, saner, after you've spent a night pretending the world hasn't gone mad and that you're on top of it—especially if you finish it off on top of a worthy man, too, not that I've had any luck finding one of those since Dancer.

Dancer. Hole in my heart that never goes away. I miss him always, especially when I'm in a location owned by a man he and I used to conspire against together endlessly.

I'd once despised Chester's, convicted Ryodan of catering to the wrong clientele. I see the place differently now.

As an asset.

The nightclub being reopened would give people a choice. Elyreum was the only club in town packed to the gills with dangerous thrills, its appeal the lethally exotic, sexually combustive Fae with their illusion, lies, and false offers of immortality.

But Chester's would offer an equally seductive draw: the immortal, basely sexual, mysterious, ferociously alpha Nine. And if a few Unseelie princes like Christian MacKeltar and Sean O'Bannion started hanging around again?

Chester's would *obliterate* Elyreum.

I'd even let Inspector Jayne in, he'd be a significant lure. And the more humans that came to party here, the more Fae from Elyreum would come sniffing around, drawn by the banquet of mortal prey. Why was that good?

We'd have control again.

We'd know what was going on. People get drunk and tongues wag in clubs, they reveal things they shouldn't. The disadvantage of being banned from Elyreum was the only info I'd ever been able to obtain on the current state of Faery came from people I questioned on the streets, and few were willing to tell me a bloody thing. I'd begun to suspect my picture hung in Elyreum's bathrooms with a block-lettered caption: DO NOT TALK TO THIS

BITCH OR WE'LL KILL YOU. With the exception of Jayne, I hadn't seen hide nor hair of Fae in . . . good grief, over a year? They were studiously avoiding me, for which I'd been grateful, given the perpetually itchy state of my sword hand.

Oh, yes, I got it now: offer to host your enemies, let them misbehave, pass no judgment. Yes, there's a price for it, you have to watch prey get preyed upon, *but*—and it's a critical but— chance favors the prepared mind; intimate knowledge of the enemy prepares. I'm all about increasing odds of success where the human race is concerned.

I saw Chester's now as I'd never been able to see it before: a vast, complicated, ever-shifting, treacherous, necessary chess- board. The White army was definitely going to lose pawns, noth- ing could be done about that. But their loss might gain the Black king's head, and checkmate the war. The moment White got dis- tracted, trying to protect pawns, the Black army would go in for the kill and take White's king.

I glanced down at the dance floors, to the elegant, wide, glass and chrome staircase that swept up to one of the many private, never-accessible-by-public levels of the club, where Ryodan's glass office was located.

In spite of my pissy mood, I smiled.

Fade and Kasteo were in position at the bottom, arms folded, legs splayed wide, two handsome, towering, scarred immortal bouncers.

The Nine were home.

I basked in the simple pleasure of that fact for a moment.

Then my smile was obliterated by a scowl. They were guard- ing the same notorious staircase from which the notorious Ryo- dan used to give his notorious nod every morning.

I knew the legend. Women never refused.

Saw. Off. Head.

I dragged my gaze from the stairs and continued scanning the club. Hundreds of laborers mulled about the interior, dismantling bars and snugs, prepping for renovations. I was pleased to see the kiddie subclub was already demolished. I couldn't look at it without thinking of Jo. Apparently Ryodan couldn't either. Nor, I'd bet, did Lor much like it anymore. Besides, it reminded me, too, of that day Ryodan had saved my life by shoving me on an elevator, sacrificing himself to fling my cabled car up to safety. I'd thanked him by slaughtering everyone in the kiddie subclub while he was out of commission. Done it to deliberately wreck his good name with the patrons he'd guaranteed safety within his walls.

I'd endangered his chessboard. No wonder he'd been so angry with me. I'd nearly cost him the information that gave him the ability to control the Nine's world, affect the world beyond it.

God, it seemed so long ago! It was a vastly different time.

A vastly different me.

I'd believed myself large and in charge in my teens, and I'd been out of control, indulging my desires without once considering their potential consequences. Here, in Chester's, I'd had a brutal epiphany at fourteen, come to understand my actions had ramifications. I'd glimpsed, for the first time, the boats I'd left capsized in my wake, occupants flailing in the water as I blasted across the whitecaps of Dublin's stormy sea.

I stood a moment, letting memories wash over me, then shook them briskly off.

I was glad to see the club reopening. I was not, however, glad to see its erstwhile owner.

I narrowed my eyes as I realized I *didn't* see its erstwhile owner. Anywhere.

Where was he? I had a bone the size of a Patagotitan's femur to pick with him.

My hands were so tightly fisted, the nails of my right hand had drawn blood. My gloved left was cold as ice and itching ferociously.

As I pushed forward through the open doors, I *felt* them fall in behind me, one on each side. I didn't even need to turn around.

Two of the Nine had been standing behind the doors on either side, and I'd not sensed them through the foot-thick steel that, I was willing to bet, was coated with the mysterious alloy Ryodan likes to use.

I certainly felt them now, an exhilarating electrical charge sizzling on every inch of my skin. But there was something more, something disturbing. That thrilling current was laced with a thing I'd not noticed when I was younger: a slow, dark, blatantly sexual burn.

They radiated masculinity, saturated the air with a palpable, primal earthiness, a promise of inexhaustible carnality. Unlike the Fae's brutal assault on the senses, there was no compulsion here. They simply exuded erotic invitation and promise, awakening in a woman's body a profound, inescapable awareness that an eminently fuckable man was near that could deliver the kind of sex women dream of, mind-blowing, earth-shattering, all-consuming, go-down-in-history as the best ever. And all I could think was, Holy distorting diode, please tell me Ryodan doesn't throw this charge off now, too.

Had something about them changed? Or was something about me different? Was this what Jo had *always* felt around Ryodan? What other women had incessantly experienced around the Nine? Had I just been too young, too sexually inexperienced, too full of myself to feel it back then?

Possible.

I turned to see who flanked me.

On my left was the one I call Shadow, as I've never learned his name. Scarred and massive, towering over me by a foot, whiskey eyes burning, he watched me in silence. To my right was, holy hell—

"Lor!" The rubber bands stringing my muscles too tight vanished and my face exploded in a hundred-Mega-watt smile.

I flung myself into the tall blond man's arms and was rewarded with an enormous, crushing bear hug as the ever-up-for-a-party Viking swept me off my feet and spun me around.

When he finally put me back down, I was still grinning like an idiot until he flashed me a wolfish smile and said, "Honey, you been running my ass ragged for two goddamn eternal years. I'm so fucking glad the boss is back. Might have time to get laid again."

My smile vanished. "Wait, what?"

"Laid. I might get laid."

"I heard that part. That's a given with you. I don't need to hear it. Two years? Running your ass ragged?"

"Watching you. Making sure you stayed out of trouble."

I strained every tendon in my right hand by fisting it too tightly. "You've. Been. Here. In Dublin. For two years? Right here?"

He nodded happily. "Thought I was gonna have to save you from those slimy bastards the other night but you took care of 'em just fine, honey."

It wasn't penetrating for some reason, probably because the thought was so odious I was barring it entrance to my mind. "Let me get this straight: for the past two years you've been here in Dublin. Like, within feet of me. Tailing me. Hiding from me." I knew he could. The Nine can outsuper me anytime. It infuriates me.

His grin widened. "Uh-huh. Damn good, wasn't I? You never caught on."

My nostrils flared. "And why would you do such an offensive thing?"

His grin faded and he cut me a dark look. "Christ. Women. I don't get you. I protect you, you get pissy. I don't protect you, you get pissy. I open doors, I'm patronizing. I don't open doors, I'm a caveman, which by the way, I am. What the bipolar fuck? Beginning to think you babes don't have any clue what you want, or change your mind constantly just to dick with us."

"I'm not getting pissy because you were protecting me— although I fail to see how you were, given you never once appeared or did anything to help me. I handled everything by myself and, while I'll never argue with backup, the precise term for what you were doing is 'snooping,' equivalent to spying on me, against my will, undoubtedly on the orders of that interfering, domineering, dickhead. I needed a *friend,* Lor. Not a bloody invisible shield."

"Boss don't listen to nobody, honey. I told him it'd piss you off."

I said icily, "But he didn't care." *Don't worry,* he'd told me in the cemetery that night, *I've taken precautions, you'll be protected.* He'd also never answered my question about whether all the Nine were leaving. He hadn't lied. But lack of disclosure can be equally offensive.

"Oh, he cared, honey. He always cares about you. Just makes up his own mind and acts on it. Kinda like somebody else I know. You two deserve each other, two of a bloody I-know-better-than-everyone-else kind."

"He and I are not, and will never, be peas in the Mega-pod. In his bloody dreams does he aspire so high. Where is he?" I demanded.

Deep, rich, baritone laughter rolled up from the dance floor behind me, down two levels. "Ah, Dani."

And there it was, the voice I hadn't heard in two long years, except in unsolicited, unwanted dreams. I shivered as it rolled through me. Same bloody charge, same instant, intense aware-ness of Ryodan as a shatteringly sexual man that I was getting off Lor and Shadow. Shit. I preferred that inexplicable shakiness I used to feel in my stomach as a teen to this painfully heightened awareness of the state of my own hormones and I. Was. Not. Shorting. Out. This. Time. I inhaled deep and full, slapped a hasty but formidable mental barrier around everything that had anything to do with sex. Boxed it, coated it with pure titanium. I was no longer a child, and wouldn't act like one.

"I'm right here. Kid."

Kid. My vision hazed crimson with bloodlust and my mind sharpened to a painful degree of acuity.

Lor groaned, "Aw, hell, honey, don't do it."

I blinked into the slipstream, graceful as a gazelle, hungry as a lion. I know every inch of this club like the back of my hand.

My percentages had shifted. I was one measly percent glad he was back. Ninety-nine percent committed to kicking his in-sufferable ass.

SEVENTEEN

How could you leave me when I needed

to possess you, I hated you

I SLAMMED INTO RYODAN AT top speed, a grenade with the pin out, fists flying. I hit him so hard we hurtled into a marble column that shuddered satisfyingly from the impact. Then I grabbed him, hurling him away from it, and heaved him into a wall.

He wasn't hitting me back, he wasn't even resisting, and that pissed me off even more.

I launched myself at him again, peeled him off the wall and flung him across the room. He blasted into a pallet of lumber with such force wood exploded and went flying in all directions.

Dimly, I registered the stunned faces of the workers. Dimly, I registered that I was behaving alarmingly like I had in my youth.

I didn't care.

"Kick up into the slipstream," I snarled at him. He wasn't even joining me. Just hanging down there in slow-mo Joe world where everyone could see him, letting me beat on him. It must have looked to them as if he was being hurled about the room by an irascible Tasmanian devil.

He stood, dusting off his crisp, well-tailored clothing, crossed his arms over his chest and cut me a hard, warning look. *Good to see you, too, Dani.*

He wasn't even bleeding anywhere. What was I—innocuous?

I thudded down from the slipstream with thunder in my boots and snarled, "I didn't say it was good to see you, and I don't think it. You bastard. Kick. Up. Fight with me."

Why would I do that?

"And don't talk to me without talking to me. You don't have the right. Stay out of my head."

His eyes narrowed. *Might makes—*

I bulleted into the slipstream again, cutting him off. That was it, I was not listening to a single word of his condescending "might makes right" or "possession is nine-tenths of the law" crap, or any of his other immortal philosophy. Sometimes there's only one way to resolve things: get down and dirty and brawl. And, by God, he *was* going to brawl with me and I *was* going to vent my outrage on his unbreakable body over the many things he'd done to prick and offend me.

I exploded into him again, hitting him so hard we erupted into the air, carrying him backward with my body to lam him into another column with such intensity the pillar cracked from ceiling to floor. We slid down it together, me gripping his collar with both hands.

He'd left me for two years. Never once texted me. Never called. Left Lor here, hidden from me, beyond my reach. It didn't appease me at all to think Lor might have kept him apprised of my well-being. That didn't count in my book.

Then he'd come back, let me save his life, and stalked off without a word.

Called me kid.

As I was about to slam my fist into his face and drive his head back into the column to see if I could collapse it with my next blow—the column not his face—Ryodan yanked me out of the slipstream, plucked me by a sleeve and smoothly dragged me down into the real world with real world consequences where the painful things are and forced me to stay still, one big hand manacled around my wrist.

"What," he said very softly, "is your problem, Dani?"

My problem? I wasn't the one with problems. I glared at him. Our faces were so close I could see the tiny crimson sparks glittering in his ice-gray eyes. Ancient, inhuman eyes, clear and cool.

He wasn't even breathing hard.

I was panting.

I drew my free hand back to smash my fist into his infuriatingly composed face but my clearly possessed hand grabbed a fistful of his short dark hair instead and yanked his face to mine while my clearly insane mouth ground itself against his.

A frenzy of lust exploded inside me. Years of loneliness, years of frustrated hunger, years of missing him.

I kissed him like he was the battlefield I was born to wage all my wars on. I kissed him like he was the only king this Amazon warrior might ever take her army into combat for. I kissed him like we were primal, lethal beasts, fearlessly stalking those violent, killing no-man's-lands where angels feared to tread, and I kissed him with a hunger that's never once been slaked, as I unleashed all the fire and fury and savagery in my soul—and there is one fuck of a lot of it.

He groaned roughly, hands slipping to my ass, yanking me

closer, if closer were even possible when I was already plastered to him like a second skin. Then my kiss changed and I kissed him with every ounce of raw, aching loneliness in my all-too-human flesh and bones, every haunted, painfully bared shred of me that was tired of reaching with the intensity and intent of life and touching nothing because I can't fuck normal men, they don't get me any more than I get them and I walk away, colder and lonelier than before. I kissed him with the rainbow-colored shattered hopes and dreams of a child betrayed in ways too damaging and numerous to count, and I kissed him with the yearning to be the one making joy blaze from his eyes.

I ground my body against his and kissed him like he was the only man I deemed complex, brilliant, and strong enough to be worth kissing, and I kissed him as if he were made of bone china, a man who'd known little tenderness in his life because he always had to be strong, like me, because he could, like me, and the world needed him, like me, and that's what you do when you fit the bill.

I kissed him with devotion, with raw sexual reverence, starved to cut loose like this. I offered him my prayer, my challenge, the one that had gone eternally unanswered: Are you there? Are you as painfully alive and aware as me? Can you feel how much I'm giving you when I touch you like this? Are you *worth* me?

In other words, to my complete and utter horror, I kissed Ryodan with my whole heart. And that fuck so did not deserve it.

I exploded backward, scrabbling away from him.

Stopped.

Stood.

He stared at me, eyes full crimson, lust burning in them with such intensity I gasped raggedly and took another step back. I'd woken a beast and, at that moment, wasn't entirely certain it could be returned to slumber. He lunged forward, checked himself and stopped, hands fisted at his sides.

I dragged my gaze from his. Looked around. Every eye in the room was on me.

I don't even know why I just did that, I thought. Then I realized, to my complete and utter horror, I'd said the words aloud.

"Well, if you're feeling the need for another moment, hour, or even year like that," said one of the strapping laborers in a husky voice, "I'd be happy to volunteer."

"You're fired," Ryodan snarled, without bothering to look at the man. He inhaled slow and deep, crossed his arms again and leaned back against the cracked marble column, staring at me with blazing crimson eyes. Not sparks. Pure, undiluted beast flamed in his gaze, fangs glinted at his mouth.

I hissed, "No, he's not. You don't fire people just because you don't like what they said. You fire people if they don't do the job right. He needs the work. You're not firing him."

"Ah, Dani," he said tightly, "you beat me. You tell me what to do. I seem to have forgotten which of us is the man. Perhaps you need a reminder."

I had no doubt what kind of reminder he had in mind.

You opened this door, bloodred eyes fired.

And I'm closing it, I shot back.

Try, woman. His lips curved with a dark smile, full of promise that he'd heard every word I'd said with my body and wasn't about to let me forget a single one of them.

My emotions were all over the place, every blasted one of them lit up, sparking. While he was gone I'd had countless conversations with him, enumerating with elaborate, scathing details the many grievances I held against him. I'd lambasted him with witty, brilliant, incisive remarks. I'd reduced him to an apologizing, contrite male, eager to get back in my good graces.

I couldn't come up with a thingle sing—I mean, single thing—to say. Bloody hell, someone had extracted my brain from my skull and stuffed cotton balls in the empty compartment.

I hefted the titanic weight of my humiliation and embarrassment up into the slipstream, blasted up the stairs, and exploded out the door with it.

"Goddamn," Lor said roughly. He cleared his throat and said again, "Goddamn. Boss, that musta been worth every ounce of the beating she gave you plus a shit-ton more. Think I need a cold shower. Nah, five blondes."

Men laughed, murmuring agreement.

Face hot, cheeks flaming, I didn't linger to hear Ryodan's reply.

EIGHTEEN

• ◦ •

A soul in tension is learning to fly,

condition grounded

THE KISS WENT IN a box.

The entire debacle at Chester's did.

I simply pretended it hadn't happened and went about my day. People waste so much time mulling over things they've done when all the mulling in the world neither undoes nor changes one iota of what you did. The only thing that alters the unsatisfying state in which you've left things is future action.

Either never see the person again, or see them and do something to set the record straight. Like, lie. Claim you were possessed by a Gripper. Backpedal hard and fast.

I had no doubt I'd see the bastard again and, since I hadn't wasted all that time in the interim annoying myself, I'd be cool, composed, and capable of redressing the facts. Somehow.

I spent several hours visiting the homes on my list and was pleased to be able to clear both of them to place children. When I called Rainey, she was delighted I'd found her choices acceptable. To date, she'd never picked a home I'd deemed lacking, her record was impeccable, and I was beginning to develop a pleasant degree of trust in our working relationship.

I also popped into the annoyingly bright, annoyingly modern Bane's bookstore (I refused to give it three B's, it didn't deserve them) and left with a bag of books: *Ireland's Legends; A Concise Summary of the Book of Invasions; When Druids Walked the Earth; Giants and Kings of Ireland; An Encyclopedia of Celtic Mythology,* plus two of my favorite iconic graphic novels in pristine condition: *Batman's Arkham Asylum,* and *Batman: Whatever Happened to the Caped Crusader?*

I was headed back to my flat to hunt for Shazam, as I'd grown increasingly concerned about his recent, long absences, when my back pocket vibrated with a text alert.

I swear to God my ass knew who it was from.

I'd received multiple texts today, from Rainey, Kat, a few of my friends and "birds" checking in. But this one was different. It practically bit my ass through my jeans.

Ryodan.

His words in my back pocket.

Even those had fangs.

Scowling, I whipped it out, tidily boxed recent events threatening to erupt in my skull.

PICK YOU UP AT EIGHT. WEAR A DRESS.

My eyebrows climbed my forehead and vanished into my scalp.

Seriously? Furious thumbs flew over the keys as I typed Barrons's words from a few years ago. He'd been right.

All caps make it look like you're shouting at me.

His reply came so swiftly, I swear he'd already had it typed and ready.

I was. You never listen otherwise.

"Wear. A. Dress," I fumed, steam building in my head. I know Ryodan and he knows me. Which meant he knew telling me to wear a dress would pretty much guarantee I'd choose anything but a dress.

But . . . you have to take things a little further with that man because that's how he thinks, always looking ahead. Since he *knew* telling me to wear a dress would make me choose something else—and he also knew I was fully aware of how his manipulative brain worked—he knew I'd ultimately decide to wear the bloody dress just to prove I wasn't being manipulated by him. So, he'd get me in a dress either way.

This was a complete clusterfuck. How did I win? By wearing a dress or not?

I now fully and completely understood why That Woman had gone into battle with Sherlock naked.

The only way I could win was by not being there to be picked up at eight. My screen flashed at that precise instant with a new text from him.

This isn't about us. Our city is in trouble. Be there.

"Oh, screw you," I growled. Right, provoke my innate, highly dysmorphic sense of personal responsibility.

I shoved my phone back in my pocket, resisting the urge to mute further texts. I wouldn't let him make me let my city down by not being there if someone in need texted me.

I was storming back to my flat to demand Shazam's presence (and counsel!) when I saw one of them: a bird with a broken wing, maybe two.

I sighed, and circled back to a food vendor, placed my order, rearranging priorities, watching her from the corner of my eye where she huddled on a bench outside a pub, trembling and pale, badly bruised.

I didn't know her story and didn't need to. I knew the look. This was a pervasive problem: the disenfranchised could be found on nearly every corner of every street in every city in our world.

Their stories were some version of this: their families/ children/lover got killed when the walls fell and they lost their job; they watched their siblings/friends/parents get seduced and destroyed by Seelie or Unseelie; the worst of humans had preyed on them.

Glassy-eyed, sludge-brained, terrorized, once victimized, they were prey magnets.

Not everyone was as lucky as me. Not everyone had a hard life, so when the going gets tough, they don't know how to get going.

"Here. Eat." I offered the woman the sandwich I'd just bought. She was young, too pretty to go unnoticed, thin.

Trembling, she raised her head and looked at me. Shock glazed her eyes, fear blanched her skin to snow. She made no move for the wax-paper-wrapped food, and if she didn't take it soon I might fall on it myself. It was one of my favorites, a hot, breaded fresh-caught fish and tartar sauce delight nestled in a sesame bun, with chips, dripping grease.

"I'm Dani," I said, settling on the far end of her bench, keeping the bulk of it between us so she wouldn't feel cornered. "I help the folks that need it. Take the sandwich and eat it. I don't want anything from you. But if you stay here, some bastard is going to hurt you worse than you've already been hurt. Do you understand?"

She flinched. Someone had beaten her. Recently. Her lower lip was split and one eye freshly swollen shut. I know bruises, her eye and half her cheek would be black before nightfall. She knew she was vulnerable but whatever happened had left her fractured, unable to make decisions. She was here because she had no ground to go to, no one to take care of her while she regained—or learned to have for the first time—fighting strength. That's where I come in.

"Seriously. You'll feel better after you eat. Here's a soda. Drink it. Sugar makes everything look better." I placed the can gently on the bench in the expanse between us.

After a moment she snatched the sandwich from my hand and took the soda. When she fumbled, trying to pop the flip-top, I reached for it to help and she flinched again.

"Easy, I'm just going to open the can," I said. The backs of her hands were scraped nearly raw, bloodstained nails broken to the quick.

She took her first bite of the sandwich with seeming revulsion, chewed automatically, swallowed hard. The second went down the same way.

Then I saw what I always hope to see but don't always get: she fell on the food ravenously, tearing off big chunks, cramming them in her mouth, shoving chips in alongside, smearing tartar sauce and grease on her chin. Her body was hungry and, despite its trauma, wanted to live. Now I just had to get her mind back in line with it.

When she was finished, she slumped against the wooden slats of the bench, wiping her face with a stained, frayed sleeve.

"I don't know what happened and don't need to," I said quietly. "I'm offering to take you to a flat I keep stocked with food, water, everything you need. I have dozens of places like it around the city for folks that need them. This one's yours for thirty days. You can stay there while you work through whatever you're dealing with, eat, sleep, and shower in peace. Periodically, I'll drop by to make sure you're okay." Usually in a week, they were ready to talk. Needed to. I offered thirty days because a time limit was pressure and a firm hand lends shape to Play-Doh. If they needed more than thirty days and were earnestly trying to recover, they got it.

She cleared her throat and when her voice came out it was gravelly, hoarse, as if she'd recently been screaming. But no one heard. And no one came. "Why?" she said.

"Because every man, woman, or child we lose in this world, I take personally."

"Why?"

"It's just the way I'm wired."

"What do you want in return?"

"For you to get angry. Heal. Maybe join those of us trying to make a difference. Do you do drugs?" That was a defining factor. Hard-core drug users I usually lose. So many broken-winged birds, I try to focus on the ones with the greatest odds of success.

"No," she said, with the first trace of animation I'd seen, a flash of faint indignation.

"Good."

"Are you for real, kid?" she said sharply, emphasis on *kid*.

Anger was common. Belittle me, drive me away. It never worked. "As if you're much older than me," I scoffed. "I'm twenty-

three," I erred on the farthest side of my age to establish credibil-
ity, "and they were hard years."

Her sharpness vanished. It took energy, and birds had little
to spare when it was all caught up in an inner cyclone whirling
around whatever horrible thing they'd endured, kicking up so
much internal debris it was hard to see anything clearly. "I'm
twenty-five," she whispered. "Birthday was yesterday."

That was harsh. I'd had a few rough birthdays myself. I wasn't
stupid enough to wish her a happy birthday. Sometimes there is
no such thing. I fished again for her name, to make that fragile
first connection. "I'm Dani."

Her nostrils flared. "I heard you the first time."

"And you are?"

"*Not* carrying a sword, assorted guns, and weapons." She
made it sound like an insult.

I said lightly, "Well, stick with me and we'll remedy the shit
out of that."

Her eyes went flat again and she said on a soft, exhausted
exhale, "I'm not a fighter."

"Then you're a die-er?" There were only two positions in my
book.

A long silence, then, "I don't want to be."

"That's a start. Do you think the world is going to get nicer?"

She began to cry, silent tears slipping down her cheeks. I
knew better than to pat her hand in a gesture of comfort. Birds
have hair-triggers. You couldn't invade their space or they half
flew, half scrabbled away. You had to talk easy. Focus on getting
them to safety. Whatever she'd survived, it had happened very
recently. From the way she'd commented about her birthday, I
suspected yesterday.

I said, "I'm standing now. I'm going to start walking. Follow me and I'll get you off the streets. You'll have thirty days—taken care of, fed, and housed—to decide what you want to be when you grow up," I flung the thorn.

It pricked, she bristled minutely. "I *am* grown up."

"If this is your finished product, you're in trouble." I pushed up and stalked off, not slow either. They had to want to come.

"Wait," she said behind me. "I'm hurt, I can't walk as fast as you."

Because she couldn't see my face, I allowed myself a smile.

π

I showed her around the flat, emphasizing the many dead bolts on the inside of the door, the food in the pantry, the way you had to jockey the stove knobs to get them to work. I didn't open the fridge; I'd grab Shazam's blood on the way out.

She walked woodenly to the bedroom, stood staring blankly at the bed, storms rushing behind her eyes. When bad things happen, you relive them for a while, keep seeing them over and over. Psychiatrists call it "intrusive thoughts" but that makes it sound like they're infrequent and intrude into "normal" thoughts. There are no normal thoughts in the near aftermath. You're trapped in a movie theatre that's playing a horror flick over and over and you can't escape because somebody locked all the doors and the film's rolling on every wall.

Unless you get angry enough to break down a door.

Some things aren't worth analyzing. You leave them behind. *Actus me invito factus non est meus actus.* Then there are those actions you chose to make that shouldn't be analyzed either.

If I can't make them angry—the right way, and there are loads of wrong ones—I invariably lose them.

She had no purse. No money. Her clothes were torn and

dirty, her oversized man's shirt an obvious pilfer, an employee shirt from an out-of-business petrol station with the name "Paddy" emblazoned on the pocket. "You got a phone?" I said.

She nodded and fished it awkwardly from the shirt pocket.

"Put my number in it." I rattled off the digits and watched her type them in. "If you want to leave the flat, text me. Me or one of my friends will come get you. My goal is to keep you safe and alive until your head clears. Got it?"

"Got it," she whispered.

"You want anything, text. Do you need a doctor?"

She shook her head. "I'll heal."

Her body would. We'd see about the rest. "Your name?"

"Roisin," she said numbly.

Connection made. "Cool." I turned to walk away when I felt her hand on my shoulder and turned back to her.

Then she was hugging me, and I thought, Shit, if she touches my head, I might blow her up, so I was even more awkward than I usually am when someone hugs me out of the blue, but I figured it out and sort of patted her comfortingly on the back while trying to keep her away from my neck and head.

She gasped with pain and stumbled away. When she turned her back to me, I saw blood on her shirt, blossoming over her right shoulder blade. A considerable amount.

"You can go now," she said. Tightly. Not because she was angry but because she was barely holding it together. I wanted to demand she show me her back, determine for myself whether she needed a doctor.

I know what it's like to have somebody try to zoom in too close to the things I don't want to talk about.

Still, I wouldn't be waiting a week to check on her. I'd be there again tomorrow. Morning. With coffee and bandages and the hope a safe night of sleep had calmed her enough that she'd let me take a look.

For now, a parting distraction. "Don't freak out if a huge . . . uh, catlike thing with violet eyes and a fat white belly pops in. I mean literally, just appears out of thin air. Don't throw things at him, and whatever you do, don't call him fat or even let him know you think he is. He's super sensitive and emotional, gets weepy. He can turn into a huge sobbing mess on you. Just tell him Dani isn't staying here right now and he'll leave."

Roisin whirled like a jerky puppet who wasn't pulling her own strings. "Wait, *what?*"

But I'd already grabbed five pints of blood from the fridge, tossed them in a bag, and was out the door. "Lock up behind me," I ordered as I closed the door.

Shazam always scanned our flats before he materialized, Roisin had nothing to fear.

But, for a time at least, she'd be worrying about a purple-eyed, emotional, very fat cat appearing, and the hours until she finally slept would pass more easily.

I learned young that moments of comedy during the horror show can be a life raft, enough to keep you bobbing in a violent, killing sea.

MURDERER

—— • • ——

S he sold me.
   To the highest bidder.
   Double-crossing Rowena, my mother sold me on the open market
like a prize pig, I learned later, with a video of me trying to freeze-
frame in my cage, of her making me crush various objects in a tiny
fist, accompanied by a detailed list of my superhuman abilities.

They came late one night, and I was so excited to see someone besides my mother or, on the very rare occasion, one of her wasted boy-
friends, someone who had surely come to set me free, that I began
vibrating, moving so rapidly from side to side behind bars I became a
mere smudge of white in the wan light of the TV.

I was so excited I couldn't even talk.

No one had ever been in our home before besides my mother and
those glassy-eyed, stoned men, and I was terrified she'd come back and
prevent my saviors from releasing me.

When I finally found my tongue, I said over and over please let *me out, please let me out, you must let me out* in a stunned kind of daze.

These were Responsible Adults like the ones on the telly.

They wore dark suits and shiny shoes, and had neatly trimmed hair above their collars and ties.

These were the kind of people that rescued other people. Who came from places like the Child and Family Agency, TUSLA, another word I always saw in my head capitalized, the color of wide-open blue skies.

But despite my pleas, they stood in the middle of our shabby living room, with its sagging plaid sofa and scuffed wooden floors, and began to discuss me as if I wasn't even there.

As if I was only super-fast and super-strong. But super-stupid. Or super-deaf.

Eventually I stopped smudging around in my stunted space and shut up.

I drew my knees to my thin chest and huddled behind bars, realizing that some people were born into Hell and just never escaped.

They said things like limit-endurance and stress-conditioning, they said things like eggs and artificial insemination and super-soldiers. They discussed how best to alter and control me.

Then they shocked me through those bars, again and again, sending extreme high voltage arcing into my small body, frying my synapses, reducing me to a quivering puddle on the worn, lumpy pallet that had once been a mattress.

They said things like surgical enhancement and discussed the regions of my brain, the possibility of dissection once they had sufficient stores of reproductive material.

They discussed the overdose they'd give my mother, erasing all ties between me and the world.

A person alone is a hard thing to be.

When I could no longer even twitch, they opened my cage.

They.

Opened.

My.

Cage.

Not since that perfect, magical-memory bubble of a night, years ago, that my mother had washed my hair and played games with me at the kitchen table until I'd been too sleepy to see, not since that night I'd drifted off in bed next to her with my tiny hands pressed to her cheeks, staring at her while I fell asleep, basking in her love, assured I was the most special thing to her in all the world, had that goddamned door opened.

OLDER and OUTSIDE awaited.

And I couldn't move.

In the periphery of my vision the outdated, faded calendar with its yellowed, curling edges, on which my mom had stopped crossing off days long ago, mocked me with the awareness that I'd been a naïve fool.

Believing—long past the time I'd been given every conceivable sign that I was nothing to her, and no one was ever going to save me—endlessly believing I mattered. That she cared.

Behind them the telly played a rerun of Happy Days *and I lay paralyzed, synapses charred, watching them bend to grab my feet and drag me from the cage, and I wondered about the kind of people that got happy days, and I wondered why mine had been so brief.*

I had no doubt their cage would be even mightier, my incarceration far more difficult to bear.

Sometimes, something inside you just breaks.

It's not repairable.

I died on the floor that night.

My heart stopped beating and my soul fled my body.

I hated.

I hated.

I hated.

I hated.

I hated with so much hate that things went dark and I was gone for a few seconds, then I was back but every single thing inside me had snapped, changed, rewired.

Me, the happy curly-haired kid with such grand dreams, swaggering about, little chest puffed out, waiting, always waiting for someone to love me.

When Danielle Megan O'Malley died someone else was born. Someone far colder and more composed even than the Other I'd slipped into so often of late. Jada.

I welcomed her. She was necessary to survive this world.

She was strong and ruthless and a stone-cold killer. She was human, all too human, yet not human at all.

Jada stared up at them, as they talked and laughed and removed the length of chain and collar from my neck.

Oh, the feel of air on my skin beneath that bloody band!

They had handcuffs and chains. A hood.

Jada coolly analyzed my brain, my body, deciding how the current had altered things, and then Jada undid it all, remaining deceptively passive, helpless, defeated.

I remember thinking, God, can't they see her in my eyes? She's Judgment. She's Death. I've seen her in the mirror since.

Don't get me wrong, I don't have multiple personalities. I learned dissociation to deal with the hunger and pain. The Other was a cooler, numb version of me. But Jada is the Other on steroids. Dani is my foundation, Jada is my fortress. Danielle was my mom's daughter. Jada, the daughter of Morrigan, goddess of war, a mother worth having.

Danielle is the one who died.

I kept the pure heart. I kept the savage.

It was the little girl who loved Emma O'Malley that quit breathing.

The moment I was clear of the cage I kicked up, flashed into freeze-frame and ripped out their hearts, one after the next, squeezing each between my fingers until they exploded, dripping blood all over myself, all over the floor.

Then, quietly, in my threadbare, bloodstained nightgown, I walked to the kitchen, washed my hands, and ate an entire loaf of stale bread.

She hadn't been home in three days.

I wasn't afraid of her anymore.

I was no longer afraid of anything.

I took a long hot shower, God, the bliss, the ecstasy of a shower and soap!

God, the bliss of merely standing upright.

I dressed in my too short, too small jeans I'd outgrown last year, a faded, holey tee-shirt, and filched one of my mom's jackets.

Then I ate every can of beans in the pantry, all three. Then I turned to the half-soured contents of the fridge.

When there was nothing left to eat, I sat at the kitchen table, folded my small hands and waited.

He came first.

The man that was supposed to pay her. He didn't bring money. She sold me for drugs.

I killed him, too, and took them.

She came shortly after.

Saw the open cage, the dead men in the living room.

My memories of that night are crystal clear.

It was three days to Christmas, the telly was showing an old black and white version of It's a Wonderful Life. *The volume was low, the strains of "Buffalo Girls" faint but unmistakable as George Bailey flirted with Mary Hatch beneath a starry sky in a world where people lassoed the moon for each other.*

She saw me sitting motionless at the table and stood in the doorway a long moment.

She didn't try to run.

Eventually she joined me at the stained, peeling yellow Formica table trimmed with aluminum, sitting across from me in an orange melamine chair, and we looked at each other for a very long time, neither of us saying a word.

Sometimes there's nothing to say.

Only things to do.

I removed the Baggie from my pocket.

She gave me her lighter and spoon.

I learned almost everything I know about life from TV. I watched things kids shouldn't see.

Taking subtle cues from her eyes, a shake of her head, a nod, with eight-year-old fingers and an ancient heart I cooked my mother's last fix and gave her the needle.

Watched her tourniquet her arm and tap the vein. Saw the tracks, the gauntness of her limbs, the flaccid skin, the emptiness in her eyes.

She cried then.

Not ugly, just eyes welling with tears. The emptiness went away for the briefest of moments.

She knew.

She knew whatever was in that needle would be her last.

If I'd understood more about heroin and fentanyl, I'd have made sure there was enough heroin in the needle to make the dying beautiful, but those sons of bitches must have brought pure fentanyl.

She closed her eyes a long moment, then opened them and poised the needle above her vein.

She spoke then, the only words she said to me, achingly slow and achingly tender. "Oh . . . my beautiful . . . beautiful little girl."

The needle pierced her skin, the poison hit her vein.

She died ugly, seizing, puking blood.

Died with her face in a pool of crimson vomit on an aged, cracking table, in her own shit on a cheap chair.

I sat at the table for a long time before I got up and disposed of the bodies.

NINETEEN

———— • • • ————

Lady in red

I WORE A BLOODY DRESS.

Not actually bloody. Although I briefly considered it.

Shazam hadn't responded to any of my endless inveiglements all afternoon, or I'd have asked his advice, figuring it was fifty-fifty I'd get a brilliant answer versus a wildly emotional one. Pretty much the same spectrum of answers I was getting from myself.

As I turned away from the mirror, I tried one more time. "Shazam, I see you, Yi-yi. Please come down from wherever you are. I'm worried about you," I told the air. "You're the most important thing to me in the world. You're my everything. If something's bothering you, we can fix it together. If you want a mate, by God, we'll go scour worlds and find you one. Please, *please,* just let me know you're okay?"

Nothing. No bodiless smile, hiss, or growl, no faint rumbling assurance he still lived and breathed. Same damned silence I'd gotten all afternoon.

"Okay, this isn't fair," I said, fisting my hands at my waist and glaring up. "How would you feel if *you* couldn't find *me* and were worried sick? How would you feel if you were aching for pets or brushes and I refused to answer you, or even pay you one tiny bit of attention? If your fur *hurt* from lack of love and kisses? If I just completely abandoned you and let your heart break all the time until you felt like you might just wither up and—"

"O-KAY!" My Hel-Cat exploded from the air above me and slammed to the closet floor on padded paws, fur spiked, back arched, hissing. "I'm here! All right?"

I dropped to my knees and held out my arms. "Shaz, baby, what's going on? What's wrong? Why are you avoiding me?"

He plopped back on his haunches and splayed his paws around his shaggy belly. "I'm just getting used to it!" he snarled.

"Used to what?" I asked, mystified.

"You leaving me! Alone again. You will. Everyone leaves!"

I frowned. Where had this fear come from? What had I done to make him think I might leave him? Since the day I'd met him, he'd always liked great chunks of alone-time and, although prone to vibrant, nearly paranoid emotion at times, had never voiced such a concern. To the contrary, he'd seemed to be growing more secure, happy, with our home and relationship. Until this recent Pallas cat incident. "You know better than that. You and me, we're *family*, Shaz. Family is forever."

"Nuh-*uh*," he said truculently and tears started to flow. "On this planet," he sniffed, "families hardly ever last. They die or leave for someone else."

"Other people's families maybe. Not us. We're different and you know that. Have I ever given you any reason to doubt my love for you? My eternal commitment?"

He wailed, "But it's NOT eternal! You're not. And I *am*!"

I blinked. I'd never thought about it that way. Was that why he'd become obsessed with finding a mate? Because he'd begun to look ahead to a day I might no longer be here?

Even *I* couldn't see that day. I never think about dying. I'm always too busy living. "Is that what this is about? You began thinking one day I'll die and—"

"STOP!" He clamped tufted paws to his ears. "I can't hear you, I can't hear you, la, la, la, la," he droned, tuning me out.

I reached for him, dragging his paws-dug-into-the-carpet-stoically-resisting pudge into my arms and hugged him hard and tight, trying to decide how to address this.

Actually, trying to wrap my own brain around it.

I was mortal. He wasn't. There it was.

It hit me like a brick in the face. I'd never projected into the future on this topic, so firmly rooted in the present I'd become future-myopic.

Hel-Cats could be killed—although I had no idea what it took and couldn't fathom it—but excluding deadly violence, Shazam would live forever.

I was mortal and he wasn't.

Neither was Ryodan.

Or Mac.

Or Barrons.

None of my crew was.

They were all going to live forever and I'd be dead in—given the intensity and velocity at which I lived my life—probably long before a ripe old age.

As a teen I used to say I didn't want to live long enough to get old and wrinkly and fall apart, but I had two sudden horrid images: me living until I was old and wrinkly and falling apart, hanging out with my ageless, immortal friends who were going to go on forever having epic adventures and saving the world, and me dying tomorrow and leaving Shazam alone.

He'd be lost without me. He'd go off the deep end. Who would take care of him? Who would be able to handle him? Who would love him like I did? Who would understand his quicksilver moods, his consuming depressions, his bombastic nature, his kaleidoscopic emotions?

Dancer, with his fragile heart, had refused the Queen of the Fae's Elixir of Life that would have healed his compromised organ and bestowed immortality at the eventual price of his soul. He died once, when he was eight, had seen something, believed in something, and hadn't been willing to sacrifice his immortal soul.

The existence of my immortal soul was debatable as far as I was concerned. Furthermore, if I lost my soul, I'd adapt. I always do. Adaptation is my specialty. I practically invented the word.

I removed Shazam's paws from his ears, ignoring the explosion of wails and hisses. "Shazzy," I said firmly, "I will *not* die on you. I promise."

He snarled around hiccupping sobs, "Can't make that promise!"

"You know Mac, right?"

"Thinks I'm fat and hates Hel-Cats," he spat.

"She does not. She'll give me the elixir of immortality. I'll ask her for it." And if for some unfathomable reason, she wouldn't or couldn't, there was always Ryodan. Or Lor, or whichever of the Nine I had to coax, bully, or keep killing until they did for me what they did for Dageus. "I will not die," I said sternly.

He squirmed in my lap and peered up at me with teary violet eyes, sniffing. "Promise?"

"Promise. I won't leave you alone. Not ever. Pinky swear."

"Pinky swear is *everything*," he said, awed, blinking back tears.

I'd taught him well. "It is. And I'm pinky swearing right now. Show me one of those adorable toes."

He raised a paw and spread fat, velvety, black-padded appendages. I hooked the pinky of my right hand around his toe—

"Not that one. Other," he said impatiently.

"It's black. It blows people up."

"Not me."

"Why is that?"

"I'm me," he said smugly. "Better, smarter, more."

Oh, yes, we belonged together, ego to ego, emotion to emotion, God, I loved this little beast! Laughing, I hooked finger to toe and said, "Shazam O'Malley, I do hereby solemnly swear I am going to love you for all of forever."

"Then nine million more days?" he demanded.

Smiling, I finished the vow we'd taken long ago, Silverside. "Uh-huh. Because not even all of forever will be enough time to love you."

"I die," he gushed, and fell over on his back, paws in the air, lolling happily.

"Never leaving you, best friend. You can count on that."

Eyes gleaming, rumbling with contentment, he followed me into the bathroom and sank back to his haunches on the counter to watch with keen interest as I did something I rarely did.

Put on makeup.

Tonight I was wearing armor. The right dress, the right hair, smoky eyes, and crimson crushed-velvet lips. Since I didn't dare show up naked to battle with Ryodan, I was going the opposite route: as the stunning, powerful, sexy woman I can be if I feel like it.

Sighing, I thumbed on my flat-iron thinking, what a bloody waste of time but my mood seems to mimic my hair. When it's a wild cloud, so am I, and tonight I wanted to be sleek and polished. It takes an unusual, thick tree sap I found Silverside to straighten my hair. I brought a leather pouch of the stuff back with me but I'm almost out. I have no idea what I'll do then.

As I began my makeup, a faint rustling sound in the shower drew my attention. In the mirror, I watched the antenna and head of a cockroach pop up from the drain. You never know if a roach is a simple Earth-born insect or part of the nefarious Papa Roach that used to hang out at Chester's, preying on the waitresses who'd permitted his vile segments to burrow beneath their skin and eat their fat away—the AWC version of liposuction. Ergo, I treat them all as the enemy.

I pretended I hadn't seen it until it cleared the grate, then grabbed a can of hair spray, whirled in freeze-frame and blasted it with a noxious burst, snarling, "Not on my turf, you little shit."

The cockroach hissed at me and gave a whole-body, violent bristle, choking and sputtering as it vanished back down the drain.

π

Not all redheads wear red well. It has to be the right shade to go with our coloring. My hair is copper flame, my skin snowy, and my dress tonight was bloodred.

My still-black arm and collarbone proved a challenge. I had to keep it covered, although, frankly, blowing Ryodan's ass up rather appealed to me at the moment and, hey, he always came back.

Still, I'd been unpredictably violent once today and I try to limit myself to once in a given twenty-four-hour period.

Ergo, my dress had three-quarter sleeves, hugged my body like a second skin, and was cut so low in the back that the tramp stamp at the base of my spine Ryodan tattooed on me years ago was beautifully framed, drawing the eye to that sensual hollow.

I'm not vain. I'll never be girly. But I do like being a woman every now and then and I'm grateful for five feet ten inches of strong flesh and bones that has an appealingly lean yet feminine shape. My ass and legs are my best feature, powerfully muscled from endless motion. After taping my neck with Gorilla Tape because black went better than silver with my ensemble, I slid black and rhinestone stilettos on my bare feet, smudged my smoky eyes one last time, swept my hair up into a sleek, high Lara Croft ponytail, blotted crimson lips, and nodded to myself in the mirror. I debated leaving my hair down to cover the tape, but in a fight—and I was certainly hoping for one or ten—my hair unrestrained is a royal pain in my ass. I added the final piece: a three-inch-wide choker of glittering diamonds and blood-stones that concealed a garrote. Although I hated that it felt like a collar, it covered the tape, held a weapon, and was easily re-moved.

"He doesn't stand a chance," Shazam rumbled.

"He, who?"

"The one I smelled on our mattress. He's back. I smelled him on you before. He makes you smell different when he's around."

Okay, that was disturbing. "Different how?"

"Like Pallas cat makes me smell."

Okay THAT was disturbing. "I don't think so," I growled.

He shrugged. "We deny at our own peril . . ."

"What? What do we deny at our own peril?"

"The cry of the flesh for the Dionysiac experience."

Eyes narrowed, I peered suspiciously at him. "Where did you

even *hear* that? Is that from some documentary you watched on theatre or history or something?"

He shrugged again. "It's why I eat. My flesh cries a lot."

"As in Dionysus. The God of Bacchae. Wine and orgy," I said stiffly.

"I chose one of your gods, not mine, better not to bofflescate you."

Good grief. "Do Hel-Cats have gods?"

"Most things do. Look suspiciously like themselves."

I wanted to have this conversation. Shazam was in an unusually lucid mood. Gods were a hot topic on my plate. And it was 8:01.

I did *not* want Ryodan in my flat. He'd have more time to look around, copy something else. "Please be here when I get back," I told Shazam. "I miss our cuddles."

His smile was instant, enormous, and swallowed his head, all fangs and thin black lips, and there was that elusive, nagging reminder of something I couldn't place again. Shazam smiling made me think of something else, something I'd once seen but apparently hadn't considered important enough to file away with a neat label. "Me, too." He bounded off the counter, stalked to the mattress, turned around three brisk times, and plopped heavily to the bed. "Can we put the mattress back up high soon? I like it there."

"Soon as I get back. I see you, Shaz-ma-taz."

"I see you, too, Yi-yi."

I tugged on opera-length black silk gloves studded with diamonds, which ended where my sleeves began, grabbed my sword, slid it across my back, tucked three blades in a thigh sheath, and stalked out the door.

TWENTY

You drive me crazy like no one else

I WENT SLOWLY DOWN FOUR flights of stairs, not because of my heels but because I was abruptly off-kilter the moment I closed the door of Sanctuary and locked it behind me.

Ryodan was picking me up. I was wearing a dress. I had no bloody idea where we were going or what we were doing.

Out of control on all counts.

For two long years I'd been mistress of the empty Mega-pod, dominatrix of every detail. There'd been no surprises. I'd not once lost hold on my emotions. Not even when I killed Bridget. I hadn't slumped into a puddle of grief and self-abasement—and I'd wanted to. That'd been one of my tougher things to box. I'd killed yet another innocent. But, no matter what happened, I went on, steady and committed, doing what needed to be done, being what people needed me to be, and I dealt with however it fractured me. I was proud of myself for that. I considered it a sign of my maturity.

Yet a few thoughts about him on the way to his club had whipped me into a frenzy of uncontrolled emotion and I'd become a tornado, whirling dizzyingly about, dizzying even to me.

I stopped, centered myself with a breathing kata, and only when I was composed did I resume descending. I wasn't about to repeat my earlier volatility. If he brought up the kiss, I'd shrug it off as PMS. Men use it against us all the time. If that didn't shut him up, I'd employ the "hangry" excuse. He knows how often I need to eat to function at peak performance, has seen me shaky and feverish.

I rounded the final stairwell, expecting to find him parked outside in the Hummer.

He was waiting at the bottom of the stairs, hand on the newel post, looking up. Looking incredible. Tall, dark, and the precise flavor of the danger I find so addictive. Standing there like we were going on a date or something. I was instantly assaulted by conflicting emotions.

I'd dreamed of seeing him standing there, somewhere, *anywhere* in my world again. And I was so damned angry, I couldn't process the complexity of it. I'm smart enough to know I can also be as emotionally myopic as Mr. Magoo is nearsighted. The more something matters to me, the less I understand how I feel about it. Mac used to help me with that. For the hundredth time I wished she were here to talk to. I missed her so much. "You could have waited in the car," I said tonelessly.

"I bloody well know what I can and can't do, and don't pull Jada-voice on me. I came to see Dani tonight."

Ryodan is beautiful. Not like Barrons, who's beautiful in a perfectly imperfect way, far more animalistic than man. You see the beast first in Barrons. You have to hunt for it in Ryodan, who pours a flawlessly human skin over his animal form, meticulously aware of precisely where each atom of his being is in relation to the world around him. He has a heightened, absolute awareness I covet and emulate. He's liquid grace when he moves. I'm damned close to it. I've admired him since the day I met him. Used to study him when he wasn't watching me. I once spent eight infernal hours trapped in his office, watching his dark head bent over paperwork, absorbing every detail of his profile, trying to figure out some way to shatter that infernal calm and grace, make that controlled face explode into uncontrolled emotion. Make him act like I always felt around him.

It hadn't eluded me that the first man to draw my gaze after Dancer died—at six feet four inches and 240 pounds, with short dark hair—resembled Ryodan. There are two types of men I'm attracted to and they're rare as hell: brilliant, sexy, full of wonder, pure as a wide-open sky and easy to be around; or brilliant, sexy, inhumanly strong, carved by ruthless experience and difficult to handle. I like extremes.

Ryodan was dark and elegant, his powerful body poured into a charcoal Versace suit, a subtly embossed white shirt, a silver and black tie that matched his eyes, wide cuff glinting at his wrist, the tips of intricate tattoos peeking above his crisp white collar, dark Italian shoes. He was as dichotomous as his club, sophistication on the surface, primal beast beneath. His jaw was dusted with dark stubble, and—I inhaled lightly—he smelled good. I didn't remember him smelling so good. The wan light of the single bulb illuminating the foyer behind him shadowed the regal bone structure of his face. Primordial, polished, pain-in-the-ass man that never fails to rattle me. Or make me feel painfully alive. I want him. He drives me batshit crazy.

He held my gaze a long moment. *Beautiful by any standards, in any century, on any world, woman,* his eyes said.

I willed my eyes blank. Emerald shallows lapping gently at a shore. Not a tsunami out of control.

As I began to descend the last flight, he said, "What did you miss the most about me, Dani?"

Aside from that dark-velvet, exotically accented voice, his clear, unfiltered way of seeing me; his ability to kick my brain up into a higher gear; his endless challenges; and how he always seemed to understand what I was feeling, even when I didn't? "Clever," I said coolly. "'Most' implies that I missed many things. I didn't think about you at all."

"You need to stop boxing the things that disturb you."

I narrowed my eyes. "How I organize my brain is none of your business."

"It is when I'm the recipient of the resultant chaos."

"I have no idea what you're talking about."

"When you refuse to think about an issue, it remains unchanged, in precisely the same state as you tucked it away."

"Precisely the point of boxing it. The issue dies. Can no longer affect you. It's a damned effective tactic."

"Short-term, yes. Long-term, a recipe for disaster. When you next encounter whatever you boxed your feelings about, you're ambushed by repressed, unresolved emotion."

"Your point eludes me," I said stiffly. It didn't. I just didn't like it. No one ever called me on my shit. I'd gotten used to that. I'd missed that about him. Even as I resented his logic for being so bloody logical.

"If you'd thought about me while I was away, you wouldn't have been a perfect storm of oppositional desires at Chester's this morning."

Truth. Wasn't about to admit it. "It had nothing to do with you. I was PMS and hungry."

He smiled faintly. "I see. So, that's how we're going to play it. Commando or thong?"

My face screwed into an instant scowl. *"What?"*

He laughed. "Ah, Dani, that's one of the many things I missed about you. When your eyes flash, your skin flushes, and you're even more fucking beautiful. I used to picture your face while I was gone, when you were on one of your rants, stalking, fierce, and high-tempered. I missed it. Tell me something you missed about me. I must have slipped out of your box every now and then."

I gave him a stony look. He'd pictured my face while he was gone? Then why hadn't he called? I wasn't a woman to be softened with a few nice words after two bloody endless years of silence. Two years in which he'd showed me precisely how little I meant to him.

As I neared the bottom of the staircase, he said, "We need a few rules."

"I don't do rules." Not true. I had an elaborate set of my own. "And certainly not yours."

"Ours," he corrected. "Mutually agreed upon. Rule number six—"

"What are rules one through five? Do I get to make those up?" I had a list ready.

"We'll get to those. I was merely making the point that this particular rule isn't the most important between us. The next time—"

"And, of course, you're the one who gets to decide what's most important."

"—you want to blow off steam, say the word. I've got a fully outfitted sparring gym at Chester's—"

"Level seven. Boxing ring, every weapon imaginable. I exploded all your punching bags. I took your guns, too. Oh, and those cool studded leather gloves with the recessed blades."

"—where we can glove up and spar, you little snoop. In private."

I was getting mad again. He sees right through me. He was right and that pissed me off even more. Putting him in a mental compartment had, indeed, left me unprepared for his return. He was here now but I was still stuck two years ago, in a cemetery, hurt and angry, with two years of additional hurt and anger heaped on top of it. I needed to address that quickly, and physical activity always helps me think. "Fine. Let's go now."

"And forgo a night with you in that dress? Not a chance. We'll have our date first."

"People like you and me, and I use that term loosely in reference to you, don't date. And rule, definition: something you don't break and certainly not the first time out of the gate. Clearly, no one but you gets to invoke the rules. Typical. You're always the only one allowed to make the decisions."

"Ah, and now we're finally getting to your point," he murmured.

I descended the final step. "No, we're not. And it's commando. Friction's a bitch when I freeze-frame. Nothing under here but skin, babe."

His laughter was soft, husky, and dangerous. "Battle engaged. Babe."

Raw current arced between us as I swept past him. I channeled that energy into a powerful, long-legged stride outside, feeling his gaze scorch my ass all the way to the car.

And that pissed me off, too. Not that he was staring at my ass. He should be. It looked terrific. The car. It was a matte black Ferrari. Sleek, sexy. Date material.

"What's wrong with the Hummer?" I demanded.

"You'd look like one of those women ascending the ladder at Chester's trying to climb in it."

He had a point. "My hands aren't broken," I said when he beat me to the car in that inhuman glide of his and opened the door for me.

"Ah, for fuck's sake, Dani, enjoy the night. It's a beautiful one. The sky's velvet, clear. Look at all those bloody stars."

His words were soft, modulated as ever, but he slammed the door before stalking to the driver's side.

I smiled faintly as I tipped my face up and glanced through the windshield at a cobalt sky, not a rain cloud in sight, not a wisp of fog, just stars glittering like diamonds on dark velvet. I'd gotten a slam out of him. A stalk. Tension ratcheting up in his body as he passed through the headlights. Life was good.

When he slid behind the wheel and started the car, the deep sexy purr of the engine was drowned out by a sudden blast of ear-shattering music, especially to someone who hears as well as me. The bass was so loud it nearly vibrated me out of the seat.

I knew that song. I loved that song.

I'd danced to it. A lot. I flushed.

Heart. The line currently blasting: *I cast my spell of love on you, a woman from a child.*

Magic Man.

I scowled thunderously, fisting my hands. Ryodan and his damn spells. Was that what he'd done to me? Was that why I was always so bloody confused around him? Because I didn't really love him, he'd just made me *think* I did? I frowned. Wait, what?

I was so not looking at him right now. I stared straight ahead.

"I like it loud," he said as he turned the volume down. "One of my favorite songs."

He was not allowed to have that as one of his favorite songs. It was mine. Still staring straight ahead, I gritted, "How constantly did that caveman of yours watch me?"

"Why?"

Teeth clenched, I spat, "'Magic Man.' I dance to it. A lot. Like, naked. In front of a wall of windows. Up high where you don't expect people or nonpeople to be lurking about on rooftops, spying on you without your knowledge or consent. How constantly?"

Ryodan was silent a long moment. Then tightly, "That fuck said nothing about you dancing."

I glanced at him. The words had come out guttural, thick. Fangs fully distended, he was the one staring straight ahead now. Hands so tight on the wheel his knuckles were white. After a long moment he rasped, "Lor wouldn't have stayed to watch."

"You can't know that."

"I can. He may have seen you begin. But I assure you, he didn't stay."

I narrowed my eyes, studying him. He was employing one of my tactics, relaxing his fingers one at a time, modifying his breath, forcing himself to regain control, fangs slowly retracting. Copycat. "What makes you so sure?"

"We may walk like humans. But we are far more beast than man."

"Your point?"

He didn't say anything for so long, I was on the verge of writing it off as one more question the great Ryodan would never deign to answer.

"Sex is the beast's greatest hunger," he said finally. "More so than blood. More even than war. It is its greatest obsession and also the thing capable of affecting it the most deeply."

"Level four. Sex for breakfast."

He inclined his head. "Had Lor stayed to watch, his beast would have taken control."

"So, what? I wouldn't have done anything with him."

"Consent wouldn't have mattered. You're not as powerful as he is. As we are."

I bristled at the reminder. I was acutely aware of it, every bloody moment of every bloody day. "You're telling me Lor, *my* Lor, who is always good to me, would have—" I broke off. "I'd have used his own club against him. Lor and me, we don't feel that way about each other."

"Lor is beast first. We all are. Never forget that. Never underestimate it. We have our limits. We do what we must to manage those limits and minimize fallout. With the exception of Barrons, none of us permit the beast to run wild. It does things we don't want it to do. With deadly consequences. Ergo, the moment you began to disrobe, Lor would have left. He cherishes you. Protects you. Calls you his little honey."

"Are you telling me the Nine can't see a woman naked without turning into a beast and assaulting them? That's lame. What kind of superhero has that kind of problem?"

He made a sound of choked laughter. "Ah, Dani, only you would call us lame. Superheroes constantly battle an inner darkness, a hunger to cast off all chains. It took Christian Bale to give us an authentic Batman. It was about bloody time the world pulled its head out of its ass and gave us a gritty, complicated version of the Bat who could champion the things that mattered, not the bloody use of seat belts, doing your homework, and eating your fucking vegetables. Champions don't spring from happy childhoods. They explode from tortured ones with a mile-wide dark streak they've learned to use for good. Superheroes aren't perfect and they're usually their own worst enemy. Yes, we can see women naked. It takes the addition of an extreme on top of it to cut the beast loose."

I blinked, trying to wrap my head around his Batman insight. It wasn't half bad. I itched to debate it, dissect details. Did he or didn't he read comics? "Extreme, my ass. I wasn't doing anything sexual. I was just dancing."

"You *are* an extreme. And I've seen you dance. It's sexual. Blatantly. Graphically. A red fucking flag to a bull. Heed the warning. Never dance naked in front of me. Unless you intend to see it through. All the way. And it's a long, lawless way."

"I wasn't planning to," I snapped. I'm entirely too visual sometimes. I had a vivid picture in my head of doing just that. Had, in fact, imagined doing precisely that while dancing to "Magic Man" in my flat over the past two years. Stunning him, dazzling him, making him lose control and vow his undying love of me. Indulged in yearnings I'd carefully boxed the moment I stalked, exhausted, from my living room floor. That was how I'd learned to vent things when sex with human men hadn't worked. Dumped my pains, my dreams, on a private dance floor, instead of in bed with a stranger. Lived out my wildest fantasies, naked and alone. Same way I lived my life.

I still found it highly suspicious that he'd been listening to my song, and told him so.

"For fuck's sake, Dani, it's not your song. I like Heart. They're two dynamic, sexy women."

My eyebrows climbed my forehead. "You know Heart? You've *met* them?"

"They used to come into the club sometimes, back in the day. Who do you think 'Magic Man' is about?"

I gaped. "No way. Your eyes are silver."

"Lor."

"His eyes are green, not blue. And I read a *Rolling Stone* interview that said it was about Mike Fisher."

"Protecting Lor's identity."

"She's a brunette."

"Occasionally he breaks his own rule. Ann Wilson was a woman worth breaking it for. He had a thing with Joan Jett for a while, too."

"Seriously. 'Magic Man' is about *Lor*?"

With a hint of irritation, he said, "According to him, yes. He says 'Crazy on You' is, too. He was hard to live with for a while. That was back when he was hanging out with the Kinks."

"Holy Hall of Fame, Lor was immortalized in classic rock and roll!" I couldn't keep the note of envy from my voice. Okay, envy liberally dripped from each word. But, criminy, what a tribute! I mean, sure it was only about how good he was in bed, but music lived forever!

Ryodan laughed softly. "Ah, Stardust, I've no doubt you'll be immortalized in far more important ways."

I stiffened. "Why did you call me that?" That was what my mom used to call me, a lifetime ago, during the hot minute she'd loved me.

"Seems fitting. Tell me the state of the world in a nutshell."

He'd done it again, changed the subject so quickly I floundered a moment, trying to shift gears. "I'm sure Lor updated you," I said tightly. He'd left for two years and I'd known nothing about him at all. But he'd been getting constant updates about me.

"I knew nothing of your life either. He was left in play to keep you alive, nothing more, and although he updated me when I got back, his mind isn't yours. I want the Mega-brain analysis."

I beamed. Since he put it that way. "We're poised on the brink of our greatest war yet. If Mac fails to gain the Fae court's loyalty, if they succeed in killing her—and they don't need the sword to do that, locking her away in the Unseelie prison would eventually kill her, too—once they seize her power they'll either eradicate us from the face of this planet or enslave us. If they've locked her in the Unseelie prison as Cruce did to Aoibheal, every moment we waste could be ushering her one step closer to death." That was a fear that kept me awake at night: Mac in trouble, needing me and, out of blind respect for her wishes, I was doing nothing. Two years of silence had turned into an end-less, gnawing worry in the pit of my stomach.

"You've not heard from Mac at all?" He sounded stunned.

"Not a word since you left."

He cursed softly. "Christ, she said she'd stay in touch. What about Rainey? I know you see her. Has she heard from her daughter?"

"I stopped asking her nearly a year ago. It upset her. I suspect if she'd heard, she'd have told me."

"Any theories on where the bookstore went?"

I offered five: "Mac and Barrons moved it for some reason. Someone else took it. The Silvers inside were changed by the Song and swallowed it up into a Fae realm. An IFP devoured it and moved on." I couldn't resist adding a Douglas Adams theory, "It got fundamentally fed up with being where it was."

"*The Long Dark Tea-Time of the Soul.*"

"I loved that book."

"The airport that blew up."

I nodded. Ryodan read books. The kind I liked.

"I think we can rule that one out."

"I'm okay with that."

Suddenly, it felt like old times. Light banter, easy comradery. "Examine the scene tomorrow, Robin?" I said lightly.

He cut me a look. "As if I'd wear that suit. Sherlock. BBC version."

My eyes narrowed. "I am so not Watson."

"I'd pegged you more as 'that woman.'"

I nearly preened. That woman was badass; sexy and lethal and one of the few to ever give the epic detective a run for his money. She'd stormed into conflict with the penultimate deductive brain wearing the most daring and formidable battle dress of all—nudity, from which he'd been able to draw not a single clue about her person or intentions. My near-preen turned into a scowl as I considered the rest of her story. "No way. Sherlock broke her code. You be 'that woman.'"

"Sherlock broke her code because she refused to admit that she wanted him. If she'd been honest about it, if she'd acted on it, there'd have been a different code—one he might not have been able to break. Instead of 'Sher-locked,' it would have been wisely nonsensical and undecipherable."

That he had a valid point pissed me off even more. "Your point is that if she fucked him she might have been thinking more clearly? Do you know how insulting that is?"

"If the shoe fits."

"Implying not fucking you makes me stupid."

"Not quite what I was saying," he said dryly.

"You do not in any way affect or dilute a single cell of my magnificent brain."

"Merely observing that we deny, at our own peril, that which we desire."

His words were eerily similar to what Shazam had said before I'd left the flat. "I. Am. Not. That. Woman."

"Hit a nerve, did I?"

"And if I was, I'm bloody well entitled to be. Sherlock wouldn't even return a single one of her bloody texts. Not one." And the alert tone she'd programmed into his phone for her texts should have melted him, at least from the waist down.

"Am I missing something? Did you text me?"

I was not ready for this argument. "Your timing sucks."

"Time has always been the problem with us."

"Am I missing something?" I mocked. "Did you text me? I'm not the one that left. The person that leaves bears the onus. Period." God, I sounded just like Dancer, when I'd finally come back from the White Mansion with Christian. I thought, My love, I'm sorry, I get it now. I get it in spades.

"I'm not the one that never called. You had a phone. You didn't call once. You were just out there having—" He terminated the sentence abruptly.

"What? What was I having that you want to throw in my face? Because I wasn't having much of a good time, I can tell you that."

"Define 'good time.'"

"Fuck, you, Ryodan." And here we were again. I don't think I ever once said those words to Dancer. I never felt the need.

"There's no reason not to. I'm here. You're here. We both want to."

I gaped at him. Christ, he'd just put it baldly on the table.

"You think I won't put it baldly on the table?"

I said with acid sweetness, "I rather thought you'd try to put it on a desk. Isn't that where you *usually* put it?"

He flinched imperceptibly and I regretted the words instantly.

Jo.

As if summoned from a grave, her ghost was there, standing between us. I could almost see her shaking her head with sorrow, telling me Ryodan was a good man and I wasn't seeing him clearly. Her gravestone loomed in the air, a solid concrete wall separating me from him. The heat of innuendo died and his gaze shuttered.

"Mac carried that one hard," he said. "I suppose I carry it, too."

I gaped again, it seemed like all I was doing tonight. "Mac ate Jo?" I practically shouted.

"When she was possessed by the *Sinsar Dubh*."

I ached for her, understanding too well the pain she carried. Bridget, all the others, my ghosts for the rest of my life. "Why the bloody hell did no one tell me? Why am I always the last to know things?"

"I'm doing everything in my power to make sure you're not," he clipped, driving his point home.

Ryodan wanted me. And he wasn't going to conceal that fact. What did he think? That he could just stroll back when I was grown up, have sex with me, then one day saunter up and tell me he was leaving again?

"When you fuck a man," I said with quiet venom, "you're giving him a motherfucking gift."

He went motionless, waiting. When I didn't continue, he goaded, eyes glittering, "Come on, Dani, say it. You know you want to. You're dying to. Fling that fucking gauntlet at me."

"You. Don't. Deserve. Me," I said with icy satisfaction.

He smiled with some unfathomable, feral light in his eyes. The bastard actually smiled. Who does that when you insult them? Then he completely changed the subject.

"No one told you because you had a great deal on your plate

at the time." He didn't say a word about Dancer but he didn't have to because instantly, another ghost popped into filmy existence between us.

Dancer. Jo. Fog tendrils curling about their transparent, forever-lost-to-us bodies.

So much loss.

I wasn't in the mood for any more.

I'm all about the things that stay.

My city. My people who need me. Shazam. Kat. Enyo. The ones who don't go tearing off on lengthy walkabouts without you, without a word of explanation.

I pulled a Ryodan and completely changed the subject. "Have you heard from Barrons?"

He didn't say anything for a long moment and I was perversely pleased to see him having as hard a time shifting gears as I'd been having. Then, "Not a word in two bloody years. I have no fucking idea where he is."

I looked at him, stunned. He'd been as cut off from news of them as me? He didn't know where Barrons was? I'd imagined Ryodan sitting somewhere, receiving constant updates from everyone. In control as always, monitoring the world. Where the hell had he been?

"What else, Dani?"

"The old gods are back. No idea how many or who. Humans are abducting adults, paralyzing them and taking them through mirrors to an unknown location for reasons unknown." He'd said "nutshell" version so I was keeping it brief.

"While you save the children left behind," he murmured. "Getting them settled into new homes. Lor told me that part."

"Where was Lor watching me from when AOZ and Jayne tried to take my sword?"

"Across the street. He couldn't hear a bloody word of the conversation. Fill me in."

I gave him the highlights, omitting the wish part because that was my business, not his, and I was still trying to figure out which wish AOZ had decided to grant that hadn't yet bit me in the ass.

"Rumor is, Jayne's being hunted," Ryodan told me when I'd finished, "the Fae put a steep bounty on his head. He hadn't been seen in a long time until he showed up in your flat. Some say he's gone into deep hiding with his mortal family, trying to protect them. Perhaps he wanted your sword for Mac, perhaps for himself."

"What does Lor say about the Fae?" Despite his claim that he wasn't getting laid, I had no doubt he'd been at Elyreum, unable to resist a party or seducing blondes with his lethally effective caveman charm.

Ryodan cut me a dark look. "Mac gave us the same mandate she gave you: no interference. We obeyed. He's not been inside Elyreum, and from what he says, the Fae don't come out."

"The Nine obeyed Mac?" I said incredulously.

"Barrons. Motherfucking shield."

I laughed softly. "Oh, how that must chafe."

"Which is why," he said, as we finally pulled away from the curb and began to drive through Dublin, "two years later, we don't know a single thing about our enemy. According to Lor, those humans that enter the club are tampered with. He interrogated a few, said they come out either unwilling or unable to discuss anything they've seen. Her mandate should have come with an expiration date. It didn't. Now that the bookstore is missing, along with Mac and Barrons, we're enforcing an expiration date. Tonight."

Surely, he didn't mean . . . "Where are you taking me?"

He flashed me a wolf smile, all teeth and hunger. "Elyreum."

Yes! Adrenaline cold-cocked my heart! This wasn't a date. It was a *mission*. I'd been aching to do this for a small eternity. Dying to stalk into their club and rattle their world. Let those bastards know we were watching and waiting, and it wasn't over.

"You do realize, I'm carrying the sword they all want."

"Bloody hell, yes, I do," he said, with unconcealed relish.

We drove in silence for a time and he turned the music back up right as Miley Cyrus was singing, *Don't you ever say, I just walked away, I will always want you.*

"Wrecking Ball." I often felt like one. His taste in music was starting to freak me out. I wanted to know if we were listening to the small, local volunteer-run station or an iPod he'd loaded with personal choices. I wanted to know if he was, like, sending me subliminal messages. He *had* just walked away. Period. End of subject. No song lyrics could change that.

There was no commercial interruption when the song ended but that wasn't a tell; nobody advertises anymore. I keep waiting for some kind of underground renegade radio station to pop up that offers both music and biting social commentary, but none has. I'd start one myself if I had more time but I no longer get to do a lot of the things I'd like to do. I have astounding taste in music, it runs the gamut all over the place, the product of watching endless discontinued and frequently retro TV shows.

"Foxy, Foxy" by Rob Zombie came on next. Ryodan snapped the radio off and parked the Ferrari half a block down the street from Elyreum.

I glanced at the club and said something to him I never thought I'd hear myself say. "Ryodan, have you thought this through?"

He laughed, and I lost my breath for a moment, watching him. "What fun would there be in that?"

"You do realize we could start a war?"

He met my gaze and held it. "Don't you think it's time we cut everything loose? See what the hell comes of it?"

I narrowed my eyes, not missing his pointed dual message but not about to address it either. "Potential gain?"

"Nothing has happened in two long years, has it? I mean, nothing of any real significance. You've changed. The world has changed. But not one bloody, meaningful thing has resulted. You pass through this city, touching everything. And nothing. And nothing touches you. You don't do a single thing that might cataclysmically alter you or the world's course. How bloody sick are you of that?"

He was speaking my language. But then he always had.

"We can sit on our hands and wait endlessly, only to find we waited too long and don't like the outcome. Or we can bloody well shape that outcome. Perhaps Mac and Barrons need help. Perhaps they need us to create a distraction, be a linchpin, turn things on their head, force the Fae court's hand. You and me, Dani, we're good at that."

I could taste the danger on my lips as I met his feral, fierce smile with one of my own. "Objectives?" I said breathlessly.

"Ascertain to what degree the Fae have changed, what we're up against. Find out where the bloody hell Mac and Barrons are. The Fae are as arrogant as they are immortal. If they have the upper hand, if they've somehow captured Mac and Barrons, they won't be able to resist rubbing it in our faces. One simple tell: if they're desperate for your sword, we'll know she's still alive."

I inhaled sharply. This was what I'd been waiting for. Backup. Someone to break the bloody rules with me because not even I am a formidable enough weapon against an entire race of immortals. Although there'd been many nights I'd nearly convinced myself I was. "I'm in like Flynn," I said fervently.

He flashed me a slow, sexy smile. "First, tell me something you missed about me."

I rolled my eyes. "I told you, I didn't think about you."

"I never escaped your box. Not once."

"Not even."

"Fine. I'll tell you what I missed about you."

"I didn't ask and don't want to know."

"I missed the way your mind works. How you're willing to make the difficult decisions few people are willing to face, the ones that cost a piece of your soul. How you suffer no hesitation acting on those decisions, despite their price, and each time you hit breaking point, you come up with a new way to put yourself back together again. How you never stop caring, no matter how badly the world treats you, and bloody hell, this world has treated you abominably. How, despite the war you eternally wage between your brain and your heart, you possess the finest of both intellect and emotion I've ever seen. You dazzle me, Dani O'Malley. You bloody fucking dazzle me. Top or bottom?"

His question didn't penetrate at first. I was too distracted by the compliments. He saw my best, the things I was proud of. Flatter my appearance? Not so flattered. I was born in my body. Praise my brain, my spirit? I melt. I've worked hard on them both. Then my face screwed up into a scowl and I nearly exploded, *What?* but swallowed it at the last second. I wasn't issuing Ryodan an invitation to continue on that topic.

He took it anyway. "Specifically, would you still need to slam down on top of me and vent that endless passion of yours in a hard, savage fuck or have you grown up enough that you could sprawl back on my bed and let me give, while you do all the taking? Who knows, maybe you'd even toss me a few pointers while I was at it. Demand what you wanted. I'd like that. Dani O'Malley taking for a change, thinking only about herself."

I was having a hard time getting a breath. Pointers. As if. I'd seen Ryodan in action. The man needed no pointers.

"We're narrowing it down to just those two at the moment. We'll move on to other positions later. Although I admit to significant interest on the topic of me behind you versus you backed up against a wall, with those long, beautiful, powerful legs of yours wrapped around my waist."

Behind. First. I grabbed my sword, shoved my door open, kicked my legs out and turned back to look at him, using his own words against him, from long ago. "Some secrets, kid," I hissed with saccharine venom, "you learn only by participating."

He threw his head back and laughed, white teeth flashing, eyes glittering.

I closed my eyes, shutting out the vision that had eternally, incessantly, escaped my box.

Ryodan. Laughing.

That was one of the things I'd missed the most about him. The rare moments I'd startled him into a laugh. Glimpsed unadulterated joy blazing in his eyes.

I definitely preferred the top. But that was none of his business. When he stopped laughing, I opened my eyes again.

"Unfortunate," he said. "Of the two, top is my preference as well."

"Stay out of my head." If he'd thought about me so bloody much, he should have called.

"We'll have to fight for it. See who wins."

An image of Ryodan and me, stripped naked, sweat-slicked

and lust-driven, battling for dominance, slammed into my brain, stupefying me for a moment. "In your dreams." As I surged from the car, I concentrated on shutting the door gently. If I slammed it, he'd know how much he'd just gotten to me.

The window shattered, glass tinkling to the pavement at my feet. I sighed. Brain/hand disconnect was clearly one of my un-written rules around him.

His laughter—that very laughter I'd missed so much—floated out the broken window into the night.

Bright side: I couldn't be more in the mood for war.

TWENTY-ONE

--- • ---

When they come for me

K AT TUCKED THE BLANKET snugly around her sleeping daughter, retrieved the worn copy of *The Little Engine That Could* from the bed, and turned to slip it back on the shelf.

As she moved to the door and turned off the lights, she glanced back at Rae and, as it always did, her heart swelled inside her chest with more love than she'd believed a single person could hold.

Rae had spent most of the afternoon into the late evening in the gardens, playing with the Spyrssidhe. *I love the Spur-shee, Mommy*, she'd said before she drifted off. *They're not like me. They're so light inside.*

Other mothers would have asked the question her comment implied. *If they're light inside but they're not like you, what does that make you?*

She hadn't asked. Time would tell. If Rae believed she was dark for some reason, yet loved as instinctively and freely as she did, there was no point in asking.

Using her gift of empathy on her daughter had proved worthless. Rae felt so much love for her mother, Kat could feel nothing beyond it.

The spots on Rae's tiny shoulders had vanished. She must have stretched out on something, perhaps lain on two rocks in the grass at just such an odd position. An unnerving freak occurrence, nothing more.

When Rae rolled over in her sleep, mumbling inaudibly, Kat's phone tumbled to the floor, and she realized she'd forgotten it on the bed. She reclaimed it, tucked her daughter back in, kissed her forehead lightly and smoothed her curls.

As she turned back for the door a radioactive cloud of

PANICFEARHORRORFEARGETRAERUN!

exploded in her head. A scream escaped her lungs, clawing its way up her throat. She choked on it to keep from frightening Rae.

Rooted to the spot by terror, she stood, sputtering softly, trembling from head to toe, staring with wide, horrified eyes.

No, no, no, no, no, began the desperate litany in her mind. *Please, God, no, I don't deserve this, Rae doesn't deserve this. I'm a good person, a good mother, but I can't protect us from this!*

He towered against the door of the bedroom, barring her exit. Trapping them within.

Enormous black wings curved loosely forward around his body. She knew those wings. She'd dreaded them. Orgasmed exquisitely, over and over again, wrapped in them.

Breathe, breathe, breathe, you must breathe, she told herself. But her lungs refused to cooperate. Everything was locked down tighter than the *Sinsar Dubh* had ever been.

It wasn't possible.

He was dead.

Mac had assured them before she left for Faery that the Unseelie Court had been destroyed, each and every one.

Including Cruce.

Especially Cruce.

Kat had asked *repeatedly*. And Mac had repeatedly told her she could feel all other royalty in existence. Not by location, just a quiet burn in her mind.

Cruce wasn't there.

Kat had gone so far as to dip into the Fae queen's heart to ascertain the veracity of her words. Mac believed Cruce dead.

But now, standing tall, dark, and malevolent, powerful arms crossed, watching her with eyes of . . . Oh, dear God.

Eyes of such finality.

She jerked and brushed blood from her cheeks. Forced her gaze away, down the thick, dark column of his neck, over the writhing, glittering torque, down his black clad, massive body. His shoulders were enormously muscled, his legs powerfully sculpted.

"Never hold my gaze, Kat," he purred softly. "I can protect you from much. But not that. It was not my intention to startle you. I sought you in private, so as not to alarm the others."

She screeched a breath into her lungs that seared them, so desperately was it needed, and angled her body as if she might conceal her daughter from him.

Had he come to take Rae away? Both of them? If that was the choice, she'd go! Just don't take my daughter from me, she thought hysterically. Anything but that.

"Why are you here?" she whispered faintly.

"Och, lass, it's Sean, he needs you."

What was he talking about? How was Cruce even alive? And

what was he doing with Sean? And why was his voice so different than she remembered from those hellish, fevered dreams?

"We've a bit of a problem, Kat. Have you someone to watch
the wee lass?"

His second use of the word "lass" finally penetrated a brain of
concrete. Kat blinked, as slow comprehension dawned. "*Christian?*" she exploded softly. "Is that *you?*"

His lips drew back in a silent snarl. Then, "Och, Christ, tell
me you didn't think I was Cruce! Do I look that bad?"

She nodded vehemently. "Yes."

"Bloody hell," he growled. "He's dead. I'd know if he was
alive. At least I think I would."

She sucked in a ragged breath and crumpled as the strength
fled her body, crippled by the profoundly worst moment of her
life—thinking Cruce had returned and was going to take Rae
away from her. She had nightmares about that happening, awakened horrified and trembling, clutching a hand to her mouth to
hold back screams.

Christian caught her before she hit the floor, swept her to
her feet and steadied her with an arm about her shoulders.

Good God, he was enormous. Seven feet at least. Massive.

"Easy, Kat. I didn't mean to frighten you. I thought you knew
he was dead."

She didn't believe it. She would never believe it until she saw
his lifeless form with her own eyes. Christian's earlier words penetrated at last and, as swiftly as horror had seized her heart, wonder blossomed and happiness flushed her skin. "Sean asked for
me?" she said breathlessly, and made the mistake of glancing up
to search his eyes.

"Stop doing that," he growled. "I can't camouflage it and I
bloody well hate wearing sunglasses at night." He swept a wing

around her and swept the blood from her cheeks with the tips of his silken feathers.

The sensation was so familiar, she shuddered and cried softly, "Stop! I'll get a kerchief."

He backed away, sensing her revulsion. "I've got the *Sidhbha-jai* muted, lass," he said stiffly. "I'll keep it that way."

As she fumbled about in Rae's chest of drawers—finding, yes, a sock would do—and wiped her eyes, she watched him carefully in the periphery of her vision.

He'd turned and was staring down at Rae. Then glanced back at her.

Her gaze went instinctively to search his eyes again—by the Saints, she was going to go blind from blood! She dabbed it on another of her daughter's socks and said faintly, "What do you see?"

He yanked a pair of sunglasses from a pocket, shoved them on and said. "A lovely wee lass, Kat, nothing more."

It doesn't matter, it doesn't matter, she's my child. "Would you know if she was more?" Fuck, she thought, and she never thought that word. But she'd asked the damned question and it was hanging out there and she waited, breath locked down again, for his answer.

He said nothing for what seemed to her an interminable time. Finally, "Not necessarily. But what are you saying, lass? Have you some reason to fear she's Cruce's?"

"No," Kat said on an explosive exhale.

"Lie," he said flatly.

Fuck, she thought again. Christian MacKeltar was as bad as she was; a walking lie detector.

Christian sighed but it turned into a darkly amused laugh. "What a world we live in, eh, Kat? I don't suppose you'd care to tell me that story?"

"You said Sean needs me." She steered the conversation away from a subject she never discussed and certainly wouldn't in her daughter's presence, not even while she slept. Some names seemed too powerful to risk uttering. She regretted that his had ever been spoken in her daughter's room. The mere syllable seemed to hold the power of a divine summons.

"Aye. Kat, have you someone to watch over the lass? I need to take you somewhere. Just for the night."

She'd suffered such a fright, she felt abject terror at the thought of leaving her daughter. But the abbey was filled with women who vied for the opportunity to babysit Rae and heavily warded against—Again, fuck.

Three times in a night. That word. She demanded, "How did you get in here without setting off our wards, Christian?"

He smiled faintly. It was a terrible smile. White teeth, sharp canines, it brought only more darkness to his eyes. "Och, lass, I'm not what I used to be. None of the Fae are. You'll be needing new wards. My clan and I can help you with that."

"Our abbey is no longer safe from the Fae?" she exclaimed softly, horrified.

"Hasn't been for a long time. Since shortly after the Song was sung."

"But we've not had a single Fae intruder," she protested.

"They've been busy elsewhere. You're not their current focus. In truth, I doubt they even care you exist anymore."

"Why?"

"You're no threat to us. We've become what we once were. So, what if you can identify us? We'll crush you. I don't mean that personally. But that's how they feel."

Kat drew a deep breath, willing her mind and heart to calm. Then she fired off several rapid texts. Regardless of whether Sean needed her or not, Christian had information—and clearly a great deal of it—they didn't possess and needed to. As well as the ability to help them re-ward the abbey. She inclined her head. "Where are we going?"

"Scotland."

She cringed inwardly. "You mean to sift me?" That meant she had to touch him, and he reminded her far too much of Cruce.

He smiled again, that haunted and haunting dark smile. "Sorry, lass, it won't be that easy. We'll need to fly."

Fly? As in hold onto him for *hours*?

"Try not to radiate abject fucking misery, Kat," he said tightly. "I'm one of the good guys."

"How certain of that are you?" she asked warily.

"Utterly," he said with finality. "And it was a bitch of a battle, I'll tell you that."

Unseelie. And one of the good guys. She wanted to believe that. "We should leave before Enyo arrives. She'll have a similar reaction."

She'd deliberately chosen her fiercest warrior to babysit in her absence. And asked Duff and Decla to be stationed beyond the door. Three women capable of extreme kindness. And extreme violence. Able to shift between the two in a heartbeat.

"I can sift us to the perimeter of the estate but we'll have to fly from there. Come, lass. And if it helps, close your eyes and think of Sean. He, too, looks like me. You'll need to be prepared for that. Revulsion could push him over the steep edge he's already perched on. But," he added softly, as I moved uneasily into the circle of his arms, "you might be surprised by how beautiful you'll find the sky at night. We'll fly above the mist that obscures the terrain, where the moon kisses the tops of clouds, turning them to silvery puddles it seems you might dance upon. You'll

see the dark, glassy lochs and the grass turned to fine-spun metallic thread. The night creatures are different than those of the
day, rarer to see. You might spy great snowy owls soaring, hoot-
ing, wolves frolicking as they woo their mates, you may even see
a playful wildcat or two."

I realized he was trying to set me at ease, distract me from
the intimacy I would have to endure. It worked. As he'd spoken,
I heard the truth of the pleasure in his words. He loved to fly at
night, he loved the land, and Cruce would never have noticed a
single bloody thing on the ground, no bird, nor animal; too
power hungry and driven to see past his own ambitions.

I snatched a last, quick glance at my daughter and murmured
that I loved her, as footsteps approached beyond my bedroom door.

"It sounds lovely Christian," I said as he drew me to his chest.

"It is," he promised, as we sifted out.

π

Lovely was an inadequate word. Once I got over the sheer terror
of being held and flown, and the fear that he might drop me, I
was dazzled by the night beneath my toes.

"I won't drop you, quit digging your nails into my shoulders,"
he growled.

I was counting on that. If he'd wanted me dead, he could
have killed me in my room.

Eventually, I relaxed, still holding tightly to his shoulders,
cradled in his arms. Distracting myself from the presence of an
Unseelie prince by watching the world unfurl beneath us, pondering the blessing his presence implied—the promise that darkness within did not necessarily equate darkness without.

I would never be able to read his eyes, one of the easiest ways
to take the measure of a person's soul—and I often wonder if

anyone else can see the many nuances in an iris that I do—but I could feel him with my gift, with my heart.

Deep inside Christian, so deep I'd almost missed it, nestled an evil black pearl within a tightly closed, blindingly white clamshell.

But it wasn't a small pearl. It was gargantuan, filling every atom of his being, and he'd compressed it somehow. He'd taken an inconceivably vast, twisted, terrifying abyss of darkness that churned within him and turned it into a zip-file of sorts, buttoned it up and locked it down. A darkness that could swallow whole, obliterate. A darkness that seethed with ambition, hunger, mind-boggling sexuality and need.

He'd managed to contain an infinity of evil within a tiny glowing white shell in which I couldn't spy even a hairline crack. "How?" I asked, as we passed over Belfast, soaring toward the ocean.

I've felt the capacity for such evil in only two other vessels: the *Sinsar Dubh* and Cruce. I've never seen such enormous darkness contained. Locked so completely away, I couldn't even get a feel for what it was. There was something, a subtle flavor of him that identified him as the prince he was . . .

"Death is my kingdom. As the Light Court is one of dreams and illusions, the Dark Court is one of realities and nightmares. The Seelie have Spring, Summer, Autumn, and Winter. We have Death, War, Famine, and Pestilence. But hold your questions, lass. It takes energy to maintain that control, and yet more to mute the *Sidhbha-jai*. So long as I'm diverting power, the most taxing of my abilities are challenging. We'll stop in the Highlands to rest and I'll tell you what I can. For now, enjoy the view."

We flew out over the angry, frothy, whitecapped ocean pounding at the shore, then farther still where the swells gentled for miles into dark starry glass.

When we passed over the lowlands, he swooped beneath the

clouds to graze clearings where night creatures leapt and played, then soared again for the bird's-eye view of patterned acreage, field and stream.

When we finally arrived in the Highlands, the beauty took my breath away. Mountains soared to majestic peaks before plunging sharply to carpeted vales, lush and burgeoning with life. The Song had awakened Scotland as vibrantly as Ireland, transforming the plants, shrubs, and trees to a verdant sprawl, giving rise to a population boom in the animal kingdom.

"Nessie's back," he said dryly. "You wouldn't believe some of the things that have returned."

"Such as the old gods?" I said.

"You know about them."

I swept a tangle of hair from my face. "A bit. We could certainly use more information."

"Almost there, lass. I've a favorite peak. We'll talk soon."

I returned my gaze to the heather tumbling in lush profusion over the hillsides, the silvered grasses, the flowers that bloomed between every crack in every stone.

I'd never been to Scotland. I'd never left Ireland. I would bring Rae to see this. I wouldn't let her grow up as sheltered as me. I wanted her to see the world, experience every wonder, know them intimately, the better to love them.

We touched down on a large flat rock atop a whitecapped ben. As he lowered me to the ground, I stumbled, unaccustomed to having my feet on the ground, and he set me steady again.

"What did you think?" he asked and, in that moment, I heard only a Highlander, proud of his country, seeking a compliment from a tourist.

"Scotland is enchanting. And now I know why angels have wings. It's their reward."

He smiled, pleased, and waved a hand. "Pull a cushion near the fire, Kat. There's a chill up this high."

I glanced where he'd gestured. A crackling fire leapt and blazed in a stone pit that hadn't been there before. A cushion and a blanket waited nearby. "How did you do that?"

"Small things are easy. I encourage matter to shift forms, become what I want it to be."

"This?" I reached for the cozy throw of purple and black tartan.

"The Keltar colors. Fashioned from a carpet of moss beyond the rocks."

"The fire?"

"A thought. Stones become logs, a combustion of air, an invitation of heat."

"I thought Fae magic was mostly illusion."

"Aye, for the Seelie. They favor form over function, beauty over value. Transforming matter takes more energy than sketching illusion, and they're lazy fucks. Still, you'd do well to never underestimate them. The moment I assume it's an illusion, I end up trapped in it."

"Then you've had dealings with them." I settled on the large flat cushion near the fire.

He dropped down to a boulder near the flames and laughed darkly. "That I have, lass. They've been trying to capture Sean and me for quite some time. When that failed, they began to offer various enticements. We're enemy number three. Mac's enemy number one. I hear Jayne is enemy number two. But I'm getting ahead of myself. There's much I need to tell you."

Wrapping myself in the woolen throw, I drew nearer to the fire to listen.

TWENTY-TWO

In a gadda da vida, baby

ELYREUM IN "FAE" LOOSELY means "the forbidden garden" or "dark paradise," depending on who you ask, and it was overload.

The only thing about the club that wasn't in-your-face erotic, enhanced by opulent illusion, was the exterior, faking normal in a faking-normal city.

Once you passed through those tall gold and alabaster doors, reality fell away and the dream began. The music was surreal, sensual, erotic, with a rhythmic, driving beat that made me think of an old Enigma CD blended with Puscifer.

The club was an anachronistic mix of exotic natural beauty and ultrasleek technology. Blossoms tumbled from stately urns, scenting the air with night-blooming jasmine, amaryllis, lily, and winter hazel. Lush vines bursting with black and red poppies twined around grand Romanesque columns. The place smelled of verdant forest, steamy tropical hothouse, and sex.

The walls, ceiling, and floor of the foyer were giant, borderless LED screens smeared with Fae/mortal porn unfolding in graphic detail, (God, I *so* did not need to see that) in off-putting, larger-than-life format, with Fae-enhanced color, texture, and sound.

As I stalked across the anteroom, two enormous, stunning Fae males having sex with seven humans ground and pumped beneath my feet and, I swear, both Fae turned their heads in the floor to look up my dress. When I stomped sharply on one of their eyes, the bastard laughed.

Exiting the foyer into the second anteroom beyond brought us out on a balustrade draped with yet more vines and drugging blossoms from which we could view the entire club. They'd further taken a page from Chester's by dividing Elyreum into numerous, individually themed subclubs, staged around a single, central dance floor that was packed with humans and Fae gyrating, grinding, having sex.

I'd never seen so many castes of Seelie before, vibrantly etched in the dazzling, seemingly Photoshop-enhanced shades of the Four Courts: the blush and rose of Spring threaded with metallic green; the dazzling, countless golds of Summer; Autumn's copper and crimson fire; a thousand frosted shades of Winter's ice. Tall, tiny, large, dainty, some flew, some glided, all hunted.

I narrowed my eyes. I'd dialed back the volume on my *sidhe-seer* senses the moment we stalked into the club, muting the cacophony of so many Fae clustered in close quarters.

Mac told me she hears the individual castes as melodies, pieces of song that play inside her head. I do, too, but my perception of the various castes is heavy on the percussion, a kind of Godsmack's battle of the drums meets Roisin Murphy's "Ramalama (Bang Bang)." There's some serious dissonance for you.

Tonight I was getting something else, too, a thing I'd never noticed before . . . or never heard. There was a low, annoying buzzing sound beneath it somewhere. A sort of distracting static on my channel.

Something about the dance floor wasn't quite right. I nudged my volume up a hair, to no avail. I dialed it higher, and still nothing. I cranked it even higher until the presence of so many Fae was deafening, charring a hole in my gut. With supreme force of will, gritting my teeth against the savage onslaught of primitive drums beating in my blood, telling me to *Kill, kill,* I punched it up yet one more notch, going wider open than I'd ever before been. I'd never needed to.

Oh!

There wasn't a single person on that dance floor.

It was empty. I could see that now.

But no other human could. Holy insidious illusions, the Fae had gotten better at glamour! The Shedon needed to know about this!

Like the foyer, the dance floor was fashioned of brilliantly lit LED screens, featuring still more graphic images of humans having sex with Fae streaming across the surface.

I dialed my volume higher, wincing as the presence of so many Fae crashed and banged inside my head with the storm and thunder of the "Ride of the Valkyries" meets the worst, most bone-chilling parts of "The Requiem."

Oh, God. There were no Fae having sex with humans in a TV screen at all!

It was only humans. And they weren't images on the surface of an LED screen, they were real live people.

Trapped beneath it.

Some were clawing at the bottom side of the floor, trying to escape. Others . . . oh, God, others were dead. There was a tangled, seething mass of humanity, some fucking, some fighting to escape, amid hundreds of corpses.

What was this? If you stepped on that treacherous dance floor, were you abruptly sucked below, never to be released again? Forced to make the choice of either dying trying hopelessly to escape or dying doing something that felt good, while the icy Fae sat by, soulless, emotional vampires feeding off the passion of human suffering, savoring each morsel of torment? I'd thought only the Unseelie were so depraved!

Was this what happened when the Light Court ran unchecked by a queen? They devolved to the worst possible version of themselves, like the worst of humans cut loose when the world went to hell, and indulged their basest urges to riot, loot, and pillage? How many people had we lost over the past two years in this damned club?

I dialed my volume back down, to see the club the way humans did. Above us, a starry sky twinkled at the high domed ceiling, around us four courts decorated as the seasons beckoned. It was utterly lovely, seductive and pain-free and utterly false.

I turned it up again, blasting my channel wide open.

We were in a living Hell. The interior was completely undecorated but for the LED panels. Concrete walls. Concrete floors. And I'd been wrong, there was only one Seelie Court in attendance at Elyreum, the iciest of them all. The others were illusion.

Winter had claimed our city.

"We're going to kill every last one of them one day," I gritted.

"Agreed. For now, objectives and get the fuck out."

"Agreed."

We glided into motion and began to descend the staircase

together. Before we even reached the bottom, heads whipped our way, conversation stopped, and a tight, suspended hush fell over the club.

The silence had fallen so abruptly, I scanned the subclubs, certain the Fae had killed their human partners. They hadn't. They'd immobilized them somehow.

They'd known we were here the moment we stepped inside the club. They'd permitted us to walk in, been waiting for us.

This was not what I'd envisioned happening. I'd imagined a small skirmish, with the majority of Fae otherwise occupied. A bit of bear-baiting. We'd saunter off. Laugh. Having stirred up enough shit to get some answers about what was going on in Faery.

As it was, we were the sole focus of a thousand Winter Court Fae, rising, approaching, closing in on us. From below, from above, behind the balustrade and the foyer beyond. They surged in a glittering, icy wave, moving with predatory, inhuman grace.

The power they radiated was exponentially greater than I'd ever felt coming from a court sans royalty, and with my sense wide open, I could tell there wasn't a single prince or princess anywhere in the club. Royalty's melody is unmistakable, drums from hell, seductive, hypnotizing, mind-stealing.

The Fae had changed. Even their gazes were different, no longer shimmering a uniform, swirling iridescence. Lethal as razors, they sliced into you, each a unique color, for lack of a better word, though I'd be hard-pressed to name the shade: here, a tint of immortal decay, rot, and graveyards; there, the precise nuance of toxic nuclear war without end; here, the hue of rabid, bone-stripping hunger; there, the stain of madness galloping down on you with thundering hooves.

I used to mock them, these strutting, beautiful, but relatively

234 KAREN MARIE MONING

innocuous Fae without royal blood. They'd struck me as poseurs who weren't what they pretended to be, bidding us believe they possessed far greater power than they did.

Now your average Winter Court Fae was—I had to force my brain to accept the truth—viscerally terrifying.

Objective one accomplished. We knew our enemy was far more powerful than they'd ever been. "The Song definitely changed them, Ryodan," I murmured as we drew to a halt half-way down the stairs.

"No shit, Sherlock," he agreed.

In spite of the gravity of our current situation, I smiled.

It was about damned time he'd finally gotten our roles right.

TWENTY-THREE

I would give everything I own

If Dancer had lived.

There's a rabbit hole I've fallen down a few times.

Sometimes reluctantly, other times, on dark nights, Shaz snoring beside me, one of his downy legs kicking restlessly in dreams, unable to sleep, I've walked deliberately to the dirt-crusted edge and plunged down. Gone exploring that fantastical, killing wonderland of madness, monsters, and maybe.

His brains, my superpowers: what kind of babies would we have made?

If Dancer's heart had been whole, if, say, he'd taken the Elixir of Life, what daring feats of bravery and brilliance might we have accomplished together on behalf of the world?

Batman didn't have a single superpower, unless you count his inner darkness. Dancer definitely didn't have that. But maybe inner lightness is a superpower, too, and he had that in spades.

Shazam could have babysat.

NOT.

He might have eaten them. But still, Shaz is the ultimate kid's best friend. The children we didn't have would have flat-out adored him, bragged about him to all their friends, and Shaz would have loved that. And if they'd zoomed around, we'd have moved somewhere I could have zoomed along with them and we'd have feared nothing.

I don't even know if my ovaries work. I don't know everything Rowena did to me. There were chronological gaps in her narcissistic journals that implied oodles of missing volumes.

Another rabbit hole: I have no idea who my father is. I'm not sure I even had one. All I do know is every journal of the old bat's I ever found contained zero mention of my patriarchy. Such a complete omission on such a critical topic is, to my brain, completely damning.

So, maybe, those adorable little kids with Dancer's dark wavy hair and beautiful sea-surf eyes were never a possibility.

Maybe Ryodan's right.

Maybe I'm not human.

But I'm getting ahead of myself.

TWENTY-FOUR

───── • • ─────

The throne belonged to Conchobar,

to Cathain, the witch's glove

"Y OU WILL FIND," A towering, pale-skinned Fae male with waist-length silver hair purred to Ryodan, pushing through the crowd, "even for an abomination like you, some of us are far more difficult to kill."

It was two against a thousand. Sucky odds.

I narrowed my eyes, modifying my assessment. Beyond the Fae, seven black beasts began to prowl silently forward from the perimeter of the room.

Yes! It took immense effort to resist my urge to fist-pump the air.

The Nine were here. Thank you, Ryodan.

Had been all along, perhaps melted into a trellised column, camouflaged as a piece of furniture. Or, more precisely, blended chameleonlike with concrete walls and LED screens.

Fae can sense their own hallows, the spear and sword, if they get close enough, which, Mac says, has to be within a dozen feet or less. But they can't sense the Nine, which makes them Fae enemy number one. One of the Nine can sneak up right behind them and kill them before they even know a threat is in their vicinity.

As far as I know, nothing can pick up on the Nine's presence. I once asked Kat what she felt when she was around them and she'd said, *Not a bloody thing. Complete and utter silence. They don't exist at all.* I'd thought at the time, what a gift that must be to a woman who never escaped the vast, combustible, and often terrible emotions of the world. Talk about a "ground zero." Hers was a gift I'd never wished to have. I pick up way too much of the world's terribleness without enhanced empathy.

A wintry Fae female draped in an ermine-trimmed snowy cloak, and a throng of obsequious courtiers, sliced imperiously through the cluster at the bottom of the staircase and moved to join the male. I committed every detail of them both to memory. Marked them as mine.

Savagery blazed from her ancient eyes, in a face so bloodless it was tinged blue. A sneer bared sharp white teeth and the flicker of a pale, restless tongue. Long lashes were dusted with glittering crystals. Her hair was so colorless, frosted with tiny, translucent diamonds, it reflected whatever shade she stood near. Her nails had been sharpened to cruel points, ten incessantly tapping ice picks.

"She's becoming a princess," I murmured to Ryodan. As she wasn't yet fully transformed, she lacked the deadly burn of the *Sidhbha-jai,* the killing sexuality endemic to royalty of the Light Court.

"Already got that," Ryodan growled.

"The only reason we did not transform into royalty before,

the only reason sniveling humans assumed our rightful places was—"

"Time on our world diminished you," I cut her off. "Making us more powerful."

"But no more," she spat, delicate nostrils flaring. "The courts are once again strong and I am Winter-born." When she stomped her foot, a thin layer of ice gushed forth, coating the floor between us. When she stabbed me with a gaze of storm and frost, my breath painted tiny ice crystals on the air. "Give me the sword, human, and I will not make you suffer." Her eyes narrowed to slits of fiery ice and she purred, "Much. At first."

Objective two: she wanted the sword, Mac was alive. But where? Every Fae in the club was glancing beyond my shoulder, staring hungrily at my weapon.

The Nine moved stealthily nearer, melting through the sea of Fae in that nearly invisible way of theirs, seeming to morph from one Fae to the next and, although inhuman heads were swiveling, alien eyes scanning, they remained just beyond Fae vision, causing a stir with no concrete point of focus. "Where's your queen?"

"She is not our queen and will never be. The pretender is worse than dead," she said, with a hard rime smile.

"In other words," I said, smiling icily back, "you have no bloody idea where she is. And it's chafing your fairy ass, isn't it, honey?"

Ryodan made a sound of choked amusement beside me.

Amusement vanished and she spun in a whirl of ermine-trimmed cloak, snarling, "Take the sword from her. Shave the bastard to pieces no larger than a newt and bring her to me. *Mostly* intact."

As she stalked away, she left a thick layer of ice in her wake and all I could think was, That's going to be a bitch to fight on, envisioning us slipping and sliding around, trying to kill each other.

We were too closely surrounded for me to kick up into the slipstream but I didn't need to. Ryodan grabbed my arm and yanked me up into his.

Straight up.

Bloody hell, I have never *once* managed to achieve a perfectly vertical ascent. Yet another challenge to work on. As we went, I kicked off my heels, in anticipation of battle.

A vast black tunnel stained with crimson blossomed around me. Then we were slamming down hard on the opposite side of the dance floor.

Winter-born spun, snarling from the far side of the club. "I said *bring* her to me!" she screamed. "What is wrong with you imbeciles? Must I do everything myself?" She reared back and flung two long, slender, icy white hands at us, releasing dozens of glittering, deadly ice picks.

"Slipstream. Now," Ryodan snarled.

"I don't think so," I snarled back.

He shoved me up so hard and fast, I went tumbling head over heels down his black and blood tunnel, where I wasted precious seconds trying to figure out how to shift out of his mode of travel and into my own. I finally regained my balance and kicked into my long starry passageway then shifted abruptly down into freeze-frame, stripping off my left glove and yanking my sword from my back with my right as I went.

I thrust my sword into the first Fae I saw, with a long-overdue roar of satisfaction.

One down, a thousand to go, I thought fiercely.

I plunged into the carnage. The bastards thought to kill Mac, thought to take our world, had been torturing and killing our people for two long years unchecked.

In the periphery of my vision I could see The Nine slashing their way toward Winter-born, leaving slaughtered Fae in their wake. She was precisely who we needed to kill, to buy time before another princess would be born, and I knew what Ryodan was thinking: kill her before she became lethal to me. The *Sidhbha-jai* is my kryptonite. If turned on me at full force, it shorts me out, renders me helpless. We'd had no idea new royalty were being born. Not a bloody clue. We'd been cut off for too long.

I spun, I stabbed, I whirled, I battled. I came back to life in Elyreum, being what I needed to be, doing what I was born to do.

Fae after Fae fell beneath my blade. Then Ryodan was behind me and we moved into flawless formation, fighting back to back.

"I told you to get the fuck out of here," he growled over his shoulder.

"Tell the sun to leave the sky," I growled back.

"It does when night moves in. I'm night."

"Scientifically untrue. The sun remains, you just don't see it."

"We've accomplished our objectives. Retreat."

"Not the boss of me."

"Bloody hell, don't I know that. Something's wrong. The bitch is losing Fae left and right and doesn't care. She's waiting for something. I'm pulling the plug. Now."

But it was too late. I'd argued too long.

The debilitating, soul-searing burn of the *Sidhbha-jai* slammed into me and charred my insides to useless ash. "J-Jayne," I stuttered. "He m-must be h-here s-s-somewhere. F-Find him. K-Kill him!" That bastard! He wasn't in hiding with his family. He'd been working for the Winter Court, likely offered amnesty, if he brought them my sword!

"I will. Get out!" Ryodan roared.

But I couldn't. Nothing was working right. I thudded down into slow-mo and crashed to my knees. Then Ryodan had me and was flinging me over his shoulder.

"Don't touch my left hand!" I screamed, rearing up on his back like a cobra, desperate to keep the ungloved, lethal appendage away from him.

A prince sifted in directly behind us, blasting me with staggering sexuality and, as he reached for me (I ached to go to him, burned to be his slave, hungered to worship my master!) I managed to retain a grip on a single shred of my mind, smiled sweetly at him with utter adoration and offered him my left hand, silently begging him to seize me from Ryodan's shoulder and take me to Paradise.

Dark, unholy promise burned in his gaze. Blood pooled in mine as I proffered my deadly hand. *Take me, take me,* I willed.

He accepted my submission as his royal due and reached.

As our fingertips met, an explosion of high voltage stabbed up into my head, shot down into my body, and as it flared to lethal life, the Fae prince exploded into a thousand fragments of pale white flesh and paler, sharp bone.

Bits of him rained down on the club and, as the killing grip of the *Sidhbha-jai* released my mind, I caught a glimpse of Winter-born's pale, incredulous face in the crowd.

Then Fae began to scream and trample each other in their haste to escape.

I kicked up, launching myself like a rocket from Ryodan's shoulder, vaulting high into the air, desperate to get away from him because the voltage was still arcing and crackling inside me.

Off-balance, I missed the slipstream entirely, slammed into the floor, rolled and sprang to my feet.

Whatever I'd set free inside me wasn't done yet, not nearly exhausted, it was still building, building, and I had no idea how to control it.

"Dani, get back here!" Ryodan roared.

I had to do something with it before he grabbed me again. Before I sent it shooting into him. I was not killing Ryodan. I'd done it twice before and hated it both times.

I spun on Winter-born and flung my hand at her, at the precise instant she thrust two pale, slender, icy hands at me.

Bolts of lightning exploded from my fingertips, one after the next, shattering her ice-summoned weapons, blasting a path through them, as I sent my power gunning for her—

Holy hell, she sifted out! I'd missed!

Furious, I slammed more bolts into the walls, into the floor. If I couldn't kill her at least I could obliterate their horrific club from the face of *our* earth. I dumped energy from my body in powerful surges of lightning, then, abruptly, I was—

Sailing in space, crystal clear and cool, surrounded by an infinity of stars on a nebula-painted canvas of black velvet sky.

It was vast but I was enormous. It was ancient but I was, too. It was timeless but I was without end.

There was wind here. Gusting, swirling waves of it buffeting my body. It felt as if I might catch one and go shooting up higher, higher, before channeling the borrowed velocity to dive beneath a moon, perhaps go ricocheting out around a star.

I'd always thought space was still but it wasn't, it was living and flowing, ebbing and changing. Not emptiness here but some kind of . . . dark matter that defied understanding, the stuff of the Cosmos, rife with possibility, as if all the hopes and dreams and desires that had ever been and would ever be were nestled deep within superdense molecules of darkness we could never comprehend, and, every now and then, something came along whose wings, or melody, rippled against that dark matter, stirring it up with lightning and song, with bolts of extreme high voltage, changing, waking, beginning something new, stitching things together in ways that defied comprehension, making connections, forging patterns and symmetry from chaos.

I felt a great breeze then and turned whatever head I had into the wind. An enormous black Hunter sailed along beside me, head rocking gently as it buffeted the waves, lips pulled back as it chuffed softly and turned its gargantuan head to fix me with a single glowing orange eye. Ready?

I frowned. For what?

I fly.

I see that.

You fly, too.

What was it saying? That I might remain here with it, flying through the greatest unexplored territory of all? Discover the secrets of the Cosmos, behold its ancient mysteries?

All of that and more.

But my people. This wasn't my world. Mine was in danger once more, and probably always would be. My world needed me. I had a job to do.

I closed my eyes, willing it all to go away.

When I opened them again, I stood blinking repeatedly, blinded by the sudden, harsh light, the jarring transition.

I was in the club but things had changed while I'd drifted in the cosmic vision. The surviving Fae had vanished; sifted, flown or run away, leaving behind only the dead, the Nine and me.

"Dani." Ryodan's voice seemed to come from a great distance.

I blinked again, staring dazedly at the destruction around me.

Walls were splintered and crumbling. The floor was cleft by a fifty-foot-wide crevice with jagged edges that dropped to a bottomless abyss. The LED panels had been shattered, spraying bits of glass and wiring everywhere, and those people trapped beneath the floor were gone. I shivered. Fallen to their deaths down the gorge I'd carved. A small part of my brain said, *A better death than the one they were facing.* A bigger part said, *Yet more people you failed to save.*

The structure of Elyreum groaned, as timbers contorted in a hopeless effort to accommodate the compromised foundation.

"Dani," Ryodan said again.

"Honey," I heard Lor say. "Can you hear us?"

I nodded tightly.

"Put your hand down, Dani," Ryodan said softly, carefully.

I hadn't realized it was still raised. I stared at it, turning it this way and that, trying to process it. My left forearm had sprouted darkly beautiful obsidian thorns. It looked like a black velvet, studded opera glove.

I forced it to drop to my side.

"Look at me, Dani," said Ryodan in a low, intense voice.

I turned slowly and met his gaze. His eyes flickered strangely, swirling with shadows and I saw, as clearly as if he'd spoken the words: *Goddamn, I was right. She isn't human. I knew it.* Then, *Shit, this wasn't at all what I expected. Fuck!*

The words hadn't come to me in the usual manner of his silent communications—deliberately telegraphed. I'd gotten an entire memory attached to his first thought, nothing with the second.

He hadn't believed I was human since he saw me outside Temple Bar as I'd stood watching street mimes, laughing my ass off, one hand shoved in my pocket, the other cramming a cheeseburger in my mouth. I'd had two black eyes and was badly bruised, still drunk on being able to freeze-frame all over the city before I learned to lock my mental grid down.

But that wasn't when we'd met. We hadn't met for some time after that.

Still, he had a flawlessly detailed memory of walking up behind me, stopping a matter of mere inches from my back, pausing for a moment, inhaling deeply, before vanishing in that eerie, instant way of his. If I'd sensed an electrifying presence behind me, I'd written it off as my own excitement at finally being free in the world.

He'd known about me long before he came to find me on that water tower, to rope me into working for him.

I tried to ponder that thought but my brain was sluggish and uncooperative. I couldn't access any of my mental vaults. Was this how normal people felt? How terrible that must be! How did they even stand it? I had sludge in my head.

My legs went out from under me then.

As I slumped to the floor, I cried out to Ryodan, "Don't catch me! Don't touch me! I'm dangerous!"

Ryodan smiled faintly but it didn't reach his eyes. "I think we've figured that out."

FALLING

Belong, etymology: Old English, "gelang," "at
   hand," "together with."

Definition: To be suitable, advantageous,
   appropriate.
To have the proper qualifications, especially social,
   to be a member of a group, to fit.
To be attached, bound by birth, allegiance or
   dependency.
To be a son, daughter, mother, father, lover.
Families belong to each other.

I have no idea what the word means.
My mom said I "belonged" in a cage.
But I know better.
I've never belonged anywhere.

                         —Dani O'Malley

TWENTY-FIVE

· • ·

What have I become, my sweetest friend

"HEY, SHAZ-MA-TAZ," I GREETED him with weary cheer, as I trudged into my bedroom and flipped on the overhead light.

He raised his great shaggy head from the mattress on the floor and peered at me, scanning me intently from head to toe. It was a look we'd often given each other after battle, ascertaining whether the other was okay.

His violet eyes widened. "You're thorny!" he exclaimed. "That'll be a tryllium scratch!"

One of my old passwords used to be thornybitch314159, a combination of how I sometimes felt plus the first six digits of pi. I considered choosing more wisely in the future. "That I am. I assume tryllium's good?"

"The best!" he enthused, but sobered quickly. "Are you all right, Yi-yi?" he fretted. "It grew again."

"I'm fine," I said, slipping out of my dress. "I'm going to wash up then I need big-time cuddles. Oodles of them."

"And we'll put the mattress back up?"

"You betcha." I headed for the shower.

Ryodan had dropped me off and left, seething, a few minutes ago.

I couldn't help it. I needed to be alone. I'd gotten used to being alone. Something was happening to me and I wanted time to focus my brain on it.

I'd had to rest for five solid minutes before I could push up from the floor, leaving the shattered, collapsing club behind. I wasn't about to let anyone pick me up and carry me out. Although I no longer felt the exhilarating, terrifying wild voltage inside me, I was taking no chances.

While I'd gathered my strength, Lor had picked through the rubble, searching for my shoes, but they were nowhere to be found, which pissed me off because I loved those shoes. I'd worn them once. The others had remained in beast form, in case the Fae decided to try to circle back for another attack, which I found highly improbable. They'd gone two years without a single threat, and we'd just killed a hundred of them, if not more. The possibility of death is something Fae avoid like humans avoid Ebola. I wanted to ponder the ramifications of our actions tonight, but at the moment all I could think about was myself.

My confusion had abated but I was still shaky and weak. Ryodan, meticulous planner that he is, had snacks stashed in the Ferrari and I'd inhaled candy bars, one after the other, before shoving half a bag of chips in my mouth.

I glanced at the mirror and raised a brow thinking, wryly, Aha *that's* why they were all staring at me like that.

Blackness had taken more of my pale Irish skin. Not only

was my left arm a thorny black glove, the stain had spread further into my flesh.

Exotic black flames arced up the left side of my neck, curving over my jaw, my cheek, to my temple and into my left brow. The pointed tip of one of those flames ended a mere inch from my mouth. The mouth that was suddenly acutely aware it hadn't done nearly enough kissing.

The Nine had closed in protectively around me as we walked to the car, which I found hysterically funny, given what I'd just done. Killed a prince without using the sword, destroyed a club.

Ryodan had argued with me all the way back to Sanctuary, demanding I return to Chester's with him. Demanding we talk.

Lacking the energy to argue, I'd looked at him and said simply, *Please, I very much need to be alone right now.*

I know Ryodan. Had I argued, he'd have debated me forever. But my quiet plea had taken the bite out of the wolf and, bristling with barely restrained testosterone and anger, he'd parked and escorted me to my door, saying tightly, *If you need me, call. Text. Throw up a bloody Bat signal. If I don't hear from you first thing in the morning, I'll be on your fucking doorstep, beating down the door.*

Only after I promised had he growlingly conceded to leave.

I stepped back and assessed my naked body in the mirror. I like my body. It's strong and lean and suits me. I should be horrified by what was happening to me but I couldn't help but think I looked kind of . . . beautiful. My entire left arm was covered with lovely dark thorns. I had no idea why I thought they were lovely but I did. They weren't ugly or scary looking. They were as gently curved as the thorns on a rose, larger with slightly blunted tips. I ran my hand over them lightly and shivered. They were cold but extraordinarily sensitive, as if entire clusters of nerve-endings were nestled at the tips.

The barbs ended just beneath my shoulder but the inky blackness had seized territory on the left side of my torso as well, from beneath my armpit to my waist, shooting more of those ebony flames across my stomach and breasts. On someone else, I'd have found it wicked cool, an otherworldly tattoo, Woman of Obsidian Fire.

On me, although it was stunning, not so much.

Unless it went away, I would never again feel a man's hands touch my breasts. Unless it went away, I would never again taste Ryodan's kiss. Faces touch when you kiss. There was no way a man could get near my mouth with more than a chaste peck and I'm not a chaste peck kind of woman, as I'd amply demonstrated this morning.

God, that felt like a lifetime ago.

I'd have kissed him harder, longer, better, if I'd known this was going to happen by nightfall.

I forced my thoughts to focus, turned from the mirror and began to tally what I knew.

Fact: I stabbed a Hunter when I was fourteen and my hand turned black for days.

Fact: It kept happening over the years.

Fact: I'd recently developed an extraordinary superpower, the ability to shoot highly destructive bolts of lightning from my hand, capable of blowing structures apart and killing Fae royalty. I smirked a little. *Ha, take that, the Nine! I'm as badass as you!*

Fact: Each time I used the power, more of me turned black and icy.

I frowned. Inaccurate. The blackness hadn't expanded when I killed Bridget. Nor when I used it to break the paralysis spell. Or had it—just not where I could see it? Staining deeper beneath my skin, opposed to wider. Were my bones black now?

Fact: When I used the power, it drained me to a degree that appeared to be increasing with use, or perhaps with the magnitude of use.

Fact: If anyone touched the black part of me, they would die. I would kill them.

"Poison Ivy much?" I muttered. That wasn't who I'd planned to be when I grew up. She was Batman's nemesis. I was supposed to be the Bat, only with superpowers.

Fact: If I kept using those incredible lightning bolts, it seemed highly probable I would turn *entirely* black. I wondered if it would affect my hair, too. Would my eyes turn black? I tried to envision myself all black. Pretty odd.

I stepped into the shower and stood under the spray pondering whether, as Shazam had suggested, I might be able to make it go away. Maybe if I never used it again the stain would retreat and I'd return to normal. It had retreated once, early on, to beneath my elbow. Was it cumulative somehow? Was its mysterious endgame inevitable and irreversible once it had begun?

I toweled my hair dry, tugged on sweats and a tee, grateful Shazam was impervious. At least I had that.

Assuming I survived whatever was happening to me, I was going to become that strange Hel-Cat lady, eccentric and alone.

It could be worse, I mused, as I headed back to the bedroom. I might not even have Shazam.

I, who at best had never known more than a tenuous connection to the world, was becoming even more cut off, more isolated. By my own skin. I'd always been dangerous. Now I was lethal to the touch.

My first year in a cage, my mother had showered me with affection. Before she'd left in the morning, and again each night when she got home. She'd washed and dried me, brushed my hair. We'd held hands through the bars. She'd rubbed moisturizer into my skin and tickled my back, and I'd known we were going to make it. That OLDER and OUTSIDE were a guarantee. I'd known it from her touch. You can feel love in someone's hands.

It hadn't stayed that way long. Her affection became more and more infrequent until, finally, she'd stopped touching me at all. Then, not long after, she'd begun to stop seeing me, too.

When I could no longer remember the feel of her hands on my body, my hair, of soft kisses pressed through bars; when those kisses had become a hazy memory that belonged to another life, some other child, I'd lain in my cage and hugged myself, turning my head from side to side, kissing my shoulders, my arms.

My small body had ached for touch. For comfort, for love.

As it did now.

I hoisted our mattress back up onto the box springs, stretched out on my back and opened my arms.

Shazam flung himself at me, landing squarely on my chest. "Ow!"

Rumbling, eyes gleaming, he head-butted me with delight, then snuggled into my killing embrace.

And, as I'd done so often Silverside, I squeezed my eyes shut to hold back tears, and held onto him with all my might.

TWENTY-SIX

◦ ◦ ◦

The rusted chains of prison moons are

shattered by the sun

"First, Kat," Christian said, "a summary of pertinent history. Try to hold your questions till the end. The timeline I'm giving you is approximate. The Fae aren't glued to the concept of time; they have an infinity of it to squander. I had to plug bits and pieces of history together with few points of reference."

"Understood," I said. We encountered the same problem with the texts we translated. Points of reference were vague at best, like tying our historical events to whatever TV shows were popular at the time and someone trying to figure it out millennia later. If he possessed an overview, I very much wanted it.

"The first significant mention of the Fae appears approximately one million years ago, although they existed long before that. Originally there was a single Light Court of Four Seasons. The Light King became dissatisfied with life at court, left and declared himself the Dark or Unseelie King. Sometime after that he met his mortal concubine, became obsessed with her and sought to make her immortal like him. Since the Song of Making was a matriarchal power, he had to petition the Light Queen to transform his lover. It was when the queen refused that everything began to go to hell.

"The Unseelie King retired to his dark kingdom, vowing to re-create the Song and make his lover immortal himself. The Unseelie or Dark Court was born as a result of his endless experiments. As far as I can tell, he spent roughly a quarter of a million years working on it. Again, approximate, I believe Cruce was born three-quarters of a million years ago, and was one of the last remaining Dark Court the king created.

"As you know, Cruce betrayed the king to the queen and told her what the king had been doing, about five hundred thousand years ago. Cruce wanted the Unseelie Court to roam freely in the world, mingling with the Seelie, which was forbidden by the king. The king knew what the queen would do if she discovered he'd created a Dark Court of his own, especially if she learned that the mortal lover she so despised was still alive, secreted away in a realm beyond time to keep her from aging.

"When the queen learned of the Dark Court's existence, it started a war to end all wars. When Seelie and Unseelie clashed, they destroyed their own planet, splitting it down the middle. The unthinkable happened: the Unseelie King killed the Seelie Queen, before she was able to pass the Song of Making to her successor.

"The Song was all that kept the Fae powerful. They, alone, possessed that ancient melody of life."

"No doubt, stolen somehow," I said, unable to resist the acerbic comment. No god I believed in would have entrusted a thing of such power and beauty to such a shallow, power-hungry, ruthless race.

"As you've seen, the Song seeps into reality and replenishes fading magic. Once they lost the ancient melody, the Fae were doomed. Over time they would have grown weaker, until they vanished on the wind, with only legends of them remaining."

"But when Mac used the Song to heal our world they were restored," I said grimly.

"Precisely. What the melody didn't destroy, it made stronger. As happened long ago in the mists of Time, the Song sank deep into the fabric of all things and crooned 'Awaken.' Another of Mac's double-edged swords. That woman does tend to wreak havoc from time to time."

I began to protest but he waved it away.

"I ken it, lass. She had no choice but to use the Song or the Cosmos itself would have been destroyed by the black holes. We're lucky she was able to wield it, and I'm grateful. But no action is without consequence. Indeed, there are times the most desirable, correct, *necessary* action results in catastrophic consequences. We're facing them now.

"Back to the timeline: Subsequent queens moved the Light Court from world to world, draining yet more power from the court each time they moved, desperately seeking a planet richly steeped in magic. They knew they were diminishing, bit by bit. Many of them drank from the Cauldron of Forgetting, to forget how powerful they'd once been, how weak they were becoming.

"Eventually, around two hundred thousand years ago, they discovered our world, which still pulsed with considerable magic. But it was already occupied by both gods and ancient man. It was a peaceful time on our planet before the Fae arrived. The gods were mostly benign and, although they occasionally warred among themselves, they cared for and tended the mortals who worshipped them and there was a strong bond between them.

"The Fae, deceitful bastards that they are, feigned far less power than they had, and begged sanctuary from the gods, claiming their world had been destroyed through no fault of their own. The gods, sensing no threat, gave the Fae a fair amount of land, and things were peaceful for a time.

"But the Fae were busy gathering intelligence, desperate to seize and rule our magic-rich world. They covertly studied the gods, seeking weaknesses. Their attack was patient, stealthy, and a shining example of slanted press on a global scale. They abducted the gods one by one, used their Fae glamour to impersonate them, and began punishing, torturing, and killing humans. To humans, it seemed their gods had turned on them.

"In kind, humans turned on their gods, and the gods that remained turned on their humans for betraying them—for refusing to listen when they tried to explain what the Fae had done. Then, the great, benevolent Fae finally stepped in to 'rescue' humans.

"The gods realized the Fae had been concealing their true power all along, but gods can't penetrate the glamour of the Fae, and the Fae gathered up and killed most of the deities on our world, leaving a scattered handful of those too powerful to kill, or those who devised ways to elude their clutches.

"I've no idea how many remain but I'd wager a few hundred or so. Those gods they couldn't figure out how to kill—unlike Fae, all gods can't be killed by two commonly known weapons, each has one unique way they can die and it's a tightly guarded secret—they captured and entombed them in the earth. They relinquished one of their most powerful shians or Fae mounds to use as a prison.

"For a long time the gods slumbered in the soil, faded to mere wisps of their former selves, but when the ancient Song was sung again, it awakened and released them from those tombs. The gods had learned from their mistakes. They came back weak, as mere shadows, and bided time as stealthily as the Fae once had, laying low, absorbing power from the newly reinvigorated Earth, until they were once again powerful. Only recently have they begun to show themselves."

I murmured, "And they despise the Fae more than ever and plot their destruction."

"Worse than that, Kat. They despise humans, too. They loathe both races and want both gone, and the odds aren't quite so against them now. The first time the gods and Fae battled, *sidhe*-seers didn't exist. The Fae weren't on our world and there was no need for them. But now they *do* exist and the gods have an enormous advantage they once lacked. Before, they couldn't have seen a Fae standing right next to them if it was glamoured as a human. With *sidhe*-seer watchdogs, they can."

I shuddered. Was that where our twelve *sidhe*-seers had gone—abducted by gods? I knew better than to assure him that our *sidhe*-seers wouldn't help them. Dole out enough torture, eventually someone will cooperate. "Have you discovered when our order was born?" Our roots were a mystery to us, I was fascinated by our origins. I knew the why of it; to protect the *Sinsar Dubh*.

"Aye, again approximately. As you know, after the Unseelie King killed the queen, Cruce stole his beloved concubine and made the king believe she was dead. In an act of atonement, the king dumped all the formidable power of his dark magic into the *Sinsar Dubh*, and cast it out into the world. But as Fae things do, it evolved and, furious with the king, obsessed with him, the dark doppelganger began to stalk the Unseelie King, wreaking havoc wherever it went. The two played a game of cat and mouse for hundreds of thousands of years."

"Wait a minute, I have to ask this: we were led to believe the *Sinsar Dubh* was nearly a million years old. It's only a half a million?"

"Depends on how you look at it. The *Sinsar Dubh* is commonly regarded as a million years old because it contains the Unseelie King's knowledge from the time he began creating his dark court, nearly a million years ago, until the time he divested himself of it, over half a million years later. Technically, it is only half a million years old. Again, this is all only approximate."

I nodded. "Go on."

"When the king finally managed to capture his dangerous alter-ego, roughly one hundred fifty thousand years ago, he needed a secure place to contain it with guards. Conveniently, there already existed a shian on a planet, rich in magic, laced with the proper elements, the perfect place to entomb it; a place the Seelie would never go because they'd already buried their ancient enemy there and abandoned it."

I gasped. "Are you *kidding* me? Are you saying . . ." I trailed off in disbelief.

He cut me a dark smile. "Aye. The Unseelie King paid a visit to our world, and hid the *Sinsar Dubh* beneath what is now Arlington Abbey, above the entombed gods, then created the *sidhe*-seers as his final Unseelie caste, to serve as his watchdogs. He gave your order the power to penetrate Fae glamour, the ability to ward your land against Fae, and various gifts to fight them if they came."

I shook my head, dazed by the thought. "The gods have been slumbering beneath our abbey this entire time?"

"Och, lass, from the hints I've gathered here and there, your abbey perches atop many powerful things. I'd like to explore the Underneath if you'd permit it. Soon. We've a mess on our hands and require every advantage we can find."

I nodded. We would find a way to work together.

"Back to the timeline. The war between gods and Fae had ravaged the earth. Queen Aoibheal, who'd once been mortal herself, had watched too many planets destroyed. Eventually, and I can't pin that event to a time, she forcibly removed the Fae to a separate realm, fabricating walls by tapping into the power of the Unseelie prison walls, striking a Compact with a clan called the Keltar, and trained them as druids to uphold it. Here's where it gets complicated. I'm going to try to explain the realm of "Faery" to you in a nutshell.

"Under the First Queen and Seelie King, Faery consisted of only the Seelie Court, a vast, resplendent land with four distinct kingdoms, with royal houses governing each: Spring, Summer, Autumn, and Winter. Over them all, the queen ruled.

"When the king left the Seelie Queen and became Unseelie, he expanded Faery to hold the enormity of his own demesne. Within his kingdom he constructed the nearly infinite White Mansion, and tied it to the truly infinite Hall of All Days. He also fabricated the Silvers as a secondary means of travel, initially for his and his concubine's use only. Faery grew from a single court to an enormous tapestry of connected worlds. Some say the battle we wage here on Earth between mortal and Fae is happening on countless other worlds with countless other Fae courts connected by this network, in a multiplicity of universes."

He saw the look on my face and laughed. "Aye, the thought boggles my mind, too. Eventually, the Silvers were cursed and the terrain of Faery became even more complex, as if it wasn't already enough of a mess. But for simplicity, think of Faery as the Light Court and the Dark Court, the Hall of All Days, the Silvers, and the White Mansion all in one enormous, otherworldly realm. But it's no longer otherworldly. No walls divide us. It exists adjacent to, spilling into, our own."

Which was why we desperately needed Mac to figure out how to use her power as Fae queen, so she could sing those walls back up and restore our world to its normal order without Fae preying on humans. "How do you know all this?" I asked. This was the kind of history we'd long been seeking.

"I sent my clan into the White Mansion, to the king's true library, and had them bring me every book and object of interest they could find. The castle, as you'll soon see, is stuffed with books and bottles and potions and endless artifacts that we've transported to Draoidheacht Keep. Heed me well, touch none of it. They're not your usual books and bottles and such. Dani can tell you a thing or two about what might be found in the king's collection." He laughed. "Ask her about the Boora Boora books. But don't ask her about the Crimson Hag, and no matter what you do, once you arrive at my castle, bloody hell, don't open any bottles you might see lying around."

"If they're so dangerous, why did you bring them out into our world?"

"Many might prove useful. Knowledge is power. So is power," he said dryly. "A controllable Crimson Hag would be a hell of an advantage. I don't sleep, Kat, I study. I learn about myself, about the Fae race. I prepare. The gods and Fae are going to war again, and that battle could well destroy our world. The gods want humans eradicated, the Fae want humans enslaved. It's a lose-lose for us either way."

I said, "What does this have to do with Sean? I'm assuming it ties in somehow?"

"We, too, were made dramatically more powerful by the ancient melody. It was months before the full transformation occurred for me, and yet another few months after that for Sean. I suspect it's moved slowly for the Seelie, as well. We all change at our own unique pace. I've learned to control what I've become. But Sean, ah lass, your Sean has not. And he must. He's running out of time."

π

We arrived at the perimeter of Christian's heavily warded kingdom just before dawn. He'd carved apart fifty thousand acres of the Highlands for his own, and begun repairing and fortifying the enormous, ancient castle he'd christened Draoidheacht Keep. It was in that great, sprawling castle he and Sean lived, in the finished parts of the crumbling ruin. As we soared over a final ben, Christian said, "Brace yourself, lass, it's not pretty."

Even prepared, I was stunned by the vision that greeted us as we cleared that final ben, broke through clouds and soared over his kingdom.

Everywhere I looked, the earth was black.

Gone was the lush greenery, the abundant profusion of foliage and life. Beneath an endless bank of low-hanging, dense, rumbling thunderclouds that stretched as far as my eye could see—a churning, crashing dark gray roof—the earth was burnt and barren, as if it had been charred to a crisp.

"What happened here, Christian?" I gasped, clinging more tightly to his shoulders as an icy gust blasted me. It was uncommonly cold, too. The temperature had plummeted thirty to forty degrees the moment we crossed the harsh line of demarcation

"Months after the Song was sung, I took a flight through the Highlands, savoring the beauty. I'd only just begun to embrace my wings. I was in a buoyant mood that day and decided to take a stroll, visit our local pub for a wee dram before returning to

Castle Keltar. I walked the last few miles, enjoying an unusual gentle hum I felt in the earth. It seemed to be seeping up through the soles of my boots, into my skin, deep into my bones. It felt good, Kat, a beautiful rhythmic vibration enlivening me. I didn't understand what was happening, didn't realize a dormant part of me was responding to the new magic in the earth, awakening. That I was becoming the Prince of Death who'd once existed three-quarters of a million years ago. When I strolled into the Cock and Crown that day, one hundred forty-two people—*my* people, under Keltar care—exploded into clouds of black dust before my eyes. I killed every single person in that pub, merely by entering it. Had I returned home instead of going for a drink, I'd have killed my entire clan, with the sole exception of Dageus."

I flinched. "I'm so sorry."

"I've spent the past two years scouring tomes from the king's library, seeking information about what I am, what power I have and how to use it. It's not as if I have anyone to ask. The Seelie would prefer us dead. Barring that, they want us on their very short leash, to be used as weapons. There are no Unseelie left to educate me."

"But don't you sort of just *know* what you can do?" My gift was simple, it slammed me in the face every day. Since the Song was sung, it had grown even more potent, but thanks to time spent with Kasteo, I'd learned how to make and hold walls, Kevlar myself in emotional armor. Before I slept each night, I deliberately and carefully walled the world out, creating a blessed fortress of silence for myself, so I might face the next day rejuvenated, strong.

"Not until I try," Christian said. "And often I'm not trying to do anything at all. The power manifests without my consent, like the day I strolled into the pub. Shortly after I imprisoned myself here, your Sean joined me. He's Famine. Wherever he walks, the earth dies, crops wither, the soil goes barren; in time enough, the world would starve. The same thing happened to him that occurred with me: he felt something seeping up from the soil and, as he walked, the earth around him began to die. Unlike me, he hasn't been able to contain that power."

I winced. "It was Sean who destroyed this land?"

"Aye. He tests himself, strolls out to a strip of what blanched green remains when he thinks he's ready to try again. Each time he destroys the earth, he returns angrier, grows more bitter. Anger and bitterness aren't emotions an Unseelie prince can indulge without catastrophic results."

"What is that? Who lives *there*?" I exclaimed. He'd soared us far to the north as we'd talked, and we now glided directly above the line of demarcation where the perimeter of his blackened kingdom met lush green again. I'd seen something like it before, the abrupt transition where the Shades had devoured everything in sight as they'd approached our abbey, but had stopped for reasons unknown.

On the charred land to my right stood a small thatch-roofed crofter's cottage in the midst of lifeless earth. On the grassy side, directly adjacent to it, was another small crofter's cottage of stone that was welcoming and warm, surrounded by neatly tended gardens where flowers bloomed.

The cottages were day and night, yin and yang, huddled next to each other. Far below us a couple walked on the grassy side, near the cottage, holding hands.

"That's Dageus and Chloe. He lives within my wards. She lives just beyond them. I've warded the fuck out of her cottage, too, but will not permit her inside my kingdom, lest we inadvertently harm her."

"You came into our abbey yet killed no one. I felt you, Christian. You have it under control."

"There is no ward, no charm, no magic solution to harnessing a prince's deadly powers. What I used to master it is the simplest yet often the most elusive thing of all: love. If I grow angry, if I allow myself any negative emotion at all, I can slip," he said quietly. "The key to success is never being bitter, never being angry, never coveting, never succumbing to any kind of desire that contains darkness. Your Sean, lass, he's consumed by it."

I blinked back a swift burn of tears. I'd wondered, so many nights, in my private garden of silence at the end of each day, where my childhood love had gone. Why he'd never texted or called. He'd simply walked away, without another word. It had pained me almost beyond enduring.

Yet, all this time, Sean had been holed up in isolation, warded away from the world, trying to learn to control the Unseelie monster he'd become. All this time, I'd thought he'd left me because he didn't want me, didn't want us. And so, I'd given him his privacy. I'd not texted or called either. Stung, hurt. McLaughlin-stubborn and unyielding.

But that wasn't why he'd left at all. Sometimes, despite the open window I have into everyone else's emotions, I can be blind and foolish about my own. "Take me to him, Christian."

"I hoped you'd say that."

TWENTY-SEVEN

Crawling in my skin,

these wounds they will not heal

I LOST ONE OF MY birds this morning.

His name was Charles James Aubry. He was twenty-three. He hung himself in my flat on Desoto after only nine days off the streets. I just dropped in on him three days ago and even I'd been fooled.

But I've seen many come and go and I've learned a bit about their ways; sometimes right before they check out, they seem better than ever, well-adjusted. Not giddy or tip-you-off kind of happy, but misleadingly balanced, and I wonder about that borrowed grace. Wonder about the enormous amount of pain they must be suffering to finally feel okay only when they decide to opt out of this crazy, beautiful world. You don't see it coming, not even me. Although I've learned to watch for an unexpected, suspicious peace.

He left a note: *I didn't ask to be born.*

I wish I had more time. I have a theory about depression. I think it comes from a shift in the chemicals in our brains because stress, trauma, and grief deplete our happy juice, disrupt the delicate, necessary balance and make the world go flat around us, get scary and monochrome, too heavy to bear. And once you're there, with depleted brain chemicals and flat colors, you're too depressed to fight your way out. I think exercise is a way to increase endorphins, rebalance the brain, and I wonder if my extreme velocity and constant motion feed my brain undiluted happy juice, constantly perking me up. I wonder if I figured out, say—the right blend of cortisol, 5HTP, and Bacopa, maybe a few other nootropics, plus lots of fun, physical activity, and loads of kindness and sunshine—then gave those people one happy, stress-free year without any responsibility, maybe I could turn their world around.

I cut him down and held him. He was still warm; I may have missed him by an hour, he must have died shortly after dawn. Lingered to watch one more sunrise. If so, that slayed me because it meant he still had joy somewhere inside, if only someone had been able to reach and nurture it. I wrapped him in a blanket and took him to a cemetery I use for the lost ones. I don't have a lot of time but I always bury them, and I always do something for them.

Dublin goes dispassionately on. This beautiful, terrifying, packed with limitless possibility and peril chronic-town chug-a-chugs on, a locomotive barreling down the tracks, with neither deviation in schedule nor pause for fallen.

They vanish, unnoticed, unsung.

I blow the horn for them. Yank that cable down and let her rip.

I graffitied his name on an underpass in three vibrant shades of neon ten feet tall telling the world that Charles James Aubry was here. It may have been brief but, by God, he was here and will be remembered. If only by me.

He couldn't stand the pain.

And I couldn't save him from it.

π

I went straight to Chester's after painting the underpass, and dashed up the stairs to Ryodan's office when I didn't find him below with the workers. I'd texted earlier, telling him I was fine and I'd be by around ten. He's not a man you don't text when he tells you to. He'll come looking for you. And he'll be pissed. I wasn't in the mood to repair my door again. I still had to fix the elevator. And I hadn't vacuumed in weeks. Shazam-hair was everywhere.

When the darkened glass panel whisked silently aside, I stalked across the glass floor that always makes me feel suspended in space, flung myself into the chair in front of his desk, kicked my feet over the side, and told him what I'd decided late last night—or rather near dawn this morning—with neither preface nor preamble.

"I think I'm becoming a Hunter." I leaned back and waited for him to deny it. I didn't actually think it myself. It was absurdly far-fetched. I was, however, quite certain I would turn completely black at some point. Still . . . the vision I'd had at the club last night seemed like . . . I don't know, an invitation of sorts, and I wanted to bounce my worst-case scenario off someone who would laugh and tell me that was ridiculous. I wasn't turning into one of those icy black demons with eyes like gates to Hell, no matter how benign it had appeared in my vision, sailing along next to me. To hear him say he knew a spell, a ward, or a charm that would make my deadly skin go away, because, by God, Ryodan knew everything.

Criminy, he was beautiful this morning. Tall and dark, freshly showered and shaved, smelling good. Looking powerful and ridiculous behind that stuffy desk. He belongs on a battlefield. Like me.

He said flatly, "You think?"

I stiffened. That wasn't the right answer, Ryodan's version of *duh*. "What do you mean, *duh*? You didn't even know I'd stabbed a Hunter."

He leaned back in his chair and folded his arms behind his head. The sleeves of his shirt were rolled up to his elbows, his forearms strong, scarred, silver cuff glinting. I know Ryodan well, the fine muscles in his face were too tight. He was pissed about something. Extremely. "I knew you stabbed a Hunter. I read every paper you wrote. And your book. All editions. Your footnotes needed work. I didn't, however," he growled, "know your bloody hand turned black afterward. You neglected to mention that."

"It was no one's business but mine. And how do you know it now?" And why was he taking this so seriously? I'd just told him I thought I was turning into one of those enormous dragons Jayne used to shoot at all the time, and I used to try to kill, species unknown, and he'd said only, *You think?* It was an absurd theory. I was small. Hunters were enormous. If nothing else, I lacked sufficient mass.

"Kat told me that part."

"Kat," I said disbelievingly. "When? What do you guys do, sit around and talk about me, or something?"

"This morning when I texted her," he said tightly. "I told her you were turning black and she knew all about it. Lor wasn't watching you every moment. He did the best he could. Christian was supposed to relieve him sometimes and he's still not fucking returning my calls. Do you know how infuriating it is to have to find out the details of your life from someone else?"

"Do you know how infuriating it is to not even be able to *find out* the details of your life?" I countered just as irritably. "At least you can butt in and text my friends. I don't have Lor's number. Or Kasteo's. Or Fade's," I said, working myself into a snit. "And if I did," I continued, eyes flashing, "you'd have told them not to tell me a bloody thing just to keep me wandering around, forever stymied by the great big mystery of R.K. bloodythefuck S. And just what the hell do the K and S stand for anyway?"

"Killian. St. James."

"Huh?" Ryodan just told me his name? I rolled it silently over my tongue: Ryodan Killian St. James. I liked it. It was polished, urbane as the man he pretended to be. *Killian* was like *killing*, sharp-edged, and intriguing. *St. James* was lofty, old money, blue-blood and power. "Oh, now that's just a pile of bull," I said crossly. "That's so bloody Irish and you're not. How could you possibly have an Irish name?" It wasn't even close to anything I'd ever come up with. And that made me even madder. I did something then so incredibly bizarre and plebian and . . . and . . . *juvenile* that I couldn't even wrap my brain around it. I thought: *Dani Killian St. James*. It had a nice ring to it. Wait, what?

"It wasn't my first," he said. "Though the initials are the same. It's the one I took when I made my home here. We change our names to fit the clime, the time. I've kept that one awhile."

"So, you talked to Kat, she told you my hand turned black, and from that mere fact alone you deduced I was turning into a Hunter?" At least I'd had the vision to go on, the *Ready? You fly, too.* Although I couldn't decide if it implied I would actually physically transform into a Hunter or just turn completely black, become lethal to the touch, yet receive the small consolation prize of being able to astral-project into the stars on occasion. Superhero rules are pretty obscure.

He inclined his head in one of those imperious nods.

"Some people might have thought it had infected me, and I was dying," I told him. I'd briefly entertained the notion myself. It hadn't resonated in my gut and, although I prize my brain, I value my gut just as highly. A lot of times more.

"I'm not some people."

"You're not even people."

"There is that. Are you so sure you are?"

I shot him a sharp look. "*You* don't think I am. And why didn't I know you met me before I thought we met?"

His gaze shuttered.

"You wanted rules? Fine, I'm making one. One of 'ours,' which means we both obey it. Full disclosure or don't bloody well interfere in my life. Don't even try to be a part of it. Don't you think," I threw his own words back at him, "it's time we cut everything loose? I might be gone soon. Soaring around in space. A Hunter. You might never see me again. I bet *then* you'll be sorry you didn't talk to me." I didn't say, *I bet then you'll be sorry you went away for two years and wasted them.* But I wanted to. Except people have to want to stay with you and he clearly hadn't.

He jerked and snarled, "I'll bloody well be sorry I didn't do more than that with you, Dani. I wanted to make love to you. I wanted to fuck you, I wanted to cut loose with you like I've never been able to cut loose with a woman in my entire existence. I wanted to explore every ounce of that brilliant mind and every inch of that powerful body of yours, learn your deepest desires, be the one to rock your goddamn world, watch the great Dani O'Malley abandon herself to passion, see her in the one place she's never conflicted, and revel in being alive."

Holy hell, he felt it, too.

"The Nine have no equals," he said, eyes glittering with crimson fire. "We always hold back. An eternity of being careful. It's not our nature to be restrained. Especially not when we fuck."

I'd never thought about it that way. Like me, he could break people without even meaning to. Restrained sex: oxymoron any way you looked at it. To have so much inside you—all coiled up and ready to explode, waiting, always waiting for someone to come along who can see it, who can handle it, and never being able to let it out—I know what it feels like.

Pain.

A pain that, unlike the others I've mastered, I've never been able to figure out how to stop feeling. I don't know that you can. It's life trying to happen.

"A woman like you is a once-in-an-eternity opportunity. Every bloody one of us was waiting to see what you'd become when you grew up. I told you, you're a fucking tsunami. I knew it even then. You didn't smell like other people."

The Nine had been watching me. Waiting to see what kind of woman I'd become.

"And Christ, you ran on pure adrenaline, unchecked aggression and sky-fucking-high dreams. The most fearless thing I'd ever seen. God damn it, Dani, everything I've done since the day I met you has been about keeping you alive. To never cage you or take away your choices, to see you rise, watch you become."

"What? A bloody Hunter?" I demanded.

"I had no fucking idea that might happen," he snarled. "If I'd known your hand had turned black, I would have factored that into my linchpin theories about you, and drawn conclusions sooner. It might have affected my actions, changed them. You withheld a critical piece of information." He was angry about it, and not even trying to hide it, his face no longer cool and composed, but savage, fangs distending.

"As if *you* don't all the time," I flung, on the verge of vibrating, melting into the slipstream without even meaning to. Papers on his desk gusted, his hair ruffled.

"Breathe," he ordered. "Get control of yourself."

"Practice the preach. Your fangs are showing." But I closed my eyes and took a moment to center myself. Then my eyes flew open and I said, "What the hell, Ryodan? What if I actually become a *Hunter*?" My voice broke on the last word, pain lacing it. Was I just one of those people who never got to belong? In this world but not of it? Never, ever *once* really of it?

He was silent a long moment, as if trying to decide what to say. A muscle worked in his jaw. Finally, he said carefully, "If you become a Hunter, perhaps you won't care about this world, or those of us in it anymore. Perhaps it's what you're meant to be. Your journey takes you somewhere else."

"You don't believe in Fate," I rejected flatly. "You believe in you."

"Ah, Stardust, I've seen too many patterns unfold during my existence that hold a startling, cohesive symmetry. There's a plan and it's way the fuck bigger than you and me. The universe has an agenda. For a long time, everything I did was in defiance of it. Then I began trying to protect that agenda, so I could, at least, have some small say in the details."

I said irritably, "I'd miss you. And I'd definitely still care about our world." I love our world. It's always my second priority. Survival is first.

"I'd like to believe that. But maybe some people are destined for larger things. And, according to you, you didn't miss me at all for the past two years. I hardly see you missing me now, if you become something even less human."

"Perhaps it's not inevitable. Perhaps I can make it go away." I ignored his other comments. I still didn't know where he'd gone or why. And I was never telling him a single thing I missed about him until he told me that.

"Perhaps. Time will tell. In the meantime, once again, we've got a world to save. Perhaps we'll need a Hunter to save it."

"Perhaps," I countered, "we'll only need a little bit of a Hunter's power. And perhaps, I can turn it off once we've fixed things, and be normal again."

"'Again' implies you once were that way. You weren't. And there's nothing in this world you'd hate more than being normal."

He was right about that. "What would you do, if you were me?"

"I'd keep an open mind, consider all possibilities. That's all any of us can do. Life is a box you don't get to open all at once. You can touch it, pick it up, shake it even, but you can only guess at the contents. There's a hole in the top of the box where things come out, on their own timetable, on their own terms. You think you have things figured out," he said, with a note of bitterness in his voice, "only to find you saw everything completely wrong, didn't understand a bloody bit of it. So, you wait to see what pops out next. And you go on living in the meantime."

Sound advice. Pretty much what I'd concluded, without the box metaphor. "What's on the agenda today, boss?"

"Ryodan. Let's just be you and me for a while. No role-playing, no superheroes. Just a man and a woman who admire each other and drive each other bugfuck crazy, spending time together. Let's make that rule number two."

"What's rule number one and who gets to make it?" I demanded.

He met my gaze and held it a long moment. Behind those remote silver eyes, storms rushed and swirled. Immense, thunderous storms. He was upset. That worried me. One of my rules goes something like this: if an Unseelie prince says "Run," run. Another is: if Ryodan looks upset, be afraid. Be very, very afraid.

But me and him, we don't do fear. We plunge back into our worlds, and wait for the next thing to pop out of the box. Prepared to face it.

"I'll leave that one up to you," he said finally. "You get to decide our number one rule." His gaze added, *Make it a good one. I'll never break it.*

We exchanged a smile then unlike any we'd shared before. An unguarded expression of warmth and respect.

Unfortunately, it did nothing at all to chase away the storms.

From either of our eyes.

TWENTY-EIGHT

———— • • ————

A momentary lapse of reason

that binds a life for life

Christian's castle was . . . atmospheric, to say the least.

It sprawled atop a high cliff, towering over the vales below, affording a clear view of potential invaders. Though it was morning, not one speck of sunlight penetrated the bank of gloomy thunderclouds overhead. That smothering, low-hanging ceiling of slate stretched from horizon to horizon, as far as the eye could see. The only illumination was wan lightning that sizzled and crackled high above, causing the clouds to briefly flicker a slightly paler shade of depression.

The castle was vast, rambling across a mighty bluff, dropping sharply away on three sides. On the fourth, the wild, crashing sea slammed into the base of the towering dark bluff.

The only way in was a winding path gouged into the side of the cliff. Once one topped that path, a long road with stone walls on each side led to a perimeter stone wall that enclosed the entire estate, broken only by a mighty drawbridge that was up and heavily barred. Then the winding streets of the keep proper began. Tall stone towers stretched up into the dense gray ceiling, vanishing within. The castle soared and ducked, towered then slumped to low garrisonlike buildings. A full two-thirds of it was crumbling, yielding to the passage of time. The remaining third had been restored.

The ocean frothed and foamed beyond it, crashing into rocks far below. The entire estate was a study in angry slates, broody grays, and dark, tension-filled shadows, broken only by that wan intermittent lightning flickering high above.

We landed atop a low turret and I moved away from him, hugging myself to stay warm, my hair whipping about my head in the wild salty breeze. "Why is it so cold and gloomy here?" I had to speak loudly to be heard over the wind. "Is it because of you?"

"Sean. We affect the climate with our mood. His mood has been foul for a long time. The sun hasn't shone on my keep since a few weeks after his arrival. What grass remains for him to test himself on is pale and sparse. He said last week if he runs out of grass within my kingdom, he's leaving."

I sucked in a sharp breath. "To go where?"

Christian shrugged. "I've no idea, lass, and he wouldn't say. He's not speaking to me right now. Perhaps into Faery, or the Unseelie kingdom, perhaps into the Silvers and beyond. We can't lose him. We have to get him back somehow." As my teeth began to chatter from the cold, he said, "But let's get you inside, lass. It's warm within. I'll see you fed and set you on the path to Sean."

π

I shivered as I picked my way up crumbling, dusty stone stairs. During a hasty meal of cheese and bread, Christian had told me a bit more about Sean, concluding with directions on how to find him. He felt it best I approach alone, as Sean could feel Christian as he drew near and grew even angrier. *Then the bloody clouds consume the entire castle,* inside and out, he'd told me. *It's not pleasant.*

As I'd wandered the eccentric keep, crammed with towering stacks of ancient books and manuscripts, chests and bottles, Ryodan had texted repeatedly and I texted back, answering his questions about Dani, wanting desperately to call him and find out what was going on. But I had my own battle here, and from what Christian had told me, it was going to be a difficult if not terrifying one.

I paused to catch my breath before topping the last few rounds of the spiraling stone staircase. Sean had retreated to the ruined part of the castle, the far tower where, Christian told me, he was wont to loom, a brooding dark shadow, staring out over the sea.

Unlike the rest of the castle, which Christian kept toasty warm somehow, it was freezing here. I tugged the woolen throw Christian had given me more snugly around my shoulders as I finished my climb.

Then only a door remained between me and Sean.

Two long years plus change had passed since I'd last seen him.

I paused again and closed my eyes as Ryodan's words from long ago floated up in my mind. Words I hadn't heeded, and suddenly I was back in his office of glass, staring down at Sean, and Ryodan was saying, *If you don't tell Sean that Cruce is fucking you while you sleep, it will destroy what you have with him more certainly than any job in my club could. That, down there,* he'd pointed to Sean serving a drink to a pretty, nearly naked Seelie, *is a bump in the road, a test of temptation and fidelity. If your Sean loves you, he will pass it with flying colors. Cruce is a test of your fucking soul.*

He'd also said: *Your god may love soul mates but man does not. Such a couple is vulnerable, particularly if they are fool enough to let the world see how shiny and happy they are. Their risk rises tenfold during times of war. There are two courses a couple in such circumstances can chart: Go deep into the country and hide as far from humanity as possible, hoping like hell nobody finds them. Because the world will tear them apart. Or sink up to their necks in the stench and filth and corruption of their war-torn existence. See things for what they are. Drop your blinders and raise the sewer to eye level; admit you're swimming in shit. If you don't acknowledge the turd hurtling down the drain toward you, you can't dodge it. You have to face every challenge together. Because the world* will *tear you apart.*

Right on both counts, Ryodan, I thought with a sad smile. I should have listened. But I'd been ashamed. Afraid. It had been utterly against my will, but I'd enjoyed it. What does a woman do with that? I'd told myself over the years that it wasn't my fault. I'd been used at the hands of the most powerful Fae prince in existence, who could make me *think* I was feeling anything. Still . . . the shame. I'd never wanted another man inside me but Sean. Yet I'd hungered for Cruce in a way I'd never hungered for Sean. Even if that was an illusion he'd forced upon me, I could still taste the memory of it. And I hated Cruce for that!

I knew why Sean was angry. I knew why he was bitter. We know each other's every gesture, every twitch, pain, fear, hope, and dream. A deception lived and breathed between us, and it had taken on a dark, rapacious life of its own. If I was to have any hope at all of helping him become the man I believed he could be, he wasn't the only one that needed to face his demons today.

Inhaling sharply, I squared my shoulders and pushed open

the door, praying there was validity to the adage "and the truth will set you free."

π

"Why have you come, Kat?" Sean said in a low, angry voice, without turning.

He stood on the far side of the circular stone chamber, framed in a tall, narrow opening cut into the stone, the wind gusting waist-length black hair around his body, ruffling the feathers of enormous raven wings. "Leave. Now. There's nothing for you here."

If I'd not seen Christian first, and felt his heart, Sean would have terrified me. My love was once a handsome, rugged fisherman, toiling on the ocean, having turned his muscled-from-pulling-nets-all-day back on the mighty, deadly O'Bannion clan. With his black hair, dark eyes, and quick, easy smiles, I'd learned to trust him in that frightened, wide-open state in which I'd spent my earliest years. Of all the people I'd met, his had been the only heart that rang true to me, void of complicity.

Despite his appearance, nearly identical to Christian and Cruce, he didn't frighten me now. I could feel him, I was close enough. He was lost within, drifting in a land far more barren and wasted than what spread, so ugly and black, beyond these castle walls. His sociopathic cousin Rocky O'Bannion's credo, inscribed on the back of a watch of gold and diamonds he always wore, had been: Isolate the mark. He'd sworn that every man and woman, regardless of education, pedigree, or wealth, would ultimately fall prey to it; that we couldn't stand alone. Yet Sean had been perched in dangerous isolation for two years and hadn't succumbed. That gave me hope. "I disagree," I said, moving farther into the icy room. "*You're* here."

"I may be. But Sean is not," he said bitterly. "He's been gone a long time."

"I don't believe you."

When he whirled in a storm of dark feathers and flashing, alien eyes, I inhaled sharply but stood my ground.

My love, I thought. Oh, my love, I'm so sorry.

Both born into powerful Irish crime families, we'd spent our entire lives running from the darkness of our own blood.

But the darkness had found him.

I hazed the vision of my eyes, the better to focus the gaze of my heart.

"Get out, Kat. I don't want you here. You're nothing to me," he said coldly. "Less than nothing. And don't bloody do that to me. You don't want to feel it. Leave now and I'll let you live."

If I was nothing, why then was the image frozen in his heart, of the day I'd insisted he accept me and my child without knowing? The day I'd erected an impenetrable wall between us and shut him out.

I blurted in a swift rush of words because I knew I'd never get it out otherwise that truth, that terrible, divisive truth that had been eating me alive inside, and cut the ties that bound us: "I lied, Sean. I lied to you. Cruce came to me while I slept. He raped me in my dreams. Rae might be his." I began to weep the instant it was out, I felt as if an enormous pressure, constantly crushing me, had vanished from my soul. I wept with relief, I wept with sorrow. I wept with confliction because I love Rae. I love her with all my heart and she might be my enemy's child. What do you do with that?

Sean jerked violently, shuddering from head to toe with the intensity of his emotion. Raven-veined ice exploded in the room, sheeting the floor, climbing the stone walls, dripping from the ceiling in dark crystal stalactites. His voice was deafening when he exploded, "Cruce raped—" He broke off, unable to finish the sentence, jerking violently, hands fisting. "That sonofabitch. That son of a fucking . . ." He trailed off, snarling, body straining from the effort to control himself.

With a mere emotion he'd turned the room into a cave of dark ice. I shivered, crying silently, but stood my ground. He wouldn't ice me. Not my Sean.

"Fuck, Kat!" he cried then. "Fuck! Why didn't you tell me?"

"I'm so sorry," I said, voice breaking. "I wanted to tell you but I was so ashamed. And the longer I didn't tell you, the longer it went on, the less possible it became." I didn't say that I felt complicit. I couldn't begin to explain how trapped it had made me feel, not without telling him why. That I'd also felt pleasure from it. "You hadn't begun to change. You were a man, he was a prince. How could you have battled Cruce? What if he'd killed you?"

"I thought she was Kasteo's!" His voice broke. "I thought you cheated on me with one of the Nine!"

"Och, no, Sean! I was pregnant before that. Didn't you do the math?"

"She could have been early!"

"She wasn't. Kasteo taught me to shut out the pain of the world, he taught me to become strong but never—" I broke off, shaking my head violently. "Kasteo's heart belongs to someone else. Not me. Never me. And my heart has always belonged to you. I love you, Sean, it's always been you. Don't you remember what we promised each other?"

"That was then. Before I became the monster I am. You'd never have pledged such a troth to what I've become. I'm what raped you!"

"If you weaken, I'll be strong," I said, through tears. It was the first line of the vow we'd taken together when we were young, the day we'd run off to Paradise Point by the lighthouse, dressed up as if it were our wedding day, had our own ceremony, pledging our hearts and souls together. Too much passion burns. Tenderness fuses. We'd always been tender with each other. And that passion we shared was rich and good and strong. Until a Fae prince had shattered it with lust inflated by illusion. And made me compare. Never compare. The moment you do, you destroy what gifts you possess, and your gifts are precious. "Let me be strong for you now."

He spun then, gave me his back, and turned to stare out at the stormy, lashing sea. "It's too late, Kat. Far too late for that."

I refused to believe that. "If you get lost, I'll be your way home," I said softly.

"Go away! I'm not the man you used to know. There's nothing left of him and I have no bloody home."

I shook my head as I wiped tears from my cheeks. Sean was not staying lost within his ugly, horrible place in this ugly, horrible land. Nor was he leaving alone to go God knew where. The Kat I'd once been would have quailed before such a creature, that looked so much like Cruce. The woman I'd been before Kasteo wouldn't have been able to handle the waves of pain, misery, and self-loathing gusting from Sean's soul, slamming into me, icy spears, piercing my heart, trying to destroy my hope.

But I'd learned, locked beneath Chester's by Ryodan, trapped with one of the Nine. I'd learned what I needed to know in order to fix the problem I'd made by failing to heed Ryodan's warnings in the first place. I wasn't the woman I'd once been. And, I was angry now, too.

Ryodan had so clearly warned me that the world destroyed soul mates. I'd not only refused to listen, I'd helped the world do it. I'd been the one to divide us. And I would, by God, put us back together.

"If you despair, I'll bring you joy," I said, speaking the third line of our vows. "Do you hear me, Sean O'Bannion? Joy. You're going to feel it again. You don't believe it now but you will. We took those vows for a reason. We made them up together, carefully paring it down to what was most important to us. We did it because we knew the taint of our own blood was strong. We knew one day we might slip. We knew how much pressure they put on us to be like them. How treacherous and sly they were, how they liked to tempt, ridicule, and bully us. We vowed to never let one another fall without helping each other stand back up and find our way. You're going to stand back up. You're going to fight what's been done to you. I'm going to fight it with you, with everything I've got. I vow that I will never again give you anything but truth. And one day you *will* take those vows with me again. And one day you *will* say that last line again. And you'll bloody well mean it. And that's what we'll use to contain the darkness within you."

"It's not that simple, Kat," he growled. "You have no bloody clue what kind of monster you're dealing with."

"You say that to the woman who was raped by one like you, and flown here by another like you. I know exactly what you are. My Sean, in trouble. But not alone. Never alone again."

"It's not possible. I've tried. Bloody hell, have I tried! I'm not Christian. I'm not that strong. He came from a line of pure hearts. I come from a corrupt bloodline."

Christian had clan who loved him, who'd fought for him, fought alongside him. Sean had no one. His entire family was dead, and I'd let him slip away, into darkness. The thing I'd vowed never to do. When had I stopped believing in us? I knew the answer to that: When I'd begun to brick and mortar a wall of shame and lies between us. When Ryodan had warned me that we were in peril. "Argue for your limitations, you make them yours. Together, we're going to argue for your possibilities. It's entirely possible Rae is your child. If you still want that paternity test . . ." That might give me a foothold, get him turned back toward the world again. And perhaps the test would be positive for Sean, and perhaps it would be inconclusive, if she were Cruce's. Perhaps whatever passed as Fae DNA didn't register. And inconclusive wasn't quite so troubling. Human hearts are funny that way. We let ourselves believe gentle lies. But it would be *his* choice this time, not me keeping the truth from him.

A tremor ran through his body, ruffling his wings. He said nothing for a long time, then, "What are the odds?"

"Fifty-fifty," I told him flatly, stung by the thought he believed I might have taken other lovers. "There's never been anyone but you and—against my will—him. You've never met Rae, Sean. You should. She's lovely, with your hair and eyes. Fun-filled, good and loving. That doesn't sound like Cruce to me. Still, she has one of two fathers: you or him, either way she has an Unseelie prince for a da. Cruce is dead." I hoped. "You're not. Wouldn't you rather my daughter, and quite possibly *yours,* as well, grow up knowing you as her father, not him?"

He turned then and looked at me, with a glimmer of emotion in his eyes, and I inhaled sharply. Deep within, I could feel a faint, weak stirring of hope. For two long years no one had come for him. Perhaps he thought I knew where he was, what he was doing, and had chosen not to come.

"I had no idea where you were, or what had happened to you," I said, fanning the flame of that hope. "I thought you didn't care anymore. I thought you'd left because you despised me. I missed you, Sean. God, I missed you more than words can say." I closed my eyes as a fresh burn of tears stung them. How many times had I imagined me and Rae walking the fields near the abbey with Sean? Being a family, no matter whose child she was. Cooking a meal of fresh-caught fish, watching the stars come out, tucking her in, making love until dawn.

"Give us one more chance, Sean," I begged. "Please, say you'll try."

TWENTY-NINE

— • • • —

There is a castle on a cloud

S OME DAYS DUBLIN IS so beautiful it slays me, and this
morning was one of those days, as Ryodan and I hurried
down cobbled streets toward Barrons Books & Baubles.

An overnight, driving rain had left puddles as still and glassy
as mirrors on the pavement, reflecting buildings and shops and
sky. Everything was glistening wet, scrubbed clean, gilded by
streaks of sunshine slicing through clouds. It was one of those
startlingly crisp mornings, done in vivid grays and blacks and
silvers, splashed with colorful flowers blooming in planters and
trees dotting the curbs.

Ryodan had asked me to narrow down the time frame of the
bookstore's disappearance but I wasn't able to give him better
than a two-week window. It had been that long since I'd last
passed by before discovering it gone, which meant it may have
vanished two weeks before, or that same day, the day before he'd
shattered my door.

We crisscrossed the lots repeatedly, searching for clues. Staring down, gazing up, poking in the few bits of debris rolling like tumbleweeds across concrete.

Aside from an impression of unnatural distortion, there wasn't a single enlightening bit of evidence to be found. The mystery of Barrons Books & Baubles had donned the equivalent of "that woman's" battle dress.

"I've got nothing," I told Ryodan a few minutes later, when we met up where the stately, transomed front entrance had once been.

"This makes no sense," he murmured as a text alert sounded on his phone. He removed it from his pocket, read it and frowned. Another alert went off and he grabbed my heavily sleeved and gloved arm while reading it and began tugging me across the lot toward the alley.

"What? Where are we going?" I demanded.

"Just come."

"You don't have to drag me," I growled.

"I'm not so sure about that." He was dashing me along so quickly I barely had time to register where we were heading, but I did and dug my heels in instantly. "Oh, no, hell no! I am *not* losing time again." My city needed me now, not months or years later. Shazam needed me.

He gave a sharp jerk and I went stumbling forward, plunging into the wall behind Barrons Books & Baubles, into that precise portal I'd once entered so long ago then spent endless years Silverside, trying to get back home.

I squished into the wall. Then I *was* the wall. Then I squirted out on the other side, into the infamous White Room, which still lacked tired starlings, where I stood, scowling ferociously at ten enormous mirrors, one of which had so nefariously dumped me into the ancient, inimical Hall of All Days a lifetime ago.

I blinked. The White Room had changed. It was no longer a completely blank, featureless room. Someone had redecorated, or, like everything else in the world, it had been treated to a magical upgrade.

Ornate white moldings crowned the walls, melting into a lavishly transomed ceiling from which a dozen chandeliers hung, glittering like ice in the sunlight. The walls were wainscoted from floor to ceiling with ornately embellished panels. The floor was glossy white marble. The mirrors, however, were exactly the same, hanging without visible means of support, some twirling lazily within elaborate frames, others motionless, in thin, welded chain-link borders. A few of the looking glasses were black as night, some milky, others swirling with unnerving shadows.

They'd once again been shuffled.

I really hated this room.

When Ryodan appeared beside me, I said crossly, "I am *not* going back into the White Mansion. Or the hall. I don't care what your reasons are."

"Barrons texted. He wanted us off site quickly so we'd stop drawing attention to it."

"Barrons!" I exclaimed. "Where is he?"

"We're going to him now."

I inhaled deeply, girding myself. I was all in, wherever he was, but I had unpleasant memories of this place. Going through a mirror and getting lost for years. Coming out chased by the Crimson Hag and killing Ryodan and Barrons. More recently, going in to save Mac, returning to an entirely different Dublin and a deeply angry Dancer. I'd lost weeks I hadn't gotten to spend with him and, bloody hell, if I'd known our time together was going to be so short—well, the truth was I'd still have gone in, because it was necessary and that's what I do. Still, I'd lost so much time in my life.

"We won't be losing time now," Ryodan said. "We're using a different stack of Silvers that bypass the White Mansion completely." When he pushed into the third mirror from the left, a Silver I'd never entered before, I rolled my eyes, shook my head, and plunged in behind him.

After a long, twisting, unpleasant stretch of myself through whatever the Silvers are made of, I stumbled out—I swear the mirrors do that on purpose to you, to keep you off balance—into the heart of Barrons Books & Baubles.

I just stood there a moment, glowing quietly, Harry Potter reunited with Hogwarts. I was in my magical place again where I'd once felt, so long ago—for the first time ever—that I might just belong somewhere. The place holds a sacred, mystical ambience for me. I love BB&B. Love, love, *love* it. It smells of high adventure bound in leather casings, crammed on shelves waiting to be freed, of Mac's peaches and cream candles, of Barrons's fine furnishings and wool rugs, and the spice of my kind of danger. The sounds of this store are music to my soul, the tinkling of the front doorbell, which I intended to bang at least once while I was here, the soft hiss of the gas fire in an enameled hearth, the quiet hum of the fridge behind Mac's counter.

Mac. I couldn't wait to talk to her. I had so much to tell her, so much to ask.

I turned slowly, drinking it all in, the elegant furnishings, the way the sun slanted through the leaded glass windows, my beloved, belled door, the strings of colored lights draping the bookcases, the stockings hung on the mantel, the tall, decorated Christmas tree in the corner—Wait, what? Had we lost time after all? It wasn't December!

"Why the bloody hell do you have a Christmas tree up, Barrons?" Ryodan growled behind me.

I spun and caught my breath, smiling. Jericho Barrons is one of the few constants in my world. Other things might change, but Barrons never does. He's impervious, immutable, a giant, obdurate stone of a man that not even water can carve. Like Ryodan.

His nostrils flared and a tiny muscle worked in his jaw. "I don't. That was Mac's idea. At least it's not pink this time."

A flash of movement caught my eye on a tall bookcase behind him. "Uh, Barrons, why is there a lemur in your store?"

His face could not have gone darker. "Mac's idea, too."

"What are you feeding him?" *Was* he feeding him? The little guy looked awfully lean to me.

"If I could catch the furry fuck, I'd throw him out the bloody window. He's been shitting everywhere. You have black flames on your face, Dani. What has Ryodan been doing to you? He knows better than to tattoo the face when there's body left."

He shot Ryodan a questioning look then, and something passed between them I didn't understand. Ryodan jerked his head once, Barrons nodded. They were having an utterly private conversation.

Years ago I'd have ignored them. I didn't this time. I wondered if I could push in, like I had at Elyreum. I stared into Ryodan's eyes, letting mine shift out of focus, and thought about the tattoo he'd inked at the base of my spine. About his blood and mine intermingled and the dangerous power of such spells, the inadvertent connections they forged. I emptied my brain of thought, expanded my senses and—wham!

—don't bloody have any idea. Think she's turning into a Hunter.

Shock and a deep undertow of sorrow. *Christ, of all the things you guessed, that was never one of them. What are you doing here? She didn't call IISS, or I'd have known. You aren't supposed to be here.*

I know.

How did you get back?

I told you, no bloody clue. One moment I was there, the next I was—

"Stop that!" They both snarled at once.

I staggered from the force with which they'd ejected me from their thoughts.

You were only in his head, not mine. Barrons shot me a dark look. *I felt you in his head and you heard me there so don't get all cocky about it.*

I arched a brow, feeling pretty cocky anyway. I'd pushed into Ryodan's impenetrable head. Damn.

Aloud, I said, "Where are we and how did you know we were in the lot?"

"I glanced out the window."

Stymied, I was headed for the door to accomplish two objectives: bang that bell and see where we were, when Barrons thundered, "Don't open it!"

I cut him a startled look and went to the window instead. I stared, blinked, stared again. BB&B was resting in the middle of fluffy white clouds, with a narrow view through them to the empty lots below. It was sunny up here, gloomy below. I pressed my cheek to the window and thought, Holy Romulan cloaking device, the store was invisible from the outside! "Good grief, we're in the movie *Up*. What did you do? How did you float BB&B?" If I'd walked out the door, I'd have plunged. "Don't you dare toss that poor little lemur out," I added worriedly.

"I didn't float it. Mac did."

I glanced around, dying to see her. This was turning out to be a banner day. Ryodan, Barrons, and Mac; my lions, tigers, and bears had returned. "Where is she?" I asked eagerly.

"That's what we need to discuss," Barrons said grimly.

π

The Fae had never had any intention of accepting Mac as their new queen, Barrons told us as we gathered in the rear seating area of the bookstore on Mac's favorite Chesterfield sofa.

Infuriated by the discovery that their past queen, who'd forcibly removed them from the human realm long ago, had begun her existence as a human, compounded by the discovery that their trusted Seelie prince, V'lane, was actually an Unseelie prince, the Light Court had gone hardcore purist. Only a Seelie would be permitted to lead in the future, only a Seelie would become the next royalty. Thus committed, they'd put a high price on Jayne's head, determined to kill him so the next prince born would be one of their own.

"There are now two Light Court princes that are full-blooded Fae," Barrons told us. "They conceal their presence from you."

"One," I corrected. "I killed one last night."

Barrons arched a brow. "You ignored Mac's decree."

"We had no choice. You left and never sent word. We had no idea if you were even still alive," I said flatly.

"No thanks to the Fae. They demanded she come to court, rolled out the bloody red carpet. For a few days they played nice, feigning willingness to accept her. Gratitude that she'd repaired the world and destroyed the Unseelie. But their ancient powers were being reinvigorated by the Song. After four days in Faery, meeting with every caste, giving Mac no time to try to learn how to access the power the queen passed to her, the attacks began.

Forty-two attacks on her life in twelve hours," he growled, dark eyes flashing.

"They came after her even though she has the spear and you at her side?" I said incredulously. "Are they nuts?"

"Stealth attacks in large numbers, trying to separate us. They were willing to die to see one of them take her place. We needed time. A queen who can't use her power is no queen at all. We returned to Dublin, I stacked Silvers, and took her to a chamber I know in the White Mansion; the first room the Unseelie King built for his concubine, long before the White Mansion came to be. A chamber where time moves so slowly it doesn't even crawl. A day in our world is decades there. Best guess, she's been sitting in that room for nearly a century."

"And you? How long have you been sitting here?" Ryodan demanded.

"Irrelevant."

"Why are you here, if she's in the White Mansion?" I asked. Barrons would never leave Mac alone, unguarded.

"She's not. She moved things. I was in the White Mansion, outside the chamber, keeping guard. Abruptly, I found myself in the bookstore with her chamber connected to it by a door that didn't exist before." He gestured over his shoulder, at a door to the right of the enameled fireplace in the rear conversation area. "Perhaps she sensed a threat approaching and moved us. Then things began to appear, change. Be glad you didn't come the day she turned everything pink. If you never see a bloody, tufted pink Chesterfield, count yourself lucky. She's testing her powers. See-ing what she can do. The lemur should vanish soon. Most of it does."

"Is she eating, drinking? Doing anything?" I asked. God, I

just wanted to *see* her. So many times over the past few years, I'd hungered to talk to her. Now especially, with Ryodan back. Me and Mac are a lot alike yet at the same time couldn't be more different. She gets emotion but doesn't always get logic. We're yin-yang and good for each other that way.

"No. Not only does time pass very differently there, I doubt she needs to anymore. She's turning Fae. I opened the door. Once. The temporal clash nearly killed me."

"When's the last time you ate?" Ryodan demanded.

"Too long."

"Go. I'll remain."

Barrons sliced his head in negation.

"You don't look good."

"We make our own choices, don't we? We don't listen to the counsel of others. How did that work out for you?"

"For fuck's sake, let it go. We argued about it then. It seemed the wisest option at the time and you know it," Ryodan said coolly.

"Time. That's always the problem, isn't it?"

I had no idea what they were talking about once again, but silently I agreed. Not enough time with Dancer. Now, not enough with Ryodan before my body had become lethal to the touch.

Ryodan glanced at me. I didn't even need him to open his mouth to know what he was going to say. "Just go," I said irritably, "have your alpha Nine catch-up time. I need to do some research anyway." To Barrons, I said, "Books on the old Earth gods, point me to them."

He did, and as they headed back to Barrons's office, I loped upstairs in the general direction of the lemur who'd just swung up over the balustrade, to educate myself on our new, ancient enemies.

π

They say that those who forget their past are condemned to repeat it. What, then, are those who *erase* their past condemned to do?

Be devoured by it?

Destroy all hope of a future?

Because that's pretty much what had happened to our past—a giant eraser had been taken to it.

The Celts were known for not writing things down, ours was an ancient, oral tradition.

Then the Romans had come along and plastered their god names over ours, and if that hadn't obfuscated our origins enough, Christianity stormed in and pasted yet more names, images, and legends over our gods until we were left with little more than the likes of leprechauns, diminutive, mischievous fairies, and trolls.

We're a stubborn people, we Irish. We don't go down easily. The only way Christianity had been able to eradicate our history so completely was by erecting churches on our sacred sites, obscuring their origin and purpose, and renaming our pagan feast days, transforming them into Christian celebrations with none of our traditions behind them.

Our gods were a hot mess of slanted, rewritten press.

I read for hours and instead of discovering answers, found yet more questions. The Fomorians had been stirred in with the Fae, blended with deities from all over Western Europe, and many allegedly defeated or converted by various saints. Saint Patrick was credited not only with driving all snakes out of Ireland, when scientific study conclusively supported that Ireland had never even had snakes to begin with, but meeting with gods from our past and after long discourse converting even *them* to Christianity.

In other words, our history was shit.

God names and the Tuatha De Danaan names had become largely interchangeable.

Oh yeah, erase that monument to whatever we did that was terrible, so it can bite us in the ass in the future. What goes around comes around, if you're foolish enough to let it. That's why I remember every single thing I've done, stare at myself in a mirror and meet those eyes that have screwed up, fully aware of my failings, because the day I let myself forget them is the day I could start doing them all over again.

Never. Going. To. Happen.

I pilfered Barrons's bookstore, gathering up tomes for further reading, jotting names in my notepad on my phone from Abhartach to Balor, Morrigan to Lugh, Dagda and Aine, Medb and Daire, sketchy scant notes about each.

I couldn't find a single mention of AOZ or a human-abducting god anywhere.

As I was scowling down at my phone, it abruptly turned pink, exploded in sparkling hearts all over the screen, obliterating my notepad, replacing it with a flowery script:

I'm getting there, Dani. Be back soon. Miss you. Love you so much!!! Mac.

I smiled from ear to ear then burst out laughing. Pink and hearts. Mac was still Mac, despite turning Fae. Mac would *always* be Mac. She'd been through so much, survived possession by the greatest evil known to man or Fae, defeated the enormous psychopathic sentience that had consumed her. Fae knowledge and power would never obliterate Barrons's Rainbow Girl.

There was no way to text her back and the note vanished, but I was quick enough to snap a screen shot of the message before it disappeared. A memento.

A *promise*. Right up there with a pinky swear.

I glanced out the window at the darkening sky, gathered up the books I was taking with me, and went downstairs to find bags to toss them in. I was rummaging behind the cash register when Barrons and Ryodan walked in.

Barrons took one look at my books and growled, "Those were in a locked case."

Duh. "I'm the one that took them out."

Dark eyes bored into mine. "No way you picked that lock."

"I know, right?" I replied crossly. I'm a superb lock picker. It's one of my specialties and the damn thing had defeated me. "I broke the glass with the hilt of my sword."

"You. Broke. The glass."

Good grief, Mac told me Barrons got pissy when you messed with his stuff. "You may as well know I took your bike and Land Rover, too, before the garage disappeared," I informed him, just to clear the air between us.

He stared at me as if I were a specimen on a slide.

"Mac texted," I said to distract him. "She's okay."

He went preternaturally still, so motionless he vanished from my sight for a moment, melting into the wallpaper behind him. Then he was back, saying softly, "She texted. You. Let me see it."

Ow, I guess she hadn't bothered to text him. Just sent him Christmas trees and lemurs. I handed him my phone, with the screen shot thumbed up.

He stared at it a long moment, shadows swirling in his dark eyes, and I saw a flash of such pure, unguarded hunger in them that it staggered me. Theirs is unity, a symbiosis, a partnership I dream of, wolves that chose to pack up and hunt together, soldiers who will always have each other's backs, no matter what, no sin, no transgression too great.

He ran his thumb over the screen as if he might somehow touch Mac through it. And I thought, Holy hell, Jericho Barrons has a . . . not a vulnerability but yes, that. A weakness, a need. Mac. I'd seen it in her, too. It was what bothered me about love. Wanting someone so much that you felt like you couldn't breathe when they went away, so intensely that your world lost half its colors and you were oddly suspended until they returned. Like my past two years. Vulnerability any way you looked at it. I glanced uneasily at Ryodan then quickly away. Losing Shazam had nearly destroyed me. Losing Dancer had taken me down again.

Then Barrons's face was remote, cool and unreadable. He pivoted sharply, stalked to the rear fireplace, rummaged about on the mantel then returned and handed me my phone back, along with an envelope. "Mac asked me to give you this when I next saw you."

I took it, a sealed white envelope with no writing on it. "What is it?"

"I have no idea. She merely asked me to make sure you got it."

I wanted to tear it open right then. I didn't. I would look at it later, in private.

"Aren't you going to open it?" he demanded.

"If it's anything to do with Mac, I'll text you."

He inclined his head. "And the moment she comes out, I'll let you know. Until then, give the bookstore a wide berth. Draw no attention to us. The Fae haven't found her yet and I intend to keep it that way."

I nodded. "Feed the lemur. Surely you have food in here somewhere. At least put a bowl of water out." Poor little guy had sat on a bookcase above my head the entire time I'd read. He was lonely. And hungry.

I tucked the envelope in my pocket, packed my books in BB&B bags, and Ryodan and I left, pushing back into the mirror, returning to dusk-cloaked Dublin below.

π

Later I sat at what remained of my dining room table, sans several leafs, with my books spread out, the envelope from Mac in my hand.

Shazam was nowhere to be seen but last night he'd promised to hang around more. I was counting on that. He was the only living thing I could hug.

Ryodan had been adamantly opposed to me returning to my flat but I'd insisted, reminding him of the stellar warding job he'd done on my bedroom, affording me a place safe from the Fae. If he had his way, I'd be living at Chester's. Nothing new there. He'd been trying to effect that change of residence since I was a kid.

I wasn't a kid anymore, I was a woman who'd grown accustomed to her own space and time. I'd agreed to meet him at Chester's after I investigated whatever was in the envelope from Mac, and spent a few more hours with Barrons's ancient tomes.

I turned the envelope over, stripped off my glove, and opened it, withdrawing two sheets of paper and unfolding them.

My breath jammed up in my throat and all I could think was, What the bloody hell—how had Mac gotten a letter from Dancer?

I closed my eyes, evened my breathing, braced myself for grief and began to read.

Hi Mega.

"Hi Dancer," I whispered.

I love you.

"I love you, too."

I thought I'd say that first so I didn't start right off with an ominous cliché like: If you're reading this, I'm dead. But if you are, I am. Don't worry about me, I'm fine and we'll see each other again.

I wanted to leave you a letter but I couldn't think of a place to leave it that A: you wouldn't find it before I was dead, and B: you'd definitely find it after I was and, honestly, I didn't want you to have it right away, so I asked Mac to give it to you when the time seemed right. I know my death will hit you hard, and I'm so bloody sorry about that.

I've suspected for a while the cosmic clock is winding down for me. I know the signs. You know them, too, and I love you to the ends of the earth and back again for ignoring them with me. That took more than courage, Mega. That took a heart of gold and a backbone of steel.

I used to worry that I'd never get to hold you and make love to you in this lifetime. That our red thread was going to have to be a platonic one because you were so young when we met and I had an impaired heart, and it drove me crazy because I knew we'd loved each other before. I knew it the moment I saw you, spitting "fecks" a million miles a minute, feeling everything in life so intensely.

Google the red thread of Japanese myth. If the Internet

doesn't work, look in my photo album, the brown leather one with all the selfies we took together when we were having crazy, stupid fun. Along with those other selfies where we were doing crazy, sexy things. I love you for those. Best. Porn. Ever.

So anyway, I printed out the myth for you, in case the world stays offline, but in brief, the Japanese believe our relationships are predestined by gods who tie together the pinky fingers of those who are supposed to find each other in life. People connected by red threads will have a profound impact on one another, life-changing, soul-shaping impact. They'll make history together. Although those threads can get tangled, knotted, and snarled, they're unbreakable. (As an aside, I think it's best not to take the "unbreakable" part for granted. Choice is paramount. Red threads are sacred. Be gentle with them.) (As another aside, those red threads shoot out from our pinky fingers because the ulnar artery runs from the heart to the little finger and those threads are there to keep our hearts connected, across space and time.)

Thank you for being my red thread. I know how damned lucky I was to get you.

I know you, wild thing. Much better than you think. You thought I loved you because I only saw the good parts of you. You thought I saw you through a filter. I didn't.

I know about the cage (I hate her for that more than you can know), the killing you were tricked into doing (I hate Rowena, too), the terrible injustices you suffered.

Yet, you came out of it with a heart so pure it takes my breath away. If I could, I'd have saved you a thousand times over. I'd have been your knight in shining armor. I'd have slayed dragons, rescued you, fought wars for you.

But no one saved you. So you save the world.

And now I'm dead and I left you alone and I hate that.

You remember when I asked you about Ryodan? You got mad at me when I said I wasn't as super as him. You said that I was just as super, just not in the same ways. Thank you for saying that.

I view you the way you view Ryodan. I worship you. I'm in awe of you. I think you're the most amazing person I've ever known.

I envied Ryodan. His strong heart, his immortal body. I envied his long life so much I nearly hated him.

Then one day he came to me, after you told him I was dying. He told me about you. The things you never let me know. He didn't tell me everything, so don't get mad at him. I know because I asked questions he wouldn't answer. He wanted me to know what a miracle you are. He was also taking my measure, trying to decide if I was worthy of you. My respect and esteem for you grew even greater that day, and I hadn't thought it possible. You're a one in a googolplex kind of woman, Mega.

Before he left, he offered to get me the Elixir of Life.

When I said no, he offered to make me like him.

I dropped the letter and sat staring blankly. He'd done *what?* I'd asked him to do that very thing. He'd said no, it wouldn't work, it might kill him. Then he'd gone to Dancer and offered to do it anyway. For me. I spent several long moments trying to process that, then resumed reading.

He said it wasn't a guaranteed success, my heart might blow anyway. I might not survive the transformation. But because

*you loved me, he would try. He said neither the elixir nor be-
coming like him was without price, both came accompanied by
significant problems. He said he would tell me those problems if
I chose one of the options.*

I've never been so tempted in my life.

*But there's a pattern and purpose to all things. I see it in
the sublime truth of math, I hear it in the perfection of great
musical compositions. This spectacular universe knows what it's
doing.*

*He also told me the definition of love you gave him when
you were fourteen—great one, by the way!—but said you'd
missed something.*

*He said love is the willingness to put the happiness and
evolution of the person you love before your own. Even if it
means giving them up.*

*Time for brutal truth: I always knew you wanted us both.
Stop sweating it, wild thing. I'm only one of the many twists
and turns of your evolution.*

*I'm getting tired now. It won't be long. I want to rest so I
can make love to you again tonight when you get home. The
way you look at me in bed, with all that fierce emotion blazing
from your eyes, the way you touch me—you're not big on words
but I feel it in your hands—and, because of you, I've gotten to
be the man I always wanted to be in this lifetime.*

*Dani, my bodacious, magnificent red thread, you rocked
my fucking world, you rattled my existence, you woke me up to
shades of life I'd never seen before.*

*I think sometimes we don't get to see our red threads for a
dozen or more lifetimes. I hope other times we get a hundred
lives together, back to back. I can't wait for the chance to love
you again.*

But it's not my turn now.
That privilege belongs to someone else.
I love you like pi.

Dancer

I dropped my head in my hands and wept.

THIRTY

— • ◦ • —

All these things made me who I am

W HEN I DECIDE TO box something, I don't fail.
I did now.

I sat at the table, staring out at the night beyond the windows, remembering Dancer. The first time I'd met him, each and every time after. The times he'd vanish for days then I'd find him again and we'd be so bloody happy to see each other, and crack ourselves up and play with the pure, wild abandon of teens in a world that had no rules except those we made for ourselves. No one to tell us when to sleep or wake, what to eat, what not to eat, no one to tell us how to live. We'd learned from each other.

We'd set off bombs and investigated mysteries. He'd invented things for me, given me a bracelet I'd lost Silverside, and I'd shown him my zany, expeditious velocity world. We'd watched cartoons, played at being Pinky and the Brain, other times I'd been Tasmanian devil with him or the Roadrunner, whizzing us around our town, twisting and carving and embedding our initials into everything.

We'd grown up and tackled even more important mysteries, saving the world together, falling in love.

I'd gotten his not-so-subtle message: we have more than one red thread.

And those threads aren't gender or even species specific, at least not in my case. Some of them are romantic, some of them aren't.

Mac's one of my threads, our lives inextricably intertwined. I think Mac and Christian also have a red thread, their interactions not always easy but definitely transformative.

Shazam is one of my threads, too. I think Kat may be as well. We have things to learn from each other; she with her enormous empathy and me with my formidable walls.

Rowena was a great big nasty thread but not a red one. I think people can invade your life and tangle themselves around you, a black rope, and if you create too much bad Karma together, maybe they become one of your red threads in a next life, and ever after, until you get whatever you're supposed to learn from your involvement with them—these people who force their way in and wreck your world. Perhaps it's a lesson in some kind of cosmic forgiveness.

I haven't learned it yet. I don't forgive her. She was one crazy bitch and I still don't know everything she did to me.

Ryodan is one of my red threads, too. He might be a massive red rope, ten times as thick as a normal thread. I'm afraid Dancer saw that.

Love is funny. Even though you don't have that person anymore, you still have the feeling. You didn't lose your *love*. You lost the tangible, tactile, sense-sational ability to experience the person or animal you lost.

Grief is all about not being able to touch anymore. Not being able to use your senses to experience them on a physical level. They've moved beyond an impenetrable veil, beyond your hands and mouth and eyes.

And . . . of course . . . that led me to another thought I tried to box and failed.

I was losing my ability to touch *everything*.

I recognize rabbit holes when I see them. That was a long, bottomless one.

I pushed myself up briskly, refusing to tumble over that edge. It was what it was. Period. Patterns, meaning, not my forte. Action, swift and sure, I get that.

I glanced at my phone for the time, grabbed my sword, shoved it over my shoulder into the sheath, and turned to the bedroom to freshen up and head for Chester's. If I didn't hustle he'd be hammering on my door.

The one who'd been willing to make Dancer one of the Nine for me. I had a brief flash of the two of them sitting together, talking about me, Ryodan offering to save Dancer, Dancer knowing I wanted them both. Holy hell. Complicated relationships. My life is full of them.

As I entered my dark bedroom and moved for the bathroom to brush my teeth and wash my face, I felt it.

There was a living presence in my room. Lurking, seething, oozing darkly in the corner behind me.

Not Fae.

Enormous malevolence, terrifying.

I pivoted sharply. It hulked in the corner to the right of my bed, filling it up, cramming it with darkness heaped upon darkness.

No, it crouched, making itself much smaller than it actually was, voracious, and suffocatingly evil.

My sword was in my right hand instantly, my left bare, upraised.

"Show yourself," I snarled.

It glided forward from the dense inky shadow it had woven around itself and, as its human-seeming form appeared bit by bit, head last, I realized it was removing a mask from its face.

I have a theory about people I suspect is universal: when someone conceals something from you, it makes you want to see it. The moment the mask cleared that side of its face, I stared, and was instantly ensnared by its terrible gaze.

There are rules in this world that you only learn by violating them. Some things you can never talk to, like the Fear Dorcha, who can steal a piece of your body if you're that kind of fool. The bastard took my mouth once, left me unable to tell the world the many brilliant things I had to say. Mac saved me from him.

And now, in addition to Unseelie princes, I learned there are other things you can never lock gazes with.

The moment my eyes met the bottomless, wet, suffocating, mist-filled gaze of the single enormous eye this creature had been concealing behind its mask, I was rooted to the ground, unable to move. No possibility of kicking up into the slipstream. That evil, consuming eye speared a piece of me and locked onto it with savage barbs that wouldn't let go.

I felt it enter my mind then, not like Ryodan, with a subtle dip, but a ruthless javelin with a shiny fishhook on the end that had multiple prongs, as it ripped into the very meat of me, yanking, pulling, wrenching something from my body.

And I knew in that moment, bloody hell I knew for a *fact*, that I had a soul because that's what it was taking from me.

The very essence of Dani O'Malley was caught on its lethal barb. The building blocks of all that I am, my strength and power, my truths and lies, my heart and brain and fabric and energy. My subconscious, my conscious, my id and ego, my entire personality was being extracted on the hooked end of its javelin. I was losing everything that was me. It was scraping me like a mussel from a shell, to devour me, absorb my strengths and abilities, and once it had me, I would never exist again. It was death so final it was beyond my comprehension. This thing, whatever it was, trafficked in obliteration of the human soul.

End of all adventures permanently. End of all red threads.

There is no greater abomination in my universe. I don't fear death. I resent the fuck out of it. I don't like commercial breaks in my programming. But I don't fear it because I know I'm a permanent, indelible, massive, fat-tipped Sharpie, I can't be scrubbed out of the Cosmos.

But this thing defied all the rules. It could erase me forever.

As it continued to rip me from my body, dragging me into its wet, suffocating mist, swallowing me whole, I caught a glimpse of the horror of it, the horror of what it contained.

Tens of thousands of souls like mine, becoming more powerful with each it stole. Tens of thousands—maybe a hundred thousand souls—screaming with panic and madness, existing in a formless half-life, as fuel for something that was erasing every shred of their individuality, molding them into a formless lump of its own will, blotting them out of existence bit by torturous bit and they were *aware* of being destroyed.

I caught a vision then, within its dark mind, of bodies shambling like zombies, controlled by it. It despised them, barely kept them alive, made them fight like dogs for scraps of food. Tormented them endlessly, laughing as they mindlessly did its bidding. It not only grew ever more powerful with each soul but was amassing . . .

An army.

Of humans.

Slaves. Countless human souls destroyed.

This thing had been taking my adults! This was the "him" on the other side of those narrow black mirrors, reeking of wood smoke and blood. But more, so much more. All over Western Europe it had been culling humans, growing in power, pursuing its dark agenda, which was . . . oh, holy hell—the obliteration of the entire human race!

It wanted us dead. Gone. Forever eradicated, never to return. It hated us beyond reason. It planned to turn its army of humans against us, then against the Fae, and with my sword it had a damned good chance at wiping both races out. Even more horrifying, it believed once it acquired a certain number of souls, it would be so powerful its demonic eye would no longer be necessary. It would only have to stroll through a city and inhale every human soul in it, its deadly reach expanding wider with each new acquisition.

I was right about you, it purred. *You are worth a hundred of them.*

I scowled. *Surely more than that.*

Its mocking laughter echoed inside my soul. It found me arrogant. It hungered to eat me, become me, assimilate me, steal everything I'd worked so hard to become.

With enormous effort, I made a box, and deposited myself within it. I ended up with less than half of me inside, it had the other half.

Battle is futile. I existed long before your puny race came along and will exist long after you are gone.

It yanked savagely.

I stretched long and painfully thin, dug mental feet beneath the rim of my box. I needed a name, damn it. I wasn't leaving without one and I *would* be leaving.

Who are you?

God, Death. Soulstealer.

But I caught a name beneath it, deep beneath. It was proud, far more arrogant than me. It wanted its name said, over and over, it commanded its soulless army to repeat an endless chant, worshipping it. That was the indecipherable chant I'd heard through those dark mirrors.

Balor.

It was a place to start. I instantly embraced the Hunter's darkness within, encouraged it to explode inside me, slam into my brain, back down to my heart, then raised both hands and flung them at it.

How are you moving? Balor screamed.

I released bolt after bolt of pale blue—

Holy hell, where was I?

Rocketing through a wormhole, achieving superluminal velocity, faster than I'd ever managed in my slipstream, exploding into open space, drawing to a sudden complete halt in the middle of a circle of Hunters.

She comes, *they gonged.* It's time.

I hovered there, feeling as if I stood in a doorway, one land behind me, one land ahead; both fascinating, both real, and all I had to do was lift my foot and take a step either way.

And for a split second I hungered to go forward not back, to feel great, black Hunter wings churning ice as I soared, exploring the

mysteries of the universe, no door barred to me, to be so bloody pow-
erful and untamed and wild and free, the biggest bad in the uni-
verse, owning the skies, tasting of stardust and eternity, and it felt
oddly as if I belonged there, as if my destiny was writ in these very
stars—

But.

My people.

NO, IT'S NOT TIME, *I roared, resisting with every ounce of*
my will. MY WORLD NEEDS ME!

Then I was rocketing back through that wormhole at a dizzying speed and I was in the room with Balor, and my beautiful
pale blue lightning was exploding, not only from my hands but
my body, crackling out in powerful bursts, jolting the god,
again and again, and Balor was roaring inside my head, screaming with pain, then he was buckling in the corner, doubling
over, clutching his leg, and he whipped his head back and
roared at me, as if insulted beyond enduring, *You wounded my*
fucking leg!

I gathered myself to hurl a bolt straight into his face.

Balor dropped his mask over his eye and exploded into a
cloud of misty, damp black dust that smelled of coffin linings
and the sterile chemicals of autopsy rooms and morgues, so cloy-
ing and suffocating that I couldn't breathe.

Abruptly, he was gone.

I tried to whirl and scan the room, in case he'd circled back
for another attack, but I had no sense of space, couldn't comprehend myself in relationship to it.

My strength was decimated, both from the tug of war over
my soul and the staggering high voltage still sparking beneath
my skin.

I drew a ragged breath then another, trying desperately to center myself.

I raised a foot to take a step but when I brought it down, it didn't feel solid. I stumbled and went crashing to the floor, cracking my head on the corner of the bed frame.

Everything went black.

VIGILANTE

———— • • ————

R owena was in my life long before I met her at eight.
      After the rejection of Seamus, a man my mother deeply
loved, a man who might have been our savior, she fell apart. Her
heart had taken too many blows.

While my mother was defeated by grief, and out of work thanks
to Seamus's spineless, vindictive way of erasing her from his life, Rowena dispatched the man who would become her pimp. Feigning love,
the bastard began his endless manipulations, treating her at first better then finally worse than anyone ever had. By then pain and despair
had become Emma O'Malley's normal. She expected to be abused by
life.

Rowena sent the next boyfriend, too, an aficionado of drugs, to
introduce her to the only escape she would ever know, besides death.

Her sadistic plan: to subject me to even more pain and suffering,
to burn my world down around me as I watched, helpless, to char me
beyond repair.

To see what rose from the ashes.

To step in as my savior and rescue me from my cage, hoping for a broken, malleable weapon. One that would despise herself for the darkness within, one so deeply fractured she would grovel for crumbs of kindness, despite the many superpowers that made her infinitely more powerful than Rowena herself.

Her plan worked.

I broke.

But I scarred stronger.

When she found me, wandering Dublin at eight, and realized things hadn't unfolded according to her careful plan, she used black arts to tamper with my mind, burying the real one beneath a false memory of her discovering me, rescuing me from my cage as I lay waiting to die. Like any good liar, she salted her lie with grains of truth; let me continue to believe I killed my mother by strangling her through the bars. She wanted me tormented by the blade of matricide.

Silverside, I meticulously ferreted out her spells and compulsions. I didn't get rid of my demons, I don't think that's possible for me. But I know them by name now. And they obey me, not the other way around.

After I moved into the abbey, even before I knew the extent of Rowena's involvement in our lives, I had a dream that I killed her.

Later, when I discovered all she'd done to us, I had that dream again.

I'd hungered to kill her.

I told myself the only reason I didn't was because the other sidhe-seers *would have ostracized me, and I'd wanted desperately to belong. I wouldn't have felt an ounce of regret; rabid animals need to be put down. My anger would definitely have ebbed.*

But there was a deeper reason that gave me pause.

Both times, as she lay dying in my dreams, I'd seen a flash of pure, evil triumph glittering in that sadistic blue gaze.

Glee. Gloating. Jubilation.

Her eyes had said: You are an animal, you are a monster, you are damaged beyond repair. I did that to you and I may be dying but I took you down with me. I may go to Hell but you'll live in it every day for the rest of your life. I shattered you and you will never be anything but a creature of impulsive reactions, a killer of innocents. You are as ugly and corrupt as me.

I'm glad Mac killed her.

I never wanted to give her the opportunity to look at me that way or feel she had a single reason to gloat.

Because I know a priceless truth: when someone has done everything in their power to mangle your wings beyond recognition, to slice them to shreds so that they can never be used, there is only one way to win.

Fly.

RISING

What the caterpillar calls the end of the world
The master calls a butterfly.

—Richard Bach

THIRTY-ONE

— • • —

Live without your sunlight,

love without your heartbeat

I WOKE IN THAT RARE, smooth, focused mood that told me I was either under attack or Ryodan had spelled me into a healing slumber again. Given my fragmented memories, it was the latter.

I sat up, glancing around in the dim light. The room was huge, with high transomed ceilings of ornate, dark tiles, the walls wainscoted black. To my right was an enormous fire in a hearth that filled half the wall, a black leather sofa and chairs, a dark coffee table, above which hung a single shimmering cut-crystal chandelier, reflecting hundreds of tiny flames.

I was alone, in a high-backed, black-velvet bed, tangled in black silk sheets.

I could smell him on the sheets. Picture him too easily here, naked, powerful, savage yet controlled, those cool silvery eyes glittering hot, bloodred with beast. I knew how he fucked, like a man on fire. Uninhibited, raw, one hundred percent focused. I'd watched him when I was far too young to have seen it, yet old enough to have shivered with awareness. Clutching a fistful of silk to my nose, I inhaled. It was a violent turn-on, slamming lust painfully awake and alive. I'd never once gotten to have the kind of sex I wanted to have, the way I lived my life, at a headlong, all-out run, wild, unrestrained.

Torture.

I thrust the sheet away and began sorting through disjointed memories.

Ryodan finding me on the floor at Sanctuary, rolling me in a blanket, tossing me over his shoulder, carrying me. A brief flash of Chester's nightclub, then darkness.

Ryodan demanding I wake, drink a protein shake, wake, drink more. Fighting with him, wanting only to sleep. A gloved hand behind my head. Liquid poured down my throat, being threatened with a feeding tube again.

No matter how far off the deep end I went, he always brought me back.

Balor. The memory slammed into my mind laced with pure adrenaline and I tensed.

Holy soul-sucking fiends, I needed to talk to Ryodan, to the Shedon! We had to find Balor but more importantly we had to figure out how to kill him, since even my staggering power had proven ineffectual against the god. My first blast alone would have blown any Fae to bits. Yet all I'd managed to do to the deadly, rapacious Balor was wound his leg.

Exhaling gustily, I scraped my long tangled hair from my face. And blinked, staring down at my hands. Both were coal black. In one of my fists was a tangle of raven curls. In the other was a tangle of red. I shoved up one sleeve, then the next. Thorns on both arms.

I surged from the bed and tried to decide which of five doors led to the bathroom. I opened the nearest and blinked, staring. It looked familiar but it was hard to tell with every piece of furniture shattered. Even the walls and floors had deep gashes slashed into them, as if massive, lethal talons had been turned against them in fury.

After a long moment I recognized the bits of furniture, so similar to mine. It was the room Ryodan had tattooed me in, that I'd thought was his private chamber but was only the anteroom to the true private chamber within. Wait—what? I stood, processing the shambles. It was furnished exactly how it had been when he'd tattooed me. Holy mimicking monkeys, *I'd* aped his taste, not the other way around! And I hadn't even realized it. I was the copycat. My mood soured.

I slammed that door and tried the next. A kitchen. He didn't have my exact counters but they were damned close. I slammed that door and opened the third then stood, hesitating on the threshold.

I'd found the bathroom and it sported an entire wall of mirrors—in anyone else's abode but Ryodan's, those silver glasses would have made me uneasy—yet abruptly, I wasn't in such a hurry to look at myself anymore. I had a damn good idea what I'd find.

Shaking my head, bracing myself, I stalked to the mirror.

And gasped.

I yanked up my shirt, unbuttoned the fly of my jeans, dropped them and stared, abruptly so angry I couldn't breathe.

The only parts of me that weren't black was half my hair, half my face, and a fist-sized spot on my stomach. My left eye was full black. Deep within fiery sparks glinted. I had a Hunter eye. Bloody hell.

I stood there a long moment, battling emotions so intense I didn't know what to do with them. I wanted to box them. Knew I could. Simply pack it all up and get back out there in the world and see what happened next. Deal with whatever did. That was the way I lived.

"And how's that been working out for you so far?" I muttered at my reflection sarcastically.

Not so well. Ryodan was right. Boxing the things that bothered me was, long-term, deadly. It was past time I faced things, and not just the state of my body.

I tugged my jeans back up, dropped my shirt, then stared at my reflection, eyes meeting eyes, telling myself what I've always told myself: it is what it is. Find the silver lining. Throw that head back and belly up a laugh. It's just another adventure. Greet it, master it.

It didn't work. Because it wasn't this time.

This adventure was stealing me away from my world as surely and inevitably as Balor had been wresting my soul from my body.

My adventures were supposed to happen *here*, in my city, with my friends who were finally back. With Ryodan. He was here. We wanted each other. We'd finally engaged in that long overdue dance of lust and . . . well, who knew what else . . . I was being yanked from the dance floor against my will.

The thing I'd hated the most about being caged was being shut away from the world, cut off from it. I'd hungered for OLDER and OUTSIDE because, deep down, I'd had the same dreams as everyone else, only superhero-sized. I'd been raised by those dreams, unfolding on the television in front of my lonely, riveted, intensely impressionable gaze. One day I, too, would have friends, a place to belong. I'd date, maybe even go to university. Dance. Fall in young love like I did with Dancer. Maybe fall in love again. That was how it worked on those shows.

But my time was running out. Fast.

I suddenly understood how Dancer must have felt, with his damaged heart, his loathing of clocks, his refusal to wear a watch, his abject rejection of the relentless march of time.

But my heart wasn't damaged, and Ryodan's was immortal, and I'd had every reason to believe we had plenty of time.

One kiss and two days later, BOOM—I was untouchable. If I were a character in a novel, I'd snipe the bitch who wrote my life this way.

I fisted my hands, staring into the mirror, pressure building in my head as I realized whether I turned solid black or actually turned into a Hunter, the end result was the same.

My life as I knew it was over.

I would never kiss Ryodan. Never touch him. Never get to lose myself in passion on that big, beautiful body of his. Never get to test his sexual limits, and mine. On him, I could vibrate at my highest intensity and never have to worry about blowing out his heart. So many desires I'd hidden, guarded in my heart, believing somehow, one day, I'd get to taste them all. When it was time.

Not.

Twenty-two years. That was all I'd gotten and, holy hell, had they been crazy. Caged, lost, fractured, soon to not even be human at all.

For whatever reason, in my mind, me and Ryodan had always been a foregone conclusion. Just as Dancer was mine, so was he. It was always only a matter of time. Or so I'd believed. Some women got a single great love in their lifetime. I'd gotten two at the same time, totally different, yet both mine. I'd known it even then. Dancer's failing heart had made my choice easier. I honestly don't know what I'd have done if he'd lived a long life. I've always been torn between the two of them. And although I'd worked hard to hide it, Dancer had seen it. Called me on it. Loved me anyway. That had taken enormous courage. To love someone you knew wanted someone else, too, but had, for whatever reason, chosen you. I can't say that I'd be capable of it. I don't think my heart is that pure.

Then Ryodan had screwed everything up by leaving. I'd almost been done working through it. The whole grief/guilt conundrum had swallowed me whole for a while. Ryodan's abrupt departure had pushed me over the edge. Any boxes that were about to open, I'd slammed shut again.

Somewhere in the suite a door opened and closed. Footfalls. He was here.

And the way I saw it, it was all his fault.

Once, I'd have freeze-framed out there, slammed into him, vented my anger on his body. I didn't dare do that now.

I turned and stalked back into the bedroom and nearly ran smack into him. We both backpedaled instantly.

He looked like hell. Every muscle in his body was tight, his eyes narrowed to slits, glittering, and there was thunder in his blood. I could hear the sledgehammer of his heart a dozen paces away. His knuckles were scraped, his hands cut but already healing, no doubt from demolishing the anteroom.

"That was yesterday," he said tightly. "Today I trashed the gym. And my office."

"What the hell do *you* have to be angry about?" I demanded.

"Clarify your emotions, Dani," he snapped. "It's not me you're upset with."

"Don't tell me who I'm upset with," I snapped back. "I know

perfectly well who I'm upset with. The person that left for two bloody years. We could have had *two years,* Ryodan, but you blew it!"

He snarled, "Don't you dare try to blame that on me! You bloody well know why I left. You won't let yourself think about it. The person you're angry with is *you.*"

"Bullshit." I fisted my hands at my sides and locked my legs down to keep from lunging at him.

"For a woman who always seizes the moment, I'm the one moment you sure as fuck never seized. And I was right there for the seizing."

"No, you weren't. That's exactly my point. You *left.* You went off into the world and had adventures and sex and a life without me and you wouldn't even be back now if I hadn't wished you back and AOZ granted it, thinking the starving black beast would bite me in the ass somehow!" I exploded in a heated rush.

"You *wished* me back? That's how I got here? Bloody hell, and you're just now telling me that? Barrons and I wasted half a day trying to figure that out!"

"And if I hadn't wished you back," I yelled, "you'd still be out there having a life while I was here by myself, trying to handle this whole bloody city alone, turning black and slipping away and you wouldn't even know it! You know why? Because you don't care! You didn't text or call me even once. You don't fucking care about me *at all!*"

His head whipped back and he roared, hands fisting, body straining, and he morphed so swiftly into the beast that his clothing exploded off him in pieces, shirt ripping down the back, sleeves and pants splitting, falling away as he transformed from a six-foot-four, 240-pound man to a nine foot, nearly five-hundred-pound beast.

Then back to the man.

Then the beast, then the man.

Beast.

Man.

Sound of bones cracking, tendons grating.

Beast. Man. Beast again. Faster.

Back and forth he went at a dizzying speed and I watched with horror, struck by the sudden fear that he might kill himself if he didn't stabilize his body fast, from the sheer stress his organs were undergoing in the rapid, incessant transformations. Not to mention his skin and bones! And, no matter how angry I was with him for ruining our lives, I can never stand to see that man die.

"Ryodan, breathe! Get a grip on yourself!" I cried, but my words were gasoline on his fire and the morphing sped up and he began to bay, jaws wrenched wide, then he was a man roaring, then a beast howling, such a terrible, desolate, fractured sound, and I couldn't think of anything else to say so I shouted, "Ryodan, goddamn it, I love you! Stop hurting yourself! Don't you dare die! I can't deal with that right now!" Not only did I hate watching him die, I'd have to wait days, maybe even weeks for him to get back so we could finish this damned fight, and who knew if I'd even still be here?

The beast jerked, stumbled, dropped to a knee, shuddering violently, then began to turn back into a man, bit by bit, first his hands, then his arms, his shoulders, and finally his face.

I held my breath, refused to say anything, in case it pushed him back into that terrible morphing of forms again. For years I'd wanted to see the great Ryodan lose control. I'd just learned a painful lesson. I never wanted to see it happen again. I'd kill anyone who ever tested his control, protect him. Never let him break.

This man was my . . . bloody hell, my hero and I wanted him to always stay strong and whole.

He knelt, gasping for breath, chest heaving, tatters of clothing hanging on his trembling body.

Then, chin tucked down, he glanced up at me from beneath his brows, eyes still crimson and ground out, "Never. Tell. Me. I. Don't. Care. You can fling any other insult you want at me, but not that one. Never that one. Everything I've done, I've done for you. Everything."

He lunged to his feet and stalked toward me, naked but for odd bits of clothing here and there. I yanked my gaze to his face, in no mood to torment myself further.

"Don't touch me!" I stepped hastily back. "And put something on."

"Don't tell me what to do," he growled. "Suggesting works better at times like these."

"You tell me what to do all the time and it's—"

"You never listen."

"—not like we'll be having future times like these because—"

"We'll always be butting heads like this. You're too goddamn stubborn and so am I."

"—our time is up, Ryodan. That's my point and it's *your* fault."

He snarled, "What did I say to you in the cemetery that night?"

"You told me you were leaving," I snarled back. "And that I couldn't come."

He stalked past me, into the bathroom, and came out with a towel wrapped around his waist, dusting part of a sleeve from his arm. "That's not what I mean and you know it. The thing you boxed. The thing you never once looked at. The final words I said to you."

"You told me to never come to you," I said hotly. He was getting too close and he was right, I was angry with myself and had been for a long time.

"After that. Goddamn it, Dani, what did I say right before I left? I know you heard it. I know how acute your hearing is."

I closed my eyes. He'd said, *until the day you're willing to stay.*

"You had my number! If you'd called me, I'd have come. But you didn't."

"You didn't call me either!"

"You wanted my brand. You wanted to know you could never get lost again. That mattered to you. I gave it to you."

"What the hell does that have to do with anything?"

"For fuck's sake, because of that brand, I feel your emotions. I felt them that night in the cemetery. You may not have wanted me to leave but it wasn't because you wanted me to stay. You wanted me to sit around, waiting endlessly, doing nothing, all for the slight chance Dani O'Malley decided she wanted to see me. I bloody well did that. I sat there four motherfucking months and you never. Once. Came. I came to find you a dozen times but you couldn't get away from me fast enough. I know exactly what you felt that night in the cemetery, I felt every bit of it. Anger that I was leaving, hurt that I wouldn't tell you for how long. But more than anything, more intensely than all the rest, you felt relieved. You were bloody fucking *relieved* to see me go!"

I fisted my hands so hard, my nails bit through the gloves into my icy flesh. "What are you saying? That you went away to punish me?"

He snorted, then laughed, a bitter sound. "Never that. And I assure you, you weren't the one being punished. I waited four months and what did you do?" He shot me a look so full of scathing fury, I flinched. "You grabbed the nearest man that looked like me and took him to bed."

I gasped, "How do you know he looked like you?"

He smiled, baring fangs, eyes flashing crimson. "I ate him."

My brows climbed my forehead. "Before or after you came to the cemetery?"

"Does it fucking matter? Before. Three minutes after you left him that night. And it wasn't because he almost raped you. The brand you wanted, the spell that kept you from ever being lost, is the mark of my beast. It binds me to you in countless excruciating ways. It mates my beast to you. Do you understand that? Let me spell it out for you: my beast abhors trespassers. My beast thinks you *belong* to it." His next words came out accompanied by a savage rattle deep in his chest, "And bloody hell, so do I. Or I wouldn't have given it to you in the first place."

I stared at him. "You put that mark on me when I was fourteen."

"As a way to keep you alive and a promise to the woman you would one day become. It was my best shot at protecting you, keeping your fearless, impulsive ass safe. And if you'd wanted the brand as a woman, I'd have let you brand me with a reciprocal mark. If you'd chosen someone else, I'd have cut it off. But I would have kept you breathing until then."

I protested, "But you didn't cut it off when I was with Dancer."

"He was a short-timer," he said savagely. "I thought I could survive it."

I flushed. "Oh, God, you could feel me when I had sex with Dancer! That's how you knew I shouldn't vibrate on him. Could you *see* us?"

"It's not like that. And I wouldn't have, if it were. I have no desire to watch you having sex with another man. I spent most of that time trying to block you two out, for fuck's sake. I felt your passion. I felt his. I felt your heat, your need, and it almost fucking killed me. I was ready. You weren't. I knew that. When you chose a man that looked like me you couldn't have sent me a clearer message. Through you, I could feel Dancer's life force. He was growing weaker every day. Had he lived, had you stayed with him, I'd have removed it. I couldn't have stood it much longer anyway."

"Yet you offered to make him like you," I said, stunned.

"How the fuck do—ah, the letter from Barrons. It was from Dancer. That shit. He wasn't supposed to tell you."

"You told me no. Why did you change your mind?"

He shrugged, muscles and tattoos rippling. "I had a moment of temporary insanity, Dani. Fuck, I don't know. I just wanted to end your pain. Maybe I knew he wouldn't accept. Don't paint it honorable. I'm not where you're concerned."

Yes, he was. No matter how he wanted to spin it. Because I loved Dancer, despite his own desires, he'd been willing to make him immortal for me. I wanted to thank him. I would thank him. But I wasn't done yet. He'd vanished then showed up at my door, nearly starved to death, and I wanted to know where he'd been and what had happened to him. No more secrets. We would, at the very least, be friends, by God, I wanted *something* with this man and friendship demands truth. Besides, I couldn't stand thinking about him out there, never once calling or texting. That was bullshit. There was no excuse. "Where did you go? Where were you for two years?" I demanded.

"Why were you so relieved to see me go?" he fired back. "There was one emotion I couldn't get to. You had it too tightly boxed. I've never been able to get into your high security vaults."

That was good to know. I closed my eyes, steeling myself. If I wanted truth from him, I had to be willing to give it myself. But this was what had created the entire mess of my boxes to begin with. Boxes are like lies, they breed like rabbits and hop around out of control. Still, it wasn't as if there was anything left to lose. Inhaling deeply, I opened my eyes and said, "I'll tell you, if you tell me."

"Agreed."

I was silent a long moment that spun out into a longer minute. Then two. We were about to do something we'd never done before. Rather than dazzling each other with our strengths, our finest qualities, here and now, in this strange final inning of a game we could no longer play, we were baring our weakness, our faults. Something I'd never done with anyone. The world ferrets out your faults often enough, I see little point in lending a hand.

I said slowly, wanting to bite back every word, "Because duration of grief seems as if it should be equivalent to the depth of love you felt for the person you lost." I paused a moment, struggling to get the next words out. "And I wanted to come to you shortly after Dancer died." I'd been ready long before he'd left. And I'd boxed it the moment I felt it. Who does that? Who moves on so quickly? I'd loved Dancer. He'd deserved better than that!

He went motionless, staring into my eyes. Softly, he said, "You crazy, beautiful, maddening woman, that's because you trained yourself to live that way. And wisely so. It's what kept you alive. It's been your saving grace. You learned young the necessity of leaving the pain behind and embracing the next good thing. Few people ever achieve that clarity. Prolonged grief is self-mutilation; a blade you turn on yourself. It doesn't bring them back and only keeps you trapped in misery. You were healing the way people should heal but they punish themselves instead. For what—being the one who lived? Those we love will die. And die. And die. Life goes on. You choose how: badly or well."

I knew that. With my head. But my heart had felt guilt so enormous and crushing, I hadn't known what to do with it. I'd been out of control from that moment on. Each time I'd passed Chester's, telling myself I was just checking on it, it was all I could do not to stalk in that door and pick up where our last kiss had left off, when he'd kissed me like I was the many complicated things that I am, when he'd shown me how completely he understood me. I'd wanted to forget my pain but any way I looked at it that was equivalent to forgetting Dancer and I was the one who *remembered* the people who died, damn it. That was what I did. I noticed the invisible people. I knew what it felt like to be one. I used to think I'd die in my cage and no one would ever even know I'd once been there. I'd simply vanish, unknown, unmourned, forgotten. Sometimes, toward the end, I'd wondered if she'd been *trying* to starve me to death.

"I couldn't forgive myself," I said softly. "It was a betrayal of the love we'd shared. I refused to see you because I knew what I'd do and I couldn't resolve the conflict. But I would have," I added heatedly. "Within a few months at most. You could have texted me, checked to see how I was. But you never did. Not once," I said bitterly. "Your turn. Where did you go? And why were you starved when you got back?"

He smiled faintly, mirthlessly. "I never went anywhere, Dani. I never left at all. I was right here in Dublin the entire time, beneath your feet, under the garage behind Barrons Books & Baubles."

"*What?*" I exploded.

"You walked above me once, feeling lost. I tried to send you a thought but the pain was so intense by then, the hunger so consuming, I'm not certain it got through. It was either make Barrons imprison me in a spelled cage I couldn't escape, where he'd once contained his son, or cut my brand off you, and risk you getting lost. I was never going to risk that. If you'd called me, Barrons would have released me. If you'd used IISS, it would have bypassed the spells holding me."

I stared. He'd been locked in a cage for two years? Barrons's son—what the hell? I knew nothing about a son! I filed that away for future questions. Right now all I could think about was Ryodan trapped like an animal, as he'd once been so long ago as a child. As I'd been. We both knew the hell of cages. I would never go back into any kind of prison again. Couldn't imagine any reason to willingly commit myself to two years of isolation, locked up. Oh, God, the whole time I'd been so angry that Ryodan had left me alone, he'd been alone, too, suffering! He'd been starved because he hadn't eaten for two years, shut away in the ground!

"I turned into the beast shortly after Barrons completed the final spell, and never changed back again. I knew it would happen when I went in. We can only go so long without eating. After that it was madness. I lost all sense of time. Marked moments by your most intense emotions. My beast raged every time you fucked. My beast wept every time you cried. With some small part of my brain, I kept thinking you'd call and it would end. I'd be free. We'd be free. Together."

The horror of it flooded my heart. All that time, waiting for me to call. But I never did. "Why?" I cried, incredulous. "I don't understand!"

Shadows rushed in his silvery, crimson-flecked gaze. *I would have killed every man you slept with, Dani. I'd have left a trail of dead men behind you, guilty of nothing more than being chosen to share your bed. You'd have hated me for that. And I couldn't control it.*

"But you controlled it with Dancer," I said.

Locked beneath Chester's. I killed three of my men the final night you spent with him. That you loved him and were loved in return was enough to give me an edge over the beast. But lust, ah, Dani, that my beast can't accept. I couldn't fight it. I couldn't win. I'm not human. Despite my appearance, despite my efforts, I'm beast first and it's not always controllable. That's what I was trying to tell you when I told you Lor wouldn't have stayed to watch you dance. We know our weaknesses. If we can't control them, we avoid them. We live by a rigid code. We didn't always. Barrons developed and enforced it and one by one we all adhered. You have always been my greatest weakness. You had every right to take men to bed. I had no right to stop it. I stopped myself the only way I could.

I stared at him and began to cry. Not ugly, just big, silent tears slipping down my cheeks.

"Christ, don't do that. Not when I can't—ah, fuck. Close your eyes."

I did, because I couldn't stand looking at him, knowing I couldn't touch him. Couldn't bear the expression in his eyes, identical to my own.

Then he was holding me and my eyes flew open but he hadn't moved.

"There are benefits to the bond we share. Close your eyes, Stardust."

I did, again, then his hands were in my hair and he was cradling my head, holding me to his chest. I could smell his skin, feel the unflinching strength of his body.

I opened my eyes and the illusion vanished.

"It only works if you keep your eyes closed."

"Ryodan, I'm so sorry," I said miserably. "If I had known, if I'd had any idea this would happen . . ." I trailed off. We'd both wasted two years. *I'd* wasted it. I'd never called. And I'd wanted to so many times.

His silver gaze locked with mine. *You, Dani O'Malley, have always been the greatest mystery of my existence, the one thing I've never been able to predict. Linchpin theory means nothing where you're concerned. My actions may not have been the wisest either. But whatever's happening changes nothing. You're so bloody beautiful to me—any color, any race, any skin, any species, woman, I will love you across all of them. If you turn into a Hunter, my beast and yours will run together. We'll fight wars, save worlds, become legend.* He smiled faintly. *I'll be the only beast in the universe in love with a dragon.*

His words took my breath away, slammed into me with a painful blend of joy and sorrow. In a moment I would pull myself together.

"As will I. That's what we do, you and I," he said quietly.

And in a moment we would get down to determining how to save our world.

"Precisely."

And maybe in a million, trillion, gazillion moments, being a dragon loved by a beast would be enough for me. But at the current moment I couldn't begin to envision that place in time.

Once before I'd waited too long and learned the true meaning of regret. I was choking on that bitter taste now.

Raw. Endless. Grief. Raining. Eternal. Tears.

I closed my eyes against the burn of it and wondered if dragons could cry.

THIRTY-TWO

---•◦•---

FOR A NOVEL CHANGE, Gustaine was happy to be small and inconspicuous.

The great god Balor was in a lethal mood today, killing the human bodies brought to him without even bothering to absorb their souls—a total waste of power!—just so he could enjoy each moment of pain and torture he inflicted upon them before they died.

Gustaine had little respect for those who reacted with ego and emotion over long-term planning for survival, it was against his cockroachian nature. Survival was paramount. Patient, subtle chesslike moves, plus yet more patience, guaranteed success. That was why he'd pledged fealty to the one called Ryodan for as long as he had. Of his many alliances over time, it was that cool, calculating beast that had commanded his respect. Like the cockroach, the beast-man would endure.

The Faerie prince was once a close second, but Cruce lied

and the lethal ice-fire he'd charged Gustaine with planting at the abbey had damaged many of his individual parts. A single mind controlled his hive of bodies, and Gustaine counted each incremental part of himself precious. Felt the pain of them all. Hundreds of his bodies sported permanent scars from that battle, had been hobbled, crippled—like Balor was now.

Dani O'Malley had injured the great god, making Gustaine wonder if he'd pledged his services hastily. The Soulstealer was limping with a raw, jagged wound in his leg, charred at the edges.

Eons past, Balor had been one of the most powerful gods to walk the face of the Earth, and a merciful one. The Soulstealer had once alleviated the suffering of humans, walking battlefields, attending the lingering dying, removing their souls from their bodies to spare them the pain of slow death.

But the Faerie had come with stealth, abducted and tortured Balor for a small eternity, trying to kill him, all the while impersonating him to his tribes. The Faerie had destroyed half his face in their efforts to gouge that great killing eye from his body. But he'd slipped their clutches, even with his shattered leg, and returned to live up to every one of the horrific legends the Fae had sown about him.

Then been captured *again* by the Faerie and entombed in the earth.

There was no god alive that despised humans and Faerie more. For that reason alone, Gustaine would remain in his service a bit longer. See if Balor could turn his recent failure around.

"Gustaine!" Balor roared. "Show yourself!"

Hissing softly, Gustaine assembled himself into a small head deep in the shadows. "My lord and master, how may I serve?"

"Find her again! Dispatch your countless bodies and locate that bitch. I want to know the instant you spot her, where she is, what she's doing, who's with her, where she's going. Get me concrete information this time!" he snarled.

He didn't point out that he'd gotten Balor perfectly concrete information last time but the god had overestimated himself, and underestimated his prey. He loathed that he would have to leave enough of his bodies here with the destructive, raging god to remain in constant communication with him. Yet another master, yet more volatility. He'd give Balor wide berth until he knew her location, stay compressed beneath rocks.

Clearing his throat, he ground out, "How will you destroy her when she possesses such power?" Perhaps he should have allied with the woman. Anyone that could injure Balor was a potential ally worth considering.

Balor gave him a terrible smile, sharp teeth, loathing and rage. "Why do you think I made my camp here of all places? The benefits were countless. I already have something she cares about deeply, and when humans care, humans fall." He turned in a whirl of long black robes and snarled, "AOZ, gather the other gods and get them here now. It's long past time we rain down hell on this world."

THIRTY-THREE

———— • • • ————

Do you wanna touch me there, where

LATER, RYODAN AND I met with Kat and the Shedon in a bona fide conference room beneath Chester's that was decorated with the same sleek blend of muscle and elegance as the rest of his club. From snooping in his files while he was gone, I knew he had vast holdings, and imagined he held meetings here, preferring to keep his business private. I couldn't picture him walking into a bank or an attorney's office.

Part of the nightclub was open again, as Elyreum was a pile of rubble, and I could feel the powerful bass thrumming beneath my boots as I irritably tapped my fingers along to "Do You Wanna Touch Me" by Joan Jett and the Blackhearts. Clearly, someone left Lor in charge of the music. Clearly, someone needed to drag him out of the eighties before he drove the clientele away. Clearly, they could pick a better song than one about people wanting to be touched. My only option right now was a Pillsbury Dough Boy poke in the belly.

When I'd called Kat earlier to fill her in on Balor, she'd swiftly proposed coming into the city for a meeting, saying she had information for us as well.

"It's possible," Kat was saying now, "this never would have happened but the Song enhanced whatever the Hunter left inside you, Dani."

"It's also possible," Enyo said, "like the Fae, when one Hunter dies, another must be born; the way Christian and Sean replaced the Unseelie princes."

"It's also possible," Colleen said, "with Hunters, if someone kills them, they automatically become the next one."

"Not only is all of that irrelevant because it is what it is, it's also possible," I said dryly, "that I'll only turn solid black and never become anything else." I doubted that. But I was sick of talking about me. I was sick of thinking about me. "We called this meeting to discuss Balor, not me," I reminded, scratching my arm through my glove. I was no longer icy to the touch but I was having random, sporadic bursts of itching beneath my skin, as if my cells were doing something I'd prefer they weren't.

I was gloved, covered from head to toe, and bloody well hot. My hair was sleeked back into a braid, because I was afraid if I turned around fast, my long waves would fly out and kill someone. Holy crackling curls, my hair could kill someone!

Everyone knew not to touch me. It wasn't as if they could forget I was dangerous when half my head was black. Obsidian flames licked across the left side of my face, streaking over my nose. With one solid black eye, dancing with low flames, I was downright fierce looking. And beautiful. Just not who or what I wanted to be.

Kat had filled us in on her time with Christian and Sean, and I'd mulled over the shocking realization that all of us—Mac,

Barrons, Ryodan, me, Christian, Sean—had been off in our own corner of the world, trying to deal with our problems. They hadn't left me. In fact, none of them would have gone if they hadn't been forced to by their circumstances. Mac needed to learn to wield the queen's power, Christian would have killed everyone if he'd come around, Barrons would never leave Mac's side, and Ryodan, oh God, Ryodan had locked himself away to give me the freedom to take lovers, to figure myself out, to grow up. *Everything I've done, I've done for you,* he'd said. Saving me from the fire at the abbey, tattooing me, offering to save Dancer, helping me rescue Shazam, forcing me to live when Dancer died, disappearing when I'd chosen a Ryodan look-alike.

I couldn't think about that now. We had a world to save.

Thanks to Christian, we finally had a reliable timeline of the history of gods, Fae, and Man. When Kat had finished recapping, I'd taken my turn and filled them in on my battle with Balor.

The Shedon furiously thumbed through the books I'd swiped from BB&B, while I talked.

"Listen to this," Decla said, reading aloud. "'Balor: king of Fomorians, often described as a giant with a large eye that wreaks destruction when opened. It's said as a child, Balor stared into a cauldron of poison, or a spell of death being brewed by druids, and the fumes caused him to grow an enormous, toxic eye. He was eventually killed by Lugh, in the battle between the Fae and Fomorians for dominion of Ireland.'"

"Here's another one," Duff said, reading from a different book. "'The demonic one-eyed god of Death. Invader, conqueror, with a single enormous leg—'"

"How does anyone even walk on one leg?" Ciara said with a snort.

"He had two," I assured her. "I injured one of them."

"'—and one huge eye—'"

"He had two," I said again. "One was much smaller."

"'—that he can use to kill merely by opening it and looking at someone.'"

"That's how he was taking my soul. I made the mistake of locking gazes with him and couldn't break it. When we find him, you must never look at his eyes. He was wearing a mask, and when he took it off, it was instinctive for me to peer beneath it."

"Probably why he wears it," Aurina said. "I'd have looked, too. When people conceal something, it makes you want to see it more."

"I don't think that was it, or that's merely an added boon for him," I said. "His face was badly scarred beneath the mask, but the rest of it was attractive. Beautiful, even. I got the impression he's vain, egotistical."

"Perhaps he got scarred like that when he looked into the cauldron of poison," Duff suggested.

"If there even *was* a cauldron," Kat said dryly. "I researched Balor myths as soon as Dani told me his name on the phone. They're all over the place. Completely different stories. I found one that alleged he was a benevolent god that came when beseeched to battlefields, to attend the lingering dying, freeing their souls so they wouldn't have to suffer the pain of death. According to that myth, he was merciful, gently removed them from their bodies and released them to the sky."

"Well, he's definitely not doing that now," I said grimly. "He's keeping them, absorbing them, using them for power and fuel. Factoring in what Christian told you, Kat, perhaps he was once a benign god, and what the Fae did to him turned him against us. Rather than using his gift for good, he uses it for himself."

Kat said, "The question is: how do we find him?"

"And how do we kill him?" Enyo said.

"The legends say by taking his eye," Decla said.

"Those same legends say Balor's dead," Kat pointed out. "Which seems to imply it didn't work."

"Not necessarily," Enyo said. "Dani said he's scarred around that eye. That sounds like someone tried but failed."

"The myths say Lugh used a slingshot to take Balor's eye with a stone," Decla said.

"Yes," Kat countered, "but supposedly Lugh was his grandson, and Lugh was Fae. Our history is a mess."

"There may be a simpler solution," I said, glancing at Ryodan. "Can you kill a god?" The Nine could kill Fae effortlessly. I'd once watched Jericho Barrons suck the psychopathic *Sinsar-Dubh* from within the body of an Unseelie princess and spit it out. I wasn't sure there was *anything* they couldn't kill.

He shrugged. "I've never tried. What few remained after the Fae killed or imprisoned them, we cultivated alliances with."

Imprisoned. Criminy. I still couldn't get over the news that the gods had been imprisoned beneath Arlington Abbey all this time. When Kat had told us that, I'd instantly flashed back to the night in the cemetery, years ago, when hundreds of dark Shade-like beings had risen from the earth, finally solving a chafing, unsolved case in my files.

I'd been standing right there when the gods gained enough strength to escape their tombs, months after the Song had been sung. I'd watched it happen, with no idea what they were.

I narrowed my eyes. They hadn't cared for my hand that night. "It's also possible I could kill him. I'd just need to get a direct hit to his eye next time."

"No," Ryodan snarled.

"No," Kat snapped.

"No," Enyo spat.

I blinked at them. "Seriously, guys, look at me. I can't be touched anymore. Do you really think I'm going to sit on my hands, literally and figuratively, and do nothing to save our world, so I don't get worse? How much worse can it get?" I had a fair idea. The difference between human and not. But they didn't know that. Not for sure.

Ryodan locked gazes with me, growling so only I could hear, *Let others tackle the enemy this time. You've done more than your share.* He looked sharply away but not before I caught, *Christ, woman, just stay with me awhile, will you? As long as you can.*

It flayed me. I wanted to stay, too. Time had always been the problem with us. I said, "I'll be the last resort, okay? I promise not to do anything unless I absolutely must, only if no one else can." That was the best I could offer. I know myself. If I can do something to save the world and no one else can, I'll pay the price. It's the way I'm wired.

Everyone in the room nodded, looking enormously relieved. Inwardly, I beamed. They all wanted to keep me as long as they could.

Kat said, "When he was trying to take your soul, did you pick up any details about where he's made his base camp, Dani?"

"Not a bloody thing. He could be anywhere. But his henchmen, Callum and Alfie, said he wanted them in Dublin for some reason and wouldn't let them move to another location. I got the impression of tens of thousands of people, perhaps a hundred thousand or more, all gathered in the same place. It's not easy to hide an army of that size."

"I've already got most of the Nine out searching," Ryodan

said. "They'll scour every inch of the city tonight and range out beyond that by morning."

"In the meantime, we'll continue researching," Kat said, pushing to her feet, "and see if we can turn up anything else."

"Can you get in touch with Christian and Sean?" I asked her. "They could cover a lot more ground from the sky." So could I—if I were a Hunter.

"Christian, yes. Sean, no," she said. "I'll reach out to him."

I said, "Ryodan and I will patrol, hunt the bastards abducting humans. If we can just find one of those mirrors, that will solve all of our problems."

"We will not," Ryodan said tightly.

Before I could even argue, Kat agreed. "Dani, I didn't tell you this because I knew you had your hands full, but a dozen of our Adepts went missing last Saturday. From what Christian said, it's a fair guess Balor's holding them as Fae watchdogs. Two people, against the god you described, plus an army of countless humans controlled by him, won't be enough. Our sisters are there. I want all boots on the ground for this mission."

"She's right," Ryodan growled. "We need a location, we go in force. All of the Nine, all of the *sidhe*-seers, Christian *and* Sean." He cut a dark look at Kat. "Fix whatever the fuck his problem is and get him functional."

She sighed. "Easier said than done. I'm trying."

"But if I kill Balor," I argued, "it's logical to conclude the humans will no longer be controlled. It could work."

"You just made us a promise," Kat snapped. "You're the last resort. Period."

"What she said," Ryodan said icily.

"But it could take too long that—"

"Dani, shut the fuck up," Enyo snapped. "We're just trying to keep you alive, okay? Let us handle this. Yes, it may take longer. We all know we're not as bloody superhero as you are. But we can do it. Think about it this way, we'll have to do it if you're no longer here. And it sounds like you won't be here soon!" Her voice cracked and I stared at her, dumbfounded, as the hardened warrior's eyes shimmered with sudden tears. She shook her head, wiping angrily at the moisture. "God, for being so brilliant, you are so fucking dense sometimes. You still don't get it, do you? You bloody saved me when you found me. I was losing it. You roped me in and put me to work and gave me a cause worth fighting for. I don't want to lose you. None of us do." She sprang to her feet and stalked from the room, unleashing a stream of curses as she went.

"You always save everyone else," Kat said quietly. "Let us save what we can of you this time."

I couldn't deal with this shit.

I shoved to my feet and stormed from the room.

π

I paced Ryodan's suite, practically gouging tufts of polished, glazed concrete from the floor with each step.

They wanted me to do nothing. Sit idly by, while they went to battle against Balor. I had no idea how to live that way. And I saw little point. My future was inevitable. The only difference between me turning now or turning later was that I'd get to spend more time with the people I loved. But what if me sitting back and not fighting ended up costing the lives of those very people I wanted to spend that time with? I'd never be able to live with that!

I felt like I was being torn in half. Part of me wanted desperately to hang on as long as I could and stay here with my friends, but there was another part of me that ... "Oh, hell, Dani, admit it," I muttered aloud. Part of me hungered for the power that was growing in me. There was so much good I could do with it. Turning into a Hunter wouldn't have been my first choice for the way my life would go. In fact, it wouldn't have even been *on* my list of choices. But if it had to happen, well, at least I didn't end up turning into any of the many other, weaker, disgusting things I'd killed. Hunters were lethal, their power astronomical. And I was pretty sure they were immortal.

I could watch over my friends *forever.* Protect them eternally. Kill Fae, kill anything that messed with them.

Then he was there, in the room with me, entering silently, stopping behind me. I shivered from raw aching awareness of him as a powerful, brilliant, basely sexual-in-all-the-right-ways man that had moved forever beyond my reach.

"Love is the one thing you've never understood," he said quietly, "because you didn't have it. You don't need to save the world to make us love you, Dani. We already do."

I exploded into tears, crying ugly.

How did he always know my secrets? That was *exactly* what I kept boxed in one of my highest security vaults.

The "Mega's" greatest insecurity: I *have* to be Mega; I have to be a superhero to be loved.

Hands fisting, he took two steps forward then jerked to a stop. We both knew he couldn't touch me. "Christ, it fucking slays me when you cry," he said roughly.

I growled through tears, "I'll get it under control, just give me a minute."

"You always do," he said flatly. I looked at him, startled by the undercurrents in his voice. Enormous respect, enormous sorrow. Gargantuan frustration at not being able to touch me.

I forced myself to breathe deep and even. I'd figured out long ago that freedom wasn't just another word for nothing left to lose.

Fearless was.

I'd had nothing to lose. No mom. No home. No friends. No life. It's easy to be fearless in those circumstances.

Now I had everything to lose, and a destructive, raging part of me wanted to go ahead and lose it right away, get it over with because limbo unravels me. Once you lose everything, you can take action: You either die or cope. But before, while you're watching it all go to hell, there's no action you can take. You're helpless, caught in a killing undertow. My mom was my entire world and, trapped in a cage, I was forced to watch her slip away bit by bit, unable to do anything to prevent it. I might have stolen food for us. With my super skills, I could have stolen money, we'd have been rich. I could have taken care of us.

But I'd had to sit there, watching, while everything fell apart.

"Close your eyes," Ryodan said softly.

I didn't argue, just let my lids flutter closed, then he was there, standing next to me. I could see him, us, as clearly as if it was actually happening. I shivered with emotion, with desire. I could smell the scent of his skin, feel the omnipresent erotic current of his body as his powerful arms slipped around me.

I dropped my head to his chest and melted into him like a second skin, savoring his strength, his heat, his big, hard body. This man was the one thing in my universe that made me feel safe.

He rubbed his jaw against my hair, his hands spanning my back, and as he began to work at my tight muscles, my tears stopped, my body stilled, my breathing deepened. Even an illusion of him could take me down to ground zero. I wondered how he'd survived his childhood and come out so bloody strong.

Careful, he said in my mind. *We're linked right now. You might see things you'd rather not.*

"You know my pain. Show me yours. I want to know."

It wasn't pretty.

"As if my life has been."

Exhaling gustily, he dropped his forehead to mine in our illusory embrace, raised his hands to my temples.

We'd been standing in his office at Chester's, years ago, when he'd shown me that, like me, he'd been caged as a child, horribly abused, kept in a pit in the ground that was dark and damp and cold.

Suddenly, I was there. Trapped. The smell of damp soil and my own waste. Never let out.

Unless he hurt me so bad he had to take me out for his "doctors" to heal me so he could do it again. It was the only time I saw the sun. I lived for the times he almost killed me. I began to pray for them. I wanted to see sunshine that badly. To feel it on my battered skin, to soak it into my broken bones, to walk "up there" with the others. Sunshine became synonymous with life.

He wasn't just giving me words in my head, he was somehow translating every nuance of the child's desperation, the hope, the hate, the pain. I was *in* that horrid, smelly, small pit with that horrid steel door above me, fitted so tightly not one ounce of light trickled in. I was cold. I was lost. I was an animal. Everyone else got to live. But not me.

I shuddered from the intensity of it. I was . . . oh! Like me, he'd gone into his brain. There'd been no place else to go. The boy had created lavish worlds in his head, lived in them. Had replayed every detail of the wonderful loving life he'd once had, milking it for what he needed to continue trying to survive.

Why doesn't she come for me? Why doesn't she save me? An anguished scream. The crack of breaking bone.

He'd not had the blessing of my TV, my infrequent mother, my glimpses beyond tightly drawn curtains when she'd walked out and slammed the door, gusting the drapes from the wall, of the world beyond, of OUTSIDE. Just endless, eternal darkness. No stimulation. Incessant solitary confinement.

How the bloody hell had he not gone mad?

I held onto my family in my mind. My mother was a beautiful woman, coveted far and wide. Barrons was her first husband's son. When he died, two wealthy, powerful suitors vied for her hand. She chose my father and was quickly pregnant with me. I had an incredible childhood. My parents adored us. No harm touched me. If it had tried, my older brother would have beaten it senseless. But it was a lawless, barbaric time and my father was killed in battle. Her other suitor came again, determined to possess her this time. She'd never liked him, always feared him, called in friends to stand her ground with her, begging for time. He agreed to leave only if she permitted him to take her youngest son until she joined him. He said it was to foster me. We all knew I was his hostage.

I saw the man then, dark and savage, from long ago, and realized Ryodan was translating things into words I could understand because people had been so much more primitive then. Wealth didn't mean a fine home. It meant a vast tribe, furs, and fire.

She never came for me because she died. Barrons says she passed peacefully in her sleep of a broken heart, that losing both her husband and son was more than she could bear. I know better. A woman unprotected by a man back then was prey. I suspect those same friends that stood with her that day descended later and killed her, seizing our lands, and Barrons barely escaped alive. He swore he would get me back. And he did. But that's a tale for another time, Dani. Our time may be short.

I drifted for a moment, linked to him, feeling him with all my senses. I'd never experienced intimacy like this before, so much more than our bodies touching, our minds mingling. I could taste the flavor of him: Danger, ruthlessness, savagery, fearlessness. And ferocious, unwavering commitment and loyalty. He was an animal first, pure, loyal, and territorial as a wolf.

Family was everything to Ryodan. He'd followed Barrons around his entire existence, determined to stay together. The Nine had become his family, too. He'd patiently reclaimed them each time they wandered off, moved them all over the globe for eons, following Barrons as he searched for a way to free the son I hadn't known he'd had.

He showed me Barrons's son then, the cage in which he (and Ryodan!) had been imprisoned. He shared the final scene with me as well: the way the tormented child had finally been laid to rest.

My eyes flew open in shock, shattering the illusion of our embrace, and I glared at him across the distance that separated us, which now seemed far too near for my comfort. I backpedaled hastily away. "Are you kidding me?" I cried. "I'm turning into the one thing that can kill you?"

He shrugged, a faint smile playing at his lips. "I always said I wanted an equal, Dani. Looks like I got one."

I stared at him in horror. "If my bare skin touches you and I blow you up, will you die *permanently*?"

He shrugged again. "I have no idea. I can, however, touch a Hunter just fine." He flashed me a wolfish grin. "At least then I'll get to ride you, woman, in one sense of the bloody word."

"Don't joke at a time like this," I hissed.

Silver ice glittered in his eyes. "For fuck's sake, Dani, unbox your sense of humor. It's one of the many things I missed most about you. Speaking of which, any time now, you can start telling me what you missed most about me. From what I understand, if you turn into a Hunter, you'll be immortal. That's a plus. I don't brood. That's Barrons's gig. Never yours and mine."

He had a point. There were worse fates. Shazam would probably like me even more as a Hunter. Ryodan and I could crack each other up for all eternity. A dragon, a beast, and a Hel-Cat, carving out our own unique way of life together.

Still, any man would eventually tire of loving a dragon.

"I'm not any man," he said quietly, as he moved to a chest of drawers and withdrew a long wooden box. "What did I tell you so long ago? Adaptability is survivability. There are ways. I didn't want you out in the streets tonight because there's something else I want you to do. Come."

He turned and walked to a table near the fire, where he removed items from the box. Inks. Needles. A complicated design etched on a piece of parchment. As I joined him, maintaining a cautious distance between us, he said, "While I can create illusion in your mind that feels real, you can't do it for me unless we complete the brand. Then the illusion will be real for both of us. Specifically," he went on, in case I was missing the point, "sex will be indistinguishable from reality. Fuck the uncertain future. Tattoo me, Dani. Let me be a beast in love with a dragon. We can still have it all."

I stood there, doing something utterly alien to me, thinking about everything that could go wrong. Love did that to you. Messed with your brain, made you think about things you'd never think about otherwise.

I shook my head hard, scattering those thoughts. I don't invite trouble. I invite the next grand adventure, and with Ryodan it was certain to be as incredible as it was unpredictable. And if we could create a convincing illusion of intimacy? It had felt exquisitely real to me with all my senses fiercely engaged. I'd known years ago that part of the reason I chose Dancer was because of how deeply Ryodan rattled me. Dancer had been easy laughter and a normal future. Ryodan was endless challenge and a future that was impossible to imagine. The future was here. I'd never had a normal life. Why would I expect a normal future?

An unexpected exhilaration filled me. I wasn't losing him, we were just changing, becoming the next thing. We were good at that, he and I. It was our strength. It occurred to me that adaptability was more than survivability; it was the foundation of love. We were all changing, every day, and those relationships that endured were the ones that rode the waves together, grew and allowed each other to evolve. Encouraged it, even when it was frightening. Adaptability in relationships was the polar opposite of a cage. It was necessary commitment wed to necessary freedom.

He dropped backward in a chair and stripped off his shirt, his back rippling sleek and beautiful in the firelight, and said in a low, sexy voice, "Come on, Stardust, brand your man. I've been waiting a long fucking time for this."

Your man. I liked that. Holy hell, did I like that. Ryodan Killian St. James had just called himself my man.

"Unless you're afraid to commit yourself to a beast like me," he goaded.

I snorted. "Hardly. I'll brand your ass."

He laughed. "Spine. It's more effective there. But finish it and you can do whatever you want with my ass. Just remember, turnabout's fair play."

I arched a brow. "You might regret that." I was a lust-driven, uninhibited woman.

"With you, no holds barred. Show me what you've got, Babe," he teased.

I'd have teased back but a sudden concern struck me. "What about my blood?" He'd had to mix ours to complete my tattoo. If my blood had changed, would it hurt him?

"Not necessary. I tasted yours years ago."

Knowing the way his mind worked, he'd taken it just in case he needed it for one of his many linchpin theories.

"Gloves are on the table by the bed," he tossed over his shoulder.

As I gloved up, I admired his wide shoulders, heavily muscled, tattooed back, tight, powerful ass and legs. He'd unbuttoned his pants, dropping them around his hips. God, he was so beautiful.

At least in illusion, I was going to get to touch every inch of him soon. Let go of all that raging, caged passion I'd been holding back for so long. I couldn't wait to explore what this bond was going to do for us.

He said softly, "Intimacy on a level you can't even begin to imagine. You should know going in, I'll never remove mine. You do this, there's no turning back. We'll know each other like humans never can. You'll be able to feel me constantly. Good, bad, and ugly, it's all there. Still want to tattoo me, Dani?"

I wouldn't miss this adventure with him for anything in the world.

THIRTY-FOUR

* • *

The best is yet to come

I worked all night on Ryodan's tattoo, racing the clock, worried that—given how unpredictable my life is—something might happen to keep me from finishing the brand before I became whatever I was becoming. I doubted a Hunter's massive talons were capable of the dexterity necessary to painstakingly ink the delicate, many-layered spell into his skin.

We talked nonstop, making each other laugh, sharing stories of outlandish adventures we'd had, subtly one-upping each other and laughing at ourselves for doing it. Ryodan is as self-aware as I am. Okay, maybe a little more. Thing is, we love the game we play, the way we provoke each other, we thrive on it. And that was a trait I couldn't wait to explore in bed with him. People say opposites attract and that's true, they do—combustively, and short-term. I think it's those with like minds and hearts that succeed long-term.

Late that morning, as I inked the final lines of the tattoo, I inhaled sharply. I felt an instant, subtle yet pervasive connection to him that I couldn't begin to put into words, an omnipresent awareness of him on a cellular level. "Is this what you've always felt since you tattooed me?"

"To a degree. Now that we both wear the brand, it's stronger," he said, turning around in the chair to face me. "You're feeling a connection to my essential energy, for lack of a better phrase."

His "essential energy" was comprised of a staggering amount of raw sexuality and tightly leashed hunger. For everything: more life, more sex, more toys, more adventure. He was one thousand percent exhilarated to be alive. All the time. Like me.

"You're on the surface. You'll always feel me now. Think of it as a bridge between us. We can stay on our own sides as we are, or we can move across it, entering each other to various degrees. Respect is paramount. If you resist my presence at any time, I'll back off. You're entitled to your secrets. You choose what to let me see. This kind of intimate connection can be beautiful or terrible. Never take, only ask, never force, only offer, respect boundaries."

Always, I vowed silently. Such access was a privilege, not to be taken for granted or exploited. I expanded my senses and, as he allowed me to delve deeper, I gasped again.

He was all around me, a great big sexy Ryodan blanket rubbing up against my mind. It felt as if I was slipping deeper inside him, not perceiving him in words, but tasting him with an unnamed sense. Discovering his nuances. There were no lies or deceptions here; it was open, raw, only what it was; good, bad, and ugly. No wonder he'd said we were going to know each other more intimately than people ever could!

The taste of him was addictive. He was proud, strong, had

often been a king during his life, determined, fiercely focused on the things he cared about and ferociously protective of them. But he was right, he was beast first, human second. I wouldn't have believed that until this moment, so flawlessly had Ryodan perfected his man's skin. His beast was savage, primitive, its law utterly self-serving, an endless roar inside that said: *I'M KING OF THIS MOTHERFUCKING JUNGLE. EVERYTHING IS MINE. I WANT IT ALL, ALL THE TIME.* His beast was ancient, ruthless, voracious, craved everything sensual and immediately gratifying, and it had absolutely no—

Careful . . . you sure you want to know that? Soft laughter rolled in my mind.

"No conscience," I said, stunned. "Good grief, your beast has absolutely no morals, scruples, or ethics. Nothing even close."

"Only those rules I make and enforce on it. It's an eternal battle. I usually win." He flashed me a feral, fierce smile. "But there are times, such as war, when I get to set the beast free."

He loved those times. Felt undivided in his own skin for a rare time. Yet always hungered for a return to the man and his world, those he'd chosen as his family.

"Dani, I feel the Hunter in you," he said quietly.

"And?"

"It's beautiful." *One more time,* his silver gaze didn't say. *That's all you've got.*

And I didn't say, *Then I'll never use it again.*

And he didn't say, *Thank you for that.*

Because we both knew I'd use it the next time it was needed. Just like we both knew he would devolve into a lawless monster the next time the opportunity presented itself.

We were what we were, and nothing could change that.

Love doesn't build cages. It builds stairways to the stars.

"Close your eyes," I said softly, ready to test just how intimate we could be. When he did, I focused on the connection between us, locking everything in the room down on my mental grid, re-creating us in a private space in my mind as I closed my own eyes.

"Christ, you're a natural," he said roughly. "I'm here with you."

Because of the way I'd taught myself to use my brain, it was second nature to re-create reality in my mind. In the illusion, I stalked hungrily toward him, straddled his lap and slid my arms around his neck, staring down at him. Sexy, brilliant, pain in the ass man, and all mine. Bloody hell, he hadn't lied, I could feel every inch of his body, indistinguishable from reality.

"I feel it, too, now that we're both branded," he said roughly. "Before I couldn't." His hands slid up my waist, stopping at the curve of my breasts, thumbs drifting up to graze my nipples. I sucked in a shallow breath, jerking from the erotic contact. "Christ, you're incredible."

It was so convincing, I wondered if it would be possible to forget which version of events was true. In the real world, he was still sitting in a chair alone while I was standing several feet away. I tested my ability to move back and forth between the reality and the illusion, stunned to find it indistinguishable. Mind-boggling.

"Get your ass back here. Practice technique later," he growled. "Fucking kiss me, woman."

I meant to kiss him with an explosion of raw, long-repressed lust, but when I raised my hands to his face they met his skin with reverence. I thought I'd lost the ability to touch him, to feel the rasp of his beard against my palm, slide my fingers into his hair. This was an unexpected gift. I lowered my mouth to his and brushed lightly, teasing, nipping, savoring the tension coiled in his body, knowing he wanted it hard, savage, and I'd get to that in just a moment but, bloody hell, teasing this man sexually was something I'd hungered—

My phone alert sounded.

"Ignore it," he growled.

I couldn't. I had to at least look. If our world was peaceful, I could shut it off. But it wasn't and it might be important so I shifted back to reality with a groan, tugged my phone from my pocket and glanced at it.

Is your last name O'Malley?

It was from Roisin. I winced. With all that had been happening in my life, I'd not circled back to check on her.

Yes why?

I need to talk to you. There's something you need to know.

I'll call you

No. I need to see you

I sighed gustily at the same moment Ryodan did and glanced at him, startled. "You can see her text?"

"No. I picked up only that someone wanted you and you'd made up your mind to go, when a split second ago there was nothing but sex on your mind. Whatever it is," he said darkly, "let's get it done."

"This is certainly going to make things easier. You can tell when—"

"Your stubborn kicks in," he growled. "Yes. We'll both know when it's pointless to argue."

"That's going to save so much—"

"Which means more time to fuck," he purred, pushing up from the chair.

"Are you going to start finishing all—"

"Good chance of it. Soon you'll stop talking."

Holy hell, I don't need to anymore!

You and me, peas in that kaleidoscopic, crazy-ass Mega-pod of yours. He flashed me one of those rare full-on smiles, blazing with joy.

It took my breath away. Maybe this beast/dragon thing could actually work.

Never doubt it, he said in my mind as we headed out to see Roisin.

π

I was pleased to hear the sound of multiple dead bolts sliding when I texted Roisin to let her know we were standing outside her flat, that I'd brought company with me and to brace herself: I looked a bit different.

Still, I suppose no warning could have prepared her for the sight of me. I'd gotten my fill of shocked, startled, and frightened looks on the way over. And notched my chin higher, put a little swagger into my step. I wasn't scary looking as far as I was concerned; Hunter-raven and obsidian flames looked good on me. I thought I looked downright dangerous and oddly hot.

Soft laughter in my mind. *That you do,* Ryodan agreed.

I sent him a wordless smile in response.

Sexy in any form, Dani. Woman or dragon.

Back atcha, badass dude.

More laughter, husky with a blatantly sexual undertone. I shivered. Couldn't wait to get my illusory hands on him again.

During the walk over I'd become aware that something deep at my core was changing, transforming, caterpillar to a leathery-winged black butterfly. I could sense subtle differences in my brain I couldn't quite grasp but it felt as if inert areas of gray matter were waking up, firing with new neurons. I could feel more raw energy pooling inside me than ever before. I loathed that the changes were taking me away from my friends, but given what Ryodan and I could do with our bond, and the power I would soon have, my inevitable transformation was more bittersweet than bitter. He loved me. He would love me no matter what I was. I loved him the same way. Love doesn't always come in tidy packages.

"What in the world happened to you?" Roisin gasped, peering intently at me.

"Hazards of the trade," I told her as we stepped inside the flat, unable to keep a note of irritation from my voice. There were no rules in our world, hadn't been for years. Who knew killing a Hunter meant you would become one? Who could even *guess* at that kind of twist? It had been somewhere between seven and nine years since I'd stabbed it. What kind of transformation took that long? I said, "How's your back?"

"Healing. The bastards dragged us down the street," she said tightly.

I blinked. "To a mirror?"

It was her turn to blink. "Yes. How did you know that?"

Balor took her? Ryodan said in my mind. *And she got away?*

Sounds like. How had this petite woman with no apparent magic managed it? To Roisin, I said, "Tell me everything."

π

Roisin, her father, and brother had been abducted by four men nearly a week ago. They'd broken into their home, shot them with paralytic darts, dragged them down the street, tossed them into a pile with other bodies near a mirror, then gone back out into the streets to collect more.

But her abduction had taken a darker turn than mine. The men who'd collected them had been sadists, raping and torturing their captives. They'd broken her father's legs and badly beaten her brother while she lay helplessly by, being raped again and again.

I will fucking kill every last bloody one of them, Ryodan snarled in my mind.

You and me both, I returned grimly.

Eventually, they'd transported them through the mirror and added their bodies to a growing mound of paralyzed, tortured humans.

"It was like something out of a horror movie," she said hoarsely. "I couldn't move. I hurt everywhere and could only see what I was pointed at. I couldn't even shift my eyes in my head. I could hear people talking." She shuddered. "The things they were saying were horrible. They hate humans and plan to eradicate us from the face of the earth. And they're not Fae."

"Why did you ask if my last name was O'Malley?" I said.

"Because the one behind it all—they called him Balor—wanted you. That was what I heard right before I crawled back through the mirror. He sent a hideous little monster that could split itself up into roaches out to find you. Balor said he was going to collect you personally."

"Papa Roach!" I exclaimed.

"The bastard keeps switching sides," Ryodan said, cursing. "I'm going to kill that fuck once and for all."

"I saw a roach in my shower a few nights ago," I told him.

"And you're just now telling me that?"

I shrugged. "I'm never certain if they're just roaches. They can't *all* be Papa Roach."

"They are," he growled.

I frowned at him. "You mean every roach in the whole world—"

"Yes. And he's dying the next time I see one."

Roison stared between us. "You guys already know about all of this?"

"Not all of it," I said. "How did you escape?"

"Because of Gustaine—that's what Balor called the roach monster. Balor had just removed the paralysis spell from a group of us when Gustaine interrupted and distracted him." Her eyes filled with tears. "I could move but my father and brother were too badly injured to escape." The tears began to run down her cheeks and she wiped angrily at them. "They kept jerking their heads toward the mirror, telling me to leave."

Oh, God, how do you leave the people you love like that; yet how do you stay? There's no point in staying. Either one of you lives or you all die. It's a horrific choice with painful repercussions either way. "I'm so sorry."

"I had to go. It was the only chance they had. I had to get back and figure out how to save them. But when I got back, I couldn't . . . I just couldn't function and you found me and brought me here and I slept for days."

"You were in shock," I told her. "Your eyes were glazed. You'd been through hell and it takes time to pull it together. I think you did it in record time."

"It's been six days!" Roisin cried. "Who knows what's happened to them in that time!"

"You did the best you could," I said quietly. "I saw how broken you were. We're here now and we'll get the bastard that did this. I promise you that."

"Describe for us where he was," Ryodan ordered. "Omit no detail."

She began to shiver as she spoke, rubbing her arms as if to ward off a bone deep chill. "We were in some kind of huge cavern. There were . . . I don't know, thousands, maybe tens of thousands of people, but they weren't . . . right. They were blank, looked nearly starved, like puppets being controlled, moving jerkily, and they chanted nonstop, saying Balor's name over and over. He was building an army of humans, controlling them somehow."

"He takes their souls," I told her grimly. "He tried to take mine."

"He already came after you?" she exclaimed.

I nodded.

"How did you escape?"

I smiled faintly. "I have a few unique talents. Back to the cavern, tell us more."

She sighed. "It was like those caves beneath the Burren, but I could see tunnels shooting off in all directions. I got the impression we were deep below the earth." She shook her head, "No, that's not quite right, they looked more like . . . corridors that had been carved out a long time ago. Tall, made of stone blocks, with high rounded arches. There were fires in the main cavern and hundreds of ancient-looking torches bolted into the walls everywhere, vanishing down the corridors."

"Metal sconces?" I said, using my gloved hands to sketch an image in the air. "With three stems going up into cups the size of my fist that had flames in them?"

"Yes, how did you know that?"

"And did those three stems shape a sort of clover?" I demanded.

"With a bent leaf," she said, nodding.

Was she fucking kidding me? "Did it feel like you were in an underground city more than a cave?" I said tightly.

She nodded again. "Yes. That's what I was trying to say. It didn't seem like a natural cave, but something that was deliberately planned—"

"Bloody fucking hell, that bastard is beneath the abbey!" Ryodan exploded.

"What abbey?" Roison said.

I shot him a dark look. "When Balor woke up, he never left. He stayed put in the one place he knew the Fae would never come, building his army, absorbing power, right beneath our bloody feet. That's how he got our *sidhe*-seers. They weren't abducted at Elyreum. He either took them on their way back in late at night or simply came up and grabbed them while they slept. That son of a bitch planned to get strong enough to destroy us all, while being protected by us, then kill us and go after the Fae!"

"But wouldn't you have heard the chanting and screaming?" Roison said.

"Not as deep as our underground city goes, no. I'm not even sure we would have heard him in the cavern the *Sinsar Dubh* once occupied, if the door was closed. Everything is solid rock and most of it dozens of feet thick." Damn the Shedon for not letting us explore the Underneath! I thought as I yanked out my phone and fired off a text to Kat:

GET EVERYONE OUT OF THE ABBEY. WE THINK BALOR IS BENEATH IT

"I'm coming, too," Roisin said instantly.

"You'll slow us down," Ryodan said curtly.

I agreed with him on that score and told her so. "Sit tight and wait. I promise to text you the moment we kill him. We'll find your family, Roisin, I promise."

I didn't tell her I was afraid there was nothing we could do for them once we did. The feeling I'd gotten from Balor was once you lost your soul, it was a done deal. Souls weren't pickles that could be stuffed back into a jar. Especially not as brutally as he'd tried to wrench mine from my body. Then there was the whole annihilating of personality facet once he had them. He'd felt like a massive pulping blender, breaking down souls into fundamental nutrients to fuel himself as if humans were his protein powder.

As we stalked from the flat, Ryodan shot off a text to Christian, a second to Lor, telling him and the others to meet us at the abbey, and a third to Barrons, though I doubted he'd be joining us. Protecting Mac from Fae attack was paramount.

We had this. One way or another.

You promised. You're the last resort, Dani, Ryodan reminded tightly.

I nodded.

I heard that, he snapped.

I smiled faintly. *Did not. I didn't say it. Boundaries, remember? You fucking felt it.*

We're going to have to make a few more rules, I said lightly. *One of them is you can't hold me responsible for my feelings if I don't voice them.* What he'd picked up was my unshakable sense of inevitability. As if this day, whatever was about to happen, had been aimed at me, trying to collide with me for a long time, and it was . . . well, I don't believe in fate but I do believe in actions and reactions. Years ago I'd made an action. The repercussions from it were bearing down on me like a cat-five hurricane whose course couldn't be altered.

I was ready. Whatever happened. Next adventure.

Fearless as always. I felt his warmth, his respect, his constant, steady love.

It's all I know to be.

You're like us in that. Becoming a beast was meant as a curse. But if I could go back to that day and choose again, I'd do exactly the same. Live forever like this? Fuck, yes.

I gasped. He'd never spoken to me of anything to do with his origins. *Does that mean one day you'll tell me?*

Tell me something you missed about me, he evaded.

Everything, I admitted finally. *Half the colors vanished from my world and I couldn't breathe right until you returned.*

Say it, Stardust. I want to hear it.

I love you, Ryodan Killian St. James. Any name, any form. Always.

Pure joy blazed inside my soul, warming me to the core.

π

Tucked beneath a base molding in the living room of the flat, one of countless roaches flooding every nook and cranny of Dublin retracted its antennae and sent a silent message back to its counterparts in the cavern, letting Gustaine know the auspicious news that the woman Balor sought had been located.

And was headed straight for him.

THIRTY-FIVE

———— • ◦ • ————

I curse the stars that take you away

BALOR HAD ALREADY TAKEN the abbey by the time we got there.

We'd originally headed for the main gate but, a half mile away, we heard the chanting of thousands of Balor's zombies and circled around to the back. We'd abandoned the Hummer behind a tall labyrinth of hedges where we now crouched, with Lor and the rest of the Nine who were already in beast form.

We eased around the side of the fortress toward the battle raging on the front lawn. It reminded me too much of another battle, between the Fae and us, when I'd melted down and raced back into the burning abbey to save a stuffed animal. The night Ryodan had charred himself to the bone to save me.

The lawn was filled with nearly a thousand *sidhe*-seers battling ten times that number of Balor's zombies, slashing and hacking their way through the crowd. It was horrific, humans fighting blank-eyed humans, and I knew every *sidhe*-seer out there was fighting their own innate instincts to do it. We're pro-grammed to kill Fae and protect humans. Yet these humans were tightly controlled killing machines Balor had loosed on us with instructions to destroy.

Balor himself was on the lawn—bloody hell, he was enor-mous! Over twenty feet tall, clad in billowing black—lumbering through the crowd, mask shoved up on his head, that terrible, enormous eye revealed as he bent, snatched *sidhe*-seers into the air by an arm as if they were dolls, drank their souls, then flung them to the ground like broken toys.

I snarled, hands fisting. There was no way I was staying out of this fight. I lunged forward, only to feel Ryodan's hand close on my wrist like a manacle.

You promised.

My sisters are dying!

Give us a chance.

"Kill him!" Ryodan snarled. He surged forward, transform-ing effortlessly, and eight beasts melted into battle, determined to take Balor down.

Scowling, hands fisted, I stayed melted into the side of the abbey, holding my breath, feeling raw power roiling inside me, demanding to be used, demanding that I do what I was born to do.

I heard that, he snarled. *Stay put.*

Then the Nine exploded out of nowhere, vaulting airborne, landing on the titanic god, ripping with lethal fangs at his flesh.

I knew which one was Ryodan, I could feel him now, and, as I watched, he hurled himself into the air and went straight for Balor's face, primal jaws wrenching impossibly wide, closing on the god's flesh, fangs sinking deep.

Balor roared, kicking and swatting at the many beasts tearing into him, howling with rage and pain. Abruptly, he focused solely on Ryodan, closing enormous hands around his throat and squeezing.

My heart clenched. I could feel Ryodan's pain as those massive fists closed tighter and tighter. Felt like I couldn't breathe, too. Could feel that whatever Ryodan usually did to kill the Fae wasn't working on Balor.

Get off him now! I thundered inside Ryodan's head. *Get all of the Nine off him. It's not working!*

But Ryodan sank his fangs deeper into Balor's face, despite the horrific sense of strangulation I could feel him suffering, ignoring me, and I suddenly understood he was trying to drain the life-force from the god, the way Barrons had sucked the *Sinsar Dubh* from the Unseelie princess's body, and I knew at the precise moment he did that it wasn't working. Whatever gods were made of, it wasn't the same as Fae.

The Nine couldn't kill them.

It didn't surprise me. I'd had a strange unshakable sense of fate riding me like a bitch all day.

I was willing to bet I could.

I inhaled deep and slow, embracing my power, calling to the Hunter within, beckoning, welcoming it. *Fill me, take me, I'm ready*, I willed. *Whatever the price.*

Energy slammed into me like a fist to my heart and my entire body bristled electric. I couldn't get a shot at the god with the beasts in the way without taking one of them out, and although they'd return if Balor killed them, there was a good chance they wouldn't if I hit them with a Hunter bolt.

Get everyone off Balor, I snarled at Ryodan. *Now, I said!*

I could feel every emotion he was feeling. Fury, grief, rage, sorrow, denial.

He didn't say *I'll miss that beautiful body of yours*, although I felt it.

And I didn't say *I'm afraid you won't keep loving a dragon*, although he felt it.

We're both too pragmatic for that. We do what needs to be done.

As the Nine dropped away, as Ryodan tore himself from Balor's grasp, I quit being the wallflower I simply can't be and strode into battle with fire in my blood, war in my heart, and extreme high voltage in my veins.

My first lightning bolt caught Balor in the chest, slamming him backward, nearly taking him off his feet.

The power inside me felt so much bigger now! And I knew with soul-deep knowing that there was no coming back from it this time. No second chances. I was going to be a Hunter when this was through.

Roaring, Balor spun to face me, stabbed me with that lethal soul-sucking gaze and began to tug at my soul.

To my surprise nothing happened. I couldn't even feel him trying to take it. I'd moved beyond his reach. Guess I wasn't quite human anymore.

I saw the look of astonishment on his face and laughed as I stalked nearer, shoving his zombies out of my way. I slammed him with bolt after bolt, in his chest, in his face, singeing and charring him, yet that damned eye remained unaffected.

Then the bastard dropped the mask back down over his eye and I heard Ryodan say, *It's not enough, Dani. You're not letting go. You have to let go of everything. Become the next thing.* He didn't say *Let go of me*, but I heard it and he was right. I was still resisting with a tiny part of me, not wanting to become something that would forever separate me from the people I loved.

I had to embrace the transition fully, accept that I was dying, so a new me could be born.

Love you, Stardust. Always. Across space and time. No ending. New beginnings.

Sorrow welled inside me. This was not what I'd planned. This was not the life I'd wanted for myself. I wiped angrily at tears icing my cold black cheeks.

New beginnings, I sent back along our bond, with a wordless expression of how I felt about him. How I'd always felt about him.

He inhaled sharply, and cursed, *Fuck. Shit. Goddamn, woman. You show me that now!*

It was now or never. Every second I wasted was potentially another *sidhe*-seer's soul. I flung my head back and threw my hands up to the sky, calling down power from the heavens. I poised on the brink of becoming something else, something so alien I couldn't even fathom it. But it was time and it was my destiny and the stars awaited. *I AM HUNTER!* I roared silently. *I ACCEPT. I WANT THIS. I COMMIT.*

My body raged with raw high voltage, I became high voltage, I quivered electric with unspeakable power, focused and hurled it all at Balor's eye in one furious bolt.

The god's head exploded in a shower of—

THIRTY-SIX

— • • • —

I would always open up the door, always

looking up at higher floors

S TARS.

 Millions, maybe trillions of them glittering on a vast, eternal black palette.

I was soaring at superluminal velocity, headed straight for a fantastical pink, gold, purple, and orange cluster of nebulae.

This time was different. In the past I'd always felt oddly disembodied.

I didn't now. I flexed my hand and glanced down. I had a hoof of sorts with black talons. It was steaming like dry ice, leaving a trail of sparkling frost in my wake. I glanced back over my shoulder and simply stared for a long moment.

I had the body of an enormous black, leathery skinned and scaled, icy, majestic dragon.

Holy hell, I was a Hunter.

I glanced right and left to see my beautiful wings. Though I'd known it was going to happen, knowing wasn't the same as seeing.

I was no longer human. And never would be again. This was my body now.

I focused on curving one of my wings. It not only obeyed, it nearly sent me into a tailspin. I snapped it rigid and pulled out of it moments before crashing into a small meteor sailing by.

Oh, God, I was in space.

I was a Hunter.

It was too much to process. I'd been too quickly ripped out of one reality and crammed into another.

My body was gone. My red hair, my arms, my legs, all of it. Just gone. Forever. I would never lace up sneakers on my feet again. Never slip into a sexy dress and high heels. Never gorge on Pop-Tarts, or access my brand of the slipstream. Never pet Shazam with a hand.

They say we deal with death in stages. I always thought I'd belly up a laugh and plunge into it fearlessly, but now I felt appallingly normal for the first time in my life, as I flashed instantly to denial. "I can't be this. Send me back!" I protested. My words came out as a deep, resonant gonging, not words at all. Where were the Hunters? They'd come in the past. Why weren't they here now?

Anger reared its fiery red head. "You can't do this to me! I had a life!"

Silence.

In case they were nearby, listening, I moved to the next stage: bargaining: "Please! I just need to see Ryodan one more time, and I need to tell Shazam what happened! I'm not ready!"

You wouldn't be here if you weren't.

The voice echoed inside my head and I turned to find a great black Hunter dropping into flight pattern beside me.

A huge Hunter! Twenty times my size. I was tiny in comparison.

It chuffed with laughter. *You've just been born. What did you expect? It will be eons before you're fully grown.*

I blinked, suffering a mind-bending disconnect. Part of me was still human, back on Earth, torn from battle, desperate to know if I'd succeeded in killing Balor, desperate to see Ryodan and Shazam, to know which of my sisters I'd lost. Another part of me was simply stupefied, trying to process and accept that I was a Hunter now. I had a new body that, fortunately, seemed to understand instinctively how to fly itself.

"Where did my other body go?" I boomed.

The Hunter snorted a tendril of fire. *Silly question. Part of you.*

"I need to know if I killed—"

Balor is dead.

"How do you know?"

I've been watching you.

I turned my (dragon!) head and peered into its fiery orange gaze. "Why?"

Protecting you. We nest our eggs.

"I'm not an egg," I said indignantly.

You were. Now you're Hunter.

"You mean because I stabbed one? Is that the deal—if someone kills a Hunter, they have to become one?"

Have to? Hardly. Hunter is a privilege. We don't birth children. We choose them. Our chosen must then choose to become one of us or not. You could have walked away at any point. You chose not to.

I blinked, pondering that, unable to argue. I have a fatal flaw: more weapons to protect my world seduces me. I'd hungered for the gargantuan power of a Hunter. I'd been enticed by the possibility of such astronomical adventures. In a deep, wordless place inside I'd been insatiably curious about what was happening to me. It's always been one of my downfalls, leading me from one extreme situation to the next.

During the past two years when I'd been so alone, I'd have plunged headlong into the transition.

But my family was back. I was in love. I had a life and a world and a Hel-Cat that needed me.

Each time you turned black, you didn't reject it. You found it curious, intriguing. When you began to transform, you welcomed it, always staring up at the stars. That's what I felt in you the day you stabbed me. You're made of stardust, destined for the skies. You belong here, with us.

I gaped at the giant Hunter that seemed somehow feminine to me. "*You're* the one I stabbed?"

She turned her head and smiled, thin black lips peeling back from saber teeth and bobbed her great leathery black head. *I am Y'rill. I have been waiting to see if you would become one of us for many years. Keeping you alive when I could.* If a dragon could look abashed, Y'rill did then. *I broke many rules for you, Dani O'Malley.*

"I thought I killed you."

Can't. We die only if we choose to become the next thing.

"What?" I demanded suspiciously, wanting to know just what was in store for me next.

It is within us to one day become planets. Your Earth was once a Hunter. You, Dani O'Malley, are one of our chosen. It is a great honor.

But my people! I peered down through space, seeing only unfamiliar moons and worlds. No sign of Earth. I had no idea where I was, no real concept of up or down. It was disorienting in the extreme.

It will soon feel natural. And they are still your people if you wish, Y'rill said.

"You mean I can return and live among them as a Hunter," I clarified. I fully intended to.

You may also live among them as a human. Half the time.

I have no idea what I did then because I didn't have the hang of my new form, but I gave an explosive whole-body jerk and suddenly I was rocketing through space in a dizzying tailspin, head over tail—Holy leaping lizards, I had a tail! A long black leathery one!

Stop fighting it, Y'rill said, chuffing softly. *You can't muscle things up here. Easy, smooth movements, small one.*

I tried, I really did. Focused on merely the tips of my wings, but I was tumbling so fast and out of control that every move I tried to make generated intense friction and I couldn't—

Dragon teeth plucked me out of freefall by the nape of my neck. Like a kitten or something, I thought crossly. Good grief, did I really have to be a child all over again?

You will learn, Y'rill said, chuckling. *Enjoy it. Unlike your human childhood, this one will be grand, with endless universes to explore and no cages. Ever.*

"*Half* the time?" I shouted the moment I had my bearings again. "I get to be human half of my life, like Persephone? I get my body back?"

I do not know of her but yes. However, if you fail to spend half your time as a Hunter, you will lose the privilege of being one. Most of us choose to remain Hunter. Few ever return.

"Why not?"

Loved ones pass. Planets die. This is home. Everything is here. We are nightwindflyhighfree. There is no place more majestic, no greater freedom to be found than among the stars. You hunger for freedom. I tasted your mind when you stabbed me. You were already one of us, sky-high dreams, no limits. You despise limits. We have none.

I wasn't hearing much past that I could be human again.

This wasn't death. This wasn't permanent.

I was like Ryodan and his beast. I was both woman and dragon—holy hell—this was the best of both worlds, better than anything I could have imagined! I hadn't lost anything, I'd gained. "*Fully* human?" I pressed. "As in, not lethal to the touch?"

You will be as you were before you began to change. But it will be some time before you can shift forms; you must bond with your new skin. The more often you shift, the more skilled you become, but that first time is terribly difficult. It may take many years.

"Years?" I exploded, bristling. That was unacceptable.

He is immortal, small one. He's not going anywhere.

It hit me then. I couldn't feel Ryodan anymore. I arched my—good grief, long scaly black—neck to peer over my shoulder but I couldn't see my back. "Do I have a brand on me?" I demanded.

Your skin is new. Nothing of his mark remains. Trinkets do not survive transformation.

I exhaled gustily, startled to see tiny, dark ice crystals puffing from my mouth as I realized Ryodan must have felt our connection sever abruptly and had no idea what happened to me. So much for our plan to love each other in illusion. It wouldn't have worked anyway. But it didn't need to. I could be a woman half the time! Exhilaration filled me. This was incredible! I was a woman who could become a dragon. And become a woman again!

But . . . Ryodan, Shazam, my friends. I had to tell them. "Take me back to Earth, Y'rill. You can teach me to shift there. I'm a fast learner." I was practically vibrating in the air with excitement. I'd soar back to Earth, tell Ryodan and Shaz what had happened, then hang out with them, learning all about my new form.

Damn. Ryodan's beast had *nothing* on me! I could feel my Hunter lips stretching into a smile as I beamed radiantly. I was badass, the most awesome superhero I could possibly be. If I'd known going in this was what was waiting for me, I'd have embraced it sooner.

Give your new world a chance. It will all be waiting for you when you return. Where did that child I felt when you stabbed me go? The one who couldn't wait for the next adventure? It's here. Look around. Is it not magnificent?

"Y'rill, Shazam will fall apart without me! He'll melt down. He's so emotional and he doesn't know where I am. He doesn't have anyone to take care of him. I have to go back! Show me how to get back!"

Y'rill chuffed softly. *Shazam is fine, tiny red.*

I jerked to a sudden stop and stared at her. "What did you just say?" I gasped.

Y'rill said tenderly, *Shazam is fine.*

"After that."

Those ferocious eyes gleamed with amusement. *Tiny red.*

Y'rill said she'd been watching over me. "But you're a she," I said faintly, trying to bend my mind into a shape it simply refused to achieve. "Shazam is a he."

You're the one ascribing genders. We have none.

Y'rill smiled then and I suddenly understood what Shazam's smile had always reminded me of, which I'd never been able to place.

Thin black lips pulling back from sharp teeth.

Same utterly alien expression.

Shazam's smile had reminded me of a Hunter. Chills suf-
fused my entire body. No way. Not possible.

I said slowly and carefully, "Y'rill, what were you before you
became a Hunter?"

*Before I was chosen for this by a great dragon soaring among the
stars, drawn by my cries of loneliness and longing for a home, I was
once the last remaining Hel-Cat in existence.* Y'rill's eyes flickered
with violet lightning. *My beloved Yi-yi.*

THIRTY-SEVEN

* ◦ ◦

Shaz the mighty fur-beast

Y'RILL WAS SHAZAM.

I just lolled there in space staring at her with my mouth open until she reached over and nudged it gently shut with a talon. *You'll catch space debris. Sorry to bofflescate you.*

I was *bofflescated* speechless; an extreme rarity for me. As I hung there, staring, I replayed my years with Shazam through my mind: his mysteriousness, his constant disappearances, his "other form" I'd known nothing about. His constant, cagey, evasive replies to so many questions, the odd juxtaposition of extreme emotion and wisdom.

We are not permitted to interfere or influence our chosen's choice in any way. We are never to have contact after the initial invitation. I've told them that's why we have so few young but they don't listen. Y'rill/Shazam looked abashed. *When you got lost in the Silvers, you were so lonely, like I once was, and I was afraid you would die. I came to you in my Hel-Cat form to help you survive.*

"All those times you disappeared?"

I had to be Hunter or I would lose the right. I could only spend half my time with you.

"But Shazam is so emotional and you're well, more . . . composed."

As a human, you strike me as quite emotional, too, Y'rill/Shazam said, sounding slightly miffed. *You saw my wisdom on occasion. I wasn't always emotional.* Then, *When we shift, we are what we once were. Flaws and all. The enormity of Hunter can't fit in a small skin. Another reason most of us choose to remain Hunter. It is difficult to get used to being tiny, driven by our biological natures again.* Y'rill shuddered, sloughing black ice into the air beneath her wings. *Being Shazam is humbling, I am a very different creature in that form, needy, tiny, lonely.* Then her eyes gleamed and she said, *You were a good mother to me. I will be to you as well, in this form.*

"OHMYGODSHAZAM!" I exploded, as it finally, fully penetrated. "You're my Shazzy-bear!"

Y'rill smiled. *I am. I couldn't tell you. They say if we breach that one rule, our child will never be born.*

"That's why my black hand never bothered you. I always wondered why I could touch you!"

Y'rill nodded. *Also why I told you to make it go away. Reminding you that becoming one of us was your choice. You said you wouldn't even if you could. I chose well with you. Your desire for adventure is exceeded only by your desire to care for worlds. We do much of that up here. One day you'll see.*

"See what?"

The threads that connect everything. We tend them. We sow them.

I began flying again, gingerly, then with greater gusto. I was flying in space! With Shazam! Holy hell! I always knew Shaz had another, enormous form and stayed "up in the air" but I'd never once imagined that form was a Hunter! I'd even written that ditty about Shaz the mighty fur-beast who lived up in the air, and us battling dragons together.

I snorted with laughter and it came out as a soft, delicate trilling gong accompanied by twin plumes of fire from my nostrils. Criminy, I just shot fire from my nose!

Hunter half the time, woman the other half; with Ryodan half the time, with Shazam the other half; with incredible adventures to be had both ways. Fierce exhilaration filled me.

I knew you'd think so, Y'rill/Shazam said smugly. *Come. I have so much to show you.*

As excited as I was to see more of my new home, Ryodan couldn't feel me anymore. "First, take me back to Earth so I can—"

Send him one of your texts, Yi-yi, and let it go. You have all the time in the universe. Others are waiting to meet you. Few are chosen, far fewer born. Most reject it. Only the fearless join us here.

"Ha ha, a text," I said dryly.

Ah, I forgot, you won't be able to do that for some time. She sighed. *I suppose I'll break yet another rule for you.*

As I watched, Y'rill turned, churning ice beneath her enormous leathery sails, and focused her attention on a nearby star. *What do you want it to say?*

I tried to nibble my lip, and gouged myself in the cheek with a fang. "Ow!" This was going to take time getting used to. "Tell him I'm okay and I'm coming home soon."

A thin bolt of pale purple lightning, fine and laser sharp, erupted from a taloned hoof as Y'rill carved a tiny chunk of the star away, etching words on the face of it that shimmered like stardust.

Then, abruptly, Y'rill vanished and reappeared far beneath

me, caught the chunk of star and brought it back, tossing it to me. Holy flour balls, she could sift! That meant I could sift, too! I'd eclipsed Batman a million times over. I caught the chunk of star, cupping it awkwardly in my hoof, marveling. One day I'd be able to carve messages on stars. Etch a twisty D for Dani all over the bloody universe. Criminy. Dancer would be beside himself if he could see me now.

Throw.

"Huh? How, where?"

I'll correct its course. Just throw it.

I did, launching it into space, then Y'rill spun midair, batted it with her tail and sent it rocketing off at such speed that it vanished from sight as if it had entered a black hole.

It is done. He has received your message.

I understood a bit about travel in space and said, dryly, "When? Five million years in the future?"

I adjusted it so that he would receive it at the proper time.

"You can manipulate time?" I was awed.

She nodded.

"I can do that, too?" I practically shouted.

Thank the stars, NO! You must grow into your Hunter powers. It takes a very, very long time.

"Do I have *any* Hunter powers right now?" It may have come out sounding a bit peevish, but seriously, I was a dragon. I wanted some juice.

Y'rill chuffed. *There's my Yi-yi. A few. But when you become human again, no.*

"You mean except for the lightning." I liked my lightning bolts. I wondered if I'd be able to use them now without turning black.

Not the lightning. That is part of the birthing process. You will be as you were before you changed.

Sucky, still, "But I'm immortal now, aren't I?" I said, and if I'd been human, I'd have been bouncing in hyperspeed from foot to foot.

You can be killed in your human form until you've spent enough time as a Hunter that you complete the full transition. You must be careful when human, Yi-yi.

"For how long?"

You would consider it a very long time. Now come, let me show you your new home.

My new home. All the worlds were my oyster, half my life. The world I loved was mine for the other half. I turned my head from side to side, drinking it all in; the velvety, exquisite, enormous expanse of space and, one day, the mysteries even of time. Beyond that, if I chose to die, I could become as a planet.

This was, I decided, bemused and stunned, the greatest superhero gig of all.

I was a Hunter.

Like the caterpillar, compelled beyond reason to spin itself into a cocoon, I'd grieved the transformation, believing I was losing my life. Deep down, in a place I never let myself feel, I'd actually been ... afraid. I'd mourned. Only to discover wonders I'd never dreamed possible. Become an entirely new thing.

I might fly Ryodan up into a starry night sky. Soar overhead while his beast hunted. A dragon and a beast, roaming the Earth together. God, the things we could do now!

It was a future I couldn't wait to explore.

"How many months?" I demanded.

For what?

"To shift."

I said years.

I said smugly, "Right, how many months? Come on, Shazzy-bear, break another rule for me."

Y'rill sighed. *You're going to be a handful.*

I grinned. "As if you weren't. I get to be the kid now. Teach me how to fly like you do. Teach me how to sift. C'mon, Y'rill, show me *everything!*"

With pleasure.

When Y'rill turned with a sharp, beautiful dark swoop of her powerful Hunter body, curving the merest tip of a wing, I imitated the motion and, together, we glided off into the starlit sky.

THIRTY-EIGHT

There's nothing left to do tonight but go crazy on you

FOUR MONTHS LATER

I LOPE UP THE FRONT stairs of Chester's, marveling at the sensation of having a woman's body again, and at just how much Ryodan accomplished while I was gone.

Chester's-above is a stunning, modern six-story building of pale limestone and vast expanses of glass. The wide, curved staircase leads to ornate steel doors, heavily etched with wards, as is everything of that man's; he likes to protect his property. As I push one open and step inside, I smile.

The domed foyer has sleek black marble floors, simple white and chrome furnishings, windows all around, and faceted skylights casting rainbows on the floor. I can feel the bass from here, rising up from the many subclubs below.

I'm a woman again. It's strange and exhilarating but I have to admit, being a Hunter, flying among the stars for the past few months was beyond my wildest dreams. Y'rill and I played with the abandon we'd shared Silverside, with one difference—no predators, no enemies, just adventures. I'd visited worlds beyond describing, drifted inside nebulae, played hide and seek in meteor fields, watched stars go supernova, slingshot around moons, played in the gaseous rings of planets, my Hunter body impervious to harm. I'd barely scratched the surface of discovering what it was to be a Hunter; Y'rill was downright mysterious about many things and full of annoying, "patience, grasshopper" sayings. According to her, I would learn when it was time and no sooner. Still, I had a fair idea my potential was virtually limitless, one day in the future.

Unlike Shazam, who lived to break rules at every opportunity, Y'rill preferred to adhere to them. It had taken me weeks to convince her to help me transition back into my human form before I'd learned to do it myself, then another four months to get her to actually *do* it.

She'd then warned me that I had a single week in human form before she came to reclaim me.

I thought it was half and half, I'd protested.

Not at first. You must settle into this skin. If you stay human any longer right now, you might lose your Hunter form.

Oh, hell, no way! I'd cried.

Still, I felt like the luckiest woman in the world. I had a whole week with Ryodan! After believing I'd lost him forever, a week felt like a small eternity to me.

We'd flown to Dublin, landed on top of the building that housed my flat, where she'd shifted me back into human form (painful!) then reverted, herself, into Shazam. We'd hurried (I was naked—now I understood why Ryodan always had extra clothing stashed in convenient places) below to my flat, where Shazam flashed me a mischievous grin and muttered a cryptic,

Go to him, he's been waiting a long time, before curling up for a nap on our bed.

I'd taken my first shower in months—not that I seemed to need one—dressed with care, weaponed up and freeze-framed straight for Ryodan, electrified with excitement.

As I push through the second set of doors, my smile deepens. The street-level bar and restaurant is lovely, with an elegant stair-case that descends to the subclubs. I dash down the staircase and stand behind the balustrade surveying the dance floor, looking for him.

It's early evening, the club is hopping as usual and I'm pleased to see not a single Fae. A part of me wants an immediate update on events in Dublin and our world, wants to head to the abbey and get all the details, but I learned a valuable lesson about time from both Dancer and Ryodan.

We don't always have as long as we think we do. Updates can wait.

It's necessary to be selfish sometimes, and tonight I have every intention of it.

It was pure pleasure to slip into a black spandex dress, heels, and nothing else but creamy Irish skin. Knowing I'm about to slip out of it and go crazy all over that man's big, powerful body.

I want Ryodan in my bed, inside me, all around me, and that's my only goal for a good long while. Before I have to leave again, I'll catch up on my world. Tonight's for me. Tonight's for us. And it's long overdue.

I descend the final set of stairs, thinking maybe I'll find him in his office, and push through the crowded dance floor, heading for the glass and chrome staircase to the Nine's private levels. I'm nearly there when someone blasts into me from behind, seizes me in a steely grip, drags me the rest of the way to the stairs, and shoves me down on the steps. Has to be one of the Nine; no one else can noodle me like that.

I toss my hair from my eyes and scowl up. Then, "Lor!" I exclaim, delighted to see him.

He stares at me in utter disbelief. "Dani?"

"Mega in the flesh," I flash him a hundred-Megawatt grin to prove it. "I'm back. And you are *so* never going to believe the things I've seen and done."

Then Fade and Kasteo are there with him, all three of them staring at me, with a mixture of irritation and disbelief.

"What's with you guys? I told him I'd be back."

"The boss," Lor says flatly. "You told him that."

I nod. "I sent him a message."

"He sure as fuck doesn't think you're coming back," Fade growls. "And I'm sure as fuck glad you are because he's been goddamn impossible to live with. Go fuck him and make him sane again." He turns and stalks away.

To Lor, I say, "He thought I wasn't—wait, I don't understand."

"Just go to him, honey," Lor says. "He's in his suite. Never comes up. Spends most of his time as the beast. Ain't eating, ain't sleeping, ain't fucking, and it's getting ugly around here."

I surge to my feet before he even finishes speaking, lope up the stairs, taking them three at a time, dash onto an elevator and tap my foot impatiently as it descends. How could he not know I was coming back? I don't believe Y'rill would lie to me. I frown, remembering her exact words: *I adjusted it so he would receive it at the proper time.* Okay, so what was the mysterious being's idea of "the proper time"?

When the door whisks aside, I explode from the elevator, freeze-frame down the hall, and blast through the door into the anteroom of Ryodan's suite.

It's still trashed. He never cleaned it up. Broken glass crunches beneath my heels as I stalk to the hidden panel that conceals the doorway to his true suite and push it open.

As I step into the room, I inhale sharply. This room, too, is trashed, every piece of furniture demolished. Savage claw marks scar the paneled walls, the chandeliers are torn from the ceiling, wires dangling, exposed, crystal splinters glistening on the floor. The bed is a collapsed jumble of wood, with slashed velvet pillows, shredded linens, pulverized mattress.

I narrow my eyes, letting them adjust to the gloom. He's here, I can smell him; that spicy, darkly exotic scent that always clings to his skin, animalistic, druggingly masculine, blatantly sexual. I can feel him, every nerve ending in my body electrified by his presence.

There's more in this room. Rage. Fury. Grief. It's embedded in every demolished item, gouged into each panel, carved in deep gashes across the floor.

He grieved me. Believed I was never coming back. But why?

All my senses are cranked up to full volume. This is my night. My choice, my long-denied, deepest desire, and I feel achingly, incredibly alive. I hear him inhale, as if questing the air, catching my scent. Then a rough laugh floats from the shadows near the fire where he sits in a tall armchair.

"Not again," he says, with a rasp of agony in his voice.

I wince. I know the power and persuasion of hallucination. I lived it in my cage. I'd wake from a tortured slumber smelling food, certain Mom had come home and I was going to open my eyes to a heaping bowl of my favorite creamed corn, topped with a crispy helping of fried chicken and green beans only to find there was nothing there for me to gnaw on but my own knuckles.

Again.

I knew the despair of the moment the brain processed the deceit, that hope crumbled to ash. That the thing you wanted so desperately wasn't there, and maybe never would be again.

He smells me and thinks I'm a dream.

I intend to fulfill every one of his wildest ones tonight.

I step carefully into the room, skirting bits of debris and broken glass, trying to decide what to say, how to convince him I'm real. Some of my hallucinations had been so extreme they'd nearly unhinged me. I'd actually eaten imaginary meals. Starvation messes with your head. Sustained deprivation of anything you desperately need does.

He desperately needed me. I like that. I feel the same about him. I decide the best approach is to simply touch him. Let our bodies do the talking.

As I skirt the shattered coffee table and approach his high-backed armchair, I inhale sharply, butterflies fluttering from my stomach to my throat. I'm . . . nervous? No. I'm exhilarated. Okay . . . a little nervous and have no bloody idea why. Just that this man has always rattled me.

God, this is it! He's here, I'm here, my skin is flawless ivory, we're free to be together, to be everything I've ever hungered to be with him. I *know* I'm real; yet even I almost can't believe this moment has come. I'd thought it would never happen. That I'd lost us forever.

Still, I was quickly disabused of my grief. He's been grieving me for months.

I clear his chair and circle to stand in front of him.

He tips his head back and stares at me with narrowed silver eyes, stained with crimson streaks. "I'm getting better at this," he mocks. "Christ, you look so fucking real. So fucking sexy in that dress." His gaze rakes me from head to toe, heat floods my body, fire ignites in my blood. "I never told you. You define beauty for me, Dani O'Malley. Copper flames and emerald ice. The snow and rose of your skin. Those insanely powerful legs. The steel in your spine. The unquenchable fire in your spirit."

Well, fuck, he'd silenced me. I'd stand unspeaking for an hour if it meant he'd keep talking like that.

"You're unbreakable, woman. None of it ever broke you. You're my fucking holy place. Do you know that? Why the fuck didn't I ever tell you?"

I swallow hard, tears stinging the backs of my eyes. His holy place. That's exactly how he feels to me. He's my temple. I slip into his presence and the world melts away and I'm safe and together we can face anything, do anything, survive anything, always find the next way to be together. I think that's what love is; holding someone sacred, honoring them, protecting them, living up to the very best of them. The grief, the pain, the fury in his gaze slays me. Humbles me. I will never doubt the depth of this man's emotion. It's evident in every too-tightly drawn line of his body, the stony set of his face, the half-wild look in his eyes.

I drop to my knees before him. Holy hell, he's beautiful. I've never seen him like this, dressed only in a pair of low slung, faded black sweats, skin poured over rippling muscle, glistening gold in the firelight. This is Ryodan slumming. His face shadowed with beard growth I've never seen that makes him look diabolic, dark, fascinating. He smells like beast and feral fury and no shower in a long time and I don't give a damn. He smells exactly right to me. Danger. Edges sharp enough to cut myself on. And I know he'll heal my every wound if I do. His perfectly cropped hair is long, messy as if he's been running his hands through it. He's too lean, skin tight against bone, and I know he hasn't fed in a long time.

I reach out and place a palm flat to his hard, chiseled chest.

No heartbeat. He definitely hasn't eaten recently. "You might want to," I tease. "I plan to wear your ass out tonight. Babe."

He cocks his head, eyes glittering, nostrils flaring. "Even if I were starved you couldn't wear my ass out. You're an illusion. I let you get away. Hell, I fucking threw you away and I shouldn't have. I should have fought for you. I should have told you everything. I should have persuaded you to reject what was happening."

I slide my palm from his chest, down over his six-pack abdomen, trailing my fingers lightly over his velvety skin. "You didn't throw me away. You did the hardest thing possible, sacrificed your own desires for my best interests. Trying to keep me here, almost completely black, unable to ever use my power again would have destroyed us both. Neither of us is wired that way. We push the limits. We adapt. It's what we do."

"And my illusion offers absolution," he says with a snort. "I *am* getting better at this."

I drop onto his lap, slinging my legs, one over each side of the chair, and take his face in my hands, stare into his beautiful eyes, fire and ice, blood and steel. "Do I feel like an illusion to you?" My dress is hitched up nearly to the top of my thighs. I lower myself, slowly, firmly, against him. He's hard. He's so fucking hard. And I'm so fucking, painfully alive and starved to have him inside me. I don't need foreplay. Not this time. I just need it done. Him. In. Me. Over and over. Maybe the next time I get to be human we'll bother with foreplay. Maybe I'm not much of a foreplay kind of woman.

His hands close on my waist tightly, fingers digging in with anger, with grief. "You never do. I've spent hours touching you, holding you, days fucking you in my mind."

I say lightly, "Do it again. But it's me. I get to be a woman half the time. Dragon the other half. Still, I only have a week. Y'rill helped me change so I could come back and tell you I was okay, spend time with you until I learn to transform myself."

"That's the most lucid, coherent explanation you've offered yet," he says dryly, gaze fixed on my lips.

"Because it's the true one. Kiss me. See how real I am."

I drop forward, brush my lips to his and my hands are at the top of his sweats and I'm so damned wet, it's glistening on my thigh.

He inhales sharply, pulls back, glances down. Then his hand is on my thigh and he's tracing the slick heat up my leg. He groans, "I don't recall it ever being quite this real. Fuck!"

"Yes, please," I say with a half laugh, half growl. "Now."

Then he's surging to his feet and he's pushing me back on the floor on a thick fur rug, and I'm sprawling with my legs spread and his mouth is on my thigh, as he shoves my dress up over my hips, then his mouth closes, warm and wet between my legs and he's licking and sucking and I hear someone screaming and realize it's me and holy hell orgasm for me is a full mind-body explosion, my brain flies open and shatters into starry pieces and my body is electrified and I buck against his face as I writhe beneath him, then I'm surging up, still coming, desperate to get him inside me, because I've come too many times by my own hand thinking of him and this is real and I want it all and I'm launching myself on top of him, shoving him back to the floor and slamming down on him with violence and lust and need, and his eyes are flying wide and flashing bloodred as he snarls, "Fuck, you're real!"

I have no idea what convinced him and I don't care and I throw my head back and half laugh, half roar as I take Ryodan Killian St. James inside me and clench every muscle in my lower body that I'm so bloody grateful to have and I don't have to be careful with him because I can *never break this man* in any way, and I can vibrate—

"Bloody hell, woman, don't do that yet!"

But he's on his back beneath me and I'm riding him and I'm in control, and I'm vibrating and goddamn, yes, he's losing control and this is the only way I ever want to see this man lose his hold on reality.

"Paybacks are hell," he snarls as he explodes inside me.

And all I can think is, I hope so. I hope he pays me back over and over again, my entire immortal life.

Then he's shuddering and his head is back and he's laughing up at me as he comes and I cup his face, that beautiful, sexy, familiar, challenging, stubborn, human skin poured over a beast face I will never tire of looking at and I catch his joy in my hands and it blazes inside my heart.

π

Later, I thumb up "Magic Man" on my cellphone and crank up the volume.

Later, I dance naked for him in the firelight and I tell him that I know it's not a spell—but it's truth that this woman-child-dragon has been waiting for him all her life.

Exaltation blazes in his eyes as he takes me down to the floor and he gets the top this time, the bastard, and he tells me something I file away but don't ask about just then because my mouth is busy and I like it being busy in precisely that way.

He tells me he's been waiting for me much longer than a

lifetime. I have no idea what he means. I don't care. He's inside me and I'm inside him and the future is as vast and enormous as the starry skies that are half the time my home now.

π

Much later, I demand to know what happened at the abbey, and he tells me that Kat and the Shedon survived but we lost one hundred and forty-two *sidhe*-seers that day. I'd indeed killed Balor with my final blast and after I'd vanished, Ryodan scratched a long-chafing itch: Papa Roach was dead, slain at last by that lethal black blade Ryodan had been threatening him with for so long. AOZ was in the battle, too, but escaped and lived to torment us another day. Still, I was back, I was powerful, and one day that cooing little leprechaun would be mine.

Roisin had joined the women at the abbey, although she had no *sidhe*-seer gifts and was working with Enyo, recruiting other displaced, disenfranchised humans, molding them into an army, giving them purpose, a cause to fight for, a raison d'être. God knows we can all use one in times like these.

Mac and Barrons were still gone. No sign of the Fae in our city for months.

Yet I knew, although neither of us said it—

"Fuck that," Ryodan says tightly. "I'll say it. And we'll print it in the *Dublin Daily* because the world needs to know and prepare. Our greatest battle is yet to come. It'll be the Fae, not the old gods. Those bastards are going to turn our world into a war zone, and soon. There's a scarce-contained violence in the earth, I feel it rumbling beneath my boots, a darkness on the wind, I can scent blood on the breeze. They're planning, conspiring to seize this planet for their own. War's coming, and if Mac doesn't gain control of her power, it's one we'll lose."

"Then we need to make sure Mac has enough time."

He growls assent.

"Any news of Christian?"

"Same. Kat's been spending time at Draoidheacht Keep, working on Sean. Still no progress there. He destroys every living thing he touches."

"People?" I gasp. I know the horror of that.

"No. As Famine, it's only living plants and crops. People and animals are exempt. Those are Christian's specialty."

"Any trouble from other gods?"

"Not yet. But I suspect we've only seen the tip of the iceberg there. Humans and gods will have to unite to have a chance against the Fae."

Somehow, I vow silently, we'll make that happen. "Bright side, we now have a Hunter on our side. And who knows, maybe I can rustle up reinforcements."

He laughs. "If anyone can persuade the unpersuadable entities, it's you."

Then he's on me again and we're battling for dominance because we always will, that's the way we're wired and I lose myself in passion and think no longer of this world or anything in it.

He's my ground zero, my mecca, beast to my dragon. Always.

π

When I was fourteen years old, I watched Ryodan having sex on level four at Chester's; the subclub devoted to providing the carnal excess necessary to keep the Nine's beasts under control.

I smile faintly. I'm Ryodan's carnal excess now.

That day, so long ago, I marked him as mine.

There it is. The truth.

Crucify me for it, if you want. I don't care.

I was never a normal fourteen-year-old.

I've never been a normal anything.

At fourteen, I'd vowed, one day, I'd be the woman making him laugh, making joy blaze from his face, so tangible it seemed I might catch it in my hands. I would trace the imperious, regal, stubble-shadowed planes of his face, close my hand around his cock and take him inside me. I'd be the one responsible for the firestorm of lust in his heavy-lidded gaze, for the savage rumble deep in his chest, the guttural, raw sounds he made when he came, half roar, half laughing, erotic purr.

Not with my fourteen-year-old body. I wasn't ready for sex then.

But one day.

With a woman's body.

The man was mine.

It wasn't just lust I'd felt the afternoon I'd watched him fuck. And yes, I'd been capable of lust at that age—for life, for the sex I would one day have, for chocolate, for being alive. I'm made of lust. We all are. Savor it. Burn with it. Never apologize for it.

It's what makes life worth living.

I know a truth: We fuck like we live. Timid people fuck timidly. Uninhibited people fuck uninhibitedly.

He'd fucked with one thousand percent focus, with savage devotion and lust. Staggeringly alive, elated to be.

It's the way I've always lived. Fully engaged, all senses ablaze.

I recognized, that day, that he and I were the same kind of people. I hadn't thought to ever find someone else in the world like me.

I'd been wandering the city, on my own, for six years by then. I'd seen and done far more than any child should. (When I think of Rae, I know how wrong my life was and I'll do everything in my power to keep her childhood pure, not that Kat needs my help, but I'll be there. Watching over her. Always.) I'd paid prices few adults ever have to pay. I'd carried sins that cut me to the core of that soul I used to pretend I didn't have. Sins that had forced me to find creative ways of rearranging myself so I wouldn't self-destruct.

Ancient eyes had stared out of my fourteen-year-old face at Ryodan, and I'd thought: This man will understand me. This man can *with*stand me.

That's something for a woman of my complicated ilk.

He's a pain in the ass. Stubborn, controlled, controlling. So am I.

He's done unspeakable things. So have I. And I suspect we'll easily speak about them with each other.

He's fascinating, brilliant, hungry for more life all the time. So am I.

He's life and death, joy and grief, mercy and ruthlessness. So. Am. I.

It was hard for me to move through those years between us.

I resisted what I knew I wasn't ready for. I resented every woman he took to his bed in a dark, possessive corner of my mind, including Jo. Even though I understood.

Then life unexpectedly gave me a man I *was* ready for.

And Ryodan had understood.

But . . . always, endlessly, I'd been pointed at this man like a beast-seeking missile, waiting for the day I was—not merely locked and loaded—but fully ready to take him on, woman to man.

That's what Dancer had always sensed in me.

And loved me anyway.

I think both my loves are better men than I. I can't share. I can't be second best. I don't know how to play that role.

"You'll never have to," Ryodan assures me, as he closes his arms around me from behind and grinds, hard and hungry against my ass.

"You should know I'm possessive."

His arms tighten around me. "As am I. You and me. No one else. If you're not okay with that, get the fuck out of my bed," he says, as he begins pushing slowly inside me.

I gasp and thrust my hips back, needing to feel him cramming me full, like earlier when he'd been part beast, so deep it nearly hurt in the best possible way. I'm not a woman to compare. We all bring unique assets to the table. But Ryodan's assets fit me stupendously well and the fact that they were . . . adjustable . . . well, that was a plus a woman had no reason to expect and every reason to thank her lucky stars for.

He laughs softly against my ear as he slides infinitesimally deeper, raking my nerves with a savage need he's creating . . . and refusing to fill, driving me mad. "I suspect the stars will always be lucky for you, Dani."

Growling, I push back, hard but his hands are locked on my hips and he won't let me gain a bloody quarter of an inch.

"Let me play, Stardust. Learn what turns you on. I want to drive you wild. I want to find your breaking points. All of them."

That makes two of us. Although I never want to see him lose control in the real world, I hunger to strip it from him in bed.

One inch, then gone, rubbing between my legs, where I'm swollen and achingly wet. Then two inches inside me. Then gone, then back and slow, so slow I nearly scream with frustration as he eases into me as if we had all the time in the world.

"We do."

Laughter explodes from me, pure joy. Eternity. I get to love this man forever.

"Fuck, Dani, stop laughing!"

"Afraid you'll lose control?" I tease and laugh again, a husky, wicked sound as I kicked it up a notch, and began to vibrate from head to toe.

"Son of a *bitch*!"

π

Later, I sprawl on top of him, staring into glittering, lazily sated silver eyes.

It's a good thing the room was already wrecked, because we'd have wrecked it anyway. I have no idea how much time has passed down here where no light of day penetrates but am willing to bet we've spent twenty-four straight hours exploring each other's bodies, testing limits, discovering what drives each other wild.

And this man is definitely wild. Hot and sexy and just the flavor of kink I like.

"I've only got one week," I remind him softly.

He stiffens and growls as I fill him in on all that happened, explaining the parameters of my new existence; his silver eyes blaze with joy.

"Half the time we'll be human. The other half, we'll be beasts together," he says, laughing softly. "What a fine fucking life."

Indeed. Still, something's bothering me. I need to know why he thought I wasn't coming back, what Y'rill did with my "text."
"Ryodan, didn't you get my message? I sent you—"

"A bloody chunk of star. Christ, that damned piece of rock has been the bane of my fucking existence."

So, he *did* get it. "It was meant to set your mind at ease."

"Your aim sucked, Stardust," he growls. He rolls me off him, surges to his feet, stalks to the hearth where he collects something from a box on the floor and brings it back, handing it to me.

I peer at it in the low light and gasp.

It says:

I'M OKAY I'M

"But that's only half of it!"

"I bloody well know that. What the fuck is the end of that sentence? You have no idea how many words I plugged in. I'm okay, I'm happy. I'm okay, I'm free. I'm okay, I'm never coming back. What the fuck, Dani?"

I turn the chunk of star over and study the edge. "It broke. It must have hit something on the way to you. Where were you when you got it?"

"On a beach."

I frown. "A beach? You went to the beach?" Lor said he'd not come out of Chester's since I left.

"I used to walk the ocean at night. It plunged from the sky and landed next to me."

"When?"

He laughs but there's a deep undercurrent of bitterness, a hint of torment in it. "Woman, you have driven me crazy far longer than you know. I got your bloody damned star three thousand, one hundred forty-one years, five months, nine days, and two hours before you turned into a Hunter at the abbey."

I gasp. "Three *thousand* years ago?" What was Y'rill thinking? Was her aim that bad? Was manipulating time trickier than she'd cared to admit?

"You're the reason I began to study linchpin theory, over three millennia ago. You're the reason I began trying to project the future. You, Dani O'Malley, have been the greatest and most irritating mystery of my existence. I smelled you on the star that night on the beach. The scent of a woman I hungered to know, unlike any woman I'd ever met. I waited to meet her. And waited. And bloody fucking waited. Found her one night in Dublin, an uncontrollable, swaggering child with a bloody death wish, balls of steel, a superhero complex, and a teenage boyfriend."

"Oh God, you knew I was the one who'd thrown the star when you saw me that night?"

"I'd given up on the whole matter long ago, decided the star was the equivalent of a text message sent to the wrong phone. Then I moved in behind you that night and smelled your scent. I knew you were her, the one who would one day throw a star at me, across time.

"My world went to hell from that moment on. I had no idea what you were or what to do with you. I only knew one day you'd toss a bloody celestial body my way. Admit it, you never wrote any more than that. I tortured you so much, you decided to torture me back for a few thousand years."

I burst out laughing. If I'd thought of it, I might have.

"That was all I had to go on. Then when you began to turn black—"

"*That's* why you were so certain I was becoming a Hunter," I exclaim, "because they live among the stars!"

He inclines his head.

"Why didn't you tell me?"

He's silent a long moment then exhales gustily. "It was mind-fuck to an extreme. I was concerned I might change things."

"Illogical. If it—"

"—already happened, yes, it would no matter what. I thought of that, too. Barrons and I discussed it endlessly."

"Barrons knew?"

"My brother is the only one I told. I've learned to take nothing for granted in this world." He's silent again then says, "I'd begun to suspect that because of my feelings for you, I'd try to sabotage whatever might happen. I questioned my motives."

I still as the enormity of what he is telling me sinks in. From the day he met me he'd known I would one day throw a star at him. No wonder he hadn't thought I was human! Then once I started turning Hunter, he'd known the what of it but not how things would end. He'd not known, even as I branded him, even as he encouraged me to embrace my destiny, if he would ever see me again. Still, he'd helped me through it.

"No cages, Dani. Ever. Not for you. It was possible being a Hunter would be everything you wanted. It was possible the final word was "happy." If it had happened then it was supposed to happen, and the only thing I could do was be there while it happened. I thought I'd lost you forever. The moment you turned, I could no longer feel you. I thought your star was your goodbye."

"Never," I say swiftly. "It was my promise to you that I was returning, to set your mind at ease. Because I didn't call you for those two years and I should have. I wasn't going to make the same mistake again. I wasted those two years because I was stubborn and proud and kept boxing my emotions instead of admitting them. That I loved you. I've always loved you."

"So, what the fuck did it say? Imagine working a cryptoquip for three thousand bloody years and never solving it."

"I'm okay, I'm coming home."

"Is this, Dani?" he says quietly. "Home? Will you live here with me?"

"Always. Well, half the time. The other half of the time—"

"Bloody hell, I'm going with you when you go."

"As high as I can take you without killing you," I promise. We would sail the night sky together, watch over our city, our friends and family.

"I might surprise you," he says, smiling faintly. "I don't need to breathe, Dani. Not all the time. Besides, I always come back."

I cup that beautiful face and kiss him, long and deep. "I always will, too. That's our number one rule, Ryodan. No matter what, we will *always* come back to each other."

"A rule I'll never break." He flashes me a wolfish grin. "All the others are up for grabs. You'll have to keep me in line. I'm not an easy man to handle."

I know that already. It's one of the things I like most about him. I'm still having a hard time wrapping my brain around the fact that he'd been waiting over three thousand years for me. Something about the length of time he'd been waiting teases at my brain. "Wait a minute, how long was it again from the time you got my star and I turned into a Hunter?"

"Three thousand one hundred forty-one years, five months, nine days, and two hours," he says flatly. "Wondered when you'd notice that."

I stare at him. "Ryodan, that's pi."

"The first seven digits of it. It was the hope I held onto. That we would somehow get all the rest of those digits, too."

I'm stupefied. Dancer was right. There's pattern and purpose to everything.

This spectacular universe knew exactly what it was doing.

"We will," I say, smiling up at him. I can feel it in my Hunter bones.

An eternity with this man was all I'd ever wanted. Whatever

comes, whatever challenges we face, we'll ride them out together. It will be intense, it will be dangerous, it will be unpredictable, but it will never be dull. Not with him.

As he surges above me, stretching his big beautiful body over mine, I let go of everything, sprawl back and tell him in great detail exactly what I want him to do. He complies with one thousand percent devotion to the task at hand as I lay back and take what I want, understanding finally that I deserve to. That I don't have to be super-anything to be loved.

Cages were funny things.

Although I'd escaped with my body long ago, only recently had my heart finally broken free.

Healed by the love of a man who'd been willing to sacrifice everything, even give me up if he had to, just to see me rise.

THIRTY-NINE

———— • ◦ • ————

Y'RILL CHUCKLED AS HER daughter disappeared into Chester's, racing to the arms and bed of the man she'd chosen for her, when she'd tied the first of many red threads in Dani's life.

Y'rill had broken Ryodan's star in half, sent him only "I'm okay I'm" to determine if he was worthy of her daughter. She'd sent it to him far in the past to ascertain if he would be there to watch over her, and to assess what he was made of.

He'd passed her tests with flying colors, helping her daughter evolve, even as he'd believed he was losing her, giving his love with no guarantee of a return.

Tucking her wings close to her body, Y'rill soared up into the sky above Dublin, watching over the city Dani loved, studying what only the most ancient among Hunters could see—the countless red threads connecting lives that were destined to make history together. There was pattern and purpose to all things.

One day, if she chose, Dani, too, would fly among the stars, studying worlds and tying those fateful threads. Only those with the purest, deepest, most resilient hearts could handle the delicate task. Her daughter certainly fit the bill and would excel at weaving happy endings for others.

But now it was time for her to enjoy her own.

EPILOGUE

———— • • ————

Let my love open the door to your heart

SOMEWHERE IN TIME...

ON A PLANET WITH low gravity and four moons, a black-skinned beast bounded across sandy dunes. He was her best friend and lover.

At the beast's side ran a Hel-Cat, both her child and mother.

Above them soared a majestic raven-dark Hunter, forged of passion, fire, and a teaspoon of stardust.

Dani O'Malley had a family. She belonged.

DELETED SCENES

———— • • ————

THE FOLLOWING SCENES WERE *written during* Fever-song, *but for one reason or another I either cut and rewrote them a different way or simply chose not to include them. As my team and I were sorting through my notes, they enjoyed the alternate glimpses so much, I decided to include them here.*

DELETED CHRISTIAN MACKELTAR SCENE FROM *FEVERSONG*:

Barrons said, "Do you remember All Hallow's Eve when we summoned the old god at the circle stones of Ban Drochaid?"

"How could I forget," Christian replied with a tight smile. "You screwed me and I got hurled into the Silvers where I turned into this."

"I was hurled into the Silvers that night, too. Because of you. I merely escaped more quickly."

"And just how did you do that?" Christian said dryly.

"Do you recall what I told you before we began the ritual?"

"Yes. Not a bloody thing."

"I told you one thing you needed to remember and you ignored it. I said: 'When it rises, greet it with warmth and respect.'"

"The foul thing came exploding out of the earth, gunning for me. It was dark and ancient and smelled of bones and graveyards. And I was supposed to smile and say hello?"

"You are dark and will one day be ancient and you don't merely smell of death, you're the most lethal horseman of the apocalypse. Your legend will forever precede you. Yes, I bloody expected you to be courteous, yet you ran as if it was the vilest thing you'd ever encountered. It responded to you in kind. Our plan that night succeeded. You didn't welcome it. It left."

"Well, why the hell was the onus on me that night?"

"You attract power."

Christian went still. He'd often felt that way as a lad, strolling the bens and vales of his Highlands, tethered by a deep bond to all of it, earth to sky, dirt to stars, feeling as if the heavens themselves sometimes shot out a milky tendril to caress him, noticed him, observed him with curiosity. His druid connection to all living things was intense. He'd not even been able to fish as a lad because he couldn't bear the pain of the pierced worm, life stolen by the hook. The worm had enjoyed its dark, sweet, rich life in the soil, comforted by the rhythms and songs of the earth. And now he was the Great Stealer. "Why do I draw it?"

"You have the potential for great good or evil. The universe notices."

"Why the bloody hell are you bringing this up now?" Barrons always had a reason. He never talked unless he needed to in order to accomplish an aim.

"You're about to meet someone. Greet it with warmth and respect. I won't tell you again."

Christian stopped in his tracks. "That thing from Samhain is here?"

"Another of the old earth gods. This one, however, will not run, they will decimate you if you fear them. The old ones can be cantankerous."

"Your pronouns aren't matching. What the bloody hell is it— one or multiple?" When Barrons said nothing, he snapped irritably, "Where the fuck do you even find old gods? It's not as if they're just hanging about on street corners."

Barrons shot him a look of dark amusement. "You might be surprised. If you were one day summoned by those in need of your services yet greeted with fear and hostility, what would you do to those who'd called you?"

Christian bared his teeth in a twisted smile. If someone dared compel his presence then treated him with horror and rejection . . . well, in his recent state of mind he might do worse than the old god had done. He'd live up to his fucking legend, every frightening bit of it.

"Be glad the one that came that night wasn't as bitter and broody as you. All things considered, it was surprisingly well mannered."

Christian narrowed his eyes. "As you've just been. You never explain." Were they becoming . . . friendly? Was Barrons capable of friendly?

"Power is gray. It goes where you will it, wrong or right, dark or light. Reviling yourself is the surest way to go dark."

Christian bristled but said nothing. The bastard had struck a nerve. Barrons didn't know he'd begun hating himself long before he turned Unseelie, when he'd been but a lad, for hearing all those truths no one else could hear, for making those he loved uneasy, for inciting suspicion and fear. But even more shaming to his character—he'd come to revile those around him, to feel contempt for their lies and evasions, their inability to face what they felt. Between despising himself and looking down on others as liars and cowards, he'd grown to adulthood with a serious chip on his shoulder. He'd donned the mask of a carefree, good looking young Scotsman, but there'd always been a streak of darkness in him, perhaps even repressed sadism, seething anger at his fellow man. Was that why he'd been one of the first to turn Unseelie prince? Had the evicted magic of the dead prince somehow sniffed it out in him and deemed him a fine fit? Had Fae power targeted him long before that night at Ban Drochaid, even before Mac fed him Unseelie?

He shifted his wings uneasily. Fuck, he had wings. He could fly. He considered that for a moment, looking for the first time past the Unseelie element of it to the simple beauty and power of having wings. The freedom. The strength.

But since the day they began to grow, he'd done nothing but bitch about the itch and the pain, the need to clean them, how he could no longer sleep flat on his back. No position was comfortable, and he'd begun to fear, like a bat, that he might need to hang upside down to get any rest at all. And sure enough, the bloody things hurt most of the time, felt wrong on his body, kept him on constant edge.

He canted his shoulders back, expanding his druid essence into the Fae appendages, as he accepted—nay, welcomed—them for the first time. When the world was safe again, he might fly a velvety night sky in the Highlands, watch wolves tussle in the moonlight with their cubs, soar beside a grand eagle for a few hours, glide across a silvery loch, tumble to a soft landing in a bed of heather.

Bloody hell, he had wings!

For the first time since he'd begun to transform into something otherworldly, he felt . . . elation.

His wings responded, lifting slightly, fluttering as if with a sigh of pleasure, as if, with the aloofness of a cat, they'd been waiting to be noticed, stroked, appreciated. Heat raced through his body into the strong, sure sails that spread and fanned without conscious thought, the powerful muscles in his shoulders rippling smoothly as they arced high before crossing down again to tuck behind his shoulders in a position he'd never before been able to achieve. Perfectly tucked precisely where they were made to be.

Effortless.

Neither dragging nor aching.

He shook his head with a wry smile. His wings had always known instinctively how to arrange themselves but his brain had been in the way. *He'd* been in the way of himself. They'd been a burden because he'd thought them a burden, and now that he thought them a gift, they behaved like a gift.

He stole a glance at his companion. If he could learn to like himself and the world around him, Barrons could learn to have friends. Thanks to Dageus, the Keltar and the Nine were practically bloody married now. They'd become clan in every meaningful sense of the word. Like the Nine, the Keltar had long been insular, secretive, staying intentionally isolated. But the world had changed and neither band could afford insularity anymore. There were too many risks to them all to shun shared knowledge and power.

Christian wanted friends. He'd missed having them as a lad. God damn it, at least he could have peers.

Barrons cut him an irritated look.

"What? Don't tell me you can actually hear what I'm thinking," Christian snapped. He wouldn't be surprised. Barrons and his men were bizarrely attuned to people's slightest nuances.

"I endeavor not to," Barrons muttered. "Sometimes you infernal creatures seem to be holding a bloody megaphone to your brains."

"What is the god's name?" Christian changed the subject swiftly. It would be easier to be courteous if he knew something of whom he was to address.

"Culsans. They are the keeper of doorways, of gates and passages, of the underworld itself, standing bastion at all that is liminal. When they can be stirred to bother themselves. Culsu may be with him. If so, beware her blades."

"What blades?"

"The ones I just mentioned."

"Why is Culsans a they?"

"You'll see."

"Are they hideous?" Christian braced himself for the worst.

Barrons cut him a mocking look. "No more so than they may find you."

"Well, where are they from? How do you find these old gods?"

"For fuck's sake, shut up."

"What the bloody hell is wrong with trying to understand my situation? Were you this much of a pain when Mac was trying to figure things out? How did she stand you?"

"She prefers me lying down. On top of her. Frequently, behind her. You want to keep talking, Highlander?"

They made their way down the long white corridor in silence.

DELETED CHRISTIAN MACKELTAR SCENE FROM *FEVERSONG*

I stole a bit of Mac's hair a while back and carry it in my wallet. Yes, Death carries a wallet. Funny the things you do to try to normalize yourself. It's not as if anything in that wallet is worth a damn the way the world is now, but when I slip it into my jeans, I get a vague sensation of being Christian MacKeltar of the clan Keltar, who has a driver's license and credit cards and a picture of my mother and one of me and my childhood sweetheart, Tara, building a fort down by the loch. I don't carry Mac's hair from sentimentality or interest in her but because with it I can sift to her location whenever, wherever, I feel like it, and keeping an eye on that woman is on my list of priorities.

I didn't mention this to Barrons. He's not the kind of man you tell you carry a lock of his woman's hair, and there's no doubt in anyone's mind that's what she is.

Sifting to her location inside Malluce's is simple. I touch her hair and let my mind go to that strange, cool place I now have that seems to connect to something deeper within the earth than I ever reached with my druid arts, draws upon it, becomes one with it, and I can suddenly step . . . sideways, in a way, because space and time no longer function the same for me once I've tapped into whatever it is I'm connected to now. One of these days I really want to be able to sit down and talk to a born-not-made Fae and pick its brain about what I can and can't do. Maybe when this is all over and we get a sliver of peace.

She's a fright, standing in the middle of an overblown, gothic nightmare of a room. Not because of what she looks like, but because I can feel some kind of dark wind inside her, and for a moment I wonder if Barrons lied to me. There's Mac, then there's a shadow within, crouching, so damned hungry, dark, velvety, and utterly seductive. I get a vague impression of enormous charm and charisma. Whatever lurks within her can be beguiling if it wishes. I expand my senses, trying to assess the emotional content of whatever it is, and get nothing.

Abso-fucking-lutely nothing. The thing that abides inside Barrons's Rainbow Girl does not feel. At all. Not one ounce, not one flicker. I can't penetrate past that. If I'd known earlier, when she approached me at the abbey, that she was inhabited by the *Sinsar Dubh,* I might have picked this up. But my expectations colored what I'd perceived. When you don't expect a monster, it's hard to see one. When you know it's there, it becomes so visible you wonder how the bloody hell you ever missed it.

"Christian!" she exclaims, then explodes in a staccato-fast rush: "What are you doing here? Where is Barrons? Is he okay? Did I hurt anyone? What about my parents? Is Jada wearing the cuff? She has to wear the cuff! The ZEWs will get her again otherwise. She's okay, right? I didn't hurt her? Did I kill anyone? Who did I kill?"

I narrow my eyes, assaulted by a veritable barrage of emotion. Genuine, unless the *Sinsar Dubh* can fake it to perfection. I relax only slightly, unwilling to make mistakes. I proceed with extreme caution. Not getting one inch closer yet.

"Jada is fine, she's wearing the cuff, and no, Mac, you didn't hurt anyone. You just bloody cocooned us all."

"But I had blood and black feathers and—"

"Tell me you're not currently the *Sinsar Dubh,*" I cut her off impatiently. This is the only other test I can perform. And it may or may not be valid, depending on the power of the malevolent Book.

She stops abruptly, blinks then says, "I'm not currently the

Sinsar Dubh. I think it fell asleep but you have to contain me with the stones. Now, Christian, while it's not aware. Sift me to wherever the stones are and lock my ass down. Do it!"

It's my turn to blink. Okay, either the *Sinsar Dubh* is playing a deep game because it wants the stones or it's really Mac and she's finally wised up.

She locks eyes with me. Tiny little dots of crimson appear in the corners then vanish. "I know I killed," she says in a low voice. "And I get that you don't want to tell me. I scrubbed before you came. I know what I must have done to end up that way. Please, Christian, you have to neutralize me."

"It's what I came for, lass." I extend my hand. When she rushes toward me, I flinch, because I also feel a dark wind rushing at me, a chilling, icy, voracious dark wind that then slices into me even more savagely than the biting wind in the Unseelie prison, chilling my already too cool heart. But she takes my hand and hers is warm, and she doesn't slap any runes on me so I focus on Chester's and blink us off into that strangely malleable liminal place the Fae can access and we're gone.

π

When we reappear in Ryodan's office, she says nothing at first, just stands and spins, her face lighting up as she observes Barrons, Jada, and Fade. She exhales gustily and seems to relax, like she's taking her first deep breath in a long time.

Then she locks gazes with Barrons and says nothing for several long moments, and I somehow know they're having an entire conversation without speaking.

Christ. The emotion I see, hell, can almost feel in the molecules of air between them—it convinces me like nothing else could that this is really Mac. I observe Barrons curiously. Does he feel? Is he capable of it? I can't get a solid read on him but the abyss that I felt within him previously is abruptly no longer empty.

She fills it somehow. And in the filling, redefines it. And him.

Her face changes then, and she scowls. "I said, who did I kill, Barrons? Don't lie to me."

"It doesn't matter," he says.

"Every life matters."

"You killed only Unseelie and a single *sidhe*-seer."

"Who?" she snaps.

Barrons shrugs. "I don't know."

"Describe her," Jada demands.

When he does, Jada murmurs, "Margery," to Mac.

Mac drops her head and deflates.

Barrons moves toward her and she stiffens and draws back. "Don't touch me. You have to contain me with the stones. I think it's asleep but I suspect it won't be long and I have no idea what will happen then."

"Mac," he says softly, "I need to touch you so I can get inside—"

"No!" she snaps. "Lock me down first, then touch me if you want to."

"I might not be able to reach you then," he snaps back.

"You're going to have to risk it. I know what the thing is capable of. I feel it inside me. Not right now, but I felt it when it took me. It's . . . amused by suffering. It feeds on it, thrives on it, draws energy from it. It's beyond sadistic and sick but it's floundering right now. It's not at its strongest. But it will be soon." Her head whipped to Jada. "The cuff is what was keeping the ZEWs from being able to find you. Never take it off. I don't know what the Book did to the Sweeper. It could be out there still."

"It sent it back in time," Jada says quickly.

"Fuck! So that part of the legend was true, it *can* manipulate time." Mac explodes: "Lock me down *now*!"

Barrons is on her. He simply vanishes then reappears with his hands on her shoulders, as if he, too, can sift. What the fuck are the Nine? Rather, ten, now. Great, Dageus was a handful before. Now he's out there somewhere and able to move like the Nine. If he hunts, nothing will see him coming.

They both freeze for a long moment, Mac looking up, Barrons looking down. Then she says softly, "You'll figure something out. This won't be permanent. Or maybe I'll figure something out. But you have to do it. I can't guarantee that if I kill myself, it won't simply jump to another body. Please, Jericho, don't let me kill anyone else. I don't want to live with the death of people I love on my conscience. I don't want to live with the fate of the world on it. I can't. This is the only way and you know it."

"Hush," he says softly and closes his eyes.

"Jericho, don't," she says. "I don't know what it might do to you. Don't go inside me after it."

"Fucking trust me to be able to survive."

"I can't carry your death," Mac says. "It would turn me into the same kind of monster that inhabits me. Once before I was willing to destroy the world just to get you back!"

He opens his eyes and a faint smile curves his lips. "I know," he says, dark eyes glittering.

"That is *not* a *good* thing," she hisses.

"In my book it is."

"Well it's bloody well not in mine," I growl. "You heard her.

Barrons, give us the stones." If he doesn't, I'll be on him in seconds, take them from him.

They ignore me. Jada stands, watching them with apparent fascination.

"Fucking try to relax, Mac," Barrons growls. "Let go. You've got walls up. Drop them," he demands. He opens his eyes, his dark gaze boring down into hers.

She locks her jaw and stares stubbornly up.

"Mac," he says softly. Then his eyes say something to her I can't read, but whatever it was, her lips curve with a slow smile of delight. "I thought you didn't believe in words," she says with a husky laugh.

"I believe in you. And sometimes you're so obtuse I'm forced to resort to them. Let me in."

With a soft sigh, she closes her eyes and goes limp against him, melding their bodies together.

And that's when all hell breaks loose.

DELETED MAC/RYODAN SCENE FROM *FEVERSONG*:

"She kissed me. She wanted . . ." He trailed off.

I shot him a venomous look. "Tell me you did *not* have sex with Dani."

"Of course I didn't," he growled.

I said indignantly, "Well, why not? What's wrong with Dani? You sleep with everyone else."

He gave me a blank look that turned instantly to annoyance. "You don't get to have it both ways, Mac. You can't be pissed at me because you think I did it then get pissed at me because I didn't. What the fuck's with that?"

"It's the principle of the thing," I said, scowling. "Dani

shouldn't be sleeping with you, at least not now. But how dare you reject my girl? She's the best thing you could ever hope to get."

"You think I don't know that?" Then he said softly, "She's a virgin."

"Oh!" Thank God. A knot I hadn't even been aware of in my stomach loosened. I'd been so afraid she'd had it taken from her as a child, or taken from her Silverside, or given it away as coolly and impersonally as a porn star. "Wait," I said, scowling again, "so *that's* the only reason you didn't?"

"I had a lot of fucking reasons. I told you she was a virgin because I thought you'd want to know. Figured I wasn't the only one worried about what might have happened Silverside. The meltdown at the abbey about Shazam made me think she might have had a child."

I softened. "Oh. So, how did it end up between you two?" My darling Dani. She'd gotten rejected first time out of the gate. I hated that. I didn't want her to ever be rejected. Why on earth did she have to pick Ryodan? When she'd first come back as Jada, I could have seen it. But she wasn't that icy woman anymore, and the more she thawed, the younger she appeared. I groaned, understanding her motive. "She always said she wanted her first time to be epic. That's why she wanted you. None of her other options were available. Barrons was out of the running and V'lane turned out to be Cruce."

He snapped, "None of her other—wait, she wanted to give her virginity to Barrons? She said that?"

I shrugged. "She was a teenager."

"Barrons and Dani would never work," he said tightly.

"Nobody said they would. That would be as wrong as me and you. *Ew.*"

He bristled. "What the bloody hell is wrong with me?"

"And there you are," I said. "See? You don't want to have sex with me but it sure burns when I reject you."

He shot me an icy look. "You didn't reject me. I wasn't offering. But if I felt like it, I could change your mind."

Oh, God, men. Sometimes there was nothing else you could say.

Barrons growled low in his throat.

"Not that I want to," Ryodan said hastily. "Or would ever want to."

Barrons growled again.

"Christ, let's just end this conversation," Ryodan said tightly. "It's going nowhere."

"Let's," Barrons agreed.

"Let's not," I said. "How did it end with you and Dani?" I pressed, worried for her.

"I left, that's how the fuck it ended. I got out of there as fast as I could."

"So, you don't know where she went?" I needed to find her. Talk to her. See if I could help with her bruised . . . pride or feelings or whatever she was going through now. I said to Barrons, "I'm going to sift to her and see how she is."

Ryodan stiffened, sucking in a harsh breath. "Ah, fuck! Don't," he growled, turning his back to me, hands fisting at his sides.

"Don't tell me what to—"

"Don't sift to her. Your timing would be terrible."

I stared at him. His back was ramrod straight and he shuddered. He turned and shot Barrons an unreadable look crammed so full of an unfathomable conversation and I desperately wanted an interpretation.

Barrons went still, closed his eyes and rubbed them.

"What's going on?" I said softly.

Without opening his eyes, Barrons murmured, "Dani is having sex."

My gaze whipped back to Ryodan. "You can feel that because of the brand on her neck?"

Ryodan said nothing, just stood there like he'd been turned to stone, nostrils flaring, eyes sparking crimson. His fangs extended, protruding from his mouth.

My gaze shot back to Barrons, and I was just about to speak when he said to Ryodan, "You knew when you tattooed her what it would do to you. You knew the price."

"What price?" I demanded.

"She went straight from me to him," Ryodan said nearly inaudibly.

"Him, who?" I practically shouted.

"Her fucking kid genius," he hissed.

I couldn't help but smile. She was with Dancer. *That* was the epic I'd wanted for the woman she'd started to become. For Dani "the Mega" O'Malley epic could only be the one thing she'd never had: normal. Then my heart sank as I remembered the condition of Dancer's heart. I got lost in my thoughts a moment, hoping she didn't ... well, surely she wouldn't be too ... vigorous. Dani was super strong, she vibrated when she got excited. Oh, I really needed to stop thinking about this. I shook my head to scatter images and said to Ryodan, "You did the right thing. You should never have been her first."

He looked at me like I was absolutely insane. "Of course I shouldn't." Then his face hardened and something I couldn't define stirred in his ancient eyes. "I'm going to be her last."

Without another word, Ryodan shifted into the beast and was gone.

DELETED SCENE FROM *HIGH VOLTAGE*:

Before I began writing the novel, I needed to see the decision Ryodan made to leave, to fully understand the emotion and motives behind it. I wrote this scene between him and Barrons to flesh it out in my mind . . .

"What are you waiting for?" Ryodan demanded.

Jericho Barrons paced the flagstones with such violence, his boots kicked up stone dust with each step. "I don't think this is a good idea."

Ryodan said coolly, "I didn't ask you to think. Just do it."

"And if we need you?" Barrons whirled on him so sharply that the fabric of his long coat cracked like a whip.

"It's five years." The corner of Ryodan's mouth lifted in a mocking smile. "Surely you can muddle through without me for so short a time. In Faery with Mac, it may pass as a mere month or two for you." Time crawled in that liminal place where the ancient Fae held formal court.

"And if something goes wrong? You haven't thought this through," Barrons snarled.

Ryodan arched a brow. He'd never been accused of that before. He considered every detail, often looking centuries ahead, patiently recalibrating. Linchpin theory was his specialty. He who knew how to destroy a thing, a person, a society, controlled it. "Have you forgotten who you're talking to?"

"I'm talking to the bloody idiot who thinks something like this is a viable option," Barrons snapped.

"I've taken precautions. Dani will be safe."

"She's not our only concern. There's also Dageus—"

"Lor will get word to you if he scents wind of the Tribunal. You know where to find me." Time also seemed to move more slowly in that strange, terrible place the Tribunal dwelled; a lair they'd never been able to find. It might be decades before retribution came slamming down. He'd sometimes entertained the notion that the Tribunal deliberately took their time, allowing the offending member of the Nine to think they'd gotten away with taking a human, so when that person was stolen from him, it cut deeper. Then again, it might be never. There had always been ten of them. The Tribunal had only ever come when that number was exceeded. With Barrons's son dead, they might never come.

"This bloody well isn't the answer, Ryodan," Barrons said impatiently.

"I killed for no reason and not to feed. I don't take life without a reason. There may be little to distinguish us from the Fae, but that's one of the defining characteristics."

"You had reason. I'd have done no less."

Ryodan smiled mirthlessly. "And scatter a trail of bodies behind her?"

"She doesn't look back."

"There is that. But one day she will. And hate me for it. She protects the innocents. She doesn't kill them because something pisses her off."

"You don't know he was innocent."

"He wasn't. But according to her rulebook, he didn't deserve to die."

"You didn't kill Dancer."

Ryodan's gaze shuttered. That was different. She'd loved Dancer. Tenderness had accompanied the erotic images bombarding him through their bond, soothing his beast just enough that he'd been able to get himself locked in a cell beneath Chester's, barricaded in, with Lor, Fade, and Kasteo standing guard beyond.

Dani hadn't felt emotion for the man he'd ripped to pieces, just a hunger in her bones to not be alone. To have a man's arms around her and pretend, with eyes closed, he was the one who'd died in her bed. To feel what Dancer had made her feel: cherished.

It hadn't worked. The man hadn't returned what that woman was capable of giving. Elysian passion had been met by dumb, plebian lust. And then when she'd stopped, the bastard tried to take what he hadn't deserved in the first place.

She left emptier and more alone than she'd gone in, and the grief she'd suffered deep in her soul had decimated the chains on his beast.

He refused to litter her life with corpses.

Barrons eyed him stonily across the room. Ryodan stared impassively back. He knew how much it cost his older half brother to be here; he'd sworn to never set foot in this place again. After an interminable length of silence during which both realized they would sit there for a small eternity before either broke eye contact, Barrons spun away and fired over his shoulder, "There's another option. Tell her what—"

"No," Ryodan snarled. "It's not her problem. It's mine. She needs to breathe, live on her own terms, define herself. Not in opposition but from choice. No boundaries. No limits. Not one bloody cage." He knew Dani. If he told her, she would either curtail her activities to accommodate it or cut the tattoo off— again—as she had in the Silvers. Neither was acceptable. Freedom was something she'd never known. He wanted her drunk on it.

"But Dani *asked* you to tattoo her."

"She didn't know what she was asking. I offered it as a weapon, a shield. She wanted protection, nothing more." A pause, then, silver eyes icy, Ryodan said, "I'll kill again. That's *my* problem. Not hers." Long ago, they'd run as beasts, obeyed no code, known no laws. They'd been a breath away from becoming no better than the immortally bored, monstrous Fae. Barrons had pulled them back from that edge. Shaped them into savages with a code that kept them south of monstrosity. On the rare occasions one of them slipped, Barrons and Ryodan did whatever was necessary to reclaim him. Divided, they were quick to abandon the canon that functioned as a conscience, protected their secrets, and ensured their prosperity. Barrons enforced the law; Ryodan kept them together. None of them had violated their code in recent centuries. But Ryodan had butchered unprovoked, goaded by primal, uncontrollable rage at a situation, not the man he'd killed.

He could carve the tattoo from Dani's skin. He hungered to escape the brutal intimacy of their bond. An intimacy she was unaware of, didn't realize worked the way it did.

Yet, if he sliced it from her flesh, he wouldn't be able to find her if she got lost.

He'd sworn to her that he'd never let her be lost.

He'd sworn it to himself. Their bond was his guarantee that she would never face danger by herself again.

Dani O'Malley had been alone in all the wrong ways and none of the right ones. Imprisoned as a child, she'd been unable to choose even the simplest elements of her day-to-day survival. He'd micromanage the hell out of her if he remained in his current imbalanced state. He'd do irreparable harm. She'd done her time in a cage. He'd do his.

"If she *does* get lost?" Barrons said finally.

Ryodan said nothing, just leaned back against the bars and folded his arms behind his head. Barrons knew if Dani used the spell etched into her phone and flesh, nothing could stop Ryodan from being sent to her, not even what his brother was about to do to him. He'd also given him instructions that if she called him at all, which would mean she was ready, Barrons was to set him free.

"You'll starve down here," Barrons goaded.

"I'll slaughter up there."

"The years will bring madness."

"I'll deal with it."

"You'll still feel it all."

Again Ryodan said nothing. There was nothing to say. It was true. He would. But he wouldn't kill again.

"You could get trapped in the beast's skin. Be unable to change back." Barrons pushed, his eyes sparking crimson as he recalled another day, another time.

"Unlike you, I prefer my human skin. I'll find my way back."

"It's dark. Underground."

Barrons knew his past. "That was a very long time ago," Ryodan parried with soft menace.

"It'll be hell."

"I know what hell is, Barrons. It's not this." A small slice of hell, however, was taking a man's life merely because Dani had taken him to her bed. A larger slice of hell was knowing he'd do it again and again. The fairest portion of hell would be the contempt in her eyes. "Do it," he told Barrons. "You owe me." Before he started to lose control again and decided he was fine killing them all. Before he convinced himself *the active caring and concern for the well-being of another person's body and soul,* as she'd once informed him love was, scorn and fire flashing in her eyes, justified eliminating all intimacy but his.

After a long silence, Barrons murmured, "When we first

transcribed that spell, we knew the mere placing of it would call a high price. It's not your fault. You gift her with the greatest protection you can give—the willingness to abandon everything, to turn into the killing machine she needs, any time she needs it. You accept sacrificing your sanity and life each time she summons you. You grant her immense control over you and open yourself to a bond that can be pure poison for us. And the mere placement of that mark loosens the restraints on your beast. It's an unavoidable side effect."

Again Ryodan said nothing. Civilized for eons, disciplined, iron-willed, he'd believed he could handle it. Nothing rattled him.

But that woman.

"We suffer incarceration no better than the Fae. It'll hurt. Worse than being burned alive," Barrons snapped.

"Pain is relative."

"What if five years isn't long enough?"

"It had better be—she's mortal." Five years wasted. Five years of her life Ryodan would never get to see. And it would be the *second* five years of her life he'd lost. A decade, total. He inhaled sharply, going rigid as curved black talons exploded from his fingertips. He slammed his hands into the floor, gouging deep gashes in the stone. His skeleton was suddenly too large for his body, his muscles shifting and elongating.

She was on fire inside, angry about something, and he felt it. He felt everything she felt, that was the problem. He wanted her to taste all the world had to offer. Gorge on it.

Then choose him.

Because he was the best the world had to offer.

To the most lawless of men, choice was golden: it didn't matter what you were, it mattered what you did with it.

"Do. It. *Now.*"

Barrons sighed, acknowledging this was one of those exceedingly rare arguments he wasn't going to win. "Our cuffs connect us. You have but to demand I release you should you change your mind."

And because of their cuffs, Barrons would feel his pain, bear it in silence and never speak of it. Ryodan dropped back on powerful black-skinned haunches with a low guttural growl.

"Ah, brother." Barrons muttered a string of curses in a language long dead, but inclined his head and closed his eyes. When he opened them again they were bloodred pools. Intricate tattoos slithered and moved beneath his skin as he chanted the words of an ancient spell.

Ryodan began to scream.

But the day came when the only sound that filled that hellish place was the tortured baying of a half-mad, starved beast in endless pain.

GLOSSARY

— • • —

PEOPLE

SIDHE-SEERS

***SIDHE*-seer (SHEE-seer):** *A person on whom Fae magic doesn't work, capable of seeing past the illusions or "glamour" cast by the Fae to the true nature that lies beneath. Some can also see Tabh'rs, hidden portals between realms. Others can sense Seelie and Unseelie objects of power. Each* sidhe-seer *is different, with varying degrees of resistance to the Fae. Some are limited; some are advanced, with multiple "special powers." For thousands of years the* sidhe-seers *protected humans from the Fae that slipped through on pagan feast days when the veils grew thin, to run the Wild Hunt and prey on humans.*

MacKayla Lane (O'Connor): Main character, female, twenty-three, adopted daughter of Jack and Rainey Lane, biological daughter of Isla O'Connor. Blond hair, green eyes, had an idyllic, sheltered childhood in the Deep South. When her biological sister, Alina, was murdered and the Garda swiftly closed the case with no leads, Mac quit her job bartending and headed for Dublin to search for Alina's killer herself. Shortly after her arrival she met Jericho Barrons and began reluctantly working with him toward common goals. Among her many skills and talents, Mac can track objects of power created by the Fae, including the ancient, sentient, psychopathic Book of magic known as the *Sinsar Dubh*. At the end of *Shadowfever* we learn that twenty years before, when the *Sinsar Dubh* escaped its prison beneath the abbey, it briefly possessed Mac's mother and imprinted a complete copy of itself in the unprotected fetus. Although Mac succeeds in re-interring the dangerous Book, her victory is simultaneous with the discovery that there are two copies of it; she *is* one of them and will never be free from the temptation to use her limitless, deadly power.

ALINA LANE (O'CONNOR): Female, deceased, older sister to MacKayla Lane. At twenty-four went to Dublin to study at Trinity College and discovered she was a *sidhe*-seer. Became lovers with the Lord Master, also known as Darroc, an ex-Fae stripped of his immortality by Queen Aoibheal for attempting to overthrow her reign. Alina was killed by Rowena, who magically forced Dani O'Malley to trap her in an alley with a pair of deadly Unseelie.

DANIELLE "THE MEGA" O'MALLEY: Main character. An enormously gifted, genetically mutated *sidhe*-seer with an extremely high IQ, superstrength, speed, and sass. She was abused and manipulated by Rowena from a young age, molded into the old woman's personal assassin, and forced to kill Mac's sister, Alina. Despite the darkness and trauma of her childhood, Dani is eternally optimistic and determined to survive and have her fair share of life plus some. In *Shadowfever*, Mac discovers Dani killed her sister, and the two, once as close as sisters, are now bitterly estranged. In *Iced*, Dani flees Mac and leaps into a Silver, unaware it goes straight to the dangerous Hall of All Days. We learn in *Burned* that, although mere weeks passed on Earth, it took Dani five and a half years to find her way home, and when she returns, she calls herself Jada.

Rowena O'Reilly: Grand Mistress of the *sidhe*-seer organization until her death in *Shadowfever*. Governed the six major Irish *sidhe*-seer bloodlines but rather than training them, controlled and diminished them. Fiercely power-hungry, manipulative, and narcissistic, she was seduced by the *Sinsar Dubh* into freeing it. She ate Fae flesh to enhance her strength and talent, and kept a lesser Fae locked beneath the abbey. Dabbling in dangerous black arts, she experimented on many of the *sidhe*-seers in her care, most notably Danielle O'Malley. In *Shadowfever* she is possessed by the *Sinsar Dubh* and used to seduce Mac with the illusion of parents she never had, in an effort to get her to turn over the only illusion amulet capable of deceiving even the Unseelie King. Mac sees through the seduction and kills Rowena.

Isla O'Connor: Mac's biological mother. Twenty-some years ago Isla was the leader of the Haven, one of seven trusted advisors to the Grand Mistress in the sacred, innermost circle of *sidhe*-seers at Arlington Abbey. Rowena (the Grand Mistress) wanted her daughter, Kayleigh O'Reilly, to be the Haven leader, and was furious when the women selected Isla instead. Isla was the only member of the Haven who survived the night the *Sinsar Dubh* escaped its prison beneath the abbey. She was briefly possessed by the Dark Book but not turned into a lethal, sadistic killing machine. In the chaos at the abbey, Isla was stabbed and badly injured. Barrons tells Mac he visited Isla's grave five days after she left the abbey, that she was cremated. Barrons says he discovered Isla had only one daughter. He later tells Mac it is conceivable Isla could have been pregnant the one night he saw her and a child might have survived, given proper premature birth care. He also says it is conceivable Isla didn't die, but lived to bear another child (Mac) and give her up. Barrons theorizes Isla was spared because the sentient evil of the *Sinsar Dubh* imprinted itself on her unprotected fetus, made a complete second copy of itself inside the unborn Mac, and deliberately released her. It is believed Isla died after having Mac and arranging for her friend Tellie to have both her daughters smuggled from Ireland and adopted in the States, forbidden ever to return to Ireland.

Augusta O'Clare: Tellie Sullivan's grandmother. Barrons took Isla O'Connor to her house the night the *Sinsar Dubh* escaped its prison beneath Arlington Abbey over twenty years ago.

Kayleigh O'Reilly: Rowena's daughter, Nana's granddaughter, best friend of Isla O'Connor. She was killed twenty-some years ago, the night the *Sinsar Dubh* escaped the abbey.

Nana O'Reilly: Rowena's mother, Kayleigh's grandmother. Old woman living alone by the sea, prone to nodding off in the middle of a sentence. She despised Rowena, saw her for what she was, and was at the abbey the night the *Sinsar Dubh* escaped more than twenty years ago. Though many have questioned her, none have ever gotten the full story of what happened that night.

KATARINA (KAT) McLAUGHLIN (McLOUGHLIN): Daughter of a notorious crime family in Dublin, her gift is extreme empathy. She feels the pain of the world, all the emotions people work so hard to hide. Considered useless and a complete failure by her family, she was sent to the abbey at a young age, where Rowena manipulated and belittled her until she became afraid of her strengths and impeded by fear. Levelheaded, highly compassionate, with serene gray eyes that mask her constant inner turmoil, she wants desperately to learn to be a good leader and help the other *sidhe*-seers. She turned her back on her family Mafia business to pursue a more scrupulous life. When Rowena was killed, Kat was coerced into becoming the next Grand Mistress, a position she felt completely unfit for. Although imprisoned beneath the abbey, Cruce is still able to project a glamour of himself, and in dreams he seduces Kat nightly, shaming her and making her feel unfit to rule, or be loved by her longtime sweetheart, Sean O'Bannion. Kat has a genuinely pure heart and pure motives but lacks the strength, discipline, and belief in herself to lead. In *Burned*, she approaches Ryodan and asks him to help her become stronger, more capable of leading. After warning her to be careful what she asks him for, he locks her beneath Chester's in a suite of rooms with the silent Kasteo.

JO BRENNAN: Mid-twenties, petite, with delicate features and short, spiky dark hair, she descends from one of the six famous Irish bloodlines that can see the Fae (O'Connor, O'Reilly, Brennan, the McLaughlin or McLoughlin, O'Malley, and the Kennedy). Her special talent is an eidetic or sticky memory for facts, but unfortunately by her mid-twenties she has so many facts in her head, she can rarely find the ones she needs. She has never been able to perfect a mental filing system. When Kat clandestinely dispatches her to get a job at Chester's so they can spy on the Nine, Jo allows herself to be coerced into taking a waitressing job at the nightclub by the immortal owner, Ryodan, and when he gives her his famous nod, inviting her to his bed, she's unable to resist even though she knows it's destined for an epic fail. In *Burned*, Jo turns to Lor (who is allegedly Pri-ya at the time and won't remember a thing) after she breaks up with Ryodan to "scrape the taste of him out of her mouth." She learns, too late, that Lor was never Pri-ya and he has no intention of forgetting any of the graphically sexual things that happened between them. Although, frankly, he'd like to be able to.

PATRONA O'CONNOR: Mac's biological grandmother. Little is known of her to date.

THE NINE

Little is known about them. They are immortals who were long ago cursed to live forever and be reborn every time they die at precisely the same unknown geographic location. They have an alternate beast form that is savage, bloodthirsty, and atavistically superior. It is believed they were originally human from the planet Earth, but that is unconfirmed. There were originally ten, counting Barrons's young son. The names of the ones we know of are: Jericho Barrons, Ryodan, Lor, Kasteo, Fade. In Burned *we discover one is named Daku. There's a rumor that one of the Nine is a woman.*

JERICHO BARRONS: Main character. One of a group of immortals who reside in Dublin, many of them at Chester's nightclub, and their recognized leader, although Ryodan issues and enforces most of Barrons's orders. Six feet three inches tall, black hair, brown eyes, 245 pounds, date of birth October 31, allegedly thirty-one years old, his middle initial is Z, which stands for Zigor, meaning either "the punished" or "the punisher," depending on dialect. He is adept in magic, a powerful warder, fluent in the druid art of Voice, an avid collector of antiquities and supercars. He despises words, believes in being judged by one's actions alone. No one knows how long the Nine have been alive, but references seem to indicate in excess of ten thousand years. If Barrons is killed, he is reborn at an unknown location precisely the same as he was the first time he died. Like all of the Nine, Barrons has an animal form, a skin he can don at will or if pushed. He had a son who was also immortal, but at some point in the distant past, shortly after Barrons and his men were cursed to become what they are, the child was brutally tortured and became a permanent, psychotic version of his beast. Barrons kept him caged below his garage while he searched for a way to free him, hence his quest to obtain the most powerful Book of magic ever created, the *Sinsar Dubh*. He was seeking a way to end his son's suffering. In *Shadowfever*, Mac helps him lay his son to final rest by using the ancient Hunter, K'Vruck, to kill him.

RYODAN: Main character. Six feet four inches, 235 pounds, lean and cut, with silver eyes and dark hair nearly shaved at the sides, he has a taste for expensive clothing and toys. He has scars on his arms and a large, thick one that runs from his chest up to his jaw. Owner of Chester's and the brains behind the Nine's business empire, he manages the daily aspects of their existence. Each time the Nine have been visible in the past, he was king, ruler, pagan god, or dictator. Barrons is the silent command behind the

Nine, Ryodan is the voice. Barrons is animalistic and primeval, Ryodan is urbane and professional. Highly sexual, he likes sex for breakfast and eats early and often.

LOR: Six feet two inches, 220 pounds, blond, green eyes, with strong Nordic features, he promotes himself as a caveman and likes it that way. Heavily muscled and scarred. Lor's life is a constant party. He loves music, hot blondes, and likes to chain his women to his bed so he can take his time with them, willing to play virtually any role in bed for sheer love of the sport. Long ago, however, he was called the Bonecrusher, feared and reviled throughout the Old World.

KASTEO: Tall, dark, scarred, and tattooed, with short, dark, nearly shaved hair, he hasn't spoken to anyone in a thousand years. There is a rumor floating around that others of the Nine killed the woman he loved.

FADE: Not much is known about him to date. During events in *Shadowfever*, the *Sinsar Dubh* possessed him briefly and used him to kill Barrons and Ryodan, then threaten Mac. Tall, heavily muscled, and scarred like the rest of the Nine.

FAE

Also known as the Tuatha De Danann *or* Tuatha De *(TUA day dhanna or Tua DAY). An advanced race of otherworldly creatures that possess enormous powers of magic and illusion. After war destroyed their own world, they colonized Earth, settling on the shores of Ireland in a cloud of fog and light. Originally the Fae were united and there were only the Seelie, but the Seelie King left the queen and created his own court when she refused to use the Song of Making to grant his concubine immortality. He became the Unseelie King and created a dark, mirror image court of Fae castes. While the Seelie are golden, shining, and beautiful, the Unseelie, with the exception of royalty, are dark-haired and -skinned, misshapen, hideous abominations with sadistic, insatiable desires. Both Seelie and Unseelie have four royal houses of princes and princesses who are sexually addictive and highly lethal to humans.*

UNSEELIE

UNSEELIE KING: The most ancient of the Fae, no one knows where he came from or when he first appeared. The Seelie don't recall a time the king didn't exist, and despite the court's matriarchal nature, the king predates the queen and is the most complex and powerful of all the Fae—lacking a single enormous power that makes him the Seelie Queen's lesser: she alone can use the Song of Making, which can call new matter into being. The king can create only from matter that already exists, sculpting galaxies and universes, even on occasion arranging matter so that life springs from it. Countless worlds call him God. His view of the universe is so enormous and complicated by a vision that sees and weighs every detail, every possibility, that his vast intellect is virtually inaccessible. In order to communicate with humans he has to reduce himself to multiple human parts. When he walks in the mortal realm, he does so as one of these human "skins." He never wears the same skins twice after his involvement in a specific mortal episode is through.

DREAMY-EYED GUY (aka DEG, see also Unseelie King): The Unseelie King is too enormous and complex to exist in human form unless he divides himself into multiple "skins." The Dreamy-

Eyed Guy is one of the Unseelie King's many human forms and first appeared in *Darkfever* when Mac was searching a local museum for objects of power. Mac later encounters him at Trinity College in the Ancient Languages department, where he works with Christian MacKeltar, and frequently thereafter when he takes a job bartending at Chester's after the walls fall. Enigma shrouded in mystery, he imparts cryptic bits of useful information. Mac doesn't know the DEG is a part of the Unseelie King until she and the others are reinterring the *Sinsar Dubh* beneath Arlington Abbey and all of the king's skins arrive to coalesce into a single entity.

CONCUBINE (originally human, now Fae, *see also* Aoibheal, Seelie Queen, Unseelie King, Cruce): The Unseelie King's mortal lover and unwitting cause of endless war and suffering. When the king fell in love with her, he asked the Seelie Queen to use the Song of Making to make her Fae and immortal, but the queen refused. Incensed, the Seelie King left Faery, established his own icy realm, and became the dark, forbidding Unseelie King. After building his concubine the magnificent shining White Mansion inside the Silvers where she would never age so long as she didn't leave its labyrinthine walls, he vowed to re-create the Song of Making, and spent eons experimenting in his laboratory while his concubine waited. The Unseelie Court was the result of his efforts: dark, ravenous, and lethal, fashioned from an imperfect Song of Making. In *Shadowfever*, the king discovers his concubine isn't dead, as he has believed for over half a million years. Unfortunately, the cup from the Cauldron of Forgetting that Cruce forced upon the concubine destroyed her mind and she doesn't retain a single memory of the king or their love. It is as if a complete stranger wears her skin.

CRUCE (Unseelie, but has masqueraded for over half a million years as the Seelie prince V'lane): Powerful, sifting, lethally sexual Fae. Believes himself to be the last and finest Unseelie prince the king created. Cruce was given special privileges at the Dark Court, working beside his liege to perfect the Song of Making. He was the only Fae ever allowed to enter the White Mansion so he might carry the king's experimental potions to the concubine while the king continued with his work. Over time, Cruce grew jealous of the king, coveted his concubine and kingdom, and plotted to take it from him. Cruce resented that the king kept his Dark Court secret from the Seelie Queen and wanted the Dark and Light Courts to be joined into one, which he then planned to rule himself. He petitioned the king to go to the Seelie Court and present his "children," but the king refused, knowing the queen would only subject his imperfect creations to endless torture and humiliation. Angry that the king would not fight for them, Cruce went to the Seelie Queen himself and told her of the Dark Court. Incensed at the king's betrayal and quest for power, which was matriarchal, the queen locked Cruce away in her bower and summoned the king. With the help of the illusion amulets Cruce and the king had created, Cruce wove the glamour that he was the Seelie prince, V'lane. Furious to learn the king had disobeyed her, and jealous of his love for the concubine, the queen summoned Cruce (who was actually her own prince, V'lane) and killed him with the Sword of Light to show the king what she would do to all his abominations. Enraged, the king stormed the Seelie Court with his dark Fae and killed the queen. When he went home to his icy realm, grieving the loss of his trusted and much-loved prince Cruce, he found his concubine was also dead. She'd left him a note saying she'd killed herself to escape what he'd become. Unknown to the king, while he'd fought with the Seelie Queen, Cruce slipped back to the White Mansion and gave the concubine another "potion," which was actually a cup stolen from the Cauldron of Forgetting. After erasing her memory, he used the power of the three lesser illusion amulets to convince the king she was dead. He took her away and assumed the role of V'lane, in love with a mortal at the Seelie Court, biding time to usurp the rule of their race, both Light and Dark Courts. As V'lane, he approached MacKayla Lane and was using her to locate the *Sinsar Dubh*. Once he had it, he planned to acquire all the Unseelie King's forbidden dark knowledge, finally kill the concubine who had become the current queen, and, as the only vessel holding both the patriarchal and matriarchal power of their race, become the next, most powerful, Unseelie King ever to rule. At the end of *Shadowfever*, when the *Sinsar Dubh* is reinterred beneath the abbey, he reveals himself as Cruce and absorbs all the forbidden magic from the king's Dark Book. But before Cruce can kill the current queen and become the ruler of both Light and Dark Courts, the Unseelie King imprisons him in a cage of ice beneath Arlington Abbey. In *Burned*, we learn Dani/Jada somehow removed the cuff of Cruce from his arm while he was imprisoned in the cage. Her disruption of the magic holding him weakened the spell. With magic she learned Silverside, she was able to close the doors on the cavernous chamber, and now only those doors hold him.

UNSEELIE PRINCES: Highly sexual, insatiable, dark counterparts to the golden Seelie princes. Long blue-black hair, leanly muscled dark-skinned bodies tattooed with brilliant complicated patterns that rush beneath their skin like kaleidoscopic storm clouds. They wear black torques like liquid darkness around their necks. They have the starved cruelty and arrogance of a human sociopath. There are four royal princes: Kiall, Rath, Cruce, and an unnamed prince slain by Danielle O'Malley in *Dreamfever*. In the way of Fae things, when one royal is killed, another becomes, and Christian MacKeltar is swiftly becoming the next Unseelie prince.

UNSEELIE PRINCESSES: The princesses have not been heard from and were presumed dead until recent events brought to light that one or more were hidden away by the Unseelie King either in punishment or to contain a power he didn't want loose in the world. At least one of them was locked in the king's library inside the White Mansion until either Dani or Christian MacKeltar freed her. Highly sexual, a powerful sifter, this princess is stunningly beautiful, with long black hair, pale skin, and blue eyes. In *Burned* we learn the Sweeper tinkered with the Unseelie princess(es) and changed her (them) somehow. Unlike the Unseelie princes, who are prone to mindless savagery, the princess is quite rational about her desires, and logically focused on short-term sacrifice for long-term gain. It is unknown what her end goal is but, as with all Fae, it involves power.

ROYAL HUNTERS: A caste of Unseelie sifters, first introduced in *The Immortal Highlander*, this caste hunts for both the king and the queen, relentlessly tracking their prey. Tall, leathery skinned, with wings, they are feared by all Fae.

CRIMSON HAG: One of the Unseelie King's earliest creations, Dani O'Malley inadvertently freed this monster from a stoppered bottle at the king's fantastical library inside the White Mansion. Psychopathically driven to complete her unfinished, tattered gown of guts, she captures and kills anything in her path, using insectile, lancelike legs to slay her prey and disembowel them. She then perches nearby and knits their entrails into the ragged hem of her bloodred dress. They tend to rot as quickly as they're stitched, necessitating an endless, futile hunt for more. Rumor is, the Hag once held two Unseelie princes captive, killing them over and over for nearly 100,000 years before the Unseelie King stopped her. She reeks of the stench of rotting meat, has matted, blood-drenched hair, an ice-white face with black eye sockets, a thin gash of a mouth, and crimson fangs. Her upper body is lovely and voluptuous, encased in a gruesome corset of bone and sinew. She prefers to abduct Unseelie princes because they are immortal and afford an unending supply of guts, as they regenerate each time she kills them. In *Iced,* she kills Barrons and Ryodan, then captures Christian MacKeltar (the latest Unseelie prince) and carries him off.

FEAR DORCHA: One of the Unseelie King's earliest creations, this seven-foot-tall, gaunt Unseelie wears a dark pin-striped tailcoat suit that is at least a century out of date, and has no face. Beneath an elegant, cobwebbed black top hat is a swirling black tornado with various bits of features that occasionally materialize. Like all the Unseelie, created imperfectly from an imperfect Song of Making, he is pathologically driven to achieve what he lacks—a face and identity—by stealing faces and identities from humans. The Fear Dorcha was once the Unseelie King's personal assassin and traveling companion during his liege's time of madness after the concubine's death. In *Fever Moon,* the Fear Dorcha is defeated by Mac when she steals his top hat, but it is unknown if the Dorcha is actually deceased.

HOAR FROST KING (GH'LUK-RA D'J'HAI) (aka HFK): Villain introduced in *Iced*, responsible for turning Dublin into a frigid, arctic wasteland. This Unseelie is one of the most complex and powerful the king ever created, capable of opening holes in space-time to travel, similar to the Seelie ability to sift but with catastrophic results for the matter it manipulates. The Hoar Frost King is the only Unseelie aware of its fundamental imperfection on a quantum level, and like the king, was attempting to recreate the Song of Making to fix itself by collecting the necessary frequencies, physically removing them from the fabric of reality. Each place the Hoar Frost King fed, it stripped necessary structure from the universe while regurgitating a minute mass of enormous density, like a cat vomiting cosmic bones after eating a quantum bird. Although the HFK was destroyed in *Iced* by Dani, Dancer, and Ryodan, the holes it left in the fabric of the human world can be fixed only with the Song of Making.

GRAY MAN: Tall, monstrous, leprous, capable of sifting, he feeds by stealing beauty from human women. He projects the glamour of a devastatingly attractive human man. He is lethal but prefers his victims left hideously disfigured and alive to suffer. In *Darkfever*, Barrons stabs and kills the Gray Man with Mac's spear.

GRAY WOMAN: The Gray Man's female counterpart, nine feet tall, she projects the glamour of a stunningly beautiful woman and lures human men to their death. Gaunt, emaciated to the point of starvation, her face is long and narrow. Her mouth consumes the entire lower half of her face. She has two rows of sharklike teeth but prefers to feed by caressing her victims, drawing their beauty and vitality out through open sores on her grotesque hands. If she wants to kill in a hurry, she clamps her hands onto human flesh, creating an unbreakable suction. Unlike the Gray Man, she usually quickly kills her victims. In *Shadowfever*, she breaks pattern and preys upon Dani, in retaliation against Mac and Barrons for killing the Gray Man, her lover. Mac makes an unholy pact with her to save Dani.

RHINO-BOYS: Ugly, gray-skinned creatures that resemble rhinoceroses with bumpy, protruding foreheads, barrel-like bodies, stumpy arms and legs, and lipless gashes of mouths with jutting underbites. Lower-caste Unseelie thugs dispatched primarily as watchdogs and security for high-ranking Fae.

PAPA ROACH (aka the roach god): Made of thousands and thousands of roachlike creatures clambering on top of one another to form a larger being. The individual bugs feed off human flesh, specifically fat. Consequently, postwall, some women allow them to enter their bodies and live beneath their skin to keep them slim, a symbiotic liposuction. Papa Roach, the collective, is purplish-brown, about four feet tall with thick legs, a half-dozen arms, and a head the size of a walnut. It jiggles like gelatin when it moves as its countless individual parts shift minutely to remain coalesced. It has a thin-lipped beaklike mouth and round, lidless eyes.

SHADES: One of the lowest castes, they started out barely sentient but have been evolving since they were freed from their Unseelie prison. They thrive in darkness, can't bear direct light, and hunt at night or in dark places. They steal life in the same manner the Gray Man steals beauty, draining their victims with vampiric swiftness, leaving behind a pile of clothing and a husk of dehydrated human matter. They consume every living thing in their path from the leaves on trees to the worms in the soil.

SEELIE

AOIBHEAL, THE SEELIE QUEEN (*see also* Concubine): Fae queen, last in a long line of queens with an unusual empathy for humans. In *Shadowfever,* it is revealed the queen was once human herself, and is the Unseelie King's long-lost concubine and soul mate. Over half a million years ago the Unseelie prince Cruce drugged her with a cup stolen from the Cauldron of Forgetting, erased her memory and abducted her, staging it so the Unseelie King believed she was dead. Masquerading as the Seelie prince V'lane, Cruce hid her in the one place he knew the king of the Unseelie would never go—the Seelie Court. Prolonged time in Faery transformed Aoibheal and she became what the king had desperately desired her to be: Fae and immortal. She is now the latest in a long line of Seelie Queens. Tragically, the original Seelie Queen was killed by the Unseelie King before she was able to pass on the Song of Making, the most powerful and beautiful of all Fae magic. Without it, the Seelie have changed. In *Burned,* the Unseelie King took the concubine to the White Mansion and imprisoned her inside the boudoir they once shared, in an effort to restore her memory.

DARROC, LORD MASTER (Seelie turned human): Once Fae and trusted advisor to Aoibheal, he was set up by Cruce and banished from Faery for treason. At the Seelie Court, Adam Black (in the novel *The Immortal Highlander*) was given the choice to have Darroc killed or turned mortal as punishment for trying to free the Unseelie and overthrow the queen. Adam chose to have him turned mortal, believing he would quickly die as a human, sparking the succession of events that culminates in *Faefever* when Darroc destroys the walls between the worlds of man and Fae, setting the long-imprisoned Unseelie free. Once in the mortal realm, Darroc learned to eat Unseelie flesh to achieve power and caught wind of the *Sinsar Dubh*'s existence in the mortal realm. When Alina Lane came to Dublin, Darroc discovered she was a *sidhe*-seer with many talents and, like her sister, Mac, could sense and track the *Sinsar Dubh*. He began by using her but fell in love with her. After Alina's death, Darroc learned of Mac and attempted to use her as well, applying various methods of coercion, including abducting her parents. Once Mac believed Barrons was dead, she teamed up with Darroc, determined to find the *Sinsar Dubh* herself and use it to bring Barrons back. Darroc was killed in *Shadowfever* by K'Vruck, allegedly at the direction of the *Sinsar Dubh*, when the Hunter popped his head like a grape.

SEELIE PRINCES: There were once four princes and four princesses of the royal *sidhe*. The Seelie princesses have not been seen for a long time and are presumed dead. V'lane was killed long ago, Velvet (not his real name) is recently deceased, R'jan currently aspires to be king, and Adam Black is now human. Highly sexual, golden-haired (except for Adam, who assumed a darker glamour), with iridescent eyes and golden skin, they are extremely powerful sifters, capable of sustaining nearly impenetrable glamour, and affect the climate with their pleasure or displeasure.

V'LANE: Seelie prince, queen of the Fae's high consort, extremely sexual and erotic. The real V'lane was killed by his own queen when Cruce switched faces and places with him via glamour.

Cruce has been masquerading as V'lane ever since, hiding in plain sight.

VELVET: Lesser royalty, cousin to R'jan. He was introduced in *Shadowfever* and killed by Ryodan in *Iced*.

DREE'LIA: Frequent consort of Velvet, was present when the *Sinsar Dubh* was reinterred beneath the abbey.

R'JAN: Seelie prince who would be king. Tall, blond, with the velvety gold skin of a light Fae, he makes his debut in *Iced* when he announces his claim to the Fae throne.

ADAM BLACK: Immortal Prince of the D'Jai House and favored consort of the Seelie Queen, banished from Faery and made mortal as punishment for one of his countless interferences with the human realm. Has been called the *sin siriche dubh* or blackest Fae, however undeserved. Rumor holds Adam was not always Fae, although that has not been substantiated. In *The Immortal Highlander* he is exiled among mortals, falls in love with Gabrielle O'Callaghan, a *sidhe*-seer from Cincinnati, Ohio, and chooses to remain human to stay with her. He refuses to get involved in the current war between man and Fae, fed up with the endless manipulation, seduction, and drama. With Gabrielle, he has a highly gifted and unusual daughter to protect.

THE KELTAR

An ancient bloodline of Highlanders chosen by Queen Aoibheal and trained in druidry to uphold the Compact between the races of man and Fae. *Brilliant, gifted in physics and engineering, they live near Inverness and guard a circle of standing stones called Ban Drochaid (the White Bridge), which was used for time travel until the Keltar broke one of their many oaths to the queen and she closed the circle of stones to other times and dimensions. Current Keltar druids: Christopher, Christian, Cian, Dageus, Drustan.*

Druid: In pre-Christian Celtic society, a druid presided over divine worship, legislative and judicial matters, philosophy, and the education of elite youth to their order. Druids were believed to be privy to the secrets of the gods, including issues pertaining to the manipulation of physical matter, space, and even time. The old Irish "drui" means magician, wizard, diviner.

CHRISTOPHER MACKELTAR: Modern-day laird of the Keltar clan, father of Christian MacKeltar.

CHRISTIAN MACKELTAR (turned Unseelie prince): Handsome Scotsman, dark hair, tall, muscular body, and killer smile, he masqueraded as a student at Trinity College, working in the Ancient Languages department, but was really stationed there by his uncles to keep an eye on Jericho Barrons. Trained as a druid by his clan, he participated in a ritual at Ban Drochaid on Samhain meant to reinforce the walls between the worlds of man and Fae. Unfortunately, the ceremony went badly wrong, leaving Christian and Barrons trapped in the Silvers. When Mac later finds Christian in the Hall of All Days, she feeds him Unseelie flesh to save his life, unwittingly sparking the chain of events that begins to turn the sexy Highlander into an Unseelie prince. He loses himself for a time in madness, and fixates on the innocence of Dani O'Malley while losing his humanity. In *Iced,* he sacrifices himself to the Crimson Hag to distract her from killing the *sidhe*-seers, determined to spare Dani from having to choose between saving the abbey or the world, then is staked to the side of a cliff above a hellish grotto to be killed over and over again. In *Burned*, Christian is rescued from the cliff by Mac, Barrons, Ryodan, Jada, Drustan, and Dageus, but Dageus sacrifices himself to save Christian in the process.

CIAN MACKELTAR (*Spell of the Highlander*): Highlander from the twelfth century, traveled through time to the present day, married to Jessica St. James. Cian was imprisoned for one thousand years in one of the Silvers by a vengeful sorcerer. Freed, he now lives with the other Keltar in current-day Scotland.

DAGEUS MACKELTAR (*The Dark Highlander*): Keltar druid from the sixteenth century who traveled through time to the present day, married to Chloe Zanders. He is still inhabited (to an unknown degree) by the souls/knowledge of thirteen dead Draghar, ancient druids who used black sorcery, but has concealed all knowledge of this from his clan. Long black hair nearly to his waist, dark skin, and gold eyes, he is the sexiest and most sexual of the Keltar. In *Burned*, we learn that although he gave his life to save Christian, Ryodan brought him back and is keeping him in a dungeon beneath Chester's.

DRUSTAN MACKELTAR (*Kiss of the Highlander*): Twin brother of Dageus MacKeltar, also traveled through time to the present day, married to Gwen Cassidy. Tall, dark, with long brown hair and silver eyes, he is the ultimate chivalrous knight and would sacrifice himself for the greater good if necessary.

HUMANS

JACK AND RAINEY LANE: Mac and Alina's parents. In *Darkfever*, Mac discovers they are not her biological parents. She and Alina were adopted, and part of the custody agreement was a promise that the girls never be allowed to return to the country of their birth. Jack is a strapping, handsome man, an attorney with a strong sense of ethics. Rainey is a compassionate blond woman who was unable to bear children of her own. She's a steel magnolia, strong yet fragile.

DANCER: Six feet four inches, he has dark, wavy hair and gorgeous aqua eyes. Very mature, intellectually gifted seventeen-year-old who was home-schooled, then graduated from college with a double major in physics and engineering by sixteen. Fascinated by physics, he speaks multiple languages and traveled extensively with wealthy, humanitarian parents. His father is an ambassador, his mother a doctor. He was alone in Dublin, considering Trinity College for grad school, when the walls between realms fell, and has survived by his wits. He is an inventor and can often think circles around most people, including Dani. He seems unruffled by Barrons, Ryodan, and his men. Dani met Dancer near the end of *Shadowfever* (when he gave her a bracelet, first gift from a guy she liked) and they've been inseparable since. In *Iced,* Dancer made it clear he has feelings for her. Dancer is the only person Dani feels like she can be herself with: young, a little geeky, a lot brainy. Both he and Dani move around frequently, never staying in one place too long. They have many hideouts around the city, above- and belowground. Dani worries about him because he doesn't have any superpowers.

FIONA ASHETON: Beautiful woman in her early fifties who originally managed Barrons Books & Baubles and was deeply in love (unrequited) with Jericho Barrons. Fiendishly jealous of Barrons's interest in MacKayla, she tried to kill Mac by letting Shades (lethal Unseelie) into the bookstore while she was sleeping. Barrons exiled her for it, and Fiona then became Derek O'Bannion's lover, began eating Unseelie, and was briefly possessed by the *Sinsar Dubh*, which skinned her from head to toe but left her alive. Due to the amount of Fae flesh Fiona had eaten, she could no longer be killed by human means and was trapped in a mutilated body, in constant agony. Eventually she begged Mac to use her Fae spear and end her suffering. Fiona died in the White Mansion when she flung herself through the ancient Silver used as a doorway between the concubine and the Unseelie King's bedchambers—which kills anyone who enters it except for the king and concubine—but not before trying to kill Mac one last time.

ROARK (ROCKY) O'BANNION: Black Irish Catholic mobster with Saudi ancestry and the Compact, powerful body of a heavyweight champion boxer, which he is. Born in a Dublin controlled by two feuding Irish crime families—the Hallorans and O'Kierneys—Roark O'Bannion fought his way to the top in the ring, but it wasn't enough for the ambitious champ; he hungered for more. When Rocky was twenty-eight years old, the Halloran and O'Kierney linchpins were killed along with every son, grandson, and pregnant woman in their families. Twenty-seven people died that night, gunned down, blown up, poisoned, knifed, or strangled. Dublin had never seen anything like it. A group of flawlessly choreographed killers had closed in all over the city, at restaurants, homes, hotels, and clubs, and struck simultaneously.

The next day, when a suddenly wealthy Rocky O'Bannion, champion boxer and many a young boy's idol, retired from the ring to take control of various businesses in and around Dublin previously run by the Hallorans and O'Kierneys, he was hailed by the working-class poor as a hero, despite the fresh and obvious blood on his hands and the rough pack of ex-boxers and thugs he brought with him. O'Bannion is devoutly religious and collects sacred artifacts. Mac steals the Spear of Destiny (aka the Spear of Longinus that pierced Christ's side) from him to protect herself, as it is one of two weapons that can kill the immortal Fae. Later, in *Darkfever*, Barrons kills O'Bannion to keep Mac safe from him and his henchmen, but it's not the end of the O'Bannions gunning for Mac.

DEREK O'BANNION: Rocky's younger brother, he begins snooping around Mac and the bookstore after Rocky is murdered, as his brother's car was found behind the bookstore. He becomes lovers with Fiona Asheton, is ultimately possessed by the *Sinsar Dubh*, and attacks Mac. He is killed by the *Sinsar Dubh* in *Bloodfever*.

SEAN O'BANNION: Rocky O'Bannion's cousin and Katarina McLaughlin's childhood sweetheart and adult lover. After the Hallorans and the O'Kierneys were killed by Rocky, the O'Bannions controlled the city for nearly a decade, until the McLaughlins began usurping their turf. Both Sean and Kat despised the family business and refused to participate. The two crime families sought to unite the business with a marriage between them, but when nearly all the McLaughlins were killed after the walls crashed, Katarina and Sean finally felt free. But chaos reigns in a world where humans struggle to obtain simple necessities, and

Sean suddenly finds himself part of the black market, competing with Ryodan and the Fae to fairly distribute the supply of food and valuable resources. Kat is devastated to see him doing the wrong things for all the right reasons and it puts a serious strain on their relationship.

MALLUCÉ (aka John Johnstone, Jr.): Geeky son of billionaire parents until he kills them for their fortune and reinvents himself as the steampunk vampire Mallucé. In *Darkfever*, he teams up with Darroc, the Lord Master, who teaches him to eat Unseelie flesh for the strength and enormous sexual stamina and appetite it confers. He's wounded in battle by Mac's Spear of Destiny. Because he'd been eating Unseelie, the lethal prick of the Fae blade caused parts of him to die, killing flesh but not his body, trapping him in a half-rotted, agonizing shell of a body. He appears to Mac as the Grim Reaper in *Bloodfever*, and after psychologically tormenting her, abducts and holds her prisoner in a hellish grotto beneath the Burren in Ireland, where he tortures and nearly kills her. Barrons kills him and saves Mac by feeding her Unseelie flesh, changing her forever.

THE GUARDIANS: Originally Dublin's police force, the Gardai, under the command of Inspector Jayne. They eat Unseelie to obtain heightened strength, speed, and acuity, and hunt all Fae. They've learned to use iron bullets to temporarily wound them and iron bars to contain them. Most Fae can be significantly weakened by iron. If applied properly, iron can prevent a Fae from being able to sift.

INSPECTOR O'DUFFY: Original Garda on Alina Lane's murder case, brother-in-law to Inspector Jayne. He was killed in *Blood-*

fever, his throat slit while holding a scrap of paper with Mac's name and address on it. It is currently unknown who killed him.

INSPECTOR JAYNE: Garda who takes over Alina Lane's murder case after Inspector O'Duffy, Jayne's brother-in-law, is killed. Big, rawboned Irishman who looks like Liam Neeson, he tails Mac and generally complicates her life. Initially, he's more interested in what happened to O'Duffy than solving Alina's case, but Mac treats him to Unseelie-laced tea and opens his eyes to what's going on in their city and world. Jayne joins the fight against the Fae and transforms the Gardai into the New Guardians, a ruthless army of ex-policemen who eat Unseelie, battle Fae, and protect humans. Jayne is a good man in a hard position. Although he and his men can capture the Fae, they can't kill them without either Mac's or Dani's weapon. In *Iced,* Jayne earns Dani's eternal wrath by stealing her sword when she's too injured to fight back.

CHARACTERS OF UNKNOWN GENUS

K'VRUCK: Allegedly the most ancient of the Unseelie caste of Royal Hunters—although it is not substantiated that he is truly Unseelie. He was once the Unseelie King's favored companion and "steed" as he traveled worlds on its great black wings. Enormous as a small skyscraper, vaguely resembling a dragon, it's coal black, leathery, and icy, with eyes like huge orange furnaces. When it flies, it churns black frosty flakes in the air and liquid ice streams in its wake. It has a special affinity for Mac and appears to her at odd moments as it senses the king inside her (via the *Sinsar Dubh*). When K'Vruck kills, it is the ultimate death, extinguishing life so completely it's forever erased from the karmic cycle. To be K'Vrucked is to be removed completely from existence as if you've never been, no trace, no residue. Mac used K'Vruck to free Barrons's son. K'Vruck is the only being (known so far) capable of killing the immortal Nine.

SWEEPER: A collector of powerful, broken things, it resembles a giant trash heap of metal cogs and gears. First encountered by the Unseelie King shortly after he lost his concubine and descended into a period of madness and grief. The Sweeper traveled with him for a time, studying him, or perhaps seeing if he, too, could be collected and tinkered with. According to the Unseelie King, it fancies itself a god.

ZEWs: Acronym for zombie eating wraiths, so named by Dani O'Malley. Hulking anorexic vulturelike creatures, they are five to six feet tall, with gaunt, hunched bodies and heavily cowled faces. They appear to be wearing cobwebbed, black robes but it is actually their skin. They have exposed bone at their sleeves and pale smudges inside their cowls. In *Burned*, Mac catches a glimpse of metal where their faces should be but doesn't get a good look.

PLACES

ARLINGTON ABBEY: An ancient stone abbey located nearly two hours from Dublin, situated on a thousand acres of prime farmland. The mystically fortified abbey houses an Order of *sidhe-seers* gathered from six bloodlines of Irish women born with the ability to see the Fae and their realms. The abbey was built in the seventh century and is completely self-sustaining, with multiple artesian wells, livestock, and gardens. According to historical records, the land occupied by the abbey was previously a church, and before that a sacred circle of stones, and long before that a fairy shian, or mound. *Sidhe*-seer legend suggests the Unseelie King himself spawned their order, mixing his blood with that of six Irish houses, to create protectors for the one thing he should never have made—the *Sinsar Dubh*.

ASHFORD, GEORGIA: MacKayla Lane's small, rural hometown in the Deep South.

BARRONS BOOKS & BAUBLES: Located on the outskirts of Temple Bar in Dublin, Barrons Books & Baubles is an Old World bookstore previously owned by Jericho Barrons, now owned by MacKayla Lane. It shares design characteristics with the Lello Bookstore in Portugal, but is somewhat more elegant and refined. Due to the location of a large Sifting Silver in the study on the first floor, the bookstore's dimensions can shift from as few as four stories to as many as seven, and rooms on the upper levels often reposition themselves. It is where MacKayla Lane calls home.

BARRONS'S GARAGE: Located directly behind Barrons Books & Baubles, it houses a collection of expensive cars. Far beneath it, accessible only through the heavily warded Silver in the bookstore, are Jericho Barrons's living quarters.

THE BRICKYARD: The bar in Ashford, Georgia, where MacKayla Lane bartended before she came to Dublin.

CHESTER'S NIGHTCLUB: An enormous underground club of chrome and glass located at 939 Rêvemal Street. Chester's is owned by one of Barrons's associates, Ryodan. The upper levels are open to the public, the lower levels contain the Nine's residences and their private clubs. Since the walls between man and Fae fell, Chester's has become the hot spot in Dublin for Fae and humans to mingle.

DARK ZONE: An area that has been taken over by the Shades, deadly Unseelie that suck the life from humans, leaving only a husk of skin and indigestible matter such as eyeglasses, wallets, and medical implants. During the day it looks like an everyday abandoned, run-down neighborhood. Once night falls it's a death trap. The largest known Dark Zone in Dublin is adjacent to Barrons Books & Baubles and is nearly twenty by thirteen city blocks.

FAERY: A general term encompassing the many realms of the Fae.

HALL OF ALL DAYS: The "airport terminal" of the Sifting Silvers where one can choose which mirror to enter to travel to other worlds and realms. Fashioned of gold from floor to ceiling, the endless corridor is lined with billions of mirrors that are portals to alternate universes and times, and exudes a chilling spatial-temporal distortion that makes a visitor feel utterly inconsequential. Time isn't linear in the hall, it's malleable and slippery, and a visitor can get permanently lost in memories that never were and dreams of futures that will never be. One moment you feel terrifyingly alone, the next as if an endless chain of paper-doll versions of oneself is unfolding sideways, holding cutout construction-paper hands with thousands of different feet in thousands of different worlds, all at the same time. Compounding the many dangers of the hall, when the Silvers were corrupted by Cruce's curse (intended to bar entry to the Unseelie King), the mirrors were altered and now the image they present is no longer a guarantee of what's on the other side. A lush rain forest may lead to a parched, cracked desert, a tropical oasis to a world of ice, but one can't count on total opposites either.

THE RIVER LIFFEY: The river that divides Dublin into south and north sections, and supplies most of Dublin's water.

TEMPLE BAR DISTRICT: An area in Dublin also known simply as "Temple Bar," in which the Temple Bar Pub is located, along with an endless selection of boisterous drinking establishments including the famed Oliver St. John Gogarty, the Quays Bar, the Foggy Dew, the Brazen Head, Buskers, The Purty Kitchen, The Auld Dubliner, and so on. On the south bank of the River Liffey, Temple Bar (the district) sprawls for blocks, and has two meeting squares that used to be overflowing with tourists and partiers. Countless street musicians, great restaurants and shops, local bands, and raucous Stag and Hen parties made Temple Bar the *craic*-filled center of the city.

TEMPLE BAR PUB: A quaint, famous pub named after Sir William Temple, who once lived there. Founded in 1840, it squats bright red and cozy, draped with string lights at the corner of Temple Bar Street and Temple Lane, and rambles from garden to alcove to main room. The famous pub boasts a first-rate whiskey collection, a beer garden for smoking, legendary Dublin Bay oysters, perfectly stacked Guinness, terrific atmosphere, and the finest traditional Irish music in the city.

TRINITY COLLEGE: Founded in 1592, located on College Green, recognized as one of the finest universities in the world, it houses a library that contains over 4.5 million printed volumes including spectacular works such as the *Book of Kells*. It's ranked in the world's top one hundred universities for physics and mathematics, with state-of-the-art laboratories and equipment. Dancer does much of his research on the now abandoned college campus.

UNSEELIE PRISON: Located in the Unseelie King's realm, close to his fortress of black ice, the prison once held all Unseelie captives for over half a million years in a stark, arctic prison of ice. When the walls between man and Faery were destroyed by Darroc (a banished Seelie prince with a vendetta against the Seelie Queen), all the Unseelie were freed to invade the human realms.

THE WHITE MANSION: Located inside the Silvers, the house that the Unseelie King built for his beloved concubine. Enormous, ever-changing, the many halls and rooms in the mansion rearrange themselves at will.

THINGS

AMULET: Also called the One True Amulet, see The Four Unseelie Hallows.

AMULETS, THE THREE LESSER: Amulets created prior to the One True Amulet, these objects are capable of weaving and sustaining nearly impenetrable illusion when used together. Currently in the possession of Cruce.

COMPACT: Agreement negotiated between Queen Aoibheal and the MacKeltar clan (Keltar means hidden barrier or mantle) long ago to keep the realms of mankind and Fae separate. The Seelie Queen taught them to tithe and perform rituals that would reinforce the walls that were compromised when the original queen used a portion of them to create the Unseelie prison.

CRIMSON RUNES: This enormously powerful and complex magic formed the foundation of the walls of the Unseelie prison and is offered by the *Sinsar Dubh* to MacKayla on several occasions to use to protect herself. All Fae fear them. When the walls between man and Fae began to weaken long ago, the Seelie Queen tapped into the prison walls, siphoning some of their power, which she used to reinforce the boundaries between worlds … thus dangerously weakening the prison walls. It was at that time that the first Unseelie began to escape. The more one struggles against the crimson runes, the stronger they grow, feeding off the energy expended in the victim's effort to escape. MacKayla used them in *Shadowfever* to seal the *Sinsar Dubh* shut until Cruce, posing as V'lane, persuaded her to remove them. The beast form of Jericho Barrons eats these runes, and seems to consider them a delicacy.

CUFF OF CRUCE: A cuff made of silver and gold, set with bloodred stones; an ancient Fae relic that protects the wearer against all Fae and many other creatures. Cruce claims he made it, not the king, and that he gave it to the king as a gift to give his lover. According to Cruce, its powers were dual: it not only protected the concubine from threats, but allowed her to summon him by merely touching it, thinking of the king, and wishing for his presence.

DOLMEN: A single-chamber megalithic tomb constructed of three or more upright stones supporting a large, flat, horizontal capstone. Dolmens are common in Ireland, especially around the Burren and Connemara. The Lord Master used a dolmen in a ritual of dark magic to open a doorway between realms and bring through Unseelie.

THE DREAMING: It's where all hopes, fantasies, illusions, and nightmares of sentient beings come to be or go to rest, whichever you prefer to believe. No one knows where the Dreaming came from or who created it. It is far more ancient even than the Fae. Since Cruce cursed the Silvers and the Hall of All Days was corrupted, the Dreaming can be accessed via the hall, though with enormous difficulty.

ELIXIR OF LIFE: Both the Seelie Queen and Unseelie King have a version of this powerful potion. The Seelie Queen's version can make a human immortal (though not bestow the grace and power of being Fae). It is currently unknown what the king's version does but reasonable to expect that, as the imperfect song used to fashion his court, it is also flawed in some way.

THE FOUR STONES: Chiseled from the blue-black walls of the Unseelie prison, these four stones have the ability to contain the *Sinsar Dubh* in place if positioned properly, rendering its power inert, allowing it to be transported safely. The stones contain the Book's magic and immobilize it completely, preventing it from being able to possess the person transporting it. They are capable of immobilizing it in any form, including MacKayla Lane as she has the Book inside her. They are etched with ancient runes and react with many other Fae objects of power. When united, they sing a lesser Song of Making. Not nearly as powerful as the crimson runes, they can contain only the *Sinsar Dubh*.

GLAMOUR: Illusion cast by the Fae to camouflage their true appearance. The more powerful the Fae, the more difficult it is to penetrate its disguise. Average humans see only what the Fae want them to see and are subtly repelled from bumping into or brushing against it by a small perimeter of spatial distortion that is part of the Fae glamour.

THE HALLOWS: Eight ancient artifacts created by the Fae possessing enormous power. There are four Seelie and four Unseelie Hallows.

The Four Seelie Hallows

THE SPEAR OF LUISNE: Also known as the Spear of Luin, Spear of Longinus, Spear of Destiny, the Flaming Spear, it is one of two Hallows capable of killing Fae. Currently in the possession of MacKayla Lane.

THE SWORD OF LUGH: Also known as the Sword of Light, the second Hallow capable of killing Fae. Currently in the possession of Danielle O'Malley.

THE CAULDRON: Also called the Cauldron of Forgetting. The Fae are subject to a type of madness that sets in at advanced age. They drink from the cauldron to erase all memory and begin fresh. None but the Scribe, Cruce, and the Unseelie King, who have never drunk from the cauldron, know the true history of their race. Currently located at the Seelie Court. Cruce stole a cup from the Cauldron of Forgetting and tricked the concubine/Aoibheal into drinking it, thereby erasing all memory of the king and her life before the moment the cup touched her lips.

THE STONE: Little is known of this Seelie Hallow.

The Four Unseelie Hallows

THE AMULET: Created by the Unseelie King for his concubine so that she could manipulate reality as well as a Fae. Fashioned of gold, silver, sapphires, and onyx, the gilt "cage" of the amulet houses an enormous clear stone of unknown composition. It can be used by a person of epic will to impact and reshape perception. The list of past owners is legendary, including Merlin, Boudicca, Joan of Arc, Charlemagne, and Napoleon. This amulet is capable of weaving an illusion that will deceive even the Unseelie King. In *Shadowfever,* MacKayla Lane used it to defeat the *Sinsar Dubh.* Currently stored in Barrons's lair beneath the garage, locked away for safekeeping.

THE SILVERS: An elaborate network of mirrors created by the Unseelie King, once used as the primary method of Fae travel between realms. The central hub for the Silvers is the Hall of All Days, an infinite, gilded corridor where time is not linear, filled with mirrors of assorted shapes and sizes that are portals to other worlds, places, and times. Before Cruce cursed the Silvers, whenever a traveler stepped through a mirror at a perimeter location, he was instantly translated to the hall, where he could then choose a new destination from the images the mirrors displayed. After Cruce cursed the Silvers, the mirrors in the hall were compromised and no longer accurately display their true destinations. It's highly dangerous to travel within the Silvers.

THE BOOK (*see also Sinsar Dubh;* she-suh DOO): A fragment of the Unseelie King himself, a sentient, psychopathic Book of enormous, dark magic created when the king tried to expel the corrupt arts with which he'd tampered, trying to re-create the Song of Making. The Book was originally a nonsentient, spelled object, but in the way of Fae it evolved and over time became sentient, living, conscious. When it did, like all Unseelie created via an imperfect song, it was obsessed by a desire to complete itself, to obtain a corporeal body for its consciousness, to become like others of its kind. It usually presents itself in one of three forms: an innocuous hardcover book; a thick, gilded, magnificent ancient tome with runes and locks; or a monstrous amorphous beast. It temporarily achieves corporeality by possessing humans, but the human host rejects it and the body self-destructs quickly. The *Sinsar Dubh* usually toys with its hosts, uses them to vent its sadistic rage, then kills them and jumps to a new body (or jumps to a new body and uses it to kill them). The closest it has ever come to obtaining a body was by imprinting a full copy of itself in Mac as an unformed fetus while it possessed her mother. Since the *Sinsar Dubh*'s presence has been inside Mac from the earliest stages of her life, her body chemistry doesn't sense it as an intruder and reject it. She can survive its possession without it destroying her. Still, the original *Sinsar Dubh* craves a body of its own and for Mac to embrace her copy so that it will finally be flesh and blood and have a mate.

THE BOX: Little is known of this Unseelie Hallow. Legend says the Unseelie King created it for his concubine.

THE HAVEN: High Council and advisors to the Grand Mistress of the abbey, made up of the seven most talented, powerful *sidhe-seers*. Twenty years ago it was led by Mac's mother, Isla O'Connor, but the Haven got wind of Rowena tampering with black arts and suspected she'd been seduced by the *Sinsar Dubh*, which was locked away beneath the abbey in a heavily warded cavern. They discovered she'd been entering the forbidden chamber, talking with it. They formed a second, secret Haven to monitor Rowena's activities, which included Rowena's own daughter and Isla's best friend, Kayleigh. The Haven was right, Rowena had been corrupted and ultimately freed the *Sinsar Dubh*. It is unknown who carried it from the abbey the night the Book escaped or where it was for the next two decades.

IFP: Interdimensional Fairy Pothole, created when the walls between man and Faery fell and chunks of reality fragmented. They exist also within the network of Silvers, the result of Cruce's curse. Translucent, funnel-shaped, with narrow bases and wide tops, they are difficult to see and drift unless tethered. There is no way to determine what type of environment exists inside one until you've stepped through, extreme climate excepted.

IRON: Fe on the periodic table, painful to Fae. Iron bars can contain nonsifting Fae. Properly spelled iron can constrain a sifting Fae to a degree. Iron cannot kill a Fae.

MACHALO: Invented by MacKayla Lane, a bike helmet with LED lights affixed to it. Designed to protect the wearer from the vampiric Shades by casting a halo of light all around the body.

NULL: A *sidhe*-seer with the power to freeze a Fae with the touch of his or her hands (MacKayla Lane has this talent). While frozen, a nulled Fae is completely powerless, but the higher and more powerful the caste of Fae, the shorter the length of time it stays immobilized. It can still see, hear, and think while frozen, making it very dangerous to be in its vicinity when unfrozen.

POSTE HASTE, INC.: A bicycling courier service headquartered in Dublin that is actually the Order of *Sidhe*-Seers. Founded by Rowena, she established international branches of PHI in countries all over the world to stay apprised of all developments globally.

PRI-YA: A human who is sexually addicted to and enslaved by the Fae. The royal castes of Fae are so sexual and erotic that sex with them is addictive and destructive to the human mind. It creates a painful, debilitating, insatiable need in a human. The royal castes can, if they choose, diminish their impact during sex and make it merely stupendous. But if they don't, it overloads human senses and turns the human into a sex addict, incapable of thought or speech, capable only of serving the sexual pleasures of whomever is their master. Since the walls fell, many humans have been turned Pri-ya, and society is trying to deal with these wrecked humans in a way that doesn't involve incarcerating them in padded cells, in mindless misery.

SHAMROCK: This slightly misshapen three-leaf clover is the ancient symbol of the *sidhe*-seers, who are charged with the mission to See, Serve, and Protect mankind from the Fae. In *Bloodfever,* Rowena shares the history of the emblem with Mac: "Before it was the clover of Saint Patrick's trinity, it was ours. It's the emblem of our order. It's the symbol our ancient sisters used to carve on their doors and dye into banners millennia ago when they moved to a new village. It was our way of letting the inhabitants know who we were and what we were there to do. When people saw our sign, they declared a time of great feasting and celebrated for a fortnight. They welcomed us with gifts of their finest food, wine, and men. They held tournaments to compete to bed us. It is not a clover at all, but a vow. You see how these two leaves make a sideways figure eight, like a horizontal Möbius strip? They are two S's, one right side up, one upside down, ends meeting. The third leaf and stem is an upright P. The first S is for See, the second for Serve, the P for Protect. The shamrock itself is the symbol of Eire, the great Ireland. The Möbius strip is our pledge of guardianship eternal. We are the *sidhe*-seers and we watch over mankind. We protect them from the Old Ones. We stand between this world and all the others."

SIFTING: Fae method of travel. The higher ranking, most powerful Fae are able to translocate from place to place at the speed of thought. Once they could travel through time as well as place, but Aoibheal stripped that power from them for repeated offenses.

SINSAR DUBH: Originally designed as an ensorcelled tome, it was intended to be the inert repository or dumping ground for all the Unseelie King's arcane knowledge of a flawed, toxic Song of Making. Using this knowledge he created the Unseelie Court and castes. The Book contains an enormous amount of dangerous magic that can create and destroy worlds. Like the king, its power is nearly limitless. Unfortunately, as with all Fae things, the Book, drenched with magic, changed and evolved until it achieved full sentience. No longer a mere book, it is a homicidal, psychopathic, starved, and power-hungry being. Like the rest of the imperfect Unseelie, it wants to finish or perfect itself, to attain that which it perceives it lacks. In this case, the perfect host body. When the king realized the Book had become sentient, he created a prison for it, and made the *sidhe*-seers—some say by tampering with their bloodline, lending a bit of his own—to guard it and keep it from ever escaping. The king realized that rather than eradicating the dangerous magic, he'd only managed to create a copy of it. Much like the king, the *Sinsar Dubh* found a way to create a copy of itself, and planted it inside an unborn fetus, MacKayla Lane. There are currently two *Sinsar Dubh*s: one that Cruce absorbed (or became possessed by), and the copy inside MacKayla Lane that she refuses to open. As long as she never voluntarily seeks or takes a single spell from it, it can't take her over and she won't be possessed. If, however, she uses it for any reason, she will be obliterated by the psychopathic villain trapped inside it, forever silenced. With the long-starved and imprisoned *Sinsar Dubh* free, life for humans will become Hell on Earth. Unfortunately, the Book is highly charismatic, brilliant, and seductive, and has observed humanity long enough to exploit human weaknesses like a maestro.

SONG OF MAKING: The greatest power in the universe, this song can create life from nothing. All life stems from it. Originally known by the first Seelie Queen, she rarely used it because, as with all great magic, it demands a great price. It was to be passed from queen to queen, to be used only when absolutely necessary to protect and sustain life. To hear this song is to experience Heaven on Earth, to know the how, when, and why of our existence, and simultaneously have no need to know it at all. The melody is allegedly so beautiful, transformative, and pure that if one who harbors evil in his heart hears it, he will be charred to ash where he stands.

UNSEELIE FLESH: Eating Unseelie flesh endows an average human with enormous strength, power, and sensory acuity; heightens sexual pleasure and stamina; and is highly addictive. It also lifts the veil between worlds and permits a human to see past the glamour worn by the Fae, to see their actual forms. Before the walls fell, all Fae concealed themselves with glamour. After the walls fell, they didn't care, but now Fae are beginning to conceal themselves again, as humans have learned that the common element iron is useful in injuring and imprisoning them.

VOICE: A druid art or skill that compels the person it's being used on to precisely obey the letter of whatever command is issued. Dageus, Drustan, and Cian MacKeltar are fluent in it. Jericho Barrons taught Darroc (for a price) and also trained MacKayla Lane to use and withstand it. Teacher and apprentice become immune to each other and can no longer be compelled.

WARD: A powerful magic known to druids, sorcerers, *sidhe*-seers, and Fae. There are many categories, including but not limited to Earth, Air, Fire, Stone, and Metal wards. Barrons is adept at placing wards, more so than any of the Nine besides Daku.

WECARE: An organization founded after the walls between man and Fae fell, using food, supplies, and safety as a lure to draw followers. Rainey Lane works with them, seeing only the good in the organization, possibly because it's the only place she can harness resources to rebuild Dublin and run her Green-Up group. Someone in WeCare authors the *Dublin Daily,* a local newspaper to compete with the *Dani Daily*; whoever does it dislikes Dani a great deal and is always ragging on her. Not much is known about this group. They lost some of their power when three major players began raiding them and stockpiling supplies.

ABOUT THE AUTHOR

KAREN MARIE MONING is the #1 *New York Times* best-selling author of the Fever series, featuring MacKayla Lane, and the award-winning Highlander series. She has a bachelor's degree in society and law from Purdue University.

karenmoning.com
Facebook.com/KarenMarieMoningfan
Twitter: @KarenMMoning

ABOUT THE TYPE

This book was set in Caslon, a typeface first designed in 1722 by William Caslon (1692–1766). Its widespread use by most English printers in the early eighteenth century soon supplanted the Dutch typefaces that had formerly prevailed. The roman is considered a "workhorse" typeface due to its pleasant, open appearance, while the italic is exceedingly decorative.